PETER AND THE WOLVES

MERRY FARMER

PETER AND THE WOLVES

Copyright ©2021 by Merry Farmer

This book is licensed for your personal enjoyment only. This book may not be re-sold or given away to other people. If you would like to share this book with another person, please purchase an additional copy for each recipient. If you're reading this book and did not purchase it, or it was not purchased for your use only, then please return to your digital retailer and purchase your own copy. Thank you for respecting the hard work of this author.

This book is a work of fiction. Names, characters, places, and incidents are products of the author's imagination or are used fictitiously. Any resemblance to actual events or locales or persons, living or dead, is entirely coincidental.

Cover design by Erin Dameron-Hill (the miracle-worker)

ASIN: B09DD8WW9J

Paperback ISBN: 9798463090096

Click here for a complete list of other works by Merry Farmer.

If you'd like to be the first to learn about when the next books in the series come out and more, please sign up for my newsletter here: http://eepurl.com/RQ-KX

❀ Created with Vellum

1

There was absolutely nothing wrong with basic table manners. Especially when one had guests. But apparently, my brothers had never heard of the concept. Which was shameful, considering our father was the Duke of Novoberg and we were entertaining two of the most distinguished families in the city. Our servants were doing their best to make the presentation of the meal exquisite, and our chef and kitchen staff had outdone themselves with delicacies. The very least my brothers could do was eat at a moderate pace and not converse with their mouths full.

I didn't have to worry about conversation. As usual, I was seated at the far end of the table, as far away as possible from my father, Duke Royale, and the lords he was entertaining at the center of the table. Father would probably have preferred that I took my meal in my room, far away from the guests who viewed me as a queer aberration, in the same way my family did. Effeminacy was seen as weakness in the rough world of the frontier, and I epitomized everything city-dwellers despised. I maintained my composure with perfect dignity all the same, even though I knew I wasn't wanted and didn't fit in, sitting perfectly straight, handling my utensils delicately, and taking small, careful bites.

Presentation was of the utmost importance, particularly when entertaining. But my brothers believed otherwise.

"Look at him," Rudolph murmured to Hans farther down the table and across from me. "You'd think he was a girl, looking the way he does."

"He should have painted his face, like our sisters, before joining the rest of the party," Hans sniggered back.

"Wait, he's *not* wearing cosmetics?" Oscar, one of Lord Beiste's sons, joined in the teasing.

The three men laughed at me, which was childish, considering they were in their twenties, but the behavior was exactly what I would have expected. I was well aware that my skin was as pale and smooth as the porcelain plates we were eating off of, and even at twenty, I had trouble growing any sort of facial hair. Worse still, the more they teased me, the pinker I could feel my face growing.

"He's like a precious little lily," Hans told the other two in a mocking voice.

"And look at the way he's dressed," Oscar said.

I was dressed in a manner perfectly befitting a formal

supper at the palace. I always dressed with impeccable care. My suits were expertly-tailored—mostly because I did the work myself when confined to my room for fear of teasing if I stepped one foot out said room—and the bowtie I wore was silk and matched the soft grey of my waistcoat. And yes, I'd embroidered green ivy on that waistcoat. It brought out the blue-green of my eyes. Perhaps my brothers disliked my soft, neatly coifed brown hair because none of them seemed to know what brush or comb was. All six of them dressed without care, in plain black or navy blue, and grew their hair fashionably long. The styles didn't suit any of them, though.

My disdainful thoughts of them were interrupted as Rudolph flicked a steamed carrot at me with his fork. It bounced off the side of my face and landed on the floor beside my chair. He, Hans, and Oscar laughed as I glared at them.

But it was my name that Father barked from the place of honor at the center of the table.

"Peter! What in the devil's name are you doing?"

"I have done nothing, Father," I answered, sitting straight and holding my chin up, even though the sound of my father's voice when he was in a temper would have withered even a mighty man. I was used to incurring his wrath. I could take it.

Rudolph, Hans, and Oscar snorted and dissolved into sniggering laughter. Most likely at the sound of my voice. Father's voice was deep, booming, and commanding. Mine was high, soft, and often mistaken for a lady. Just the sound of it made my brothers laugh and my father's face pinch in disgust.

"That's right, you've done *nothing*," Father sneered. "Your brothers have captured championship cups and prizes for archery, swordplay, and marksmanship, whereas the last time you were handed a knife, you fumbled it and ran away crying."

My throat went tight and I lowered my head. The last time I had been handed a knife was when Father had ordered me to slit the throat of the kitten I'd rescued from the stables and kept hidden in my room. I'd had Boots for a month before Father discovered her and ordered her murdered. I had been utterly incapable of doing the black deed myself. Animals were the only friends I had.

"Official records list me as having four sons and three daughters, but the truth is that I have three sons and four daughters," Father growled.

His guests laughed, sending sneers and looks of derision down the table to me. I was used to those as well. I couldn't hide what I was, and what I was invited scorn and disgust from city-dwellers who believed all men should be brutish and masculine. All I'd known through my entire life was that disgust. Hans kicked my shin under the table as if to demonstrate how nearly everyone I'd ever know felt about me. I fought to keep a straight face, but I could feel myself losing the battle not to cry.

Father wasn't wrong. I was as self-aware as anyone, perhaps more so. I was a man in every way that mattered —even well-endowed, for anyone who cared to notice—

but I was a different kind of man. I cared more for books and my study of the law, art and beauty than blood and fighting. I took great care with my appearance, unlike my brothers. And yes, I was aroused by men, not women. Very much so. I always had been. And for that, I was cursed. Not by myself, mind you. I knew I could no more change who I was than I could change the stars in the sky, and I'd grown accustomed to my differences. No, I was cursed to be born into a family and a place that reviled men like me as though we were plague carriers.

"Tell me more about these forest-dwellers causing problems for you," Father said to Lord Beiste, resuming his seat. I wasn't even important enough to sustain his wrath.

That wasn't the case for my brothers and Lord Oscar, though.

Hans kicked me under the table again. "What do you suppose he looks like in a dress?" he asked Rudolph, staring at me, eyes narrowed.

"Very pretty indeed, I'd say," Rudolph replied. "I bet he wears them when he's secreted away in his room."

"I bet he'd wear them all the time, if given half a chance," Oscar added.

"He'll wear them under his judicial robes when he joins the courts," Hans snorted.

"Judicial robes?" Oscar snorted in derision. "He's going to be a Justice?"

"It's Father's idea," Rudolph said.

"He can't very well sire heirs, after all," Hans sniggered. "Although since he wears dresses, I wouldn't be surprised if he managed to get himself with child at that."

"I do not wear dresses," I muttered, trying with everything I had to maintain my composure and carry on with the best manners possible while ridiculous things were being said about me.

The young man seated next to me, Lord Neil Beiste, glanced askance at me and inched away. He was around my same age and, while not effeminate, like me, he wasn't as tough as his brother or mine. He had the same dark hair and eyes as his brother, but presented himself in a more subdued manner. He likely thought that sitting too close to me would cause whatever pestilence I had to rub off on him. I didn't hold his wariness against him. I'd always liked Neil Beiste, and if I'd ever had such a thing as a friend, it would have been him. Which was why I ignored him for his own good. There was no use in getting Neil in trouble along with me.

Supper continued, and I did my best to be dignified and polite. Rudolph, Hans, and Oscar continued to stare at me and whisper amongst themselves as dessert was served, right before the party broke up so that guests could take themselves off to different parts of the palace for drinks, cards, gossip, or whichever other activity they preferred. I didn't like the way the three men stared at me. They were plotting something. The closer the time came to stand and leave the dining room, the more anxious I became.

Whatever they had planned, it wouldn't be the first

time I had ended up as their target. At various points in the last year alone, I'd been dunked in the well, had my head stuffed in a privy, been stripped naked and shut out of the palace on a faire day, and had most of my personal belongings dumped out of my bedroom window. And those were only a handful of the indignities I'd been subjected to on a regular basis. My brothers and Lord Oscar had the same look they usually got in their eyes when they were plotting some cruel, new endeavor. It was coming, I could feel it, and there was nothing I could do to avoid it.

"And now, ladies and gentlemen," Father said, standing once he finished his chocolate soufflé, "it is time to adjourn for the evening."

I figured I had only a slim chance of escaping my brothers, and only if I moved fast. As the rest of the guests stood, I rose and immediately stepped away from my chair. I glanced to both ends of the room, mind racing to form a plan of escape. Already, my brothers and Lord Oscar were standing and skirting around their chairs with the clear intent of coming after me. The grand exit to the formal hallway was clear at the other end of the room. The only chance I had was to break for the servant's entrance.

Attempting to draw as little attention to myself as possible—which wasn't difficult, as barely anyone in the palace ever bothered to acknowledge my existence—I headed for the servants' door.

Every hope that I'd been fast enough to get away was

crushed as Rudolph, Hans, and Oscar darted around the table and chased after me. As soon as I was fully out of the dining room, I broke into a run.

I was not athletic, but I kept myself fit. I was nimble and had greater stamina than my brothers, so I was able to zip forward, ducking and dodging around servants carrying trays or clearing dishes from the butler's pantry. I knew the twisting back hallways of the palace better than my brothers too. I had more than a slim chance of being quick enough to avoid whatever cruel plan they had in store for me. If I could just reach—

"Ha!" As I turned the corner into the kitchen hallway, my oldest brother, Frederic, leapt out from a side hallway and caught me. I hadn't even noticed him in cahoots with the others. I should have known. When one brother ganged up on me, they all did.

"We've got him," Rudolph said, catching up.

The three others joined Frederic, grabbing me and jostling me along to the kitchen.

"What do we do with him this time, lads?" Hans asked.

"Dunk him in the scullery sink," Oscar suggested.

"That's not good enough," Frederic said.

"Toss him in the midden heap," Hans suggested.

Frederic shook his head, "Too easy."

They pulled and shoved me along the hall and through the kitchen. The palace staff stopped what they were doing, looking on in helpless alarm as I was kicked, pushed, and dragged out to the back courtyard. They would have done something if they could, but the last time any of them had intervened on my behalf, they'd been sacked and banned from working in any respectable household for the rest of their lives.

"I've got it," Frederic said once we were all outside. The deep of winter was over, the thick snowfall that the frontier received every year had melted, but we hadn't yet reached the balmy days of spring. It was a cold night, and I shivered without a coat. I shivered at the evil look in Frederic's eyes as well. He narrowed his eyes and bared his teeth at me. "Let's throw him to the wolves."

Fear like nothing I'd ever know sank through me. "Not the wolves," I whispered, shuddering. I loved all of Nature's creatures, but wolves terrified me. I'd seen one at a village faire once. It was lean and menacing, even though it had been in a cage. Its fangs were horrible, and its eyes bright yellow and filled with hate. And everyone knew that the deep forest surrounding the city was filled with vicious, wild wolves. It was why no one ever ventured beyond the carefully-maintained boundaries of the cities. To set foot outside of the cultivated areas of the cities was a death sentence, and everyone from Tesladom to Good Port knew it.

I tried to make a break for it, ripping out of Hans's grip and shooting back toward the palace. My brothers caught me once again, and instead of being satisfied with pushing and kicking me on, they hoisted me above them. It didn't matter how much I wriggled and fought and squirmed to get out of their grip, the four men carried me over their heads, like a sacrifice being taken to the altar, out of the kitchen courtyard, beyond the palace grounds, and into the city streets.

Novoberg was a small city, but it had a few thousand inhabitants. Those inhabitants all knew who I was, knew who my brothers were, and likely knew what sort of torture I endured at my brothers' hands. Not one of them, man, woman, or child, lifted a finger to stop them as they carried me through the city as their prize. Even though it was small by frontier standards—let alone by the standards of the Old Realm on the other side of the mountains, far to the east—the city was prosperous and solid, which meant it was surrounded by a high, stone wall to keep vagabonds, thieves, and, yes, the wolves out. There were four huge gates in the wall, all of which were shut and locked after dark, by my father's decree. Forest-dwellers couldn't be trusted, or so the rumors went. They would rob city-dwellers blind or kill them without a second thought, so the gates were a necessity. No one—not even my brothers, had the authority to order the gates opened once they'd been closed for the night.

They carried me to the south gate—the last gate to be shut and locked every night. I could see the gatesmen heaving the huge, iron-studded doors closed as we approached. My struggles renewed. I panted, desperate to delay my brothers, willing to do anything if it meant they were too late, that they couldn't get me to the gate before it was closed. They seemed to feel the urgency as well.

"Hurry, lads," Frederic ordered. "Run!"

"No! Please, no!" I cried, too frightened to stop the tears from streaming down my face.

It was no use. When my brothers were intent on torturing me, nothing could stop them. Not even the shouts of the gatesmen as we grew nearer. The doors in the gate were so large and so heavy that once they started moving, it took immense strength to stop them. The gap between the doors grew smaller with every second. My cries of fear took on a whole new urgency as my brothers shifted me, ready to throw. There was a good chance that I could be crushed between the doors if they were even a second too late.

"Now!" Frederic shouted.

I screamed, the sound undignified and piercing, as I went hurtling through the air. I felt the brush of one side of the door against my leg a split second before I landed with a thump that knocked the wind out of me. On the wrong side of the gate. A resounding thud sounded from behind me as the gate closed. A second later, it's great, iron lock was clapped into place.

"No, no!" I shouted, breathless and panicked. I wrenched to my feet and turned around, throwing myself against the door and banging with my fists. "Please, let me back in. Please!"

The only sound I heard on the other side of the door was my brothers' and Lord Oscar's muffled laughter.

"Please, let me in, let me in!" I continued to shout and pound, but it was no use. I knew they wouldn't open the gates. Not for anyone, and especially not for me.

I twisted to press my back against the tightly-shut gate, breathing hard and weeping freely. The cold bit through my thin, formal dinner attire. I hugged myself, staring into the black of the night. The forest started a mere hundred yards from the edge of the wall and extended in every direction. Novoberg was one of several cities that dotted the vast, some said endless, forest on the other side of the mountains from the Old Realm portion of the kingdom. All of our farmland was contained within the wall, on the other side of the city. There was absolutely nothing at all between me, the mysterious forest-dwellers, and the wolves.

The only redeeming feature of the night was the full moon. It shone down on the wilderness like a cold beacon. But that also meant I was desperately exposed, without any weapon, and ill-dressed for the elements. I couldn't stay where I was, against the bare, stone wall. I had to move forward. My only hope was to find some sort of shelter within the forest, some sort of shrubbery or cave, anything that could keep me out of sight, away from the wolves for the night. I might be able to find wood and kindling for a fire as well, if I was lucky.

Within an hour of walking through dense trees, I knew my luck had utterly run out. It was a forest, there was wood everywhere, but none that could be made into a fire. And that was assuming that I could figure out how to light a fire without a match or tinderbox. There were no caves either. Our part of the forest was verdant, with only a few, sloping hills and no caves or cliffs to speak of. I knew there were geological resources underground from my studies, but gems or gold would be of no use in keeping me warm and safe from the wolves.

The only sign of hope I had as I grew colder and colder, shivering, unable to feel my hands or feet anymore, was the gurgling of a stream. I followed the sound, traipsing through nearly pitch darkness. The tiny slivers of moonlight coming down through the trees were the only guidance I had, though before too long, I could see moonlight reflected off a narrow creek in the distance.

It was so dark, in fact, that I almost didn't see the man standing facing a thick tree until I was almost on top of him.

"Oh!" I yelped stumbling back from him.

The man turned to me, and only then did I realize that he'd been relieving himself against the tree. There was just enough moonlight to make out the size and shape of his cock.

"Oh," I repeated, blinking, my throat going dry.

As soon as the man straightened, my eyes drew up to take in how tall he was. He had inches on me. He was well over six feet, with broad shoulders and thick arms. A shiver shot through me—one that was more than just fear. The man was all muscle and sinew. He could have snapped me in half without breaking a sweat. I could tell that much, even though he was wearing a hooded cloak.

He pulled his hood back a moment later, revealing a

swarthy, and not entirely unattractive face. He had hair as black as the night, blue eyes, and high cheekbones. He swept me with a glance from head to toe, then broke into a wide, interested smile.

"Well, well. What have we here?" he asked in a gravelly voice.

"M-my name is P-peter," I said, my voice high, light, and shaking. "Peter Royale. I've…I've been locked out of the city."

"Have you?" The man took a step closer to me.

I inched back. There was something vaguely menacing about him. But of course there was. He was a stranger in the forest at night. One who seemed perfectly at home there. Although the menacing thing about him could also have been the fact that he still had his prick out from relieving himself and appeared to be stroking himself as he studied me.

I swallowed hard, suddenly feeling warmer than I'd been moments before. I tried not to look at his prick—it was shockingly large. Instead, I fell back on the one thing I knew better than anything, manners.

"I do hope you can help me," I said, trying with everything I had to stand straight and maintain a polite, genteel attitude toward the stranger. "It was a cruel joke on the part of my brothers. Me being out of the city after the gate has been closed. As you can see, I am not dressed for the wilderness, and I was hoping you might be able to direct me to some sort of shelter for the night. I would be ever so grateful."

"Grateful, you say?" The dark man's eyes lit with... excitement. "How grateful?"

"I suppose my gratitude would depend on the hospitality of the offered shelter," I said with a breathy laugh, trying to keep things light. The man didn't reply. He continued to watch me, licking his lips. "If you please," I went on, still polite. "I wish to avoid wolves. They—" I gulped, not too proud to admit it, "—they frighten me, you see."

The dark man's smile grew even wider. "Wolves aren't anything to be frightened of, boy."

"Peter," I reminded him as demurely as possible.

"Peter." My name on his lips sent a shiver down my spine.

He stalked closer, rubbing a hand over his mouth, still handling himself. I tried not to look. The sensations his activities aroused in me were entirely inconvenient and inappropriate for the moment.

I was ready to turn and run when the dark man said, "I know where you can pass your night, boy."

"Peter," I whispered.

"Peter," he repeated. "I most definitely know where you can pass the night. We'll keep you nice and warm."

A surge of relief nearly had me sagging before I asked, "We?"

"My...brothers and I," he answered.

Disappointment shot through me. I had had very little luck with brothers in my life. But at the moment, I didn't see many options presented to me.

"I thank you for your kindness," I said with a slight, formal bow. It could have been more graceful, but I was shivering so hard from the cold—and yes, from fear—and something else I didn't want to name—that it was stilted.

"Oh, you will, Peter, you will thank me," the dark man said.

I held my breath, trying not to think about what he could mean by that.

A moment later, the dark man tucked himself back into his trousers and turned, gesturing to me. "Come along," he said. "The others will be pleased with the results of tonight's hunting."

2

*D*mitri—as the dark man informed me his name was—led me through the forest on a long and wandering path. I was in awe of how well he knew the miles of black and twisted trees. The deeper we journeyed into the forest, the less moonlight penetrated through the leafy canopy above. Several times, I was nearly left behind, Dmitri moved so fast. He finally ordered me to grab hold of his cloak and follow close behind. He smelled like wood smoke and musk, and I did my best not to be distracted by his scent.

I spotted a faint glow between the trees before we reached the odd house. By that point, I had no idea how long we'd been walking. My feet hurt, my legs were like rubber, and I was hungry again, which told me it had been hours. I was just on the verge of worrying that I would never be able to find my way back to Novoberg alone, and that I had inadvertently landed myself at the mercy of a man I knew nothing about, when we stepped out of the trees and into a clearing.

With moonlight shining down again, I was able to make out the strange house and the land and gardens around it. It was too early in the year for the gardens to be planted, but someone had begun to till the ground to prepare for planting. I could just make out a section near the edge of the woods that had recently been cleared and still held stumps as well.

But it was the house that fascinated me. One would expect to find a crude hut or a mud dwelling so far away from civilization, but the house before me bore all the signs of expert, modern construction. It had sturdy walls that seemed to be painted in a beige color and a thatched roof. Several chimneys stuck up from the roof, smoke emitting from all of them. What surprised me was the size of the house. It was as if someone had stacked at least four farm cottages together. From the outside, I guessed it must have held at least a dozen rooms.

The inside was an even more astounding sight to behold.

"Sascha, look what I found in the forest," Dmitri announced as we stepped inside.

The room immediately on the other side of a strong, well-constructed door took my breath away. It was as big as any of the parlors in the castle and had smooth, wooden floors, paneled walls, and stained, exposed beams across the ceiling. A massive fireplace was built into one side of the room in what I assumed was a wall that divided it from the rest of the house. That main room seemed to serve the purpose of parlor and dining room, and the kitchen off to one side was open rather than being separated by walls.

The massive room was furnished with a sofa and chairs nearer to the fireplace, a long, wide table with seats for ten around it, and several shelves and sideboards. The kitchen had multiple counters and cupboards, and at first glance I could see everything from food preparations to what looked like an herbal apothecary spread over the countertops. The entire house was surprisingly civilized for being in the middle of the forest.

But what captured my attention and held me stunned were the other men in the room. One stood by the stove in the kitchen. He had ginger hair and a beard, and appeared to me stirring something in a pot. Another was at the apothecary's table, pounding some sort of herbs. He had blond hair and a goatee. Another man with brown hair and stubble on his chin stepped out from a hallway leading to the rest of the house as Dmitri and I entered. But it was the man who stepped forward from the fireplace who arrested my attention the most. All of the men were well over six feet tall and stacked with muscles. Any one of them could have crushed the life out of me.

The man who Dmitri had addressed as Sascha, while not the largest of them, was by far the most attractive. He had chestnut hair and green eyes that I noticed seemed to be flecked with gold as he stepped right up to me to have a look. He towered over me, at least eight inches taller and twice as wide in the chest and shoulders as I was. His face was chiseled, and the way he looked at me, eyes blazing with interest, had my cock standing up to take notice, much to my embarrassment.

"What do we have here?" Sascha asked in a rich, tenor, smiling widely at me.

"I found him wandering alone in the woods," Dmitri said with an equally hungry grin. "Says his brothers locked him out of the city."

"Now why would they lock out such a lovely boy?" Sascha cupped his hand under my chin, forcing me to look up at him.

"My name is Peter," I gasped, nearly losing my balance. It didn't help that the man's hand was warm and calloused and forceful against my face. "Peter Royale. My brothers seem to think it's a lark to torture me," I added, in a near whisper.

"Who would torture someone like you?" the man with the goatee said, moving away from his apothecary counter. He, too, grinned at me as though I were the winning pie at a village faire.

I blinked, glancing around me as the two other men approached as well. They encircled me, which made me highly aware of just how out of my depth I was. The men were taller, thicker, and far, far more powerful than me. And they all had that heady, woodsy, masculine scent that was hard to find in the palace. I did my best not to be overwhelmed, but I also found myself regretting the choice of such close-fitting trousers for supper.

To be honest, as I continued to peek up at the men around me, I had a curious feeling that I'd walked into something monumental that I didn't quite understand. And I was the only one in the room who didn't understand it.

"I beg your pardon," I said in a wispy voice, my throat gone dry, "If it wouldn't be too much trouble, might I ask for your hospitality for the night? I won't take up too much space or require too much attention. I merely wish to keep warm for the night, until I am able to make my way back to the city in the morning."

The men chuckled. A chill shot down my spine. Fear wasn't the only emotion I felt, or the only physical sensation either. But the situation required politeness and refinement. I was in their home, after all.

"Where are our manners?" Sascha said, surprising me a bit. "Our pup is shivering. He needs something warm to fill him up." The others brightened, as if Sascha's words meant more than what they seemed. "Ivan, fetch young Peter some of that stew you're making. Sven, Gregor, settle Peter in by the fire."

I repeated each of their names in my head so that I could remember them, as manners dictated. Sascha seemed to be in charge. Dmitri was the dark one who had found me while hunting in the forest. Ivan was the cook, Sven was the one who had come in from the back rooms, and Gregor was the one with the goatee who was, perhaps, an apothecary.

"You have no idea how much this means to me," I said demurely as I sat on the sofa—which was surprisingly comfortable. Sven and Gregor sat on either side of me. They sat quite close, which made me feel tiny. Though not in a way that was entirely unpleasant.

"Tell us more about yourself," Sascha said, sitting in the largest chair across from me. He sat with his thickly-muscled legs open…which drew my eye inexorably toward the bulge in his breeches.

I swallowed hard and smiled benignly, folding my hands carefully in my lap to hide my reaction. "Well, as I said before, my name is Peter Royale, and I'm from the city of Novoberg," I began. I had no idea what these large, strong men around me would want to know. I could hardly think of a single thing to say as it was. I knew they were forest-dwellers. They were the first forest-dwellers I'd ever met. I suddenly realized just how sheltered my life in Novoberg and the palace was. "My father is Duke Royale," I added in a quiet voice, bowing my head slightly and wondering if revealing my family was a good idea.

The men exchanged surprised expressions and their smiles widened as they focused in on me once more.

"A son of the duke," Dmitri said, as if just realizing the sort of prize he'd brought home to the others.

"Youngest son," I clarified politely. "I have three older brothers."

"The ones who cast you out of the city and closed the gates behind you?" Gregor asked in a growl.

"Yes." I glanced to him at my side.

"The ones who torture you," Sven added. I turned to look at him on my other side.

"And your father allows this?" Sascha asked with a frown.

It would have been rude of me to speak ill of my father when I was a guest in someone else's house, so I tilted my head slightly to the side and said, "My father does not approve of me."

The men exchanged another set of looks. "Why not?" Dmitri asked.

I felt myself blush hot. "I am not the sort of son he wanted."

"But he has three other sons who, I assume, are what he wanted," Gregor said.

"They are," I agreed. For some reason, thinking about it made me sad.

"You're exactly the sort we want," Sascha said, stroking a hand over his jaw. He was the only one of my hosts who was clean-shaven.

The way he regarded me sent a shiver down my spine that had nothing to do with the cold. I was glad I had my hands placed just so over my lap.

"Here you are, Peter." Ivan joined us, handing me a bowl of delicious-smelling stew.

That forced me to move my hands to reach for the bowl and spoon. It would have been impolite not to. It would also have been rude to draw attention to anything other than my appreciation of the hospitality that had been offered to me.

"This is delicious," I said, meaning it genuinely, after finishing a few mouthfuls of stew.

"Ivan is an excellent cook," Sascha said as I continued to eat. "He was once an apprentice to the head chef in the castle at Klovisgard."

My eyebrows went up, but my mouth was too full to inquire about that further. I was hungrier than I'd thought and finished the stew with a few more bites, half wishing they'd given me more to eat.

"This house is fascinating," I went on making conversation. A good guest always found ways to complement his hosts. "It feels so solidly constructed, and it's so large."

"Sascha was an engineer and carpenter in Telsadom as a youth," Dmitri answered.

"You designed this house?" I blinked at the huge man across from me. He seemed restless somehow, unable to sit still, as if he were waiting for something.

"And built much of the furniture as well," Sascha answered.

"I'm impressed," I answered. "I assume wood is easy to come by in the forest." I laughed nervously at my own joke.

The men laughed with me, as if what I'd said was far funnier than I knew it to be.

"I think tea is in order, Gregor," Sascha ordered, his eyes still fixed on mine.

Gregor leapt up and moved into the kitchen.

I still felt it was incumbent upon me to carry the conversation as thanks for the gracious way the men were hosting me. "I've never been out in the forest before," I said.

"We would have noticed you," Sven said, then licked his lips.

"I bet there are a lot of things you've never done before," Dmitri said.

A fluttery sort of feeling swirled through me. The man couldn't possibly mean anything by his comment that was untoward, but my trousers felt unbearably tight all the same.

"I will admit, I've lived a sheltered life at the palace," I said, high-pitched and hoarse.

"Let me take that from you." Ivan stood to take my empty stew bowl back to the kitchen.

"Thank you once again," I whispered to him.

"Virgin?" Sascha asked.

I nearly choked on my own tongue. My face was so hot that I was certain my cheeks shone bright pink against my pale face. I gaped at him, unsure I'd heard him correctly. "I beg your pardon?" I squeaked.

"Never mind." Sascha waved vaguely. "You've answered my question." And he seemed exceedingly pleased with the answer.

"Your tea." Gregor returned, handing me a mug of warm, mint-scented tea.

I lifted it to take a sip—it was sweetened with honey,

which I loved—then paused. "I feel rude to eat and drink without you. And we've yet to discuss arrangements for tonight and tomorrow."

"Don't you worry about us," Sascha said. "And tonight and tomorrow will take care of themselves."

"Very well." I smiled and drank my tea. It really was delicious. Definitely mint, a touch of honey, and a few other herbs that I didn't think I'd ever tasted before. "So, how long have you lived here in the forest?" I asked. It was important to take an interest in one's hosts.

"Many years," Sascha answered. He glanced to the others. "Some more than others. All of us since we were younger than you."

"How old are you again?" Dmitri asked.

"Twenty," I answered, feeling suddenly light-headed. "Though, yes, I know, I look much younger. I've been told I'll consider it a blessing once I'm older, but at the moment, I fear it makes my brothers see me as even weaker and more fragile."

I finished the tea in a few gulps. It was too delicious not to. At the same time, it had a slightly intoxicating effect on me. A fast one at that. I was hardly aware when Gregor slipped the mug out of my hands and carried it back to the kitchen.

"Thank you," I managed to say. A faint bit of dizziness was no excuse for impoliteness. "That was lovely. What kind of tea was it?"

"It's my own blend," Gregor answered with a particularly bright smile. "It tends to...relax things a bit."

"Ah." I nodded.

That might not have been the best gesture to make. I suddenly felt off-balance. No, it was more than that. I felt...good. Very good indeed. Contended. Relaxed. Aroused.

That last bit came as a surprise—one that had my heart beating faster. It was more than that. I felt...eager. As though my balls were filling up at an alarming rate and begging to be emptied.

"Oh, dear," I said, shifting uneasily in my seat. "I feel a bit—"

"We'll help you," Sascha said, his voice deep and sonorous.

For some reason, the men helping me involved Sven sinking to his knees and pulling my shoes and socks off. Not that I minded, really. My feet had warmed up nicely since sitting in front of the fire. I didn't need shoes and socks anyhow.

When he stood, Sven lifted me off the sofa to stand as well. I wasn't sure I'd be able to support myself, but I needn't have worried about that. Sascha got up from his chair and stepped toward me.

"I think, perhaps, I'd better—"

I got no further than that. Sascha clasped the sides of my hot face and slanted his mouth over mine. My eyes went wide at his kiss, though the intoxicating effect of the tea remained. I'd *seen* plenty of kissing in my life, but I'd never actually *been* kissed myself. It was far more invasive than I expected, but infinitely pleasanter. Sascha didn't just caress my lips with his, he parted them and thrust his tongue into my mouth. That surprised me, but I found it to be invigorating. Even if I didn't know what to do in return. It wasn't every day that one found oneself with a strange man's tongue in their mouth.

If that wasn't distracting enough, Dmitri soon stepped up behind me. He reached around to unbutton my dinner jacket, then pulled it from my shoulders. As he did that, Gregor—who had returned from the kitchen —tugged at my bowtie, loosening that and pulling it away. After discarding my jacket, Dmitri reached around for the buttons of my waistcoat and undid those. Sascha broke away from my mouth as he did, starting on the buttons of my shirt once Dmitri pulled my waistcoat away.

I was still reeling from the way Sascha had kissed me —and from the effects of the tea—but as soon as Sascha finished with the buttons of my shirt and Sven stepped in to lift said shirt over my head, baring my torso, I began to get the idea that I was in trouble. Perhaps that was because of the way Dmitri and Sven and Ivan all ran their hands over my exposed flesh, causing goose flesh to spring up. Or perhaps it was because Sascha reached for the fastenings of my trousers to undo them. Or perhaps it was because, in between taking turns touching and caressing me, my hosts for the evening had begun to remove their own clothing.

Everything that had been said to me that evening and more came rushing back in on me. The way Dmitri had stroked himself at first sight of me—something I'd tried to forget—made more sense now. Even the tea had a logical place in what I knew was happening. Logical in that I realized it was intended to make me unable to protest what my hosts were about to do to me. And I knew exactly what that was. What came as a shock to me was that the shiver of fear I felt was rather delicious. I wanted it. I wanted them.

So much so that when Sascha finished with my trousers and pushed them down my legs, I was already hard.

"Look at you," Sascha said, his eyes hungry, his tone impressed. "You're impressive for such a sweet young pup."

"Thank you, I—" My instinct for politeness was cut short as Sascha cupped my heavy balls and squeezed them ever so slightly. I gasped, then let out a plaintive cry as he stroked his hand up my shaft. I'd never had another man touch me—not like that and not like anything. If I'd ever had a shred of doubt about my sexual preferences, that ended it.

If that wasn't telling enough, Dmitri stepped into me from behind, pressing his front against my back. My eyes —which had turned heavy-lidded—went wide when I realized he was naked. His hard cock pressed into the small of my back. And God helped me, I found myself wishing I were taller or he were shorter so that that magnificent cock that I'd had a peek of pressed against something else entirely.

"That's it, pup," Sascha cooed, stroking me slowly as Sven pulled my trousers the rest of the way down my legs and helped me to step out of them. "You're such a good boy. Such a good, sweet boy."

Those words did something to me that the mere touch of them men alone couldn't have done. It was the first time in my entire life that I'd ever been complimented, that I'd been told I was good and not some horrible, disappointing aberration. My heart felt warm in a way that the rest of my body didn't, and I smiled as Sascha captured my mouth in a kiss once more. My back was still flush against Dmitri—who was grinding himself sensually against the top of my ass—so I closed my eyes and leaned into him, simply enjoying the moment, mad though it was.

While my eyes were still closed, Sven and Ivan moved in closer at my sides, and I discovered that they were both naked as well. They each took one of my hands and wrapped it around their hard, hot cocks. That snapped my eyes open again. I glanced quickly at each of them, overwhelmed by how big both of their pricks were. In fact, all of my hosts were exceptionally well-hung. They were all naked now too—except Sascha. But within moments, he stepped back to hastily remove his own clothes.

As he did, Gregor moved in to kiss my neck and shoulders, then to tease my chest and nipples with his teeth and tongue. All the while, someone had their hands on my rigid cock and around my balls. Then Dmitri moved in from behind to nibble my shoulders and back, and even Sven and Ivan kissed my face or traced my ears with their tongues. There were so many hands and mouths on me that it all blended into a mass of erotic sensation.

I loved it. I wasn't even ashamed to admit it, though perhaps that was the tea. It was amazing. I rubbed my hands up and down Sven and Ivan's cocks, enjoying the chorus of moans and sounds of pleasure we were all making, even me. Everything was pleasure, inside and out.

"Gregor," Sascha ordered in a hoarse voice, gesturing to the kitchen. "Sven." He nodded to Sven.

The two moved away, and for a moment I felt as though I'd lost something. I was still feeling hazy from the tea and lust, but I heard a heavy scraping. Sascha pulled me away from Dmitri and Ivan a moment later, commanding my mouth again, but also tugging me to walk forward with him. I would much rather have feasted on the sight of his naked body. He was perfect and golden, even in the dead of winter, with a broad chest, trim waist, and a cock that had me breathless.

I only had a brief glance at him before being led to what appeared to be a workbench of some sort. Sven had pulled it out from the corner, then rushed to find a blanket and pillow to lay over the narrow top. As soon as that was done, without being entirely certain how I got there, I was bent forward over the bench.

"Be gentle with him," Sascha said. "That virgin ass

will be tight. It's mine first, but we'll all get our chance. And go easy on his mouth too. He won't come to love it if all he does it chokes and gags."

I had an inkling of what he meant, particularly as the way I was bent over the bench put my face at the level of my hosts' waists. My hunch was proven correct a moment later when Dmitri came to stand in front of me. He cupped his hand under my chin, brushed his thumb over my lower lip, then tugged my mouth open enough to move his cock inside.

I gasped at the intrusion, especially since he slowly filled my mouth until I felt as though I might gag, in spite of Sascha's cautions. I knew that men did these things, and secretly, I'd always wanted to try, so the shock wasn't unwelcome.

"That's a good pup," Dmitri cooed in his deep bass, as he rocked in and out, urging me to take more, bit by bit.

I hummed in response, which caused him to suck in a breath. My mouth felt stretched and full. The taste of him was salt and musk. I kept swallowing reflexively, and every time I did, I could feel a reaction in Dmitri, so I tried doing it deliberately.

"Fuck, he's a quick learner," Dmitri groaned.

"Let me," Sven said, nudging Dmitri out of the way.

I had two seconds to catch my breath as Dmitri stumbled back before Sven offered his prick for me to swallow. I let him slide it in deep, but when I choked, he pulled back.

"I said careful," Sascha snapped.

That sharp command, given on my behalf, only made me eager to try again. Sven came back to me, and I glanced up at him, opening my mouth eagerly. He slid in more carefully, and we worked together to find a way that pleased us both.

The whole time that was going on, I was only barely aware of Ivan and Gregor finding cushions for the floor under me, and of my legs being spread apart as they did. I cried out—even though I had Sven's prick filling my mouth, as someone moved to kiss and lick my ass, focusing with increasing intensity on my hole. That wasn't the only thing. My eyes went wide at first, then heavy-lidded, and a muffled sound of surprise turned into long moans as someone positioned underneath me closed his mouth around my throbbing cock the same way I had mine around Sven's.

"Move." Dmitri pushed Sven aside—I had two seconds to breathe and cry out with pleasure—then pushed his prick deep into my mouth. "Whatever Gregor is doing to you, do that to me."

I nodded in obedience—which was somewhat difficult to do with a fat cock working in my mouth—then tried to concentrate enough on what was happening to me to duplicate it. I did my best, but that proved impossible when Gregor's sucking and swallowing brought me off so suddenly and so hard that I cried out around Dmitri's cock. It only helped things that whoever was behind me—likely Sascha—was tonguing my hole perfectly.

My whole body went limp in the aftermath, but that didn't stop my companions.

"Fuck, he's sweet," Gregor panted from somewhere under me.

"Thank God for your tea," Sascha said, confirming he was the one playing with my ass.

A moment later, still feeling hot and liquid and disjointed, the cycle of arousal seemed to begin all over again. I wondered if I was right when I'd speculated that my balls seemed to be filling up with unusual intensity. My prick was hard again in no time, which was unnatural, but seemed to suit my companions just fine.

"I want to put him to the test," Dmitri said with an insistence that sent that delicious sort of fear through me again. "Push him to his limit."

The way he jerked in my mouth turned more intense, bordering on choking me again, but I concentrated enough to stave off gagging—perhaps helped by my physical focus being split by someone sliding their somehow slick cock into my right hand. Dmitri's sounds grew more desperate, and moments later, I swallowed reflexively as he shot into my throat.

I barely had time to enjoy the sensation—or, once again, to breathe—as Dmitri stumbled back. Sven took his place once more, and I hummed eagerly as I accepted him. Though at the same time, something cool and silky slid over my hole. That was followed by a thick finger penetrating me. It was a surprise, but a welcome one.

I tried to move into it—in spite of Sven working in my

mouth—but found I couldn't move. At all. I didn't know if it was because I'd been fastened into my position somehow or because the tea had, at last, rendered me incapable of movement. All I knew was that I was completely and utterly relaxed, aroused, and at the mercy of the men around me. And they were merciless.

Sascha's single finger turned into two as he stretched my asshole in what I knew was preparation for more. I was vaguely aware of some of my companions switching positions around me, until once again, someone was swallowing my cock.

It took longer the second time, which made everything more enjoyable—the man who was using my hand to pleasure himself, Sven pumping in my mouth, and Sascha fingering my ass wide. We were all making sounds of pleasure, all enjoying every second. When Sven came in my mouth I sputtered a little, but only because I was so close to coming myself. I did shortly after he withdrew, crying out with a sound that was both primal and melodic. Cum spilled through my right hand a moment later.

And just as before, within a minute, as the others shifted around me, touching, stroking, and petting me, I went from feeling spent and limp to vibrating with tension all over again as my prick surged back to life. It definitely wasn't natural, but I wasn't complaining.

"You're ready, little pup," Sascha told me as I'd finally caught my breath, arching over me. His hands rested on the bench by my sides, then I felt the hot tip of his cock—seemingly impossibly large—against my hole.

I drew in a sharp breath, then let it out in a long moan as he invaded me. It was as if my body couldn't make up its mind whether it wanted to resist or not. Sascha seemed so much bigger than I ever imagined a man would feel in me. Sweat broke out down my back, as I arched as best I could. He jerked hard, and pushing past the resisting muscles of my hole and sinking in deep. So deep that I felt his balls slap against my ass.

"Oh!" I gasped. "Oh!"

"Does it hurt, little pup?" he asked in a voice that was more like a caress.

It did, but not in a bad way. Or perhaps I was damaged enough that I liked how it hurt. Burned would be a better way to describe it. I felt possessed, filled, claimed in the most intimate way. And that was before Sascha started to move in me.

"Oh," I sighed again, my eyes rolling back in my head, my mouth staying open.

It stayed open, but it was filled a moment later by Ivan. I felt as though I'd lost my mind—with Sascha in my ass, Ivan in my mouth, and moments later, with each hand wrapped around someone else's cock and someone under me, taking my prick to the hilt. It passed through the only remaining shred of my brain capable of thought that I was pleasuring all five of them at once in some way. We were like one, unified animal of pleasure, grunting, moving, sighing, and, soon enough, coming. Sascha let out a cry, and filled my ass. A moment later, I swallowed a thick stream of cum from Ivan.

When Sascha moved away, someone else took his place, and I cried out all over again as another cock filled me. Whoever that was moved faster, as though they were already near to bursting. I was so close again myself that when they came, I exploded as well. Whoever was under me moaned as they swallowed me, then moved to take their turn at my ass. With just that sensation to concentrate on, I was able to appreciate the paradoxical pleasure of being penetrated and used and filled. And when that man was done, the last of them took his place. I could do nothing but sprawl over the workbench, ass on fire—but in the best possible way—and let him pummel into me until he, too, cried out and spilled into me.

I was so spent once he was done that I could only lay draped over the workbench. I didn't even care that it was horribly uncomfortable, that my inability to move was because I was drugged, or that I felt bruised in a dozen different ways. The sensation of spunk dripping out of my ass and running down my thighs captured every last bit of attention that remained to me. It felt so good I wanted to cry.

"That is the most beautiful thing I've ever seen," I heard Sascha's voice say behind me.

"God, look at that ass," Gregor agreed. "So creamy and perfect."

"I'm never going to forget that sight," Ivan added.

Even though I was draped over the workbench, arms

hanging down in front of me, I smiled. Not with mere politeness, but with a joy that sank all the way to my heart.

"Our pup is fucking amazing," Dmitri said.

That curled around my heart like an embrace. I hurt all over. My ass throbbed in pain. My stomach felt vaguely sick, and my jaw was sore. My mouth tasted musky and dirty, and my cock—which was finally satisfied—felt rubbed raw. And I was utterly exhausted besides. But I was being complimented, praised in a way I'd never been before. I was being revered and appreciated for the very things that had made people sneer at me, call me disgusting, and turn up their noses at me for my entire life.

As I floated off to sleep—in spite of the hurt and my awkward position over the workbench—I wondered when we'd be able to do it again.

3

The first thing that caught my awareness when I awoke—even before the morning light filtering in through what passed for curtains in a window several yards away from me—was the warm, firm, and very large body against my back. It startled me at first. I'd never shared a bed in my life, but there was definitely someone in bed with me. Someone much, much bigger than me. Someone naked, as I was naked too.

I sucked in a breath in a moment of panic before remembering where I was—in general, because I had no idea where I was specifically—and what had happened the night before. That memory caused the panic to morph into a dozen scattered emotions, all of which had my heart beating faster. I'd been thrown out of the city by my brothers and found by Dmitri. Dmitri had taken me home and introduced me to his brothers? Friends? Companions? I still wasn't sure what they were. They'd given me something to eat and a tea that had intoxicated and immobilized me. And then they'd used me sexually until I was sore and bruised and senseless with satisfaction.

And now there I was, in bed with one of the men. He had me tucked against him, my head cradled on one of his massive biceps, his arm draped possessively over my side, his hand on my lower belly, my ass—which throbbed painfully from use—nestled against his hips. His erection pressed hot against my ass, but seeing as his breathing was slow and steady, I guessed he was still asleep and unaware of his morning wood.

Perhaps more surprising was my own morning erection. Waking in that condition was common enough, but considering the details of the night before and my current position, it unnerved me. It didn't help matters that the more I recalled of my activities with my hosts the night before, the harder I became. Which felt wildly inappropriate to me.

In the palace, I was always considered the least sexually interesting man possible. My preference for academic and artistic pursuits, my detailed study of the law, the care I took with my appearance—not to mention the androgyny of that appearance—and my soft-spoken manner had caused everyone to assume I was neither interested in or any sort of object of sexual desire. It wasn't true on my part. I had those feelings and impulses as much as anyone, maybe more, but I'd always assumed I would never have a chance to act on them. Ever.

Now, there I was, lying in a naked man's arms, pulse quickened with the wild notion that I'd stumbled into a situation where my primary value was as a sexual object. For five different men. And whether it was something narcotic in the tea they'd given me or my own latent impulses, I had not disappointed the night before.

The whole thing was overwhelmingly surreal.

The man in whose arms I slept stirred and stretched as he awoke. The ripple of his considerably muscled form against my much slighter body, both aroused me and made me aware of every part of me that was sore and bruised. I turned my head as much as I could to see that I was with Sascha. That lined up with the few things I was able to determine about my hosts the night before—namely, that Sascha was their leader somehow, and would, therefore, have first rights to me.

I shivered a bit at all the implications of that thought.

Sascha must have felt the slight tremor in my body. A lazy smile spread across his face, and he held me tighter against him. "Good morning, little pup," he said, the words sounding contented. "Did you sleep well?"

Come to think of it, I had. "Yes, thank you," I answered. My voice sounded so small and gentle compared to his, just as my body felt delicate compared to his mammoth form. And I wasn't overly skinny or boney. Sascha was just so large.

He chuckled deeply, as if amused by my politeness. The vibrations left me buzzing.

"I...I don't remember how I got to bed," I said, not sure what else I could say.

"I brought you here," Sascha said. "After cleaning you up a bit." His hand began to wander my stomach, chest, and side, making me short of breath and hot. "You slept like a babe through the whole thing."

"I suppose I was exhausted, after the evening I'd had," I said. Or, at least, I tried to say. The words came out between gasps and sighs as he continued to explore me.

His touch made me restless. I could count on one hand the number of times in my life when I'd been touched with anything even slightly resembling tenderness. I'd certainly been manhandled, shoved, and beaten by my brothers and many others, but I couldn't remember ever being embraced, or even receiving a pat on the back or so much as a handshake. The people of Novoberg had always treated me as though touching me would give them plague.

But now, Sascha was stroking and caressing me as though I were a cherished pet. Logic told me I should be terrified, particularly as he was simultaneously grinding his thick erection against my backside. His intent was clear—even before he slipped his hand over my hip and between my thighs to fondle my balls. Sense told me his interest was carnal, but instead of protesting or thrashing to get away, I let out a supremely sensual moan as he toyed with me.

His rumbling laughter sounded against my back as he

curled himself so that he could nibble on my neck. "You're hungry for it, aren't you, pup?"

"I—" I had no idea what to say. I didn't think I'd be capable of saying anything for a while when he drew his hand up the length of my throbbing cock.

"You're big for being such a sweet little thing," he said, wrapping his hand around me. He moved with slow, almost tender strokes, swiping his thumb over my head, which was leaking pre-cum. I could already feel telltale signs of orgasm building in me. "Big and eager and oh so sweet," he murmured against my ear. "But not as big as me."

I'd closed my eyes while he stroked me, focusing on the pleasure he gave, but opened them reluctantly when he rolled suddenly away from me. Instead of feeling relief, like good sense told me I should, I felt bereft without him. That rush of feeling embarrassed me, and my face heated.

It heated even more when I twisted to look over my shoulder, only to find him retrieving a small bottle from the table beside the bed. For a moment, I was aware of the room. It was a simple bedroom with no adornment. The two windows on the wall I faced as I lay on my side were covered with unhemmed squares of muslin that didn't do much to keep out the morning sunlight. The room contained a wardrobe, a fireplace, the bed we lay in, a table beside it, a chair, and a chest at the foot of the bed.

I had only a second to notice that the bed's headboard was elaborately carved with wolves—something that inspired a spike of fear—before Sascha twisted back to me, the bottle in his hand. He nudged me to roll nearly all the way to my stomach, then tipped the uncorked bottle over my ass.

I gasped as cool, viscous liquid slipped over my crack. I gasped again as Sascha parted my ass cheeks. I'm not even certain what the noise I made was as he smoothed the liquid over my hole, teasing and massaging.

"Your poor, sweet ass," he said, his voice more proud than sympathetic. "It's bright red. I should have told the others to hold off last night. Does it hurt?"

"A bit," I confessed breathlessly as he dripped more of the liquid onto my hole. I couldn't shake the feeling that it would have been rude to tell him the full truth— that his touch felt like fire. "I...I have a high tolerance for pain," I admitted with a gasp as he pressed one finger into me. "Thanks to my brothers' mistreatment of me over the years."

"The last thing I want to do, pup, is mistreat you," Sascha said.

He slipped a second finger inside of me to join the first. I winced and made a sound that was something between a groan of pain and one of pleasure.

"Do you want me to stop?" Sascha asked, his fingers still inside of me.

"Please, no," I panted, surprising myself. That wasn't any tea talking. I genuinely didn't want him to stop. My cock throbbed, and my balls had drawn up, aching for release.

Sascha chuckled and spread my legs apart, kneeling between them. "Eager little pup," he growled. "You're going to wear us out long before we tire you out."

My instinct to reply was cut short as he lifted my hips and flexed into me. I sucked in a breath at the contact of his cock's head against my hole, then grimaced, fisting my hands in the bedclothes, as he breeched me. It wasn't any easier than the first time he'd split me open, even though the liquid he'd used eased and cooled things considerably. He pushed past my body's resistance, and once he did, I let out a cry of pleasure as he pushed in to the hilt.

"Tell me if I'm hurting you," he said in a voice impatient with need, then started to move.

It was extraordinarily painful...and incredibly pleasurable. It occurred to me that if I hadn't been so sore from being had by five men the night before, there might not have been any pain at all, just ecstasy. The way he filled and stretched me felt so good. His increasing speed and accompanying sounds of pleasure added to everything I felt. He shifted the way he was fucking me just slightly and touched on a spot inside of me that sent white-hot pleasure through me.

He shifted again, reaching around to hold my throbbing cock. "Fuck, pup, you want it so badly. You're desperate for it."

I gave him perhaps the most appropriate answer possible. I came hard in his hand, crying out plaintively as I did. He responded in kind by jerking hard into me a few more times before letting out a guttural cry. His warmth spread inside of me. I felt exhilarated by it. His body grew heavy over mine, but at first, he stayed sheathed inside of me.

"You are mine, pup," he panted against my ear. "I might let the others play with you, but make no mistake, you belong to me."

A shiver passed through me. I absolutely believed him. The way he had me bent forward under him, his softening cock still in my ass, his weight holding me almost immobile, my cock and my cum in his hand, and his breath hot against my neck made me believe it. Again, I knew I was supposed to be terrified in that moment, but it felt so good that all I could do was close my eyes and smile. I was in so far over my head that I didn't think I'd ever see the surface again.

Eventually, Sascha pulled back. I winced and grunted with pain as he left my body, then sagged onto my stomach, overwhelmed with physical sensations. I was tempted to drift off to sleep again, but when Sascha touched my ass, sliding his finger through my crack, my hole leaking his cum, I flinched.

"Peter, you should have told me it hurt too much," he scolded. "You're obviously in pain. I shouldn't have done that."

"I didn't want to disappoint you," I panted, rolling to my side.

Sascha stared incredulously at me, then shook his head. His expression of tenderness was almost paradoxical. "Your purpose is pleasure, not pain."

As he moved off the bed and over to a closet that I'd only barely noticed earlier, my heart thumped against my ribs. My purpose was pleasure. That seemed to confirm what I was doing there. A dozen other questions popped into my mind with that realization.

I was about to ask the first one when I heard the sound of running water from the closet. That surprised me enough to sit up—which wasn't, perhaps, the best idea. I was sorer than I'd realized, and sitting was a challenge.

Sascha walked back into the room with a damp rag. He brought it to me, but rather than handing it off so I could clean myself, he did the job for me. He washed my stomach and cock—which were sticky with my own spunk—then gestured for me to turn over so he could gently wash my ass. I was too startled by the possessive care he showed me as he cleaned up the remnants of what we'd done.

When that was finished, he helped me to stand. I wasn't sure I needed help, but once I was on my feet, I was highly aware of not only my throbbingly sore ass, but my tender joints as well, probably from all the positions I'd been bent and folded into since arriving at the house in the forest. My clothes were in the other room and it was highly unlikely that any of Sascha's clothes would fit me, so he fished a fur-lined robe out of his wardrobe and dressed me in that. He dressed me, complete with tying the robe's sash, then dressed himself. I studied the overlong arms of the robe with a curious look as he did. The robe smelled like Sascha as well, which wasn't a bad thing.

Once Sascha was dressed, he took my hand and led me out of his bedroom and into a long hall. I tried not to wince with each step I took, figuring that if Sascha saw I was in pain, he might try to carry me. While that was appealing on one level, my dignity wouldn't allow it.

The hall contained several doors, some open to show other unadorned bedrooms, some closed. The hall ended in the main room of the house that I'd seen the night before. In the morning light, it looked even more home-like and inviting than it had the night before. Not only that, scents of coffee, bacon, and fresh bread filled the air. My stomach grumbled in response, and I realized I was ravenously hungry.

Dmitri sat in the same chair by the fireplace he'd occupied the night before. He was fashioning arrows of some sort, but the second Sascha led me into the room, he looked up, an unmistakable hunger in his eyes. His smile was equally hungry. I knew full well what that portended, and while part of me thrilled at that look, I moaned inwardly at it on behalf of my burning ass.

The others gave me similar looks, though each in their own way. Gregor was sitting at the dining room table with a collection of dried herbs and empty bottles in front of him. He wore spectacles as he made notes on tiny slips of paper next to each bottle, but when he glanced to me, it was with clear thoughts of what activities he could engage in once his work was done. Ivan and Sven were in the kitchen, preparing breakfast. They both smiled at me, and then at each other, as though all three of us would get to know each other much better later. I almost regretted the stirring in my prick at the way the four other men took such notice in me.

"Our little pup is probably starving," Sascha said, leading me to the table.

"I must confess, I am," I said in a modest voice, blushing slightly. "But I don't want you to go to any trouble on my account. I'm not picky. I'll eat whatever you've made. I could even help set the table, if you need me to."

I started toward the kitchen, but Sascha stopped me with one of his huge hands on my shoulder. "You'll do no such thing. That's not your place here."

I gulped and nodded up at him—I couldn't decide if he seemed bigger when he was standing above me or lying beside me or balls deep inside me. "Please let me know what you'd like me to do," I said quietly.

I think I might have accidentally sounded far more submissive than I'd intended to, but the result was fascinating. Sascha drew in a breath and grinned as though I'd uttered words of wisdom. Dmitri got up from his seat by the fire and came to the table. Gregor lowered his glasses to stare at me.

I glanced nervously to each of them in turn, even to Ivan and Sven in the kitchen. "Have I...have I said something wrong?" I asked, gulping in the middle.

"Far from it," Dmitri said, his smile wolfish, rubbing a hand over his mouth.

"You've said everything exactly right," Gregor added, laughing and shaking his head.

I didn't understand why my simple offer was remarkable. I was far more interested in the swiftness with which my hosts told me I'd done something right. I was much more used to constantly being told I was doing everything wrong.

"Sit, Peter," Ivan said, bringing a plate of freshly baked and sliced bread, dripping with butter to the table. "I've been up for hours making breakfast for you."

Sven stepped in to hold out a place at the table for me. Baffled by their hospitality, I moved to sit. "Oh!" I cried out as soon as my ass hit the chair and flinched up. It was worse than I'd thought.

"Dmitri, a cushion," Sascha ordered, snapping his fingers.

Dmitri frowned at him, but moved to fetch one from the sofa. He placed it on my chair, and I was careful when I sat the second time. It was still uncomfortable, but at least I was able to manage it.

What caught my attention more was the tension I sensed between Sascha and Dmitri. I hadn't noticed it the night before, but it was plain as day now. I watched them for a moment, then covertly glanced to the others as Sascha moved my chair closer to the table as Sven poured my coffee.

"Do you take cream and sugar?" he asked.

"Yes, please," I answered with a smile.

What I really did was study the way he, too, peeked at Sascha and Dmitri as they took their seats for breakfast. It didn't take much to guess what was going on. Sascha was the leader of the group, but Dmitri was second and eager to take over as first. I'd seen the same sort of rivalry among my brothers. Frederic was the eldest and heir, but Rudolph was less than a year younger and constantly envious. I'd often wondered if Frederic would one day fall down a long staircase or have an accident while out riding, and if he had, I would have known who was to blame. The same energy was there between Sascha and Dmitri, but as far as I was aware, there wasn't any precedent of birth holding them to their positions. Anything could change at a moment.

"I hope I've made enough," Ivan said, bringing two heaping platters of food to the table. I caught his flicker of a glance toward Sascha and Dmitri before he sat down.

"This looks delicious," I complimented him with a smile. "I'm certain it's more than enough."

I reached for the platter of bread, but Sascha grabbed my hand from his seat beside me and shoved it back. He then chose two of the fattest, butteriest slices from the platter and put them on my plate. I almost tried to help myself to some of the bacon that was being passed around the table, but I already knew how that would go. Sascha served my entire breakfast without blinking an eye. He was waiting on me as surely as my father's footmen had.

"Enjoy your breakfast, pup," Dmitri smiled from the head of the table. "And then we'll enjoy our dessert."

I opened my mouth to express my curiosity about dessert being served in the morning, but realized a moment later what he meant. My face flushed—which must have made me look like a painted porcelain doll—and the stirring I'd felt earlier increased to the beginnings of an erection under the table.

"His ass if off-limits until he heals," Sascha said, as if that were the sort of thing that was discussed in ordinary conversation.

"I've got a salve for that," Gregor said, also without a hint of embarrassment or guile.

"There are plenty of ways our pup and I can get to know each other better that don't involve injuring him further." Dmitri frowned at Sascha, then smiled at me.

I swallowed some of the coffee Ivan had poured for me awkwardly as I wondered what those things could be. Once I'd recovered, I asked, "Begging your pardon, but why do you keep calling me 'pup'? My name is Peter."

My hosts exchanged grins, giving me the feeling that there was an entire world of things I didn't know but was about to find out.

"Because you're our wolf pup," Dmitri answered, as though it were obvious.

I felt sheepish for not understanding him—and a bit unnerved by the reference to wolves. "I'm terribly sorry," I said, trying not to speak with my mouth full, but as interested to know what was going on as I was to eat everything in front of me to stave off hunger, "but I don't understand."

"Haven't you ever heard of the wolves in the forest?" Ivan asked from his seat across the table from me.

"Don't go into the forest or the wolves will get you," Sven growled.

The two of them laughed, but I sank into my seat. "I'm afraid of wolves," I admitted in a tiny voice. "I love animals of all sorts, but not wolves. They terrify me."

My hosts exchanged looks as though I'd said something hilarious.

"You liked wolves enough last night," Gregor said with a grin.

"I didn't encounter any, thank God," I told him. "Dmitri found me first, and then I was safe from them under your roof."

All movement at the table stopped for a moment before my hosts burst into laughter.

"Peter, *we're* the wolves," Sascha explained.

My eyes went wide and I nearly choked on my eggs.

"The men who live in the forest are called wolves," Gregor said, seeming quite academic all of a sudden. "At least, a certain type of man living in the forest. We live in packs throughout the vast forests that separate towns and cities."

"The city-dwellers gave forest-dwellers that ridiculous nickname generations ago," Sascha continued the explanation. "Mostly to frighten sweet little pups like you out of running away to join us." He placed his hand on my leg under the table.

I felt a warm jolt at his touch that made me glad I was sitting at a table. Though one would think I'd been touched quite enough for one day, especially intimately. I knew I hadn't, though. I suspected that after going for twenty years with hardly any touch, I wouldn't be able to get enough of it now.

That is, if....

I swallowed my bite of bread. "Am I to understand that you are referring to me as your pup because—" I caught my breath before going on, "—you intend to keep me?"

"Our pup is clever indeed," Dmitri said, winking at me from his end of the table.

My heart raced as I glanced around the table. All five of them were looking at me with a possessive fire. I was clever, I'll admit it. I always had been. In that moment, I was clever enough to understand that I'd gone into the forest after dark and the wolves had gotten me...and eaten me alive, just as the legends said they would. Though perhaps not exactly according to legend. And now that they had me, they weren't going to let me go. Sascha had even whispered to me that I was his now, in spite of what the others might think. *His*.

Forever a possession of a wolf pack. One that was intended to be used the way I had been last night, and by Sascha that morning. I reached for my coffee and took a gulp, fighting to reconcile why my insides hummed with excitement at the idea instead of roiling in fear. I couldn't decide if I'd sunk horribly low in the world or if I'd been lifted up beyond any expectations.

"There are many kinds of people living in the forest," Sascha went on. "Most of us live separate from each other, for our protection and for the protection of others. We look and behave like most others, though, so we are able to attend village faires and even walk through the streets of cities, purchasing whatever wares we need, or even working temporarily, within city walls. Most of us choose not to do that, though."

"Wolves are a particular sort of forest-dweller," Gregor picked up the explanation. "Wolves are men who like other men, as we all do."

"Which I'm sure you figured out last night," Sven said, exchanging a wink with Ivan. It occurred to me that the two of them had a deeper connection between themselves than the other members of what I assumed they called their pack did.

"I see," I answered, slightly hoarse, finishing the bacon on my plate. I was careful to maintain a look of curiosity to encourage my hosts to go on.

"Wolves have appetites," Dmitri said, arching an eyebrow hungrily at me. "Occasionally, we require fresh meat."

Sascha sent him a disapproving look. "It's not as dramatic as all that. Packs sometimes take on new members. Sometimes those new members are a certain type of man—young, gentle, fey." He nodded to me.

I certainly fit the description. "I wasn't aware that men like me wandered into the forest with any frequency," I said.

"They don't," Gregor answered with a touch of irony. "Pups are extraordinarily rare. And you're a thousand times rarer than any pup I've ever heard of."

"For several reasons," Dmitri added, just slightly menacing, as usual.

He was clearly—at least to me—referring to my willingness to pleasure them all the night before. Which begged the question, what was the fate of pups who weren't as embarrassingly willing as I had been? Unless that was the purpose of the tea. I couldn't help but admit to myself that I would have been willing even without the tea, though. Perhaps. Five was a lot of men for a virgin to take on at once, as my aching body screamed at me. Would I have allowed so much to happen if I hadn't been drugged?

I drank the last of my coffee thoughtfully before saying, "I suppose this spares me coming up with an excuse for where I've been all night once I return to the city gates."

"You're not going back to the city gates," Sascha said with a wry grin.

"Yes, I'd gathered as much," I said in a wispy, equally wry reply.

My hosts—or should I refer to them as my pack or my captors—chuckled. Gregor winked at me. Sven and Ivan exchanged another look that seemed to confirm my suspicion they were a couple within the group—though one that didn't mind sharing an occasional pup.

"I almost wish I could hear my brothers attempt to explain my disappearance to my father," I said, reaching for the coffee pot to refill my cup. "Not that my father will care one way or another. He'll probably be thrilled to be rid of me."

Sascha pulled my hand away from the coffee pot and gestured for Svan to pour for me. I'd forgotten that I wasn't supposed to serve myself. Only them. I would most definitely be expected to service the pack. All five of them. My ass felt sorer just thinking about it.

My cock wasn't as reticent. I was embarrassed at my body's enthusiasm for capture.

"Are there other wolf packs living nearby?" I asked, suddenly nervous. They might not have been actual wolves, but Gregor's hint that pups wandering in the woods was rare and that I was rarer still immediately set me to wondering whether there was a code of honor among wolf packs or if pups were stolen and put to use by hordes of strange men. The thought was even more terrifying than real wolves.

"Not for miles," Sascha said, resting his hand on my leg under the table again. This time, he must have brushed up against my erection. A grin tugged at the corner of his mouth, and he slipped his hand between the folds of the robe I wore to be certain.

I fought not to let it show in my expression when he

cupped his hand around me. Thankfully, he withdrew a moment later and went on.

"We live remotely for several reasons. No one is entirely sure of our numbers or where other packs live. We are spread throughout the forest, though. There are rumors of greater numbers of wolves to the south, but I've never cared to investigate."

I didn't think that could be true. There was nothing but wild forest to the south, too thick to traverse. Everyone knew that.

"Wolves tend to carve our their territory and then stick to it doggedly, if you'll pardon the pun," Gregor said.

"We don't tell others where we live for the most part. Not all wolf packs are as prosperous or well-equipped as we are," he explained.

"If some of the other packs I know of were aware of half the things we have that they don't, I shudder to think what might happen," Gregor said.

"Oh?" I asked curiously.

Dmitri pointed to Gregor with his fork. "Gregor here was training to be a court physician in Seymchan before being found out and ostracized."

"It was one of my patients," Gregor sighed. "A duke's son, like you. He was young and nubile. How could I resist a cock like that?" He glanced to me with a wicked look. "I love the feel of a good cock in my mouth. I might not ever get tired of yours."

I swallowed my coffee wrong and spent the next

several seconds sputtering while Sascha thumping my back and the others laughed.

"Gregor's healing abilities are legendary in the woods," Sven explained. "But there are some groups who aren't content to purchase his remedies or see him by appointment at the occasional village faire."

"How many kidnapping attempts have we thwarted now?" Ivan asked.

"None since I passed the flower of youth," Gregor laughed.

None of that was remotely reassuring where my safety was concerned.

"Dmitri here is one of the most skilled hunters in the forest," Sven said, nodding across the table to him. "Not only can he track the animals with the finest pelts, he can kill them without leaving a mark. His furs fetch a pretty penny, as does the meat."

"But there are too many thieves who would gladly raid our stores before I ever get those furs and meat to market," Dmitri said.

I ran a hand over the robe I wore, assuming Dmitri was partially responsible for it.

"Don't let Ivan and Sven fool you either," Sascha said. "As I think was said last night, Ivan was once an apprentice to the head chef in the castle at Klovisgard."

"And I was apprenticed to the head gardener," Sven said, reaching across the table to take Ivan's hand. "They stripped us naked and threw us out in the middle of the night when we were discovered in bed together."

My jaw dropped. It had never even occurred to me that anyone would be brave enough to so much as attempt that sort of relationship in a city.

"Sven is the reason our kitchen garden flourishes," Sascha explained. "And Ivan is responsible for how well we all eat."

"And for the baked goods we sell at village faires," Ivan added.

"And Sascha was a carpenter and engineer," I said, happy that I remembered that much from the night before. "You built the house."

"I did." The way Sascha smiled at me sent swirls of warmth through me. "And the furniture. I also have a workshop in the back where I make furniture to sell at—"

"Village faires," I finished for him.

"You're a clever little pup." He leaned in and kissed me soundly.

My brow flew up and my eyes went wide, not just because of the kiss, but because of the ridiculously pleased feeling in my gut at having guessed right. I was twenty years old. I should not have been responding to simple compliments and petting like I was a child.

But it felt so good I couldn't help myself.

It took me a moment to catch my breath once Sascha pulled away from kissing me. "There's a workshop in the back?" I asked.

"There are a lot of things in the back," Dmitri answered, standing. He pushed back his chair and started around the table to me, one hand extended. "Come on.

I'll show you." The fire in his eyes said he'd show me more than that.

I peeked at Sascha, highly aware of the claim he'd made on me that morning.

Sascha looked as though he were trying to marshal his patience. "Just remember that he's still recovering from last night," he said at last.

"How could I forget?" Dmitri smirked.

It wasn't that I was reluctant. Far from it. My heart pounded and my cock stood up before I did. It was the undercurrent of tension between Dmitri and Sascha that made me anxious. That and the feeling that even if I hadn't been a willing pup, I would have had no choice about whether to go with Dmitri or not. Dmitri was the hunter, Gregor the doctor, Ivan the cook, Sven the gardener, and Sascha the carpenter. I had a role too, and it was inescapable.

4

I followed Dmitri away from the table and over to a second, shorter hallway than the ones where the bedrooms were located, equal parts curiosity, trepidation, and excitement pulsing through me. Sitting at the table had done nothing to ease my aches and pains, but a warm meal had me feeling better in general.

"Looks like a clear day today," Dmitri said as he opened a door at the end of the short hall and took my hand to pull me outside. "I should be hunting. Perhaps later."

He raked me with a look, but I was too overawed by what I found waiting behind the house to pay it much mind. I'd approached the house in the dark the night before and had mistakenly thought the forest hedged it all around. Perhaps it had been made to appear that way on purpose, but that was far from the case. From the front, the house itself concealed a huge complex of outbuildings and garden beds. I'd noticed one garden bed toward the front of the house, but there were several more in the back, all arranged methodically.

There was a barn which must have contained horses or other animals I couldn't see, a chicken coop, and three main buildings behind the house, which Dmitri gave me brief tours of. Sascha's workshop was bright and smelled of resin and woodchips. Several pieces of furniture were in the process of construction. Gregor's apothecary workshop stood next to that. It smelled richly of herbs of all sorts. Bunches of them hung from the ceiling and even more were waiting to be categorized on shelves along the walls.

Both of those shops amazed me and had me wanting to see more. Dmitri's workshop, on the other hand, nearly made me vomit up everything I'd had for breakfast.

"A little squeamish, are we?" he asked as he stood in the workshop door.

I nodded quickly and backed away, swallowing bile. Dmitri's workshop smelled of blood and raw meat. I told myself that there was nothing to be afraid of, Dmitri was a hunter, and meat had to be processed. I wanted nothing to do with it, though. There were some processes that I just didn't need to know about, even if I benefited from them.

Dmitri chuckled and shut the door. "The hunter's life isn't for everyone. I bring in quite a bit of money for what I do, though."

"I'm sure," I croaked.

"I suppose I won't be inviting you to come hunting with me," Dmitri went on, slipping his arm around my waist and leading me away from his workshop.

"I don't think I could." I tried to be as polite as possible.

"There are related shops behind that building," Dmitri went on, taking me in the opposite direction. "A smokehouse for the meat and a tannery for the skins. Thank God for Gregor's herbs or I would never be able to get the stink of the tannery off of me."

"He makes more than medicines?" I asked, desperate to find something else to talk about to take my mind off of death and suffering.

"He makes all sorts of things." Dmitri ushered me through some of the empty garden beds to a large, flat area made out of flagstones. "You had one of his teas last night."

"What was in it?" I asked, suddenly curious. "It clearly had an intoxicating effect."

Dmitri shrugged. "I don't know Gregor's exact recipe. I'm not entirely certain what he mixed up for you. Judging by the effect it had, my guess is that it was an aphrodisiac mingled with some sort of psychotropic element, possibly mushrooms." He sent me a wicked grin. "I don't know where Gregor finds those mushrooms, but they're amazing."

Nothing Dmitri said surprised me at all. I'd read about all sorts of narcotic mushrooms and herbs. It stood to reason that they were available in the forest. Or maybe

Sven grew them. Perhaps that was another reason Sascha and the others wanted to keep their home hidden.

We reached the circle of flagstones. A smaller, wooden circle lay in the middle. Curls of steam emitted from around the edges. I studied it, then glanced around at the entire complex and the surrounding trees.

"Is there some sort of concealment around the house?" I asked. "Something so that even if intruders were nearby, they wouldn't be able to find it?"

Dmitri chuckled as he toed off his boots. "Are you afraid word about you has gotten out already and other packs are on their way to steal you?"

I was too embarrassed to admit that, yes, I was.

A moment later, I was too interested in what Dmitri was doing to care. Once his boots were off, he pulled off the crude sweater he wore and his shirt with it and tossed them aside. My breath hitched in my throat at the sight of him. His chest was broad and covered with dark hair that formed a line across his flat abdomen, leading down. His arms were not quite as thick as Sascha's, but they were close. He was gorgeous in his own way, and my body responded immediately.

I could have looked at him for much longer—and judging by his smirk, he knew I was looking—but he leaned over to grab a leather handle on the wooden circle and tugged it aside. I was fascinated by the ripple of his muscles as he removed the heavy covering, but even more fascinated by what he uncovered.

"It's fed by the hot spring," Dmitri explained as I

stared into the wide, bubbling pool. "Sascha rigged it up, of course. Two years ago. It's brilliant, even in the dead of winter, when the forest is covered in snow."

It was still cold, even though winter was mostly over. I was shocked for more than one reason as Dmitri shucked his breeches and stood, straight and naked, in the crisp morning air. His cock was as long and thick as I remembered it and already well on its way to being erect.

"Come on, pup." He kicked his clothes aside and approached me slowly, licking his lips. "Let's enjoy each other."

When he reached me, he tugged the tie of my robe, instantly loosening it. I shivered and sucked in a breath as he pushed it from my shoulders, exposing me. Part of me wanted to shield myself from his devouring gaze. I didn't have any tea to make me receptive to whatever he wanted to do. The rest of me didn't need tea at all.

"God, you are unbelievable," Dmitri growled, coming close enough to run his hands up and down my sides. Touring the outbuildings had softened my prick considerably, but the sweep of Dmitri's hands across my sides and around my backside reversed that in a hurry. "How is it possible for one man to be so perfectly formed in every way? Soft, pretty—but not too soft or too pretty." He drew a hand around my hip and between my legs to stroke my cock and handle my balls. "You're definitely a man, with a cock like this, but you're so, so delicate."

Instinct said to thank him, but I was panting too hard for speech as he stepped closer to me. His hands were calloused, and felt amazingly good as they stroked my cock and roved my body. Yes, without a shadow of a doubt, I liked being touched that way. I loved it.

I loved being kissed too. Dmitri moved his body fully against mine, squeezing my ass with one hand—and eliciting a small yelp of pain that he silenced by closing his mouth over mine. He cradled the side of my face with one hand as his mouth devoured me and his tongue explored. I closed my eyes and leaned into it, accepting him and giving him more and more. I knew so little about what I was doing and wondered whether I should be trying to take a more active role, but no, it was my job to let him do whatever he wanted to me and not to resist.

I had to put my hands on his hips, though, if only to support me as my legs threatened to give way. Dmitri hummed in approval, but stepped away.

"The pool," he said in a hoarse voice, taking my hand. "Get in."

I moved quickly to do as I was told. I wanted to. Something about being ordered to do something sexual by a man so much larger than me was irresistible. I was certain I would have qualms about it later, but at the moment, I had none. The pool had steps or seats built into it, and I stepped down into the steamy water without hesitation.

"Oh, that's nice," I said, surprised, sinking deeper into the water. It was slightly warmer than a bath, which felt good with the cold nip in the air.

"All the way," Dmitri said, his eyes dark with passion, as he stepped in himself.

I glanced down into the water, assessing how deep the pool was. I was a strong swimmer if it came down to it, but the deepest part of the pool only reached my waist.

"*All* the way," Dmitri said again as he moved to sit on the lip of the pool. He settled in with his legs apart, gripping the pool's edge.

I knew what he wanted without him having to ask it. That was either due to sharp observation and listening to everything said and unsaid earlier, or simply because my mouth watered to taste his cock again. I sank into the water up to my neck, moving in between his legs. The water was unusually buoyant, and part of the wall of the pool where Dmitri sat, waiting, seemed to have been purposely constructed for someone in my position, so it didn't hurt my knees too much.

I tentatively rested my hands on his thighs for balance and let out a shaky breath as he gripped the base of his prick and pointed it at me. I could see so much more of it in the sunlight—its flared head and the texture of his skin, and the slick of moisture already leaking from him. The sight and scent of it alone was unbelievably arousing. He was intimidatingly big—even more so with me submerged in the pool with him sitting on the edge—but I'd swallowed him the night before, so I could do it again.

I closed my lips around his tip, tasting him with a flicker of my tongue.

Dmitri tensed and growled. "Yes, little pup," he growled.

I was encouraged by his approval and went on, licking him and sucking on his tip before daring to take him deeper. His hairy thighs flexed under my touch, and he fisted a hand in my hair. A titillating sense of helplessness swirled through me. I couldn't have backed out if I'd wanted to. I liked it. He arched his hips in short thrusts, growling as he did, forcing me to take more and more of him.

I moved my tongue in a way that had been done to me the night before, and Dmitri tipped his head back and let out a moan of pleasure. "Fuck, pup. You're such a quick learner."

I hummed in answer, since I couldn't say thank you. He took that as his cue to push deep. I let out a cry, which he answered with another sound of pleasure. It was just on the verge of too much, so close to gagging me, but I was determined to rise to expectations. I breathed carefully through my nose, swallowing so that I didn't choke, as Dmitri moved more and more insistently. I focused on his taste—salt and musk—on the way he pulled my hair, and on the increasing pressure building in by balls as he moved in and out with increasing urgency.

"Fuck, pup," he groaned, letting go of my hair so he could grasp the side of the pool with both hands to brace himself. He tipped his head back farther, jerking his hips up with abandon and groaning as if his soul was about to leave his body. I kept on as best I could, letting him fuck my mouth hard, until his soul really did leave his body as he came.

His cum hit the back of my throat, and I swallowed him, eyes going wide. He jerked a few more times with diminishing strength as he emptied his balls all the way. With a final, satisfied groan, he pushed me back until his cock popped free of his mouth, then sank into the pool with me.

"Fuck, that was good." He panted as I floated back a few inches.

It might have been good for him, but I was still throbbing and in desperate need of release. Dmitri's eyes were half closed as he moved slightly around the pool to find a steadier place to sit. I wasn't sure if he remembered I was still there, still hard as a rock. I didn't think it would be acceptable to bring myself off, not under these circumstances.

At last, when I was starting to get desperate, Dmitri opened one eye and grinned at me. "Come here, pup."

Relieved beyond telling, I floated toward him. He caught me as soon as I was close and tugged me so that I straddled him. He caressed my ass for a moment—maybe it was the hot spring, but it didn't hurt as badly surrounded by warm water—then closed a hand around my cock.

I gave him what I was sure he wanted and made every appreciative sound I could think of as he stroked me. He watched me with an amused look as I came closer and closer to the edge.

"You really do like it, don't you, pup?" he asked. Unfortunately for me, he also stilled his hand, leaving me throbbing. "Don't you?" he asked again.

I nodded quickly, but that wasn't enough for him. "I do, I do," I panted, figuring out that he wanted me to ask for it.

He rewarded me by resuming his strokes, even if they were so slow all they did was make me more desperate without giving me release.

"You would have fucked all of us last night even without the tea, because you're just gagging for it, aren't you?" he asked, his tone slightly sinister.

"Yes," I confessed. "I would have. I am."

He moved his hand slightly faster. I might have been able to come if I'd reached for it, but Dmitri was playing with me, and more than ever, I knew it was my sole purpose to indulge him.

"You probably sat, all alone in that palace, dreaming of the day when you would be fucked senseless by wolves."

I hadn't, but I might have if I'd known it was possible. "Yes," I answered anyhow. I moved my hips, trying to urge him on.

He caught on to what I was doing and clamped a hand over my thighs to hold me in place. He was in control, not me. "You want to come right now, don't you?"

"I do," I panted. "So badly. I need to."

"Then beg me for it, pup," he said, his voice dark. "Beg me to let you come."

"Please, Dmitri," I said, rolling my eyes back in my head as I came closer and closer. "Please get me off. Please let me come. Please. *Please.*" I sounded weaker and more desperate with each plea, but I was certain that was what he wanted.

"Good, pup," he said, suddenly stroking fast. "Good boy."

I let myself go, bursting so hard the edges of my vision went black. I moaned with pleasure and glanced down to see thick swirls of white shooting into the water from my cock. It was erotic and kept me transported as Dmitri milked the last of it from me. For a moment, I was too sensitive and his touch was uncomfortable. But overall, it felt so good, and when he finally let me go, I sagged backwards. I would have sunk into the water with a spent sigh if Dmitri hadn't caught me.

He kept his hands on me as he held me, laughing to himself. "Aren't you glad I captured you in the forest last night?" he asked with self-congratulatory smugness.

I nodded blearily and gasped, "Yes."

I was telling the truth.

5

We didn't stay in the pool for as long as I would have liked afterwards. Dmitri seemed to lose interest as soon as he was satisfied and climbed out. He moved quickly in the chilly air to a small chest that I'd barely noticed off to one side of the pool, taking out a handful of thick towels to dry off with. I hoped he would ignore me and leave me to study the pool. It was fed by some sort of ingenious means from what I assumed was the hot spring Dmitri had mentioned earlier. I'd read about such natural phenomenon in my studies and would have loved to have explored more. Most hot springs were made of mineral-infused water which could be put to a variety of uses. I knew of a hot spring in one of the larger cities that was used to feed extensive medical baths. I'd once been audacious enough to ask Mother if I could go there someday, which elicited a slap and a typical response of—

"Get out and come back into the house," Dmitri ordered, cutting short my thoughts.

I climbed out of the pool, noticing that the warm water had soothed my aching body a bit. Which is why it would have been nice to spend more time in the pool. I still felt disjointed and shaky as Dmitri tossed me a towel to dry myself.

The difference between Dmitri and Sascha was marked. Where Sascha had carefully washed me after our activity that morning, Dmitri was content to stand back and observe me with a rapacious smirk as I dried myself. I hadn't finished swallowing him more than ten minutes ago, and he'd only just brought me off, but I could see as plain as day he was already looking forward to next time. That observation sent an expectant shudder through me—one that was perhaps slightly more fear than arousal. I forced myself to breathe steadily as I finished drying and donned my robe, though, already resigned to my position as pup.

"Come along." Dmitri turned once my body was covered and walked ahead, back to the house.

I scurried to keep up with his long strides, wincing slightly as my tender, bare feet stepped across cold stones and sticks hidden in the withered, winter grass between the garden beds. It was a relief to step back into the house in more ways than one. My hair was wet from the pool, and being indoors, in a warm house, fragrant with the scent of fresh bread and wood smoke, was vastly pleasanter than being out in the chill.

But a chill of a different sort snapped through the air in the house's main room as Dmitri and I entered. Sascha stood by the fireplace, transferring a load of logs from a wide leather strap he must have used to bring them in from outside—I remembered the sight of stumps and felled trees at the edge of the property from the night before. He straightened at the sight of me and Dmitri, his eyes narrowing for a fraction of a second.

Dmitri returned Sascha's look with a smug grin. "Our pup has a mouth like heaven, and he's eager to use it," he bragged.

Heat flooded my face and I hunched in on myself slightly. It wasn't as though what Dmitri and I did in the pool was any sort of secret or even unexpected. I was ready to wager scenes like that would be repeated frequently with all of my hosts. But having it spoken of so bluntly, almost as though I wasn't in the room or wouldn't care that something so intimate relating to me was being spoken of so cavalierly stung somehow.

"You were careful with him?" Sascha pulled himself to his full height, facing Dmitri squarely.

"Of course I was." Dmitri smiled. Or perhaps that was a sneer. "Ask him yourself, if you don't believe me."

I understood those words to be a challenge of their own, Dmitri calling Sascha out for potentially disobeying rules of some sort. The struggle between the two men was palpable. And I felt as though I'd landed in the middle of it when Sascha glanced to me, one eyebrow raised.

"He was," I answered quickly. I swallowed, scrambling for a way to diffuse the situation. "I enjoyed the pool immensely. I take it it's fed from an underground hot spring?"

There was a pause, a hesitation, as the two powerful men stared each other down. I hugged my robe tighter around me. A situation like that was untenable at the best of times, and now an element of possession and conflict had been thrown into the mix, like a bone tossed between two snarling dogs—and that element was me. Conflicts like that never ended well for the bone.

"The entire house is constructed atop a deep hot spring," Sascha explained, opting to give his full attention to me and ignoring Dmitri. "That's why we built here. You haven't seen it yet, but I've engineered the kitchen and washrooms with running water as a result."

"Really?" My interest was genuinely piqued. Not only by the house's fascinating plumbing.

Dmitri marched on toward the front door. "I'm going hunting," he announced in a deep voice. "Since the only thing I caught yesterday is more likely to eat us than we are to eat him." He chuckled at his own joke, then moved to fetch his cloak and hunting gear from its spot near the door.

"Speak for yourself," Gregor chuckled from where he sat at the table, once again surrounded by herbs and making notes in a ledger.

My cheeks burned even hotter.

Sascha followed Dmitri with his eyes for a moment

before stepping toward me. "When we came across this patch of land, there were several outlets for the underground spring. The house was constructed to make use of those outlets. That's why it's such an odd shape."

I frowned, aware of Dmitri leaving, but pretending not to be. "Wouldn't that cause an unstable foundation for the house? Surely the area is prone to sinkholes."

Sascha's brow inched up. He swept me with a glance from head to toe, as if reassessing me. "What do you know of geology?" he asked.

I cursed myself inwardly, careful to keep my expression neutral, perhaps even ignorant. It was never a good idea to let people know you were smarter than you looked. I was well aware that I looked like a pretty young thing, fragile, easily teased, tormented, or—in the case of my new companions—fucked. I was also self-aware enough to know, in most circumstances, I was the smartest person in the room. At the moment, that was the only weapon I had against men who were larger and more powerful than me.

"I was educated by private tutors at the palace in Novoberg," I said harmlessly. "One of my tutors was fascinated by geography and geology and overemphasized that area of my education." I was also an excellent liar. I could lie with a straight face and look like an angel while doing it. In reality, I had been brought up to be a member of the ruling class, which meant I had been educated at the palace school and taught everything about the resources of the land and the laws that governed them.

"Sinkholes were a concern when I was drawing up the designs," Sascha went on, evidently believing me. He crossed back to the woodpile he was building near the fireplace. "I had some experience constructing on difficult terrain before being cast out of Tesladom. The area around that city is pocketed with similar springs. The foundation of the house stretches deeper than the footprint of the rooms and is reinforced with crossbeams, just in case a sinkhole should form." He shrugged as he unloaded the last of the wood he'd brought in, then reached for a thick fur coat draped over a small table nearby. "The design isn't foolproof, but it should prevent the entire house from being sucked down, if it ever comes to it."

"The hot springs are perfect for irrigating the garden beds," Sven chimed in from the kitchen, where he was helping Ivan prepare what could very well be lunch later on. "And the mineral deposits make for incredibly fertile soil."

"Soil that you should be preparing for the first planting instead of flirting with Ivan," Sascha said with a grin.

It was a genuine grin too. I could see Sascha was on good terms with both Sven and Ivan, in spite of a little teasing. Gregor had relaxed since Dmitri left as well. I began to wonder if one of the elements that prevented Dmitri from wrestling control of the pack from Sascha was the fact that the other three men seemed perfectly at ease with Sascha in charge. If he attempted a coup, it would be one against four. But that also begged the question of why Dmitri stayed in a group to which he brought so much tension.

"You're right, of course." Sven kissed Ivan's cheek, then strode toward the back hallway. "I should be able to start planting the first crops in a week or so, if I stay on task and get the tilling done."

"So early?" My brow flew up.

Sven smiled as he plucked a coat from a peg near the entrance to the hallway. "It's the hot springs. We can't have a cold storage cellar anywhere near the house, but I can plant weeks ahead of when I'd be able to plant without them."

I tilted my head to the side, considering. That would be incredibly useful, especially if the pack relied on the garden's produce to feed themselves and to sell at market. Early vegetables could fetch a higher price since people were usually desperate for them in the early days of spring. But how they managed to produce everything that they'd hinted the area produced with just five men to do all the work was a mystery.

One that prompted me to action. "I can help, if you'd like," I said, moving to where my formal dinner suit was draped over the back of the sofa. It was neither warm nor sturdy enough for labor, but it was all I had, aside from the robe.

"No." Sasha stepped into my path to stop me. "You're not working in the gardens, Peter."

A flutter passed through my gut as I looked up at him. He was at least eight inches taller than me, which made me feel helpless in the best possible way with him standing so close. In fact, the way he grinned down at me made me clench my ass in anticipation of having it pounded raw all over again. I wasn't against the idea, but I wondered how long it would be before I was seriously injured.

"You're not to do any manual labor," Sascha went on, glancing past me to Gregor and Ivan, as if telling them too. "Not even scrubbing pots," he said to Ivan in particular. He clasped my wrist and held my hand up. "These hands are staying as soft and smooth as they are now."

He traced my fingers with his large, calloused ones. The fluttering in my gut intensified, and—God help me—my cock stirred again. As if it hadn't done enough for one day. I couldn't help it, though. Any sort of tender touch at all was such a treat for me that I responded on instinct.

Which was exactly what made me such a valuable asset to the pack.

"If I'm not to do manual labor," I began, clearing my throat when my voice came out hoarse, "what am I to do?"

"We'll find something to keep you busy," Sascha said with a wink.

I heated all over. Though I did wonder how long it would be until I grew bored of being used.

Sascha called to Gregor, "You can find something quiet and restful for Peter to do this morning, I assume. What with all the labels you need to make."

"Absolutely," Gregor glanced up from his work with a smile. "I assume you have good penmanship?"

"Excellent penmanship," I confirmed with a smile.

"Then go help Gregor," Sascha ordered me. "We'll figure out the rest later."

I joined Gregor at the table—sitting gingerly and trying not to wince—as Sascha headed outside and Ivan went back to preparing whatever food we'd be having later.

"Your ass is still sore?" Gregor asked with an apologetic half-smile.

I nodded sheepishly.

"I've got a salve for that. Let's just finish up these labels and I'll get it for you."

Gregor showed me what needed to be written out, and I got right to work. As I'd expected, Gregor was impressed with my handwriting and raised his eyebrows in surprise. What he'd given to copy me was simple, and I was able to work quickly.

As I did, Ivan brought me a large glass of water flavored with herbs that I eyed suspiciously at first. "You'll need to be mindful of your fluid intake," he said with a knowing look.

Gregor laughed at the way I sniffed the water. "It's not laced with anything like last night," he said. "We save that particular concoction for special occasions."

Relieved, I took a long drink, thirstier than I'd thought I was. "Dmitri said you know of all sorts of herbs with...interesting effects."

Gregor's grin widened. "I do. Every good medical apprentice learns the entire lexicon of herblore. I can mix up a tincture, tonic, or poultice for every kind of ailment under the sun. Some are for recreational use as well." He tapped the side of his nose with a mischievous look.

I smiled in return. I liked Gregor immediately and felt safe with him. At least, safer than I'd felt with Dmitri. The emotions I felt around Sascha were something else entirely—something I didn't want to think about at the moment. Instinct told me that Gregor could give me whatever information I needed to answer whatever questions would arise. He would probably figure out how intelligent I was in the process. But for the time being, I made up my mind to give away as little as possible.

"Do you sell these mixtures at the village faires?" I asked. It was always safer to get someone to talk about themselves than to ask direct questions, and since most people were more than happy to talk about themselves interminably, the diversionary tactic always worked.

"Of course," Gregor answered proudly. "Some I'm able to sell openly, but tinctures like the one we gave you last night are best left for deals under the table." He grew serious at the end of his explanation. I could only surmise that not every recipient of the sort of tea I'd been given the night before was as willing as I'd been. The fact that

that seemed to bother Gregor only raised his estimation in my eyes.

"What is this mixture we're labeling do?" I asked, directing him to our work.

"This is a simple healing tincture for the common cold, a mild flu, and the like."

I kept Gregor talking about the various herbs and mixtures spread across the table for the better part of an hour. I remembered everything he said as well, which was helped by writing things down as he instructed me. I did the best I could to appear only politely interested, but in actuality, I drank in everything he said, beginning an inventory of things I might find useful later if the relative peace and accord of the pack were ever to crumble. I made plans to convince him to teach me how to mix a few of the concoctions as well.

As the hour wore on, though, I found it more and more uncomfortable to sit on the hard chair. My mind started to drift to the pool in the back and how nice it would have been to sit in it for a long time. My squirming didn't go unnoticed, though.

"That's it," Gregor said eventually, putting down his pen. "Sascha was right. We shouldn't have used you so hard last night. You're clearly in pain." He stood, pushing his chair back.

"It's nothing, really," I said, downplaying my discomfort.

"It's more than nothing." Gregor came around the table gesturing for me to get up. I set the pen I'd been working with down and rose. "Trust me. You'll be much happier once the salve I have in mind for you does its work."

"Does it work that quickly?" I asked in a high, small voice. If it did, I was certain I'd have someone's cock deep in my ass in no time at all. But on the upside, if it worked, I'd have someone's cock deep in my ass in no time at all.

I grinned at my private joke as Gregor explained, "Not instantly, but I've fine-tuned the formula over years for maximum efficacy. It helps that you're young. Young bodies heal faster than old ones."

He led over to his apothecary counter, which I could now see was lined with drawers and cubbies containing a staggering variety of dry herbs, unctions, and jars. Ivan glanced over his shoulder at us with mild interest as he chopped vegetables for some sort of stew. The entire kitchen area smelled so wonderful that it put me at ease.

"This is the stuff." Gregor took a medium-sized jar down from the cupboards above the counter. "Now, bring that stool closer to the counter, take off your robe, and lean over, resting your arms on top of the stool."

I did as I was told—though it occurred to me with a smirk that Sascha wouldn't have liked me moving my own stool—and untied the robe. I hesitated for only a moment before handing it off to Gregor, who moved to drape it over one of the chairs at the table. Once again, I was naked in a room with men I barely knew, both of whom immediately looked at me with interest. I fought the instinct to shrink or hide myself, knowing it would be completely pointless. I was there to be looked at as much as anything else.

"Bend over the stool and stand with your legs apart."

The command would have sounded much more erotic coming from Sascha or Dmitri, but it still affected me as I did what Gregor asked. It felt utterly surreal to settle onto the stool with my ass presented. I hung my head slightly, forcing myself to breathe steadily instead of shaking my head at the madness of it all.

Ivan whistled slowly behind me. "I didn't know that shade of red was possible," he said.

"I should have applied this first thing this morning," Gregor said with a sigh.

I was about to suggest that maybe he was right when I was jolted by the cool, sticky sensation of a large dollop of salve touching my throbbing hole. I nearly went up on my toes and had to hold my breath to keep from moaning in pain and delight at the feeling. I was embarrassed by my reaction to Gregor's touch, but as I'd learned so well since the night before, practically any touch set me off.

I whimpered slightly as Gregor spread the salve, biting the inside of my lip to keep from making an utter fool of myself by groaning.

"Does it hurt that badly?" Gregor asked curiously.

Ivan laughed. "I don't think that's it. Look how hard he's gone."

I winced slightly as he pointed it out. Sure enough, my prick had filled to throbbing in a matter of seconds and stood out as my balls drew up.

Gregor muttered an oath under his breath. "You certainly are responsive," he said, as though it were a wonder. The way he applied the salve suddenly took on a slower, sensual feel. "Have you always been this way?" he asked, as though it were a medical question.

"I've never had an opportunity to find out," I said, letting out the breath I'd been holding. "I've rarely been touched before in any manner, let alone a sexual one." He'd asked a clinical question, so I gave him a clinical answer.

"Not at all?" Gregor's hand paused on my ass. I could hear the incredulity in his voice.

I shook my head and tried not to push against him, asking for more. "I was considered unsavory and was barely tolerated."

"Even by your own family?" Gregor resumed massaging my hole, and I had to bite my lip to stop from moaning again. "Your own mother?"

"Mother despised me," I confessed in a tight voice, breaking out in a sweat as Gregor pushed a finger into my tight pucker. "She didn't want me in the first place, and as soon as she realized I would turn out more like my sisters than my brothers, she tossed me into the care of an elderly nursemaid."

"How old were you?" Ivan asked. The gruffness of his voice told me he, too, was affected by what Gregor was doing to me.

"Three or four," I panted. "Before I remember. I'm certain they would have tossed me to the wolves much sooner if they'd thought they could get away with it. But my father is well-connected in the frontier and I have an uncle who served in the king's army a decade ago, so—"

I sucked in a breath hard as Gregor's probing touched on something inside of me that sent a blaze of pleasure through me. In my current position, I could see pre-cum bead on the head of my prick. Whether he was attempting to spread the salve to parts inside me that were inflamed or whether he was trying to massage that spot, he kept going.

"That feels good, doesn't it," Gregor said in a deep, heavy voice.

"Oh, yes," I groaned.

"Did Dmitri bring you off earlier?" he asked as he kept going.

That image on top of what he was doing rocketed me close to the edge. I nodded sharply, then let out a wildly sensual groan.

"And already you're about to spill again." Gregor was both aroused and curious. "I don't think I've ever known anyone so reactive."

In that moment, I didn't care if he had or not. I was moments away from coming, especially now that the herbal salve had my entire ass tingling.

"I couldn't possibly resist this," Gregor said, both humor and desire in his voice. "Stand straight, pup."

As soon as I did as he asked, ass clenching around the salve, prick springing up, Gregor grabbed my shoulders and maneuvered me until the small of my back rested against his apothecary counter. I hardly had time to blink before he dropped to his knees, nudged my legs apart, and took my cock into his mouth.

I cried out at the pleasure of it, tilting my head back, and gripping the counter for all I was worth to keep me upright. Gregor was an expert and, in spite of my length, took me to the hilt. His mouth was hot and wet and encompassing. It felt so uncommonly good that I wanted to scream with pleasure. He only barely had a chance to do something with his tongue that I would have to remember for later when something like lightning that had been gathering at the base of my spine shot through me. I came with a loud cry that echoed in the cavernous room as he sucked me dry.

The force of my orgasm left me stunned and barely able to hold myself up. Only gradually, with Ivan's pitched growl of, "Fuck," did I notice he had his trousers down and was bringing himself off as he watched.

Gregor rose shakily to his feet, the front of his breeches wet. "You do beat all, boy," he panted. "I've never even heard of anything like it."

I wondered what they'd heard of in the first place. Men were naturally sexual creatures. I supposed it was the novelty of my inexperience that made me so eager, as they were constantly telling me I was. Or perhaps I did just have a stronger than natural affinity for pleasure. It was the whole touching thing. I loved to be touched.

"Do you think," I began, panting and struggling to stand taller as my cock, damp with Gregor's saliva, settled. I swallowed, changing what I'd been about to say. "Would it be too impolite of me to ask to take a short nap?"

Ivan laughed. A moment later, Gregor did as well.

"I think you deserve it," Gregor said, rocking back. "I might need one too, after that."

"I...I could sleep with you in your bed," I suggested bashfully, no idea what was proper in that situation.

Gregor laughed louder and thumped my arm. "And risk Sascha cutting my balls off? I don't think so. You'll nap on the sofa." He moved uncomfortably to the table to retrieve my robe. "It's actually quite comfortable."

"Oh?" I accepted my robe and pushed away from the counter. I was breathing more evenly, but the heaviness of exhaustion pressed down on me. And my ass still tingled from the salve, but in a way that gave me hope it was working. I threw my robe over my shoulders, tied it in front, and headed for the sofa.

"You'll be warm by the fire too," Gregor said, walking with me and making sure I was settled comfortably. Once I was nestled on my back with a pillow under my head and a quilt tucked over me, Gregor bent down to kiss my forehead. "Nap well, little pup," he said, then chuckled. "I think you'll need all the rest you can get."

6

The morning sunlight had turned to mellow afternoon light by the time I awoke. I'd slept heavily, still worn out from the night before as well as my eventful morning. The first thing I noticed was that neither Dmiti's nor Sascha's coats were hanging on the pegs by the door. The next was that my quilt had been removed, my robe untied and pushed open, and that I'd been lying naked and on display as I slept. A wry grin pulled at the corners of my mouth. I was on display, like an erotic piece of art. At least I wasn't hard. But knowing me, I probably would be soon.

I sat up, noticing that my ass felt considerably better, though definitely not back to normal. The table was spread with what looked like the aftermath of a midday meal, complete with uncleared plates that indicated someone other than Sven—who still sat at the table while Ivan cleaned up in the kitchen—had been there for a meal without waking me. My guess was that Sascha and Gregor had been the other two there, though they were gone now. Instinct told me Dmitri would be gone for most of the day hunting. Everything I knew about hunting suggested it was an all-day affair.

"Oh, good. He's awake," Sven said with a broad grin. He stood and started toward me.

"Is he?" Ivan glanced over his shoulder from the kitchen sink. The look he gave me was mischievous.

"I'm so terribly sorry," I said, still groggy from sleep, swinging my legs off the sofa to stand. "I slept through lunch." I closed my robe and reached for the ends of the sash to tie it.

"No!" Ivan and Sven called out at the same time.

I nearly stumbled as I stepped forward. Panic instantly gripped me. I didn't know if I'd done something wrong or there was some sort of danger in the room or if one of the sinkholes Sascha had mentioned was about to open.

"Keep your robe open," Sven laughed as he walked toward me. I couldn't decide if the look he had in his eyes was lascivious or giddy.

I fought not to sigh and roll my eyes, dropping the sash and pulling the garment open again so that it concealed nothing. I was there to be ogled, after all.

"I've got the razors and soap ready," Sven went on, chuckling. He marched past me to one of the smaller tables placed under a window.

"I'll fill a basin with warm water." Ivan abandoned

the dishes he was washing. He wiped his hands on his apron and fetched a large, wooden bowl from the cupboard next to the sink.

On the one hand, I was curious to see how the running water Sascha had mentioned in the house worked. There wasn't a pump in the sink, but rather a spigot of some sort. The pressure from the spring must have been enough to propel it through the spigot. On the other hand, the mention of razors had my heart thumping in alarm.

"Have I done something wrong?" I asked in a tremulous voice. I didn't know whether to stay where I was or go to the kitchen, so I moved hesitantly forward, nearly bumping my foot against a low table as I did.

"No, no, nothing wrong," Ivan and Sven said, talking on top of each other.

"We had an idea," Ivan went on, filling the bowl with water.

"You'll like it." Sven came forward with what looked like a shaving kit. He gestured for me to sit on the sofa again. "You should probably just take the robe off."

I did as he'd asked, draping my robe over the back of the chair nearest the sofa, then sitting. The pieces came together in my mind as the two men converged on me with the bowl of warm water and shaving things.

"Thank you so much for your consideration," I said in a soft, polite voice, "but I rarely need to shave." I ran a hand over my jaw. "I'd say I have weeks to go before my face shows anything more than peach fuzz."

My lack of facial hair had always been a point of ridicule for my brothers. It set me apart from most other men. I tried not to resent my inability to grow a beard, but secretly I'd always wanted one.

Ivan and Sven continued to chuckle, exchanging impish looks.

"That's not what we're going to shave," Sven said.

They both looked pointedly at my body. Specifically, my genitals. I tried not to sigh in disappointment or roll my eyes. Not only would it have been rude, for all I knew, there might have been some unspoken rule about pup grooming that I didn't know about. All I knew was that I had been so secretly proud of myself for finally growing hair in interesting places once I'd hit puberty, and I had a bad feeling it was all about to be shaved off.

"Hand me the soap," Ivan said as he sat on the sofa beside me.

Sven sat on my other side, reaching for the soap. As Ivan lathered it in a small bowl, Sven shifted so that he could drape one of my legs over his thigh. Once Ivan handed the bowl off to him, he hoisted my other leg over his own. The effect was to spread my legs wide and to render me far less capable of significant movement than I wanted to be.

"Sascha is going to love this," Sven chuckled as he daubed shaving soap around my groin.

"Does Sascha prefer his pups shaven?" I asked to distract myself from the utter indignity of Ivan picking up a straight razor and going to work removing the hair I was so proud of.

Sven shrugged, and, to my dread, continued spreading the foamy soap across my abdomen and onto my chest. They were going to shave all of my hair. "Honestly, I don't know," Sven said. "We've never had a pup before, and I don't know if his previous pack had one."

"Previous pack?" I asked to distract myself. It wasn't just undignified, it was nerve-wracking to have first one, then two men scraping sharp razors so close to my balls and cock. And, of course, the whole thing instantly aroused me. Ivan and Sven noticed that as well, I could tell. Their breathing changed, and Sven's hand wasn't as steady as I would have wanted it to be.

It took several beats for them to remember I'd asked a question.

"Our pack formed about five years ago," Ivan explained as he slid the razor into a dangerously tight area. "Sven and I were with Gregor in a pack of six, miles and miles from here, closer to Hedeon in the west."

"It wasn't a healthy environment," Sven said, too emotional for my comfort. I held perfectly still so that he wouldn't nick a tender area.

"Pack dynamics change all the time," Ivan resumed the explanation. "Some groups are happy to stay together for decades. They've formed veritable villages of their own out there, though those villages are usually ruled with an iron fist."

"Sascha was from a village like that," Sven said. "He chafed under the leadership."

I breathed a little easier when they finished with my pubic hair and moved on to my belly and chest. A maudlin sort of sadness rang through me as I stared down at myself, smooth and pink.

"Sascha was lucky that the pack leader of that village encouraged ambitious young men to go off and start their own packs instead of crushing them, like some leaders do," Ivan went on. "He brought Dmitri and his twin brother, as well as another man called Jakob, with him."

"Dmitri had a brother?" I would have sat up straighter, but Ivan and Sven had their razors a little too close to my nipples for me to consider sudden movement.

"Mikal," Ivan nodded. "The two couldn't have been more different, even though they were identical. Dmitri is...." He let his words drop and sent a significant look to Sven.

"Dmitri can be difficult and strong-willed sometimes," Sven filled in.

"That's one way to put it," Ivan murmured.

I relaxed back against the sofa as they shaved away the last of my meager chest hair. "What happened to Mikal, then?" I asked, blinking up at the ceiling beams and wondering how long it would be before either Sven or Ivan noticed my erection and played with it—like they were most definitely playing with me now. I was clearly little more than a toy in their eyes, which, I'll admit, chafed. "And the other one...Jakob?"

"Mikal and Jakob loved each other," Ivan said.

"Like the two of us do," Sven said with charming sweetness. He leaned forward, and he and Ivan met in a kiss over my soapy, half-shaved chest. It would have been infinitely sweeter if they weren't both holding sharp razors over my skin.

"Dmitri didn't like it, of course," Ivan went on as the two of them leaned back and continued with their task. I hoped they were almost done, but when Sven set down his razor and reached for more soap to spread over my legs, I nearly groaned. And not with pleasure. Their intention was to completely denude me. "Dmitri and Mikal had a hard time of things when they were younger. They wouldn't have survived if they hadn't clung to each other. But then Mikal met Jakob. Some forms of love trump even that between brothers. So Dmitri and Mikal argued, and—" Ivan looked as though he'd said more than he should. "Mikal and Jakob set out on their own around this time last year."

"That was recent," I said, shifting to a slightly more comfortable position as the two men started in on my legs. There was more to the story than that, I could tell. I sent a mournful look to my now-smooth chest and groin. My erection looked almost lonely without hair around it.

"A little too recent, if you ask me," Sven said, arching one eyebrow.

"How so?" I asked.

The two exchanged a wary look. "Dmitri is still bent

PETER AND THE WOLVES

out of shape because Sascha not only allowed the affair, he encouraged it," Ivan said.

"Sascha has a bit of a sentimental streak," Sven said with a wink. "If you ask me, he's always longed for a lover of his own instead of satisfying himself in the usual way of a pack member."

That piqued my interest. "What is the usual way?" I asked.

Ivan shrugged as he focused on dragging his razor down my leg with a long stroke. "Men have urges. They find ways to satisfy them. And since everyone in a pack is in the same situation, they usually just fuck whoever they want when the need arises."

"Or wait until a faire and fuck everything in sight at the revels," Sven added with a knowing flicker of his eyebrows for Ivan.

My cock jumped at the suggestion—which was embarrassing, considering the position I was in. "Would I be correct to assume that that is why pups are so highly prized?" I asked hoarsely. "Because they're available to be fucked whenever?"

"Correct," Sven said with a teasing grin. "Of course, there's more to it than that. There's status and bragging rights too, since young, attractive men are rare in the forest. And I still maintain that you are a complete rarity, even among pup-kind."

"You're nobly-born, for one," Ivan said before I could bring myself to ask. "And as we discovered this morning, you are—what did Gregor call it? You're 'highly reactive'."

"I'll say." Sven pointed his razor at my erection. "He's already weeping for it."

Sure enough, sheepish though it made me feel, pre-cum was already shining at the tip of my cock, and my pale skin was flushed pink from more than just the scrape of razors and the chill of being naked and damp.

"I can't help it," I said quietly. "It feels good to be touched." I didn't feel like explaining my cold past again, so I left it at that.

"Most men aren't cast out into the forest until they're older, when they do something to be found out," Ivan went on. "Cities have this mad notion that they can either educate or beat the desire for other men out of us. They don't usually toss us out with the garbage until they've exhausted all resources."

"That's why a good half of pups are captured or bought at faires."

"*Bought?*" I stiffened so fast that Ivan's razor cut into my calf.

"Shit," Ivan hissed. "Sascha is going to murder me for cutting you."

"Just put a plaster on it," I said dismissively, then went right on to, "Young men are purchased at faires? Do you mean…as slaves?"

They both glanced guiltily at me. "'Slave' is such a charged word," Sven said.

I sank back into the sofa, letting them finish shaving

my legs. The pieces that came together in my mind were so alarming that it withered my erection a bit. No wonder Gregor had looked guilty when he mentioned how much the tea mixture that they'd given me last night fetched. Out there in the forest, young men—perhaps no more than boys—were likely kidnapped or captured and forced to do all the things I was willing to do voluntarily. That was my nature, but what if it wasn't for some of the boys who were sold as slaves? Even if they did like men, what if they didn't like the ones they ended up with? Dmitri intimidated me, but I was still excited by him. I realized it was because I instinctively felt that Sascha and the others would hold him back from doing me any real harm. But what if I'd ended up in an entire pack of Dmitris?

The thought made me shudder.

"Oh dear, we've upset him," Sven said, sending me an apologetic look.

"It's not as bad as all that, Peter," Ivan said, putting his razor down now that all of my hair was gone and dipping a rag in the warm, soapy water. Whether I was disturbed or not, as soon as he started wiping off remaining bits of shaving soap, my cock began to fill again. "Everyone integrates into a pack eventually. There's safety in numbers."

"And then you have groups like ours," Sven added. "Prosperous, content, and blessed with a find like you." He took the rag from Ivan and rubbed it over my chest.

I sucked in a breath as Ivan stroked his hands over my smooth, bare thighs, inching up toward my balls. "Look what a beautiful boy you are," he smiled at me. Or rather, at my bare groin.

I glanced down at myself. Except for my once again throbbing erection, I looked like I was about twelve years old. Without exaggerating. I should have been disturbed by the way Ivan and Sven drank in the sight of my denuded body as though viewing a favorite dessert, but as soon as they laid hands on me, feeling my soft, clean skin, I knew I was gone. One man's touch was like fine wine to me. Two at once was more than I could hope to resist.

"Fuck me," Sven growled, cupping my balls and rolling them slightly. "Gregor was so right about you."

"Reactive," Ivan said as though it were a deeply off-color oath.

"Highly." Sven shifted so that he could nibble on my shoulder, then run his tongue along my newly hairless chest. He sought out my nipple and closed his mouth over it, licking and sucking.

"Oh!" I moaned, tilting my head back and sinking into the sensation. "That's nice."

"Yes, it is," Ivan rumbled.

I arched up a moment later as he closed his mouth over the head of my cock and licked its weeping slit. He reached back to dip his hand in the bowl of warm, soapy water, then closed it insistently around my shaft, stroking slowly.

Ivan and Sven's combined efforts not only had me close to coming within a minute, they had me close to weeping too. Because I was forced to admit that every sensation they imparted was heightened without hair to stand in the way of hands and mouths and tongues. My senses were overloaded with pleasure, and I couldn't have stopped myself from vocalizing it if I'd tried.

I couldn't hold still either. As Sven licked my nipples and stroked my belly, and as Ivan sucked with agonizing gentleness on the head of my cock while fisting my shaft, I writhed against them as if begging for more. I should have been ashamed of myself—truly, deeply ashamed of myself—but I didn't have it in me to resist.

As my panting and mewling grew more desperate, Ivan pulled back and focused on stroking me off. I convulsed and pushed into his fist as cum streamed out of my cock like a fountain, spilling across his hand.

"So fucking beautiful," Ivan gasped in appreciation.

I sagged against the sofa, spent once again, without realizing that things weren't entirely over. Ivan and Sven were worked up, but instead of turning to me for satisfaction, they unceremoniously dumped my legs from their laps and lunged for each other. I was pinned awkwardly between them as they tugged at each other's clothes, shoving down trousers, until they'd both freed their thick hard cocks.

My brow shot up as they moved into each other, mouths crashing together, sighing with arousal, and grinding together. Watching them was a revelation, and if I'd been anything but fully spent, I would have wanted to find a way to get involved.

But no, Ivan and Sven were lovers, and what I was

witnessing was private and intimate. Ivan grasped his hand around both of their pricks together and stroked fast and hard as they continued to kiss. Sven caressed Ivan's face as they groaned and panted into each other's mouths. Ivan's hand moved faster, and first he, then Sven erupted onto each other and Ivan's hands.

With deep moans of satisfaction, the two of them collapsed onto the sofa beside me. I was almost too transfixed to move out of the way and to save myself from being crushed. Up until that point, I'd never so much as seen two other men kiss. It was fascinating to see how things could be between two men in love. I found it sentimental and lovely, not to mention arousing. And with a bit of a surprise, I found myself wondering what it would be like to get off with Sascha like that. I wanted to be as intimately connected to him as Ivan and Sven were to each other.

It was a strange thing to think about. I barely knew Sascha. I'd hardly spoken to him alone—only that morning, when I'd awaken in his arms. There was something about him that drew me inexorably toward him, though. He was the handsomest of the pack, in my opinion, and the strongest—in authority, if not in body. Maybe I had a natural inclination to be attracted to the most powerful man in any grouping. I also sensed a kindness about Sascha and an intelligence. That never failed to appeal to me.

Which was why I felt as though I'd been struck by lightning for doing something wrong when his voice boomed, "What's been going on in here?" behind the sofa as he came in through the short hall at the back of the room.

I was the only one who reacted as though all three of us might be in trouble. I scrambled away from Ivan and Sven, glancing around and wondering where my robe had gone.

"We got you a present," Ivan said, still panting as he and Sven twined together, stealing an occasional kiss.

"Well, we made you a present," Sven said, chuckling and nodding toward me.

I was more self-conscious about being naked than I'd ever been, now that I was also hairless. The sensation sent a chill through me as Sascha strode over to the sofa to take a look. I scrambled to my feet, ready to defend myself and Ivan and Sven's mischief, but the fire in Sascha's eyes stopped the words in my mouth.

Sascha also seemed speechless. His eyes devoured every inch of me, studying my denuded groin in particular. I didn't know what to do with my hands, but it definitely wasn't cover myself. My breath caught in my throat and my heart pounded at the thought that he was pleased and aroused by what he was seeing. I wanted him to be pleased with me. I wanted him to be very pleased. Which was ever so slightly humiliating.

"How's your ass feeling?" he asked with a lascivious glint in his eyes.

I opened my mouth to tell him it was just fine, thank you very much, and that if he wanted to put his cock in me I wouldn't mind at all, but Gregor marched into the room and said, "Give it another day at least. I was alarmed by the state of it earlier."

"Oh?" Sascha pulled his gaze away from me, perhaps a bit disappointed, and glanced to Gregor.

"I should probably reapply the salve, then he should rest for the remainder of the day," Gregor said, sending Sascha a particular look.

Sascha nodded. "Whatever it takes to get our little pup back in fighting shape as soon as possible." He winked at me, then continued on to the pegs by the front door to hang his coat. As he removed it, I could clearly see his trousers were tented.

I took a step forward and opened my mouth once again to offer to suck him off, but stopped. Twenty-four hours ago, I had been morosely dressing for a formal supper I knew would make me miserable. Now here I was, on the verge of offering to swallow a man so much bigger than me that it made me shiver. And that was after sucking off someone, being brought off myself, and being fucked until I was sore so many times that I had lost track. And enjoying it. It was utterly mad.

"You look cold, Peter," Sascha said, walking to the chair to fetch my robe, then bringing it to me and draping it over my shoulders. His warmth and his scent surrounded me again. "And you look beautiful," he whispered against my ear.

I was so ridiculously pleased with the compliment that I felt like a fool, standing there grinning up at him. I was such an easy target. Sascha chuckled at my grin and wrapped his arms around me, bringing me into a tender hug. I could have died right then and been perfectly happy. I didn't care one bit that I'd apparently lost every shred of self-respect I'd ever possessed. A gorgeous, massive, powerful man had his arms around me tenderly, and he was delighted with me.

7

I spent the rest of the day staying as close to Sascha as I could. And not just because I was deeply attracted to him and anticipating going to bed with him that night. Sascha was the leader of the pack. If I wanted to know and understand the dynamics of the unit I was now a part of, I needed to know and understand him. Perhaps better than any of the others. And if I was to stay safe and make the most out of my delicate position within the group, I had to know what he wanted from me. Aside from the obvious.

The rest of the pack was simpler to figure out. Dmitri was the challenger to the throne. He chafed under Sascha's leadership, but he must have had a reason for staying with the pack. I needed to discover what that reason was. When he returned home shortly before supper with a brace of hares, he sent me a hungry smile and Sascha a look that dared him to say something about it.

"It was a fruitful afternoon," he said, holding up the brace.

I tried not to flinch at the caked blood on the hares' fur and their dead eyes. It was obvious to me that Dmitri was waving his catch in my face in order to frighten and intimidate me. Dmitri wanted me to be afraid and perhaps in awe of him. Our activity of the morning suggested that he wanted to master me. He was the same sort of man as my brothers, which, paradoxically, put me somewhat at ease. I knew exactly how to interact with men like that. One played dead with them, so to speak, gave them as little reaction as possible. Do what they asked, submit when it was required, but don't put up a fight. They got bored and found another target eventually.

"Take that out of here," Sascha growled at him from where he sat close to the fire, fitting together the pieces of what I assumed would be a chair. I sat close by and had been watching the process for the past hour as Sascha explained his craft. "You'll drip blood on the floor."

"I just thought our sweet young pup would like to see what I've brought home for him." Dmitri started across the hall, sparing a toothy smile for me. His teeth were in fine condition for a man who had lived in the forest for an indeterminate amount of time. Everyone's in the pack were. I suspected Gregor's medical expertise was probably the explanation for that, which made me relieved for the future state of my own teeth. "We'll have rabbit stew for supper, and once the skins are treated, I could make our pup a rabbit fur coat. Not that he'll have much use for clothing." He chuckled as he passed through the house and out the back hallway, presumably to his workshop.

I glanced down at my robe, then over to the table in the corner where my suit from the night before had been discarded. Contrary to what Dmitri believed, I rather thought I would need suitable clothing at some point. I doubted anything owned by any of my companions would come close to fitting me. But that was a problem for another time.

Sascha watched Dmitri like a hawk until he disappeared down the back hall. Once he was gone, Sascha let out a heavy breath through his nose, lips pursed, brow knitting in thought. He glanced to me with a look of concern.

I kept my expression carefully innocent. Sascha didn't know what Ivan and Sven had revealed to me earlier. He didn't know what Gregor had said before that. In fact, none of my companions knew fully what the others had said to me. My heart raced as I contemplated the importance of finding out as much as possible about, well, everything, while letting on to no one what I knew. I would have to learn what I needed to know piecemeal. The longer my companions operated under the assumption that I was just a pretty, innocent, ignorant piece of ass, the more of an advantage I would have.

Perhaps it was a very good idea indeed that Ivan and

Sven had shaved me bare. Perhaps Sascha and the others would forget that I was twenty and had been educated for a career as a Justice, and that they assumed I was barely out of the schoolroom. I hated lying to Sascha—not just because my cock was more interested in him than the other four, but because he was the leader, the alpha. The benefits of becoming his favorite were huge, but the dangers of him discovering I was being dishonest with him were monumental.

It was a risk I had to take to save my own, newly-hairless hide, if my situation became untenable. And as long as the threat Dmitri presented was still there, it was only a matter of time.

"You do need clothes," Sascha said after studying me for a long time. He stood from the stool where he'd been working and set his newly finished chair aside. "You can't walk around in my robe forever."

"It'll be fine," Ivan said in a jolly voice from the kitchen, where he was finishing the final supper preparations. Dmitri could think what he wanted about hare stew, but from the scent of things, we were having some sort of roast of lamb. I'd seen chickens and goats in the backyard earlier, but not sheep. There must have been a place for cold storage somewhere on the property that I had yet to discover, even though Sven had said the hot springs prevented it. Ivan went on with, "As soon as the weather warms up, our pup can go without clothes entirely."

He chuckled to himself, and from his place at his apothecary counter, Gregor grinned and shook his head.

"Peter is not walking around naked all the time," Sascha said, amused by Ivan, but with just a hint of wariness. "It wouldn't be comfortable for him, and I don't want any visitors getting ideas."

My heart thumped against my ribs, and my amused smile dropped. "Visitors?" I asked, holding my robe tighter around me. I'd been under the impression that Sascha had chosen the site for the pack's home because no one would find it.

"We live apart from others," Sascha explained, offering a hand and helping me up from the chair where I'd been watching him, "but that doesn't mean we don't visit each other. The forest might not be densely populated, but it is populated."

"And we've been known to hire extra help for planting and harvesting when we need it," Sven added. He'd come in from working outside a short time earlier and was now helping Ivan set the table with our supper.

"Lone wolves are always looking for work in the busy seasons," Sascha went on, as though what he was saying was common knowledge. "We're on good terms with several who include our home in their range. We have some friends who will stop in now and then. Katrina and her friends live just an hour away."

"Katrina?" I blinked. There were women in the forest?

"We have some friends who we need to convince to

move back, if you ask me," Ivan said. As Sascha steered me toward the table and helped me into a seat as if I were a princess who needed to be deferred to, Ivan nodded to me and said, "We told him about Mikal and Jakob."

"Did you?" Sascha arched one eyebrow as he took the chair next to mine. I couldn't tell if he was upset or not.

Sven shrugged as he brought a large wooden bowl of roasted root vegetables to the table. "I didn't see that it would cause any harm. We were explaining packs and the ways of the forest."

"I take it you were a good student," Sascha said, grinning fondly at me.

Again, I had the feeling that he wanted me to be as sweet and innocent, and perhaps dependent on him, as possible. "I have much to learn," I said in a high, gentle voice.

His smile broadened. "You do." He winked and rested a hand on my thigh.

I sucked in a breath at the touch, and Sascha seemed to change his mind about withdrawing his hand. On the contrary, he rubbed it across my thigh, on top the fur of the robe, his fingers brushing against my cock, as if contemplating a snack before supper. I stirred against his touch, but perhaps not as quickly as I would have if I hadn't spent so much of myself earlier in the day. Sascha eventually pulled his hand away and cleared his throat, focusing on the feast that was being set out for us.

"Ivan, you've outdone yourself," Sascha said, carving the roast that Ivan set in front of him. I also had the impression he was avoiding talking anymore about Mikal or Jakob, or anyone else who might appear at the house someday.

"I figured I'd cook as though we were celebrating," Ivan said, winking at me before returning to the kitchen for the chicken pie he'd spent the better part of the afternoon making. "Though our darling little pup had better be careful about eating too much."

"Unless Sascha has plans for cleaning him out before taking him to bed," Sven added with a laugh.

My face heated in mortification, and I shrunk into my seat. In fact, when he'd taken me into one of the house's astoundingly modern bathrooms to reapply the healing salve to my ass, Gregor had also showed me a collection of enemas and explained their benefits for avoiding untoward messes, once my ass was back in the sort of condition that would allow for fucking. It made perfect sense that something of that nature would be appropriate, but it was so painfully personal that bringing it up at the supper table went beyond my ability to keep my emotions in check.

"Enough of that." Sascha frowned in disapproval as Ivan and Sven chuckled over their teasing. "The two of you might be full of shit, but there's no need to assume Peter is as much of a mess as either of you."

That only made my face burn hotter. Sascha didn't actually think I was too delicate to have normal bodily functions, did he? He clearly hadn't been in the bathroom with me earlier. But if that was the fantasy he wanted to operate under, I could play along.

"I'll be careful of what I eat," I said modestly as he put the first slice of roast on my plate.

"You'll do nothing of the sort," Sascha said, handing the platter with carved meat off to Gregor and reaching for the root vegetables to continue filling my plate. "You'll eat your fill, as much as you want. You need to keep your strength up." He paused, sending me a wicked look. "And if you need a little refreshing before going to bed, I'll do the honors myself."

I hadn't thought it was possible for me to flush any hotter. I wasn't used to that sort of rough conversation—at the dinner table or anywhere else. And imagining myself draped over Sascha's legs while he used an enema on me had me squirming with guilty pleasure. I must have taken complete leave of my senses if something like that seemed erotic and desirable.

I was certain from the secret smile he gave me that Sascha knew what I was thinking and was probably contemplating it himself, but the intimate mood was shattered as Dmitri marched back into the room.

"You started without me," he growled, yanking his chair away from the table.

"The food was ready," Ivan said, losing his jovial mood.

"And you didn't wait for the hares I caught for the stew," Dmitri plopped into his chair.

"I'll make it for supper tomorrow." Ivan turned back

to the kitchen to fetch his latest loaf of bread. I had the feeling he also didn't want to spend another second longer than he had to listening to Dmitri.

"Did you wash your hands?" Sascha asked Dmitri.

Dmitri answered with a look of mutinous offense. "I'm not some pup that has to be told to wash up before supper." He glanced to me. I avoided meeting his eyes as I started in on my supper. "Of course I washed up." Dmitri turned back to Sascha. "I'm not some half-mad lone wolf."

Hearing the term "lone wolf" again sent an uncomfortable shiver through me. I assumed those were men who lived by themselves in the forest. Perhaps some of them did by choice, but I was certain some had been shunned from all good society and bad society too. It was something I'd never known to consider before, but now that I was, those sorts of men frightened me as much as actual wolves.

"Are you truly planning on keeping the hides to make something for Peter, or will you take them to the faire to sell?" Sascha asked as he, too, started in on his supper.

Dmitri hesitated for a moment before seeming to accept the normal flow of conversation. "I'll prepare them for the faire," he said. "The sooner I can earn all the money I need to set off on my own, the better."

I nearly choked on the vegetable I was eating. So Dmitri did have plans to leave Sascha's pack. It shouldn't have come as a surprise to me that money was his chief obstacle. Everything in the entire world required money, as I'd seen growing up. But if the forest was filled with lone wolves—not all of whom could possibly be as well-off as Sascha and his pack—then how much did Dmitri truly need to set off on his own? Or had he just become so accustomed to the coziness of Sascha's house that his threats to leave were only that, threats?

I happened to glance up at him as I contemplated the question and found him watching me. It took everything I had not to let the fear inspired by that look show on my face. Perhaps Dmitri suddenly had another reason to stay in Sascha's pack, even though it chafed. For all I knew, he might have been days away from leaving before he found me and changed his mind, deciding to stay.

The mood around the table was tense. It had always been impressed on me to put people at ease whenever I could. It was somewhat of a risk to speak without being spoken to, but I took that risk and said, "To think, this time yesterday, I was attending a formal supper in the palace of Novoberg at which my father hosted the grandest families in the city."

The statement had exactly the effect I'd hoped for. Sven and Gregor chuckled, and so did Ivan as he returned to the table.

"I wonder what that father of yours is thinking now," Gregor speculated, chewing on a bite of roast.

"I'm not sure he would notice my absence," I said, my appetite suddenly vanishing.

"Any man would notice his son's absence," Sascha said in a sympathetic voice. When I glanced up at him, he added with a smirk, "If only so that he could rage at someone for misplacing his property."

I laughed when the others did. "You may be right," I said. "In which case, I wonder what sort of punishment he's eked out on my brothers."

"He should shut them all outside of the city gates for the night," Ivan laughed.

"Especially if they're all as sweet and fine as you," Sven agreed, nudging Ivan with his elbow.

"Believe me, they're not," I said, rolling my eyes slightly and taking another bite of lamb. Ivan truly was an excellent cook. Or perhaps, as Sascha had implied, I was hungry because I really did need to keep my strength up.

"If they were my sons, I'd stick them in the pillory for a day," Dmitri growled, ripping a piece of bread in half. "See how they like it."

My brow inched up. "You know something about the pillory?"

Dmitri laughed ironically. "They kept me and Mikal in there from dawn til dusk before dragging our broken, stinking bodies outside of the city gates and slamming them on us."

Of all things, I suddenly felt sorry for him. The pillory was a strange punishment. How someone fared in it depended entirely on the mob that came to watch the punishment. Someone who had been accused of a crime but had earned the sympathy of the crowd might feel nothing but a bit of discomfort as they sat with their head, hands, and feet in the stocks for an hour or so. Others weren't as fortunate. I'd seen men—and women—killed by mobs throwing stones, rotten vegetables, and dead animals at them while hurling invectives. Someone like Dmitri—someone like me—would be lucky to survive in one piece.

"You're just lucky Murdoch's group found you when they did," Gregor said with a sad smile. He peeked at Sascha.

A few more pieces of the puzzle fit together for me as I remembered a few details from earlier. Sascha and Dmitri had been part of the same pack before. If Sascha had been involved in saving the life of Dmitri and his brother, that could be another reason Dmitri stayed even if he wasn't happy. It could be out of reluctant gratitude.

"I doubt Duke Royale would allow any of his sons to be punished publicly," Sascha went on when a somber silence fell over the table. "More likely, he'd mete out whatever punishment he had in mind for them in private."

"That way, he wouldn't have to admit he'd lost a son at all," I said, but only as a side thought.

Sascha, however, saw more in my comment than I did. "I wonder," he said.

"You wonder what?" Dmitri asked.

Sascha turned to him. He wasn't antagonistic as he went on with, "I wonder if Duke Royale will admit that Peter is gone or if he'll spend the next several years pretending he's hale and hearty and living blissfully within the palace walls."

My jaw dropped open. "Good lord. I bet that's what he'll do."

I blinked into the space in front of me. It was the ideal situation for Father. He could pretend I was still there without ever having to actually admit to me. It was worse than if he'd rejoiced to find me missing. Now he could just ignore me entirely, making an excuse now and then when I wasn't at a city function, and perhaps even kill me off, thanks to some mysterious illness, in a few months or a few years. I would be effectively erased.

I couldn't stand Father, or any of my family, but it hurt to think they could forget about me with impunity.

"I think we need to pay a visit to Novoberg tomorrow," Sascha said, startling me out of my sorry thoughts.

"I beg your pardon?" I sat a little straighter.

"Not you, of course," Sascha said. "I wouldn't allow you to go anywhere near the place. But someone has to go retrieve your clothes and belongings."

I was speechless. I couldn't imagine how Sascha would be able to sneak through the city gates and creep into the palace. How would he even know where to find my room? And what would he think of the remnants of my old life once he found it?

"I'm going with you," Dmitri said, as if Sascha had already said he couldn't.

"Us too," Ivan and Sven said, exchanging a look.

"There's safety in numbers," Sven said.

"And they won't be able to ignore us if we stand united," Ivan finished the thought.

Once again, I nearly choked on my food. "Do you intend to simply walk into the palace and demand my things be packed and handed over?"

Sascha grinned. "Yes."

I gaped at him. Strangely, along with disbelief and wariness, I was worried for him. I couldn't imagine what might happen to him and the others if they strode into the palace, bold as you please. I didn't want to imagine it. They might have been my captors, to a degree, but the last twenty-four hours of my life had been unlike anything I'd ever experienced before. Mad though it was, they'd been the happiest of my life. I didn't want the promise of what my life could be cut short by people who had never cared about me half as much as the five men sitting at the table did, though they barely knew me. Even Dmitri.

"Don't worry, pup," Dmitri said, as if he could read my thoughts. "We'll go in armed." He winked, sending me a bloodthirsty and lustful grin.

"Please do be careful," I said in my most cautious voice.

"We will," Sascha promised, stroking a hand over my head.

The gesture was somewhat infantilizing, but I didn't care as long as he was touching me. The conversation turned to more mundane things—Sven's work in the garden beds and speculation about when planting could be done, an inventory of Dmitri's recent catches, and how much space Sascha would need in the wagon to take the furniture and other things he'd made over the winter to the faire that was coming up in a fortnight. I listened to it all with interest, particularly the mention of the faire.

Underneath it all, I was still trying to assess not only the pack and my place in it, but more about the workings of packs in general. Honestly, the more my companions talked, mentioning business they'd have at the faire and other people they knew they might see there, I began to feel as though packs were nothing more than very small cities of their own. By the end of supper, as Ivan and Sven cleared, I was determined to find a way to convince Sascha to let me go with them to the fair in a fortnight. I wouldn't be able to bring it up right away, though.

"I can help," I said, rising from my chair as the others got up to go about their business.

I reached for my own plate and cup, but Sascha plucked them out of my hands. "I said I don't want you doing any manual labor."

"Clearing a table is hardly manual labor," I argued before I could think better of it.

Sascha's eyes widened by a fraction, and a faint grin pulled at his lips. "You've got a bit of bite in you after all," he said quietly.

I quickly glanced around to see if the others had heard the comment. Dmitri had already moved to his chair by the fireplace and taken up what looked like supplies to make new arrows. Ivan and Sven were all the way in the kitchen and out of earshot. Gregor was close, but either hadn't heard or was pretending he hadn't.

I glanced back to Sascha, meeting his eyes. "Please, let me do something," I said, trying to sound deliberately weak. "I truly do want to help, to do my part."

"You'll do your part soon enough," he rumbled near my ear, sending shivers through me. He straightened and went on with, "But you have a point." He glanced around the room, then started toward a small bookcase against one wall. "I assume you can read?"

"Of course," I answered, following him.

He reached the bookshelf, perused the titles, then took out a book and handed it to me. "You can read aloud while the rest of us finish up for the night."

It was a relief to have something to do that didn't involve an erection. Not only was reading aloud a way to provide entertainment for my companions, it gave me the opportunity to observe them as they went about their evening tasks. Reading didn't take that much of my attention, after all.

I watched Ivan and Sven cleaning up from supper in the kitchen as I began a classic tale of heroes and gods from the ancients. The two of them flirted and wasted their time as much as they worked, nudging each other and even splashing water from the sink at one point. They were in love, which was sweet. Love would make them less inclined to jealousy where I was concerned. After their antics of the afternoon, I had the feeling I was more of a diversion for them than a serious object of affection or possession. They likely just wanted me to play along with them, but I knew already that they would lose interest in me first.

Dmitri, as I had noted before supper, wanted me to submit to him. He was the most dangerous of the pack. No doubt, I had many, many days of sucking him off and being used roughly by him ahead of me. Knowing it was coming, I could handle it. I did feel a visceral attraction to him and a fascination with rough play—or, at least, my body did—so whatever was to come, I would probably enjoy it.

I wasn't certain about Gregor yet. He was the oldest of the group and perhaps the most educated, aside from me, as a former physician's apprentice. He'd participated in the bacchanal the night before, but had only wanted to suck me off that day. If I'd had to guess, I would have said he was the recipient of the others' lusts before I arrived. Perhaps he would lose interest in me even faster than Ivan and Sven, if his interest was even that keen in the first place. Not every man was a ravening beast who required sexual satisfaction every moment of every day.

Which brought me around to Sascha.

"That's enough for one night, Peter," he said, rising from his seat near the fire, where he'd been carving decorations into the back of the chair he'd finished that afternoon. "It's time for bed."

I nearly dropped the book in my hands. Dmitri chuckled as I scrambled to stand, putting it aside. "I hope you follow your own advice and spare that ass so that there's enough of it left to go around tomorrow," he drawled.

Sascha sent him a scathing look, but didn't say anything. He took my hand and led me away from the warm fireplace and along the hall to his bedroom. I did a quick assessment of the state of my body and decided that, though it wasn't quite back to what it should be, my ass was soothed enough for whatever Sascha might want to do with it. The possibilities had me well on my way to being hard before we reached his bedroom.

"How did you enjoy your first day as the pup of our pack, Peter?" Sascha asked as he shut the bedroom door behind us. I noted that the door didn't have a lock, but he made sure the latch was in place.

"Am I a member of your pack?" I asked, inching backward as he stepped toward me.

He was so much taller and broader than me that glancing up at him left me breathless in anticipation. "In a manner of speaking," he said with a smile, cupping a hand against the side of my face. "Not quite a full member, though I'll make sure your member is full soon enough."

I smiled in spite of myself, at his ribald humor and clarification of my place. Even if I wasn't an equal, it felt good to belong to a group I actually liked. My family certainly didn't fit that description. But I didn't have time for a more complex thought than that as Sascha closed his other hand over my face as well, tilting my head up, then bending down to kiss me.

Sascha's kisses were ten times more erotic than any prick thrust into my mouth. His mouth was larger than mine too, and his lips full and demanding. I sighed as he brushed his tongue against the seam of my lips and parted them for him. He took immediate advantage of that, thrusting his tongue into my mouth to claim me. He wasn't forceful, though. He explored me, savored me, and had my blood pounding through every part of me.

"You really are the most delicious morsel I've ever tasted," he said in a gruff voice. "I want you in every way possible."

My knees went weak. I grabbed the front of his shirt for support, but that only made me aware of the broad, firm muscles of his chest. The room was already spinning around me, and we hadn't even made it to the bed.

"It's impossible for me to take my time with you," Sascha growled, backing me another few steps toward the bed and tugging at the sash of my robe. "You're too enticing for me to resist."

"I—" I wanted to say something polite or obedient, or even witty and dazzling, but my mind was nothing but a jumble of emotions and lust.

Sascha chuckled low in his throat but didn't say anything either. My robe sagged around me, and he sucked in a breath as it fell to the floor when he pushed it off my shoulders. His hands roved over my shoulders and down my back to my sides, then spread across my smooth chest.

"They should have asked me before they did this," he said, hoarse with desire, "but I like it."

So much for ever having hair like a grown man again. If Sascha liked me denuded, I was going to stay that way. Though if it meant he touched me like he was doing just then, I wouldn't mind.

"On the bed," he ordered me. The growl in his voice had me trembling and hard.

I followed his command, turning to pull back the bedcovers—it was still technically winter, after all, and nights were cold. Those gestures had me bent forward just a bit.

"Your ass looks much better, though I don't care for that green stuff," Sascha said, humor in his voice.

I pivoted to find him staring at my backside, bare-chested, having just pulled his shirt off over his head. "It feels much better," I half-lied. "Good as new, even."

Sascha tossed his shirt aside and gave me a flat look. "You said that this morning, and I ended up hurting you. I'm not falling for that enticement again. If you want my cock in you, you'll have to provide a different hole."

My mouth dropped open as I scrambled for a reply.

"That one will do," Sascha said, even more humor sparkling in his eyes.

He kicked off the moccasins he'd changed into before supper and unfastened his breeches, pushing them down his legs. The breath stopped in my lungs as his massive cock leapt free, standing straight and thick. I didn't have the strength to even attempt to resist him when he reached me by the bed and pushed me slightly. I sat hard on the side of the bed, which had my face close to the level of his groin.

Without a hint of hesitation, he gripped the base of his cock and held it out to me. I was so overcome with excitement that I went right for it. He was so thick and long, and already his flared tip shone with moisture. I licked at it with a broad stroke, and he sucked in a breath of pleasure. That only encouraged me to explore more with my tongue and lips. I'd just had a day's worth of education about what felt good, and I was eager to practice what I'd learned.

He let me take my time, working his tip until I was salivating for more. The tension of holding back rippled off of him, which made me feel powerful. I'd had that effect on him. I drew in a long breath and took more of him in, bit by bit. He filled my mouth, testing my limits. I needed several tries before I could get my tongue to do what I wanted it to and stay flat enough to swallow him deeper.

My efforts were rewarded when Sascha let out a shaking breath and pulled out of my mouth quickly. "If we keep going like that, sweetheart, I'll be done too fast. And I have much more planned for you." He sank to kneel before me, pushing my knees open wide. "This, for example."

He stroked his huge hands up my shaved thighs to close a hand possessively over my heavy balls. I let out a sound of pleasure and tipped back, barely catching myself on my elbows. Sascha grinned, using my new position to pull me forward until half of my ass hung off the side of the bed.

"I shouldn't like this, but I do," he growled, brushing his fingertips over my denuded groin.

I liked it too. So much that my prick dripped precum onto my belly as it throbbed in expectation. He noticed with a grin, running the flat of his hand up my length, then teasing his fingertips over my head before closing his hand gently around me. I groaned with the pleasure of it, letting my head fall back.

"Fuck me, Peter. You don't know what you do to me when you look like that," he growled, stoking me gently.

I used all of my strength to lift my head enough to ask, "Like what?"

"Like you want my hands on you so desperately you're about to come out of your skin."

"I do," I panted, jerking instinctively against him. "I am." And I was nearly crying I wanted it so badly.

Sascha chuckled deep and slow, teasing my hole with his other hand. "Peter," he said scoldingly, "don't you know that I'm your captor? You're my prisoner here, and I won't ever, every let you leave."

"I don't want to leave," I panted, breaking out in a sweat.

He seemed amused by that answer. "You know I could do anything I wanted to you. Anything. Depraved things."

"I don't care," I whimpered. "I want you to do them."

Fire flared in his eyes. "Why? You're not here willingly. You were captured and brought here."

"I am here willingly now," I insisted. "And I want it. It feels so good. You feel so good." I met his eyes as I spoke.

Something shifted between us. I might have been completely submissive to him, but we were equals. Equals in lust.

I expected him to suck me into his mouth. I wanted him to. So desperately tears were leaking from the corners of my eyes as surely as precum was from my cock. But he didn't. Instead, with a sleek, powerful movement, he stood and pulled me across the bed, covering me with his massive body.

The feeling of him on top of me, my legs spread wide, was a breath away from being terrifying. Even more so when he grasped my wrists and forced them above my head, holding them locked there with one hand. He stroked the side of my face with his other hand before bearing down on me and punishing my mouth with a kiss. He was less gentle with his tongue this time, invading and claiming me with kisses that had me so aroused I was on fire.

At the same time, he ground his erection against mine, trapping our burning cocks between our bodies. Flashes of what I'd watched Ivan and Sven do went through my mind, and I groaned into Sascha's mouth. I wanted what they'd done, what they had. I wanted to feel that wild intimacy with Sascha, to feel how much he wanted me and wanting him with equal ferocity.

"I can't hold back with you," he panted. Breaking away from my mouth and reaching between us. "You're everything I've ever wanted."

I cried out loud as he wrapped his massive, calloused hand around our cocks together and started to move it. Something about the whole thing felt unplanned and wildly pleasurable. I fought with everything I had not to come too soon, but between the way he pinned me, the way I was so helpless under him, and the way my mouth throbbed from his kisses, I knew it was a losing battle. I wept and mewled with need, pushing into his grasp and even wrapping my flailing legs around his thighs.

"Oh, Peter," he growled, fisting us faster.

I came with a wrenching cry, spilling across both of our stomachs as we rested so close together. It felt so good to empty for him like that that my entire body went limp in the aftermath. His didn't. Instead, he let go of me and balanced himself above me, groaning as he finished himself off while drinking in the sight of me. He caught his breath and let out a sigh milking himself onto my smooth chest.

A few drops of him splattered across my chin. I reached my tongue out and licked them in.

Sascha's eyes went wide, then hazy. "Fuck almighty, Peter," he growled from the depths of his chest. "I just finished, and you make me want to go again."

"We have all night," I panted, feeling as though I was made of golden sunlight and infused with his cum.

"Fuck," he gasped again, collapsing on the bed beside me, then rolling around until his head was on the pillow and the bedclothes covered us. He tucked me against his side, stroking my back and lifting my leg across his hips. "You weren't lying when you said you liked it."

"I wasn't," I panted as exhaustion settled over me.

"And you swear you were a virgin until last night?" he asked on.

"I swear it, I was." I wasn't sure if he believed me, so lifted my head until I could stare hard into his eyes and said with deadly earnestness, "I swear I was a virgin until you had me last night."

He studied me, fighting to catch his breath, then said, "I believe you," as if he were surprised that he did.

That was a good enough answer for me. I sagged against him, resting my head on his shoulder and closing my eyes. "You'll keep me, won't you?" I asked, sounding as small and innocent as a mouse. "You'll keep me safe and touch me and make me come like that forever, won't you?"

I was already half asleep when he answered in a deep, impassioned voice, "God help me, I will, Peter. I'm your prisoner now as much as you're mine."

I smiled and let myself fall into oblivion. That was everything I could have possibly wanted.

8

Contrary to my assertion that we had all night, I didn't awake again until morning light cut through the squares of muslin that Sascha called curtains on his bedroom windows. Once again, I'd been so exhausted that I'd slept like a log through the night. Or perhaps I'd slept that well because, as I had the night before, I'd slept in Sascha's encompassing embrace. The same as my first morning in the forest, I awoke with his large body cradling mine, my head resting on his shoulder.

"You sleep the same way you do everything else, sweet Peter," Sascha hummed against my ear as soon as he saw I was awake. "Masterfully."

I grinned widely and sucked in a breath, stretching off the night before. Sascha groaned at my movements, pressing a hand against my belly and grinding his morning erection against my backside in tandem with my movements. I sighed in bliss at the sensation, closing my eyes again and relaxing into him as he kissed and nipped at my neck and shoulder.

"I like that," I sighed, still too sleepy to check my words.

Sascha's rumbling chuckle stirred my already filled cock harder. "You like everything."

"Because it feels good to be touched," I agreed.

It was dangerously bold of me, but I brushed my hand against his as it rested against my stomach, pushing it lower. Sascha continued to laugh as he obeyed my unspoken request to fondle me. His hand roved the smooth flesh of my groin, teasing my balls enough to make my breath catch in my throat, before he made his way to my cock slowly.

"This really was a good idea," he sighed, exploring my smooth skin with enthusiasm. "I can't get enough of touching you like this."

And I couldn't get enough of being touched. By Sascha, at least. His touch was so much more than any of the others'. It was sensual, designed to pleasure both of us, not just him. I wasn't just a toy or a tool for him, I was a willing and equal participant, and that made all the difference.

I twisted in his arms, seeking out his mouth with mine. He knew what I wanted and covered my mouth with his, kissing me with a sigh of passion that was almost vulnerable. He fisted his hand around my cock, and I gripped his powerful thigh as we moved together.

He stopped immediately when I winced though. "What hurts?" he asked breathlessly.

I wanted to laugh. "My penis. It's been rubbed raw."

"We can't have that off-limits as well as this." He stroked between my crack, rubbing my hole—which felt considerably better. "Perhaps this," he said, then shifted quickly.

Before I was fully sensible of how I was moving, Sascha had me on my back with my legs spread, my head against the pillow. He positioned himself between my legs, taking possessive hold of my cock and sliding it gently into his mouth. I let out a pleasured cry and threaded both hands into his thick, chestnut hair. He let me know how much he liked that with a moan that was muted by my cock.

The way he sucked me was so gentle, in spite of how overused I was, that I was primed and ready to burst in no time. His lips were soft on me and his tongue moved in just the right way to drive me wild. He was able to take me deep as well, so deep that I was worried I'd choke him when I instinctively jerked into him. As soon as I did, he held my hips firmly to the bed, rendering me unable to move, as much as I wanted to. It felt amazing to be restricted that way, so that he was the one in control of giving me pleasure.

"Sascha," I sighed his name as heat and energy gathered at the base of my spine. "Oh, Sascha, yes."

I came with a grunt, and he answered with a moan as he swallowed. I knew I was awake, but I still felt like I was dreaming. My body felt warm and fluid as he pulled away, panting and kneeling above me between my legs. My arms flopped to my sides above my head, and I smiled lazily up at him. He reached quickly into the open jar of ointment at the side of the bed, hurriedly stroking it over his leaking cock, then slowed down, pleasuring himself as he feasted on the sight of me.

"You're so beautiful like this," he grunted, stroking slowly at first, then faster, like he was beyond ready to come. "So soft and pale and pink. And that mouth, Peter, that smile."

"It's for you," I said, high and sweet, without quite having caught my breath. It was impossible to catch it while watching Sascha stroke himself off.

His body was intoxicating—strong, muscular, and large. His thighs alone were almost as big around as my waist, and I was no beanpole. I envied the hair that covered his chest and stomach. His nipples were taut with pleasure. His face was contorted with it as he drew closer and closer to climax. He was simply the handsomest man I'd ever known with his high cheekbones and green eyes, and his lips were swollen from kisses and from being around my cock.

It was his cock, so immense and slick as he fisted himself hard, that I was interested in. I loved the way his foreskin rolled as he worked himself and the drip of precum that shone on his dark head. I wanted to burn the image of him worked up and panting like that into my memory forever. The more I smiled sinfully at him, body completely limp and on display for him, the more I liked it.

And I knew exactly what Sascha wanted from me. He wanted me to pretend to be utterly submissive while actually telling him what to do. He wanted the illusion of control over me while knowing I was as strong as he was.

That in mind, I tilted my head just slightly to him, barely winking, smile wide. He came with a ripping cry, spilling his seed over my chest and belly, then sagging. I brushed a hand lightly across my belly, wetting my fingers with his cum.

I thought about sucking on those fingers, but he collapsed to the bed beside me before I could, gathering me into his arms, face to face, and kissing me lingeringly. Those kisses started urgently, but quickly turned into a long, slow mating of our mouths. He drew my leg up over his hips and threaded his fingers through my hair. I was more than happy to stay that way with him all day, for the rest of my life.

"I feel like we've been like this for our whole lives," he whispered at last, resting his forehead against mine. "Even though it's barely been more than a day."

"I know," I murmured back, my heart so light it felt like singing. Sascha was smitten with me, and a man who was smitten would protect me with his life. I'd never felt so safe. I might even be able to be smitten with him too, once my life settled to the point where I knew what the shape of it would be. In the meantime, it was nice to pretend.

"I knew the moment I saw you," he went on, "looking so frightened and innocent and—"

A fist pounded on Sascha's bedroom door, followed by Dmitri growling, "If you two are done fucking, we need to get to Novoberg as soon as they open the gate."

Sascha let out an answering growl of frustration, flopping to his back. "I'd murder him if he wasn't right."

I pushed myself to sit, gazing down at him. "You don't have to go to the palace to get my things," I said, letting my worry show. "I...I don't know what I'd do if something happened to you." That much wasn't a lie. There was no telling what my fate would be in a forest full of wolves and wolf packs without Sascha to protect me.

He lifted himself with one arm and surged against me, kissing me soundly. "I'll be fine, Peter. I've got more tricks up my sleeve when it comes to marching into a town like Novoberg than you think."

"You do?" I eyed him warily as he rolled out of bed and stood.

"I do," he said with a perfectly wicked look. "Now, get yourself out of bed, wash up, don that robe, and come have breakfast."

I did as he'd asked, although it was a tight fit for both of us to use the washroom adjacent to his bedroom to clean up at the same time. I positively refused to relieve myself while he was in there, or vice versa, which Sascha thought was hilarious.

"I was raised to value manners and decorum," I

explained as he came out of the washroom after using it so that I could go in.

"I'll show you manners and decorum," he said, smacking my bare ass hard as we crossed paths.

I jerked up to the tip of my toes, my eyes going wide. I didn't think I was the sort to go in for that kind of thing, but the tingles that spread across my backside weren't all of the painful variety.

There wasn't time to think about anything like that once we joined the others at breakfast, though. Dmitri was already fully dressed and practically pacing, he was so ready to leave. Ivan and Sven were busy setting the kitchen in order.

"There's an extra loaf of bread from yesterday," Ivan explained, arranging things on the kitchen counter, "and there's a sausage you can have for lunch. We should be back by supper, but maybe not in time to prepare an elaborate meal."

"Are you all going?" I asked, wispy with alarm. The idea of being alone at the house was both intriguing and terrifying.

"Not on your bloody life," Dmitri said. "We wouldn't want you to get the idea that you could run off while no one is looking."

I sent a look to Sascha meant to tell him there was no way I would do that now. He replied with a look that said he knew, and that he knew why.

"I'm staying with you," Gregor said from the table, where he was still eating a leisurely breakfast. "I've got too much work to do before the next faire to miss a whole day of it."

"I can help," I said, tugging my robe tighter and crossing to the table. My stomach rumbled as soon as I saw the spread of pastries and sausages laid out there.

Gregor glanced to Sascha, one eyebrow raised in question.

"As long as you don't do any manual labor or get your hands dirty," Sascha said. "You were raised with manners and decorum, after all."

I let out a laugh before I could stop myself, then clapped a hand over my mouth, blushing. Sascha flushed with pleasure at my reaction.

The others all took note. Ivan and Sven exchanged knowing winks. Gregor looked uncommonly pleased. But Dmitri narrowed his eyes and clenched his jaw. "Yes," he said. "I want those hands fresh as a daisy when they're around my cock later. And I trust that ass of yours will be healed enough by the time we get home for me to fuck it again, at last."

He glanced pointedly at Sascha.

Sascha looked downright murderous, but he didn't say anything.

I bit my tongue over the myriad of questions I suddenly had. I bided my time, pretending nothing was out of the ordinary as I joined Gregor for breakfast. The others ate quickly, filling a small pack with extra food, and preparing to leave.

Before they headed to the door, Sascha came over

to the table and closed a hand under my chin, lifting my face up to his. He kissed me soundly, his eyes lingering on mine when he stepped away. "Don't get into any trouble," he said as he backed away, pointing at me.

"I won't," I said sweetly, knowing full well I was flushed pink.

My smile faltered when I glanced past Sascha to find Dmitri staring at me in calculation. I smiled for him as well, sensing a great many things depended on me keeping the peace between the two alphas in our pack.

A few more goodbyes were said as Sascha, Dmitri, Ivan, and Sven headed out. As soon as they were gone, my smile dropped and I turned to Gregor.

"I have questions," I said.

Gregor laughed wistfully. "I'm sure you do." He put down his fork and leaned back in his chair, narrowing his eyes assessing at me. "Go on." He nodded. "Ask them."

I didn't know where to start, so I reached for my coffee and took a long drink as things organized themselves in my mind.

"Will Sascha forbid Dmitri to touch me?" I asked, figuring that was the best place to start. Gregor would think I was mostly concerned with myself, not the power dynamics of the pack.

"Do you want him to touch you?" Gregor asked with a slow smile.

I took another sip of coffee. Gregor was smarter than I'd given him credit for. Answering a question with another question was the best way to stay in control of a situation.

"It's too soon for me to say for certain," I answered carefully. "I don't think I would mind Dmitri having his way with me."

"But you've formed a fast bond with Sascha," Gregor finished for me.

I looked calculatedly guilty, interested to hear what he thought of the situation.

Gregor shrugged. "I don't blame you one bit," he said. "Sascha is gorgeous. He's also kind and intelligent, and he's the leader." Gregor's pointed look hinted that he could guess my motivations.

"He makes me feel safe," I admitted. Gregor had earned that much. "And for someone who has been bullied, teased, and even beaten for his entire life, nothing is more valuable than feeling protected."

"Oh, believe me, I understand," Gregor said, moving back toward his place and resuming his breakfast.

A lick of suspicion hit me. "Are you in love with him?"

"Sascha?" He looked startled, then laughed. "God, no. He's a good man and a considerate lover, but I don't have those kinds of feelings for him."

I was surprised by how jealous I was at Gregor's admission he and Sascha were, or had been, lovers. It was obvious, though, based on what I'd learned about pack dynamics yesterday.

"Don't worry," Gregor went on with a laugh. "I'm as content to go without sex as I am to have it when it's offered. It's nice, but there are more important things in life."

"So I don't have to worry about you ravishing me all day while the others are gone?" I asked.

Gregor laughed out loud. "No, certainly not." He paused, tilting his head to the side. "Though I suppose I could, if that's what you wanted."

"Not particularly," I said, reaching for the buttered bread on my plate. I'd actually had a chance to butter it myself, since Sascha wasn't there. "I hope that doesn't offend you," I said as an afterthought.

"Not at all." Gregor shook his head. "I see the way you and Sascha look at each other."

I continued eating, but said, "I've only known him one day."

"And how many times has he fucked you in that one day?" Gregor asked, one eyebrow raised.

I looked sheepish as I reached for my coffee.

"You're a clever lad," Gregor went on, inadvertently hinting that he'd forgotten how old I was. "You're smart to have figured out where to cast your lot so quickly. And if you want my advice, cling to Sascha like a burr on a cat."

It was nice to have my suspicions about the situation confirmed. "But what about Dmitri?" I asked. "He's made it clear he wants me too."

Gregor sighed and sat back in his chair again. "Dmitri

found you," he said. "Technically, according to unwritten rules, he has first claim on you."

My ears pricked at the mention of rules. Rules and laws were the things I knew best. "So, if he were to decide to leave the pack, would he have a right to take me with him?" The very thought put me off the rest of my breakfast.

Gregor squinted and tilted his head to the side. "Maybe. Sascha is the pack leader, though. He has the right to claim you belong to him. That rule is also unwritten, though."

"Someone needs to write a definitive book of pack laws," I said, rising and gathering my dishes to take to the kitchen area.

Gregor laughed and followed suit. "I've been saying that for years."

We walked on to the kitchen, tidying as we went. It felt good to be able to fend for myself instead of being treated like a porcelain doll.

"I can tell that what you really want to know is whether there's going to be a fight," Gregor said as we stood at the sink, washing plates.

"That is what worries me," I said.

Gregor snorted and shook his head. "One day here, and you can already sense it. Because that rivalry has been going on for years."

"It has something to do with Mikal and Jakob, doesn't it?" I asked.

Gregor drew in a long breath. "That's a whole other story."

I stared at him, silently ordering him to tell it.

Fortunately, it seemed like he wanted to.

"Mikal and Dmitri are brothers, of course. Twins," he said as we moved back to the kitchen. I sat as he set up the work we would do for the day. "Dmitri and Mikal were close. Then things heated up between Mikal and Jakob. Dmitri grew jealous. He demanded Sascha cast Jakob out."

"Of the pack?" I asked. "That can happen?"

"It happens all the time," Gregor said. "Sascha didn't want to get in the middle of it. He avoided the conflict for as long as possible. We were still building up the house and the land around it, and the last thing we needed was that sort of conflict. Finally, Dmitri demanded the matter be settled. There was a huge argument, the case was made on both sides, and ultimately, grudgingly, Sascha agreed to cast Jakob out."

"He did?" I blinked in shock. I questioned the wisdom of caving in to Dmitri's demands.

"Believe me, it wasn't an easy decision," Gregor said, holding up a hand. "And the only reason he did was because he knew Mikal would go with him."

"Oh." I sat back in my chair, imagining what the conversation would have been like back then.

"That, of course, infuriated Dmitri," Gregor went on.

"Of course, it would," I said, taking the pen Gregor handed me once our work was set up.

"He demanded that Sascha forbid Mikal from leaving," Gregor said.

"Could he have done that?" I asked.

"Yes." Gregor said. "A leader has full control over everyone in his pack. It's a huge amount of power, but good leaders, like Sascha, take it as a grave responsibility."

I was even gladder that Sascha was so taken with me. I admired him more now, as Gregor told the story.

"Sascha has a sentimental streak, as you might have noticed," Gregor said with a wink. "He could no more part Mikal and Jakob than he could throw a wedge between Ivan and Sven. In fact, I think that's part of why Ivan and Sven have been so loyal to Sascha. Not every leader is as sentimental about love."

"I'm not certain I would want to live under the leadership of someone who wasn't," I said.

"No one does," Gregor chuckled. He started in on his labels, handing me a few sheets of paper to do the same. "It was the right decision," Gregor went on with a bit of a frown. "Dmitri couldn't exactly defy it. He would have been in the wrong if he had. There really weren't solid grounds for Jakob to leave the pack, besides Dmitri's jealousy over suddenly coming second in his brother's eyes. To tell you the truth, I've been expecting Dmitri to pack up and leave as soon as winter is over." He paused.

"But now I'm here," I sighed, finishing his thought. "And Dmitri was the one who found me."

Gregor hummed. "Indeed."

"So I might have just prolonged a conflict that was about to resolve itself." My shoulders sagged.

"You couldn't have known, lad." He chuckled. "You didn't end up here deliberately. Technically, you're Dmitri's prisoner."

I shuddered at the thought.

Gregor must have seen it. "Don't worry, I know Sascha. Even though it's only been a day, he would go to war to keep you with him. He's always wanted a pup. And I truly don't think you understand how rare and valuable you are, and not just for fucking."

"So rare and valuable that I might start a war," I said wearily.

Gregor seemed to think that was funny. "All of the great love stories of history start with a war. And if you ask me, I still think Dmitri's desire to forge out on his own will win out in the end. He'll be gone by midsummer."

"And in the meantime, he's going to take every opportunity that he can to use me, and then rub it in Sascha's face," I sighed.

"If you don't want him, Sascha will stop him," Gregor said seriously.

I paused my work to look at him frankly. "Do you think it would be better to refuse Dmitri's advances and to cause a confrontation immediately, or would it be better to let Dmitri have his way with me in the hope that he'll lose interest and give me up?"

Gregor's brow raised in surprise. "Rare as a precious gem," he said. "You're a sharp lad." I didn't take the bait and fall for his compliment. I continued to stare at him until he sighed and answered, "If you're fine with Dmitri fucking you, then it would probably be best to ride it out. So to speak."

I grinned at the off-color pun. "As much as I would rather save myself for Sascha alone, I think it would do much more for the pack as a whole, to keep the peace, of course, if I capitulated to Dmitri for the time being. And there is a certain...appeal to his appetites."

"I think you're right," Gregor agreed. "And you're a brave lad for going on with it. Now. Let's finish up these labels, and then we'll defy Sascha's orders by feeding the chickens and goats and collecting eggs and milk."

It was a pleasant way to pass a morning—almost enough to make me forget the reason Gregor and I were alone in the house. As the sun hit its zenith and then started toward the opposite horizon, I began to grow nervous.

"Novoberg is no short walk from here," Gregor tried to reassure me as we sat near the fireplace in the early afternoon.

"Yes, but they took the horses," I said in a hushed voice. The chickens and goats weren't the only animals I hadn't noticed during my first day at the house. The pack owned four horses as well, all of which were away with Sascha and the others now. "Surely, they could have gotten there and back by now."

Gregor smiled sadly at me. "Most freshly-caught

pups would be wishing death on their captors if they were in your position."

"Yes, but as you've told me, I'm not most pups," I replied, sitting straighter and allowing myself just a hint of smugness.

Gregor's grin returned. "No, you're not." He set his book aside and inched forward in his chair. "And as the unusual treasure that you are, would you like to learn some skills that will help you in your endeavors to keep Dmitri distracted and win Sascha's heart?"

I eyed him askance. Throughout the day, I'd all but written off Gregor's interest in me sexually. "I suppose that would depend on the lessons you're offering," I said demurely.

Gregor chuckled and stood, crossing to his apothecary counter to retrieve a jar. He brought it to the sofa where I was reading, then knelt on the floor in front of me, setting the jar on the floor. "Let me show you a few tricks for blowing a man."

I arched one eyebrow, fussing with my robe, trying to decide if I was disappointed with myself for being aroused by the offer or not. I wanted to be loyal to Sascha, but my cock was a libidinous traitor. "By way of demonstration, I suppose?" I asked.

"Of course." Gregor sent me a cheeky wink. That dissolved into a more practical look. "Come on, untie that robe and spread your legs. I'll show you a few things that will make it more comfortable for you and more pleasurable for them."

"If you insist," I said, barely above a whisper.

Oddly enough, I felt far more self-conscious untying my robe and spreading it open to present my prick to Gregor with no one else in the house or on the property than I had when others were in the same room, looking on. There was something far more intimate about doing such a thing alone with a man than having an audience.

"You're not the only one who likes to be touched," Gregor said, shifting me forward and gesturing for me to put a cushion behind my back. He found the position he wanted as well, then gently stroked his hands up my inner thighs. "Every man likes a little finesse when he's being pleasured," Gregor explained. "Think of it as building a fire slowly instead of throwing paraffin on a blaze."

"Oh!" I wriggled under his touch, understanding exactly what he meant. My cock filled quickly, rising to meet Gregor's challenge. He took a small bit of ointment from the jar he'd fetched and slicked it over my prick. I gasped at the sensation and settled back into the pillow.

"I recommend using something like this jelly every time," he said. "It makes things easier, and some of the concoctions I've formulated enhance the pleasure."

In fact, a delicious, warm tingle started to spread through my cock where he spread the jelly.

"I don't know how I'm supposed to last long enough to learn my lessons when you've employed that," I gasped.

Gregor sent me a flat look. "You have more natural control than anyone I've ever known."

It was time for me to confess. "I might have been a virgin before Dmitri found me the other day, but I've had a lot of practice with myself."

Gregor laughed out loud. His amusement made me smile, but I was also ready for him to get on with his instruction.

"Never forget that there's more to play with than just the shaft when you're pleasuring a man," he explained, cupping my balls and working them gently. "A little bit of pressure is good if you aim to please." He demonstrated by tugging them just a bit to send my eyebrows flying up at the sensation. "Different sorts of pressure have a different affect." He gripped them tighter, causing a flash of pain that somehow managed to be erotic. That had me squirming and breaking out in a sweat. "It all depends on who you're with and what they like."

"Duly noted," I gasped.

"And there's nothing to say you can't do a little fingering while you're in the area for a blow-job," he went on, stroking his fingers lower to toy with my hole. The sensations he evoked in me were stunningly good, and I had a hard time swallowing the sounds of pleasure I wanted to make. "Oh, and never hold back from vocalizing your pleasure," he advised. "Whether you're on the giving or the receiving end. It's a compliment to your partner."

"All right," I mewled.

He laughed, then scooted closer. "Now, it's best to start with a bit of teasing, get them ready, and leave them wanting more."

He leaned in, closing his mouth over the head of my cock to lick and suckle it as though it were a sweet. I let out a sigh of appreciation which doubled as victory. I'd done something right while pleasuring Sascha the night before. And if Sascha had felt anything half as delightful as what Gregor was causing me to feel, I'd done a good job.

"Some will tell you to pay special attention to the underside," Gregor said, growing breathless, then licking a particularly sensitive spot just at the base of my head, "but I say, why focus on just one spot when you can go for the whole?"

"Why indeed?" I panted, then sucked in a breath when he closed his mouth over my head again. Gregor was fantastically good at what he was doing. I was having a hard time paying close enough attention to learn his technique, but I forced myself to try.

"Now, I'm not sure how to describe this next bit," he said, more breathless still. I noticed his trousers were tented as well. "The best way to handle a full-sized cock is to keep your throat as relaxed as possible and to breathe steadily through your nose."

I nearly bucked off the sofa when he bore down on me again. He managed to swallow me almost to the hilt, as he'd done the day before, in one, long movement.

"Can you feel that?" he panted, coming off me. "It's all in relaxing. Now, observe what I do with my tongue."

He bore down on me again. I watched, eyes wide, as my throbbing erection disappeared into his mouth. He didn't look even a little bit distressed as I disappeared into him. When he started to move his tongue in what I could only describe as an undulating pattern, swallowing as he did, he drew me in even farther.

It was almost impossible to pay full attention after that. The way he moved on me, drawing me in and out with increasing speed, had me near the edge within minutes. I took his earlier advice and let out every manner of thoroughly erotic sounds, and he did the same. He was right, the experience was doubly enjoyable when one's partner made sounds of enthusiasm.

I was seconds away from bursting when he pulled back to catch his breath.

"Now," he panted, holding up one finger. My eyes popped in disbelief that he could leave me hanging where he had. "There's a different between sucking someone off and fucking someone's mouth."

"There is?" I asked, a bit desperately and high-pitched.

He nodded. "It's all in who controls the motion. That was me sucking you off. This time, you do the thrusting. Hold onto my head as you do if it helps you control the movement."

I felt instantly naughty for what he was urging me to do. I was supposed to be the submissive one, after all.

What he was teaching me to do felt taboo. But when he took a deep breath and bore down on me, giving me the signal, I jerked my hips into him.

He made a sound of approval and signaled with a thumbs up that I was doing it right, then gestured for more. A thrill of excitement rocketed through me as I thrust into his mouth—slow at first, but with increasing speed as I grew more confident. To start with, I was nervous about being too forceful, so I held back. But as the tell-tale signs of orgasm began to grow at the base of my spine and my body prepared to climax, I threw myself into it with abandon. I held the sides of Gregor's head and pumped my hips for all I was worth until the pleasure became too much and I came with a shuddering cry. I was too transported to pay even the slightest bit of attention to how, exactly, Gregor swallowed my stream of cum.

"Good boy," he panted as I sagged back. "Sascha is in for a surprise one day where you're concerned."

"Yes," I gasped. It was the only response I was capable of at the moment.

"Do you want to switch places and, you know," Gregor asked with a flicker of one eyebrow, "practice what you've learned?"

I nodded quickly and slumped off the sofa, letting Gregor take my place. More than just feeling obligated to him, I wanted to see how I ranked at my new skills in an expert's eyes.

"I can't promise I'll be able to hold out long," Gregor

said as he unfastened his trousers and shoved them down to his knees. "After all that, I'm already—"

His explanation ended on a long sigh as I went straight to work. We'd already gone far enough that there was no point taking my time with touches and licking. I went straight to what he'd showed me with his tongue and attempted to swallow him all the way. My eagerness resulted in gagging, though.

"Easy, easy, pup," Gregor cautioned me, breathing heavily. "You've got to work your way up to taking the whole thing. Don't push yourself."

I nodded, then tried again, slower. I found that if I concentrated on relaxation and breathed through my nose, as he'd said, I could bring him in quite far. I tried the trick with my tongue—understanding it now more than I had the day before—and was able to swallow him deeper than I'd been able to take anyone up until that point. The whole thing sent a thrill of triumph through me. I would be a master at this in no time, and then wouldn't Sascha be pleased with me.

True to his word, Gregor didn't last more than a minute. I wasn't completely ready for his eruption and sputtered a bit as his cum hit the back of my throat. He apologized profusely for not warning me sooner, but there were no hard feelings. Nothing was hard at all between us once we were both satisfied. Gregor brought me a glass of water and fetched one for himself, then we spent the next several, bizarre moments in a question-and-answer session about what we'd done, as if he'd just taught me how to form letters or make a bird out of folded paper.

We were in the middle of discussing exercises I could do to improve the depth to which I was able to take a cock when a commotion sounded outside.

I jumped out of the chair where I'd been sitting, heart racing, and hugged my robe around me. For a split-second, I worried that the noise was from someone other than Sascha and the other pack members. I needn't have worried, though. A moment later, they burst through the door, triumphant smiles on their faces. Ivan and Sven carried a large chest that I recognized from my bedroom in the palace between them.

"We're home," Sascha said, smiling wickedly at me.

"And we've brought presents for you, pup," Ivan said.

"You're safe." I breathed out, happier than I'd ever been when Sascha strode across the room to fold me in a tight embrace.

"Boy, do we have a story for you," he said, excitement in his eyes.

9

*O*nly after the fact did I feel self-conscious about how quickly I'd run into Sascha's embrace. It was more than just a matter of dignity—I wasn't actually a twelve-year-old boy, even if I'd been made to look like one—it was a matter of discretion. I was highly aware of the narrow-eyed look that Dmitri gave Sascha as he held me and rubbed his hands over my back, then kissed my forehead before stepping back. Whether they'd been allies in taking on my father at the palace or not, they were antagonists now that they were home.

"You would have laughed if you'd seen the looks on those city-dwellers' faces when we marched into Novoberg," Sven chuckled as he and Ivan set my trunk down in the space between the sofa and chairs. "You'd've thought they'd never seen a forest-dweller before."

He and Ivan shared a humorous look. I stepped away from Sascha as he set about removing his coat. It would have been rude to point out to Sven and Ivan that the only time I'd ever seen forest-dwellers in my life was at the occasional village faire, and even then, I hadn't been aware that they were wolves. Although, if I'd thought about it, I would have realized there had to be other people in the frontier besides the ones who lived in the cities. I'd always assumed the vendors and craftsmen at faires were from other cities, but after learning about how all the things my five packmates caught, grew, or crafted were destined for sale at faires, it dawned on me that I'd been around forest-dwellers my whole life without realizing it. In fact, I'd've wagered that my life and the lives of everyone in all of the cities depended on wolves more than anyone realized. And it also occurred to me that perhaps such things were kept from young people of my social station deliberately.

"It's not as if we look any less civilized than they do," Ivan added as he, too, removed his winter things. "I've seen much rougher-looking sorts."

I blinked on my way to examine my trunk as I realized he was right. Sascha and the others were dressed no worse than tradesmen or more prosperous farmers in Novoberg. Their clothes were well-made and fit as though they'd been custom tailored, though they wore unforgivably drab colors. Since I hadn't seen so much as a sign of sewing equipment in the house—not that I'd gone through every cupboard and chest the way I wanted to—I assumed everything they wore was purchased at village faires. It was more proof that trade between the cities and the wolves thrived to a degree that I'd been unaware of, and I was highly educated. Why were such things kept a secret?

"We don't need to dress the part to let everyone know we're not to be trifled with," Dmitri said, taking his bow off his shoulder and shrugging out of his coat. He sent me a toothy grin. "Even Peter knew at first sight that he was in trouble when I found him."

I pretended to be eager to see what was in my trunk as a way to avoid the multiple lies and misinterpretation of Dmitri's words. I'd been terrified when I stumbled across him because I was alone in the dark in a deep forest and afraid of wolves. The real kind. My first reaction to him had been wariness and curiosity, particularly since his cock was one of the first parts of him I'd seen. I stifled a wry laugh. I should have known. But if he wanted to believe himself to be a terrifying force, I thought it wise not to disabuse him of that notion.

"So they let you through the gates all right?" Gregor asked as the entire pack gathered to sit near the fire.

I knelt in front of my trunk and unclasped the leather straps holding it shut so that I could open it.

"They did," Sascha said with a nod, sinking into the chair closest to me. "But to be fair, we weren't the only ones entering this morning. Novoberg is a bustling city, as it turns out."

"We do a great deal of trade with the surrounding cities, and lie along a major trade route," I said, finishing with the clasps and opening my trunk. "Even though our faires are smaller than most." Of course, now I questioned exactly who our trading partners were, but since I was no longer in Novoberg, I ignored the questions that poked at me.

"No one so much as batted an eyelash as we walked right in," Sascha continued.

He was kept from going on with his story when I let out a cry of delight that was so sentimental it was mortifying. It didn't help that I could feel my cheeks go pink and was certain my eyes looked huge and glassy as I snatched up the item sitting on top of a haphazard pile of my clothing. It was a stuffed squirrel made out of a furry, russet material, with glass eyes and a soft, bushy tail. I'd thought the toy was gone forever, snatched from me by some of my brothers when I was ten and they were tormenting me. I used to carry Nutty around with me everywhere, sleep with him at night, and talk to him, telling him my sorrows. So, of course, my brothers had made it a point to take him from me. They'd threatened to burn him, dip him in manure, give him to the palace dogs, and tear him to shreds. I'd wept bitterly, begging them not to hurt him, then cried for days after I believed him gone.

"Where did you find this?" I asked Sascha in a hoarse voice, ashamed down to the tips of my toes that tears had formed in my eyes at the sight of a child's toy.

Sascha studied me with a soft look that was all heart. "One of the servants ran to give it to us as we were departing the castle. She said she'd kept it for years so that your brothers wouldn't destroy it, but the time had come to give it back."

"What was her name?" I asked, finding it almost impossible not to hug Nutty like I was still ten.

"Mina," Ivan said. "She was also the one who gave me the cookbook."

I twisted to gape at him. "Cookbook?"

Sure enough, he had removed a thick book from his coat when he took it off, and paged through it now, as he joined the group by the fire. "She marked your favorite recipes, told me I should prepare them for you," he chuckled.

"Your family might be a bunch of sodding pricks who think their shit smells better than anyone else's," Sven laughed, "but the servants in that palace think the world of you."

"I've never seen a group of people so relieved to find out a young man had been claimed by a wolf pack," Sascha laughed.

I pivoted back to him, stunned, and shook my head. "What happened?"

Sascha sighed and sank into his chair. "Like I said, no one so much as batted an eye when we marched through the gates with the intent of storming the palace."

"Which is a pity," Dmitri said, studying the blade of a knife I hadn't seen him take out of his coat before sitting down. "I would have liked to put this to good use."

I swallowed hard, remembering too well the last time

I'd held a knife, when Father had wanted me to kill my kitten.

"We only met resistance when we reached the palace itself and demanded to be let inside," Sascha said.

"I'm surprised you met resistance at all, if you were there asking about me," I said, setting Nutty on the floor and examining the rest of the contents of my trunk. It contained most of my clothing, as well as several books and random items—like brushes and a hand mirror—that someone might have thought were important to me. "I'm surprised they didn't toss you out of the city, once they heard you were there on my behalf."

I held the hand mirror up, surprised by the first look at myself I'd had since becoming part of the pack. There weren't any mirrors in Sascha's house that I'd discovered. I supposed the pack had no need for them. I was just vain enough to admit I liked checking my appearance now and then to make certain everything was in order. My hair needed washing and brushing—which I did by combing my fingers through it—but what shocked me was how red and swollen my lips were. It didn't take a scholar to figure out why, but even I could see how erotic my mouth looked in its current state. Also, I had several dark, red marks on my neck that I never would have seen without a mirror. I looked even more debauched than I'd thought.

I realized that Sascha and the others were watching me appraising my appearance when the silence in the room stretched a little too long. I quickly put the mirror down, cleared my throat self-consciously, and said, "I beg your pardon. Please go on."

Sascha grinned slowly, as if I'd done something deliberately sensual to tease him. He adjusted himself as he sat, cleared his throat, shook his head slightly, and continued the story.

"We were stopped at the door by some sort of pages or servants or something," he said.

"That spry, blond one would make a fine meal," Dmitri growled.

I knew exactly who Dmitri was talking about. Jesper had the same, regrettable problem that I had with appearing younger than his years. Jesper also had a sweetheart who worked in a bakery in town, a woman, so he wasn't exactly pup material. Though if what I'd been able to read between the lines was any indication, that wouldn't have stopped someone like Dmitri with kidnapping him and forcing him into the position.

"From there, an old man was fetched," Sascha went on. "Some sort of butler."

"Did he have a black moustache and silver hair?" I asked.

"He did." Sascha nodded.

"Then it was Heidelberg, my father's steward," I said, sifting through the pile of my clothes. I couldn't wait to put on real clothes again.

"Whatever his name was, he was surprisingly polite," Sascha went on with a grin. "He told us to wait in the front part of that first hall while he inquired whether Duke Royale was at home."

I glanced up and smiled at the way he imitated Heidelberg's affected accent.

"He wasn't, of course," Sascha went on. "Which was a lie."

"Father likely wasn't home *to visitors*. That doesn't mean he's not in residence at the palace. He's almost always home, unless he's attending to official business. Even then, he requires all business be brought to him."

"Which was exactly what we did," Dmitri said.

I glanced up from where I'd started to refold and sort my clothes into piles.

"That steward thought we would go quietly when we were denied entrance, but boy was he wrong," Sven laughed from behind me.

I looked to Sascha. "What did you do?"

Sascha shrugged. "We helped ourselves to a tour of the palace. That's quite a home you lived in, Peter." He grinned indulgently at me.

"It wasn't much of a home," I admitted, continuing with my sorting and choosing an outfit to put on right away.

"It didn't feel like one," Ivan agreed. "All cold marble and hoity-toity artwork."

"Ancestors staring down at you from their portraits miles above your head," Sven added.

"It was laughable how no one lifted a finger to stop us as we went in search of your things," Dmitri chuckled.

"They followed us, mind you. We gathered quite a crowd. That pillock, Frederic, nearly shit himself when I grabbed him by the shirt and chucked him out of my way."

A sudden wave of joy swept through me. "Frederic is my eldest brother," I explained. The mental image of Dmitri manhandling Frederic and frightening him was enough to leave me inclined to let him do whatever he wanted to me later as thanks.

"We eventually met the rest of your brothers, and your father as well," Sascha said with a vicious smirk. "No wonder they spent so much time bullying you. Not one of them has the balls to stand up to anyone stronger than a delicate pup. No offense, Peter."

"None taken," I said, grinning myself. "You're right."

"You should have seen the way your brothers were ready to throw each other under the wagon when your father found out you were with us and not in your rooms at the palace," Dmitri went on.

My grin dropped, and my heart with it, even though I felt like a fool for being disappointed. "My father didn't realize I was missing?" I asked.

"Sorry, Peter. He didn't," Sascha said. "No one had told him your brothers locked you out of the city."

"Not until that moment," Dmitri said. He laughed, and went on with, "You should have seen them scramble to blame each other. They were like babies accusing the others of taking a pie from the kitchen window."

"So, my father was angry with them for what they did to me?" I felt pathetic for hanging onto that hope.

Sascha must have seen how wounded I was. "He was upset that they had behaved so immaturely," he said, gesturing for me to come closer to him. "Your absence was more of an afterthought to him."

I got up and moved to him as he'd asked. Once I was close, he caught me around the waist and drew me to sit on his lap, like a child. I had mixed feelings about the gesture. I liked being close to Sascha, but I was increasingly uncomfortable with being infantilized by him. I was a man, and I wanted him to want me as a man, not a pup.

"So what did you do next?" I asked, hoping the continuation of the story would prove that at least someone in my family was sad to see me gone.

Judging by the way Sascha grimaced slightly, I knew that wasn't going to happen. "First, your father asked who we were and why we were there."

"And we told him," Dmitri chuckled. A lump formed in my gut as he went on with, "We told him I'd found you wandering in the forest and brought you back to our pack and that you belonged to us now."

"What did they say to that?" I asked, dreading the answer.

Sascha's hesitance before answering proved I was right to dread. "Your brothers laughed at first, saying they couldn't have asked for a more perfect outcome and that you were probably in heaven being fucked senseless by a bunch of brutal forest-dwellers."

They weren't wrong, but at the moment I didn't appreciate their derision.

"That's when your father realized what they'd done and flew off the handle," Dmitri said.

"Your brothers argued that you deserved it, but as I said, your father was more concerned about their bad behavior than your capture," Sascha said. "Like Dmitri said, each tried to blame the other. I think the argument would have gone on even longer, if I hadn't stopped it to demand your clothes and possessions be handed over to us."

"Do I want to know how my father reacted to that?" I asked in a quiet, hurt voice.

Sascha showed his sympathy by slipping a hand between the folds of my robe and laying it on my bare thigh. It hadn't been more than half an hour since Gregor had sucked me off, so I wasn't as fast to react as I might have been. In fact, my heart was so gloomy that I barely reacted at all.

"He told us to take what we wanted and to get out," Dmitri said before Sascha could. "And a right prick about it he was too."

"I was astounded at how little someone could care for their own son," Sven growled.

"Especially a son as wonderful as our pup," Ivan added.

"We showed them in the end, though," Sven went on.

I twisted to stare at Sven and Ivan. "You *showed* them?"

Sascha's hand tensed on my thigh. I pivoted back to him, wary of the guilty look in his eyes. "Your father ordered servants to take us to your room and to help pack your things," he said. "That's when the maid brought us that stuffed toy, and the cookbook."

"And once we'd packed up your belongings and left the palace, we went straight to the city square and announced just who we were and how we'd come to find you," Dmitri said with a triumphant snarl. "We stood up there on the edge of that fountain for a good fifteen minutes, shouting to everyone in that city that your father is a heartless bastard who let his own son be turned over to the wolves, and how vile your brothers were for the way they've treated you all these years."

My heart sank, and my shoulders sagged. "You didn't," I sighed, wanting to squeeze my eyes shut and hide my face in embarrassment.

"We did," Sascha admitted sheepishly.

I frowned at him. "I'll be a laughing stock. I can never go back there again. People will laugh at me—Peter Royale, son of the duke, turned into a sexual plaything for wolves—for the rest of my life."

"I know," Sascha said, wincing. "I'll make it up to you."

I'm sure he would, and I was certain I'd enjoy it. But at the moment, all I felt was humiliation.

Until I noticed that Ivan, Sven, and Gregor were watching me with varying degrees of discomfort and shame in their eyes too. I'd effectively just called them out for what they'd done to me as well, even if I had been a willing participant. From the looks of things, they hadn't fully digested the implications of my position as pup as juxtaposed to the glimpse they'd had of my former life and position, and now that they had, their consciences were pricking them. Seeing what sort of a life I'd been destined for, a life that was now dead to me, might have added to their sense of guilt.

Not so for Dmitri, though. He still wore a smirk, as though the entire thing were amusing, and not a little bit arousing. He shifted as he sat, giving the bulge in his breeches more space to grow.

"We may have caused more trouble for your father than for you," he said at last, studying me with a wolfish look. "Those guards who arrived to shut us up stayed to listen to what we had to say."

I glanced to Sascha. He nodded. "A lot of people listened to what we had to say."

"I wouldn't want to be your father this evening," Ivan added. "That entire city felt like a pile of kindling just waiting for a match."

"And you were that match, Peter," Sven finished the thought. "At least, your absence was."

"It's a good thing the faire in a fortnight is in the opposite direction, in Berlova," Sascha said.

There was something final about the way he spoke, as if that would be the last I heard of what had happened in my home city that day. I doubted I'd hear anything more about Novoberg or my family for a very long time, perhaps ever. That didn't stop me from loathing the fact that my brothers had probably made a joke out of me. The indignity of it stung.

"Where should I store my things?" I asked Sascha as the others got up to go about finding supper. Without Ivan there preparing something all afternoon, it would be a simple feast instead of something my father's kitchen staff would have laid out for a state banquet, as Ivan had served the night before.

Sascha grinned, rubbing my back for a moment, then brushing the backs of his fingers across my cheek. "In my room, of course," he said.

I smiled at his touch, certain I was blushing too. It still felt wonderful to be touched like that, but annoyance at his and Dmitri's lack of discretion with my family and Novoberg crushed any full enjoyment I might have felt.

"Is there a place for it all there?" I asked, squirming on Sascha's lap. I wanted to get up, but perhaps not quite yet.

"Peter, for you, there will always be a place," Sascha said with a smile.

I didn't think he would with the other four in the room, watching us out of the corners of their eyes, but Sascha held his hand firmly at the back of my head and leaned in to close his mouth over mine in a searing kiss. It was deep and probing, possessive, and a bit apologetic. He sucked my tongue into his mouth and bit it gently. At the same time, the hand he'd slipped into my robe earlier traveled up my thigh to close around my balls. I breathed in shakily, my annoyance chased away by lust, and relaxed.

Only when Sascha ended the kiss and gestured for me to stand did it occur to me that he'd done all of that deliberately to distract me. I felt like I'd lost a small battle of wills, but the means of my defeat had been so sweet—not to mention clever—that I didn't mind losing. I stood when Sascha did and returned to my trunk to gather an armful of clothes.

"You don't have to do that," Sascha said. "Dmitri, Sven, you can carry Peter's things into my room."

Once again, I was to have everything done for me, even if I could have done it myself. I drew the line at handing back the armful of clothes I already had, though. I could carry that much into Sascha's room. Once there, I made the case that I should put my things away in the place he cleared out for me, since I knew the proper care of my own clothes. It was heaven to be able to put on a clean shirt, a normal pair of trousers, and a sweater again.

It would have turned into a smoothly domestic scene, if not for the way Dmitri continued to watch me as the work was done. I started counting the minutes until he took me aside to have his way with me—which meant I was also counting the minutes until the next confrontation between Dmitri and Sascha happened.

That confrontation didn't come until supper was finished.

"After that decidedly mediocre meal," Dmitri said, tossing down his napkin and standing, "it's time for me to have some well-deserved dessert." He fixed his eyes on me as he stepped away from his chair and skirted the table. "Come along, pup." He gestured for me to get up.

I peeked at Sascha, wondering how he would react.

"You don't have to ask his permission to go with the man who found you in the first place," Dmitri snapped, gesturing again for me to hurry along.

I stood slowly, nerves bristling, anxious to see if Sascha would stop me. He was the leader, and as such, he should have stopped what he didn't want to see happen. I didn't want to look too eager as I inched away from my chair, biting my lip and sending Dmitri a worried look. As I'd discussed with Gregor that afternoon, I was content to let Dmitri have his fill of me until he grew bored and looked for amusement elsewhere. I was even excited by the prospect.

Sascha, who sat rigidly in his chair, fist clenched around his fork as he stared at his supper plate. I couldn't tell if he was merely stewing because he was unable to stop Dmitri from having what he wanted or if he was attempting to think of an excuse to deny him. Either way, he didn't turn his head to look at me. I didn't know what to make of that either. He could have been angry that I would jump to do as Dmitri asked—although I would have called it moving gingerly rather than jumping—or if he felt guilty for being unable to negate Dmitri's claim on me.

Within a few seconds, the moment of greatest tension

had passed, and I walked away from the table, following Dmitri when he continued down the hall to his bedroom.

"I've been looking forward to this all day," Dmitri growled as soon as he'd snatched my hand and drawn me into his room. He shut the door behind us, then backed me against it. "I've been driven to distraction imagining all the ways I might have you."

I was only human. His aggressive sexuality was exciting—in the same way that thrusting one's hand into a mystery box that could have been filled with cotton balls or worms or poisoned shards of glass was exciting. He towered over me, resting one hand on the door above me and scooping the other under my chin to force me to look up at him.

"Now that I've seen where you lived and what kind of a life that was, I'm inclined to show you what life is like for those who haven't been raised with a silver spoon to feed them," he murmured against my ear, then sucked on my earlobe. "I'm tempted to show you how rough life can be, since all you've known is softness and comfort."

He was most definitely going to fuck me hard. I couldn't help but shudder in expectation, hungry for every sort of experience, since all of it was new.

"If you want your pretty, soft cloths to remain intact, little pup, I suggest you remove them before I'm able to get my clothes off," he growled, pushing back.

He wasn't joking, and his vest, shirt, and breeches would be far simple to remove than my finely tailored things. I rushed to do as he'd suggested, tugging my sweater off over my head and tossing it over a chair standing nearby. Dmitri probably mistook the speed with which I unbuttoned my shirt and pulled it out of my breeches as eagerness to be with him. Part of it was. I was still so fascinated with all things sexual that part of me ached for whatever would come next.

I wasn't fast enough, though. Dmitri shed all of his clothes and left them on the floor where they'd dropped before I could discard my shirt or do more than unfasten my breeches. He closed in on me, ripping my shirt the rest of the way off my arms, then attacking my trousers. I was only lucky that trousers were so much more difficult to rip to shreds than a shirt would be. The worst he was able to do was jerk them down my thighs. And without hair on my legs, they came off relatively easily.

Dmitri made a sound of surprise when he saw I was now hairless. "Whose idea was this?" he said, running his hands over my chest and thighs before centering in on my groin.

"Ivan and Sven," I gasped. It didn't matter who he was or how aggressive his hands were, his touch was enlivening. My cock went hard right away.

"I like it," Dmitri said, studying my nude groin ravenously. "The first boy I ever had was about your age," he growled, fondling my balls. He met my eyes with a look that challenged me to be shocked or offended. Which only proved that he, too, had forgotten how old I actually was. He chuckled and went on with, "I wasn't much older myself, though. We were mates at school, playing silly schoolboy games. He liked it when I pinned him down and stroked him off. He started out trying to fight me off, but he submitted in the end. They all submit in the end."

I kept my expression neutral. My earlier thoughts about Dmitri wanting to frighten me seemed confirmed, as did my theory that if I was supremely submissive, he would lose interest. As his story seemed to demonstrate, he wanted his prey to struggle first before giving in. Dmitri would get no struggle from me.

"I will submit to you," I said, taking extra care to make certain my voice was as soft and young as I could make it.

"Yes, you will," he insisted, as if I'd sworn I would fight.

To prove his point, he pushed on my shoulders until my knees buckled. I landed as softly as I could, which still bruised my knees as they hit the floor.

"You'll put my cock in your mouth, and you'll like it," he sneered.

I answered with a short nod, glancing up at him with as innocent an expression as I could muster for good measure. I even opened my mouth wide, inviting him in. Dmitri was either playing games to amuse himself or had a short memory indeed. I'd already sucked him off more than once, but he seemed to want to pretend that he was forcing me to do something I was against.

He chuckled as if he were the one in charge and grabbed a fistful of my hair, then inched forward, holding himself so that he could guide his prick between my lips. "That's a good pup," he sighed as he pushed deep.

So much for Gregor's careful lessons about how to tease and entice. Dmitri wasn't looking for an erotic interlude. At least, not in that way. He wanted to express his dominance, and it didn't take much to figure out why.

"I bet you don't swallow Sascha like this," he growled, working in and out of my mouth, going deeper with each thrust. "I bet he thinks you're too sweet, too precious to like your mouth fucked."

Another of Gregor's lessons popped to mind, and I had a hard time not smirking at its relevance. I wouldn't have to do any work at all for Dmitri. All I had to do was practice the relaxation and breathing techniques Gregor showed me to keep from choking as Dmitri jerked in and out. It was oddly arousing to test myself and to see how much I could endure without breaking. I even managed to make sounds of enjoyment and grip Dmitri's broad thighs tightly as his pace turned downright brutal.

And as an added touch, I managed to glance up at him, eyes streaming with involuntary tears, playing on his need to feel like he was punishing me. I schooled my face into a mask of fear, even as I continued to make muffled, mewling sounds of pleasure as his thick cock slid between my lips.

My acting did exactly what it was intended to do. Dmitri let out a sudden cry and shot his cum to the back of my throat, presumably before he'd intended to. "Fuck,

PETER AND THE WOLVES

pup. You're too much," he panted, staggering back once he was empty. "That face."

I didn't have to guess what he meant by that. As he shifted to the side, staggering toward his bed, I noticed a tall, broad mirror standing to one side of the bed. I hadn't even noticed it when we'd first come in. I'd never so much as peeked into Dmitri's room before. But now, not only did I see the mirror, I saw my reflection as I climbed to my feet. I was a curious and erotic sight with no body hair. I assumed it made me look boyish, but my enormous erection, standing straight up against my belly told a different story. My pale skin was flushed pink, and my cheeks were downright scarlet. And my mouth and the area around it was red and swollen, even more than the glimpse I'd caught of myself in my hand mirror. Looking as I did now, I would have made even the most stalwart straight man want to fuck me raw.

"Don't just stand there admiring yourself, pup," Dmitri panted as he collapsed onto the bed. "Come here and let me play with you until I'm ready to fuck that sweet ass of yours into next Sunday."

I did as he'd ordered immediately, lying on the bed with him. He wasn't joking when he said he wanted to play with me. Dmitri's version of playing with me turned out to be holding my legs as far apart as he could and teasing me until I was a hair's breadth from coming. He fingered my ass, massaged my balls, and stroked my cock until it wept, then backed off and watched me sweat. I wouldn't have moved one way or another, but he took great enjoyment in pinning my hands at my sides and keeping me from closing my legs so that I was helpless.

As soon as my breathing began to slow and the urgency subsided, he repeated the entire process, taking me right up to the edge. It was wildly pleasurable, but maddening at the same time. And it went on and on. By the time he was hard again, I was so desperate for release that my whole body ached and my sighs of pleasure had turned into tearful sobs.

"I could blow on you right now and you'd come in my face," he laughed, enjoying having me at his mercy. He wasn't wrong. "I've got other things in mind for you, though, pup. Get up."

I was incredulous, and I was so hard that shuffling off the side of Dmitri's bed and standing was nearly impossible. He rolled off on the other side, retrieving a jar from the stand beside his bed as I stood there panting in anticipation. Curiously, he adjusted the mirror beside his bed before walking around to my side. Immediately, I saw why. He wanted to watch himself fucking me.

"You'll like it," he murmured in my ear, then shoved me so that I doubled forward. "You'll like watching yourself get fucked."

He kicked my legs wider, jerked my hips up, and adjusted my arms the way he wanted them, then uncorked the jar and poured something cool and viscous over my crack. He slathered a generous amount over his huge cock before setting the jar aside, then came back to study his handiwork. I let out a groan as he thrust a finger into my ass, then two, testing and stretching me. At least he had the courtesy to do that much before—

I'd thought too soon. He positioned himself behind me and thrust his cock into my ass so fast and hard that I cried out with the burst of pain. He answered my cry with a long, gratified one, biting his lip as he tested me with a few more hard, slow, and deep thrusts. I forced myself to breathe and accept him. I knew it would start to feel good if I could just do that. I was already so aroused from his earlier teasing that I had something erotic to focus on.

"See, pup," Dmitri gasped as he changed the rhythm of his thrusts to be short and insistent. He grabbed a handful of my hair and forced my head up so that I was watching us in the mirror. "This is what you look like when you're being fucked."

I wasn't prepared for how erotic the sight was. Dmitri was merciless in his movements, punishing my ass and clearly enjoying every moment of it. But the way I was bent over, I could also see my own thick cock, swinging in rhythm to his thrusts, feeling as though it would burst at any second. God help me, I loved it.

The other advantage of seeing what I looked like was that I could perfect my submissive expression, working with how the sensation of Dmitri's body slamming into mine made me feel to come up with the perfect look of defeated acceptance. I knew it was working because of the pure erotic enjoyment in Dmitri's eyes as they met mine in the mirror.

The moment I realized I had more control than he did, everything my body felt became magnified. I liked it. I wanted it. Even the faint pain. And watching it happen in the mirror only heightened the madness. It felt so good that the edges of my vision began to blur. I lost all inhibitions and made sounds that would probably embarrass me when I thought about them later. And I came so hard I felt as though I might turn inside out.

"Fuck, fuck, fuck," Dmitri hissed with increasing intensity, until he, too, cried out as he came deep inside of me. He emptied everything with a groan, then pulled back, his back hitting the wall a few feet behind where I was still bent over.

My knees were on the verge of giving out, but instinct told me to stay in the position I was in until he bade me move. I felt his cum trickling down my thigh and figured he would want to look at me that way for a moment. Indeed, when I peeked in the mirror, that's exactly what he was watching.

"I wish Sascha could see this," he chuckled as he pushed himself straight. "I want him to see how eager you are for me, to hear how you begged for it with your moans, and to know how hard you came with my cock up your ass. Maybe then he'll drop his arrogant notions of being better and more magnanimous than everyone else. As if he's the only one who knows who is right for who around here."

I was certain his words were significant and that I'd be occupied for hours contemplating what they could mean, but at the moment I was too hazy from being toyed with and fucked to be able to think about much of anything. Dmitri moved forward, grabbing my sides and wrenching me to stand.

"You soiled my sheets," he said with a frown. "I'll have to put a towel down." He pushed me to the side again as he walked past me to a chest at the foot of his bed. Almost as an afterthought, he glanced over his shoulder at me. "Get out of here. I'm done with you, and I want to sleep."

Still trying to catch my breath, I quickly gathered my clothes, then headed to the door. Maybe Dmitri would get tired of me quickly. Maybe I didn't want him to after all. But maybe his interest was not so much in me but in making Sascha pay for past wrongs.

10

I didn't bother putting my clothes back on. I gathered them to my chest and crept out to the hall. Dmitri flopped into bed with an exhausted sigh, and that was the end of that. I shut his door quietly behind me, then tiptoed down the hall to Sascha's door. The house was silent. I'd been with Dmitri longer than I'd thought, or else everyone had decided to go to bed early. The house was mostly dark.

Sascha was in bed when I entered his room, but clearly not asleep. He'd been lying on his back with his arms behind his head, staring at the ceiling with a clenched jaw, but as soon as I opened his door, he shot bolt-upright. His eyes widened, then narrowed as I slipped into the room and shut the door behind me.

"Are you all right?" he asked, deep concern in his voice.

It was an odd question, under the circumstances. He must have known full well that Dmitri had spent the last hour or so fucking me. And I was walking on my own power, and I wasn't exactly covered in cuts and bruises.

"I'm fine," I said, choosing the most neutral answer possible. I hoped my face didn't betray any emotion.

Sascha let out a breath and held one arm out to me. "Come to bed, then."

I sensed he wasn't asking me to come to bed so that he could fuck me, but all the same, I said, "Give me a moment in the washroom first."

For half a second, he looked embarrassed, as if he realized of course I'd want to clean up after Dmitri. Then he let out a breath and nodded, lying back with his hands behind his head again.

I dropped my bundle of clothes on the chair near the fireplace, then skittered into the washroom. Once I'd relieved myself and washed in the ingeniously-designed sink, I took a moment to clean my teeth and brush my hair. I wished I'd thought to bring my hand mirror with me so I could use it to get a good idea of how red my ass was after the way Dmitri had used me. I wished my heart didn't pump with quite as much excitement over how the whole thing had felt either. I didn't have any particular feelings for Dmitri. I wasn't certain I even liked him. But, as I'd discovered in the last few days, I liked sex, and with Dmitri, it was good.

All the same, I was infinitely glad he'd tossed me out

of his room when we were done and that Sascha was the man in the bed I crawled into once I came out of the bathroom.

"You would tell me if he hurt you," Sascha said, gathering me into his arms as soon as I hit the mattress.

I found it sweet and comforting. I hadn't realized I even needed comforting after Dmitri until I was nestled in the protective warmth of Sascha's body. He was naked, of course, and half hard, but there was nothing aggressive or needy in the way he settled with me. We were just lying together, which was better than the lust-filled rush of what I'd done with Dmitri. I had the best of both worlds.

"I promise you, I will tell you if Dmitri ever hurts me," I said earnestly, looking into Sascha's eyes as I did. Or rather, if I minded being hurt.

Sascha let out a breath of relief, pulling me tighter against him so that he could kiss me. It felt wonderful. I relaxed against him, sliding an arm over his broad side and letting him catch one of my legs between his so that our genitals nestled against each other's thighs—not demanding satisfaction, just connected. Sascha cupped my ass gently, but seemed more focused on exploring my mouth with his.

Until he sighed and inched back. "If he didn't hurt you, that means he *didn't hurt you*," he said in a flat, disappointed voice.

I suddenly felt like I held all responsibility for

Sascha's happiness in my hand. "Would you rather I feel pain instead of pleasure when I'm with Dmitri?" I asked bluntly.

His expression soured. "No."

I could feel plainly that he wanted to go on to say that he'd rather I was never with Dmitri at all. It was curious to me that he stopped himself from saying it. It was interesting that he hadn't forbidden Dmitri from fucking me in the first place. As leader, I was certain he could.

I looked for an answer to some of my questions by the most circuitous route possible by asking, "What is it like for pups in other packs? And does a pack only ever have one pup at a time, or can there be more than one?"

I hoped the onslaught of questions would distract him, and they did. Sascha frowned in thought before saying, "I've only ever heard of a pack having one pup at a time. They're so rare to begin with."

"Because hapless young men don't go wandering alone in the forest where they can be scooped up at random every day," I said with a teasing tone.

"No," Sascha laughed, then delayed the rest of his answer by kissing me again. I could effectively distract him with questions, but he knew how to spin my head with kisses.

Eventually, he went on with, "I don't know why effeminate young men ended up being seen as such a prize among wolf packs." He shifted to prop himself on one elbow, stroking my side with one hand and contemplating. "How does anything end up with more value than anything else in this world? Who was the first person who saw a shiny golden rock in the ground and decided it was more precious than an ordinary grey one? Or who came up with the notion that marble floors were better than wooden ones?"

I'd never thought about it like that before. "It's like the way my brothers somehow decided that green olives are better than black olives."

"They think that?" Sascha laughed.

"They're insane about it," I told him. "It's ridiculous. Olives are olives, but with that lot, you'd think green olives were sent down from the heavens on a golden plate and blessed with powers of virility."

"So I guess it's the same with fey young men being so highly prized in the forest." He shrugged. "It could have easily been tall, burly men winning that coveted status."

"There's nothing wrong with tall, muscular men," I said, my voice betraying just what I prized above all when it came to the male form. I spread my hand across Sascha's enormous pectoral muscle, feeling his nipple harden under my palm.

"Careful, Peter," he said in a warning voice. "I'd planned not to fuck you tonight, since you need a rest, but if you keep that up, you'll make it impossible for me to resist."

I laughed, sounding as young as I currently looked. I could see by the look in his eyes that wasn't helping his resolve. "So young men of my type have been arbitrarily assigned a high value in the forest and are considered the most desirable," I said, prompting him to go on.

"Exactly," Sascha said. "Though I will admit that, for me, it's a deep, personal preference as much as it is a societal ideal."

I arched an eyebrow and grinned smugly. It felt good knowing that I was exactly what Sascha fancied.

"But, yes, you're a rare type in the rough existence that is forest life. It takes a lot of grit to survive and thrive out here, though perhaps not as much as it did a few generations ago, before any sort of society or structure was created. We don't exactly live a hand-to-mouth existence here."

"No," I chuckled. "This house is quite comfortable."

"It wasn't always like this, though." Sascha's expression took on a faraway look again. "Two or three generations ago, the frontier was a wilderness. Survival wasn't a guarantee. It wasn't even the norm. Which is why packs formed."

"Safety in numbers," I said. Which was exactly how I felt about the pack I was now in.

Sascha nodded. "Men are sexual creatures. The reason most of us were cast out of society was because we want sex with other men. Which is not hard to come by. So I suppose the whole practice of having a pup in any given pack wasn't so much about sex as it was about having a shared, valuable commodity."

"Sascha." I fixed him with a flat stare. "It's about sex. And if you don't think so, then ask my ass."

He laughed. The sound was rich and the vibrations of his body against mine were almost enough to start me back down the path to arousal.

"All right." He stole another kiss. "It's about sex. But it's also about commodities. A pack shares all its resources. Everything from food to shelter to—"

"A sweet young ass," I finished his list for him.

He laughed, even though I'd been dead serious. "Satisfied men are even-tempered men," he said. "More wars are caused by restless, frustrated energy than by border disputes or money."

I wasn't so sure about that, but I let him go on.

"I've seen it with my own eyes." He must have also seen my doubt at his statement, because he argued the point. "I've been in packs where resources were harder to come by and tensions were high, but as long as every man could find that release when he needed it, things remained peaceful."

I still didn't entirely believe it. "So why doesn't everyone just pair off, like Ivan and Sven or Mikal and Jakob?"

"I've often wondered that myself." The way Sascha looked at me as he spoke seemed to imply that he would be perfectly happy pairing off with me in some way. I don't think I would have minded either, though it was too early to tell. "Not everyone has the same desires, though," he sighed as he went on. "Some men like possessions, trophies. They define their superiority by how many things they can collect that other men can't have. Their need for power outstrips their need for love or companionship."

I sensed we were getting closer to the heart of Sascha's beliefs, but also to answers to some questions that continued to linger with me.

"You asked what it's like for pups in other packs," he said, reaching for my hand and threading his fingers through mine. "It's not like this. In fact, I've heard of some situations that sound like the way your brothers treated you, only with sex as the endgame of the teasing instead of being dunked or locked out of a city."

I shuddered at the thought. It was what I had expected, but I was still horrified and disappointed. And grateful I'd been found by Dmitri—even with his problems—than someone from that kind of pack.

"They're not all like that," Sascha reassured me. "I've known packs with pups that are perfectly content with their role. And they all grow up eventually and lose that pup status."

I blinked. "So, if I'm around long enough, I'll be just a regular member of the pack instead of a pup?"

"Of course, you will," Sascha laughed, kissing me again and brushing a hand across my smooth chest. "But not anytime soon."

I stopped short of reminding him I was twenty, and that Ivan and Sven were responsible for my lack of hair, not age. Instinct told me to hold onto that truth, that I might be able to use it to my advantage someday.

Instead, I said, "So, as long as my official status within the pack is that of pup, you're required to share me with the others."

Sascha stiffened. He let out a tight breath before saying, "That is the precedent."

"But if you chose to change that precedent?" I remembered the contradiction in the rules that Gregor had mentioned that afternoon.

Sascha's brow furrowed. "There are other complications. Things you don't need to worry about. The situation with Dmitri is...tenuous. A few things happened last year that make him a liability as much as an asset. He's like holding a wolf by the ears—it would be just as dangerous to let him go as it is to hold onto him."

My curiosity was beyond piqued, but I couldn't ask any further questions without giving away how much I knew. And with the position I was in, knowledge was the only power I had.

"How big are packs usually?" I asked instead, seeking out more knowledge. "I only ask because I've noticed there are more bedrooms in this house and more chairs around the dining room table than there are men to fill them."

Sascha relaxed and let out a breath, letting go of my hand so that he could draw his down my side to cradle my ass again. "It varies wildly," he said. "Everything from lone wolves to pairs striking out together to small villages with dozens of men or more."

I shuddered to think what life would be like for a man in my position in one of those packs.

"If you ask me," Sascha went on, "it's only a matter of time before some of those packs drop the name and simply start calling themselves villages and towns. I know of a few that have accepted women and children that have either been cast out of their cities, bought as slaves at a faire, or fled their abusers in cities."

The mention of slaves sent a wave of dread through me, as did the idea that women would need to run from their abusers. But it also occurred to me that a wolf pack would be the safest possible place for them.

"Those villages would be outlawed, of course," Sascha went on. "We couldn't have anyone competing for resources and prestige with the likes of your father, now, could we."

"Certainly not," I answered in a mock grave voice. My study of the law included an entire list of things that made someone an outlaw.

"But the day will come," he said with a sense of finality. "If I can enlist the help of a handful of men to construct a house this well-equipped in the middle of the forest, and then keep it running with even fewer men, and if we can all produce enough goods to sell at faires, allowing us to live in comfort and peace, others can do it too. And if we all connect into functioning networks, well," he shrugged, squeezing my ass gently, "I believe that's what they call a society."

I let out a breath, contemplating the idea. How wonderful would it be to create a society where everyone was accepted and no one was ostracized, cast out, or even killed for being who they were? And where other unfortunate souls could find safety and protection from the darkness.

"So are there women living in the forest too? Women who desire other women, or just those who fled their old lives?" I asked.

"Of course," Sascha said. "I know several. There are a few nearby too. Katrina and her sisters. I helped build their house, and they'll probably be here before too long to help Sven with the planting."

"Really?" My brow flew up. "I'll get to meet them?"

"Are you so eager to meet people?" Sascha asked with a wry grin. "Don't I get to keep you all to myself?"

I laughed, though I sensed a thread of seriousness in his joke. That and his cock had steadily been growing harder against my thigh as we moved together while talking. "There is so much of the world that I'm only now discovering," I said. "It makes me insatiable for more."

"Insatiable, you say?" Sascha growled, rolling me to my back.

It felt good to be trapped under him. Good enough that my cock was well on its way to making an effort to rise to the occasion, in spite of my thorough exhaustion. It would never not feel good to be the object of Sascha's desire.

"Weren't you going to let me rest tonight?" I asked, teasing him with a coy look.

"I was," he hummed. "But my prick has other ideas." He ground his erection against my hip.

I pretended to be far too refined and well-mannered for such things. "I suppose if your prick has other ideas...." I sighed dramatically, glancing wickedly up at him.

A rumbling laugh rolled through Sascha as he continued to grind against my hip. "I told you that you are everything I desire in a man, didn't I?"

"You did." I wriggled under him, lifting my legs over his massive thighs and digging my fingertips into his back.

"And that just the sight of you drives me wild beyond my ability to restrain myself." He thrust harder and with purpose.

"Not in those words, but I understood your meaning," I gasped.

"And that, in spite of rules and precedent, you are mine?" He grew more serious as his body rippled with tension.

"Yes," I sighed.

That was all Sascha needed. He muscled himself to his knees and fisted himself furiously until cum erupted from his thick cock spilling over my stomach. He let out a satisfied sigh and drank in the sight of me, messy with that sign of his possession. I loved it too, loved being marked as his. The feeling that I was a possession that belonged to Sascha was as erotic as watching myself being fucked by Dmitri in his mirror. Both presented their own kinds of guilt. It was one thing to get off on being used hard, but feeling so utterly pleased and downright giddy to consider myself to be another man's possession was a blow to my self-respect that I wasn't ready to think about.

11

The ten days were more than enough to establish how things would be in my new life. I slept in Sascha's bed. Every night ended with kisses and passion, and every morning began with the same. But Dmitri claimed several afternoons a week or an occasional evening. I learned to be extraordinarily discreet about what I did with both men, hiding from each other what I felt about their attentions. The fact of the matter was that I adored the passion I experienced with Sascha. It went deep into my heart, urging me to fall head over heels in love with him, at least on a superficial level. But in spite of that, pure, raw sex with Dmitri excited me in ways that were deeply gratifying. Dmitri touched on a dark side of me I hadn't known I possessed, and I always wanted more.

Perhaps unsurprisingly, neither Gregor, Ivan, nor Sven bothered to make any sort of advance on me after those first two days. They must have understood as well as I did that, as the analogy I'd come up with before suggested, I was Sascha's and Dmitri's bone to fight over.

Except when it came to keeping my body smooth and hairless.

"You look uncomfortable, pup," Ivan observed as he worked in the kitchen, mincing huge bowls of dried fruit for the pastries he would stay up all night making in a few days, right before the village faire in Berlova.

I sat on a stool near the end of Gregor's apothecary counter, repairing a pair of Sven's breeches that had split months before. Sewing was one of the things Sascha not only didn't forbid me from doing, my skills with a needle proved highly useful. Father would have been mortified.

I squirmed on the bench, sending a sheepish look to Ivan. "I'm itchy," I admitted.

"Itchy?" Ivan blinked.

My face heated. "I did not realize that hair itches like the Devil as it grows back in."

Ivan laughed out loud. "The best way to prevent that is to shave it all off again."

"Please tell me you're talking about shaving Peter clean again," Sascha laughed as well as he walked through the main room. He, too, was busy preparing for next week's faire and had only come in from his workshop to fetch a whetstone to sharpen his woodworking tools.

"That's exactly what I was suggesting," Ivan said. He

paused in his chopping and glanced over his shoulder at Sascha. "You wouldn't mind me doing the job again?"

Sascha shrugged as he headed on toward the back hall. "No. I trust you."

Those words sent an odd combination of humiliation and pride through me. Sascha trusted Ivan enough not to mishandle his prized possession, so I could trust Ivan too. All the same, I said, "I could do it myself." And really, I would have preferred it.

Sascha paused halfway through the room and sent me a flat stare. "I won't risk you cutting yourself somewhere important," he said. "Or at all. Gregor might be a magician with his herbs and concoctions, but if you had a cut become infected and poison your blood...." He blanched slightly instead of finishing. "Ivan is an expert with a knife or razor. He'll do it."

"Whatever you wish," I said, pretending to be agreeable when I actually regretted my imposed helplessness. More than regretted it, I was beginning to chafe under it.

"I'll make it up to you later," Sascha said with a wicked grin before continuing on and outside.

His promise thrilled me, but also hinted that he knew I resented his rules for me, in spite of how I pretended I didn't. He was swiftly getting to know me more than I necessarily wanted him too. Although the trade-off to that was that I had come to know him much better in the past ten days as well. I'd learned that he was naturally inclined to be quieter and more thoughtful than the others—except perhaps Gregor—and that he enjoyed coming up with new, clever designs for the furniture he constructed. I also learned that his creations were prized at faires as unique pieces of art rather than being serviceable chairs or tables, and that they fetched extraordinary prices. Which was another explanation for how affluent such a small pack was.

"All right," Ivan said, finishing with the pile of dates he was chopping and washing his hands under the spigot in the sink. "Get those pretty clothes of yours off and spread out on the sofa. I'll fetch the shaving soap and razors."

I sighed as I slid off the stool, setting my mending aside. Admittedly, the noise I made and the sullen look I sent at Ivan's back as he walked down the long hall to his and Sven's room was as adolescent as I looked without hair. At the rate I was going, I would regress to being twelve instead of just looking like it.

I carefully unbuttoned my fine jacket and folded it neatly over the back of one of the chairs after removing it. At least I had been able to wear real clothes since mine were retrieved. I'd always loved clothes, and now that I'd been made to go for two days without them, I appreciated them even more. Everything I owned—from the navy-blue jacket I'd just taken off to the red trousers and embroidered waistcoat I removed after—were bright and colorful. Dmitri had dismissively called me a porcelain doll the first time I'd stepped out of Sascha's room in the morning wearing pink and green. Sascha had told me I was beautiful and kissed and pet me in a way that made me want to throw off every piece of clothing I'd just put on. I was bound and determined to wear every stitch of clothing that I loved so much, though.

By the time Ivan returned to the main room with his shaving things, I had my clothes lovingly folded over the back of the chair and had flopped onto the sofa and spread my arms and legs.

"All right," I sighed. "Do your worst."

Ivan laughed as he deposited the soap and razor on the small table by the sofa, then went to fetch a bowl of warm water. "Don't you like having a smooth, touchable body?"

"I like the touchable part," I confessed. I held my tongue over the complaint that it was infantilizing.

Ivan continued to chuckle as he rejoined me at the sofa and went to work lathering up the soap. "Well, Sascha and Dmitri like it, at any rate."

"And that's all that matters," I grumbled.

Ivan smirked and scrubbed shaving suds across my groin and thighs. "What, no immediate erection for me anymore?" he teased me when I didn't instantly go hard.

I grinned and shook my head. "Give it a minute. I've gotten slower in the last week, since the novelty of being a sexual object has worn off."

"Don't tell me it's worn off so quickly," Ivan said with mock hurt.

I laughed. "Oh, it hasn't, when the mood is right. I'm as eager for it as ever." As both Sascha and Dmitri were constantly reminding me—Sascha as a tender compliment, Dmitri as a needling taunt.

"Well, you can react to me or not as you see fit," Ivan said, setting aside the brush and going to work with his razor. "I'm plenty satisfied with Sven. You're the one exhausting yourself by juggling two intensely proud men."

"The fate of all pups, I assume," I said, making light of the way he so casually touched on what was now the single most important and dangerous balancing act of my life.

"Probably," Ivan sighed, eyes focused on his work.

The scrape of his razor and the care he took with my body did eventually cause my cock to stir, but after more than a week of frequent use, it was as banal a process as breathing.

"Do you think Sascha will let me go to the faire with the rest of you next week?" I asked as Ivan moved on to shave my chest. "I have the feeling he's not eager for the rest of the world to know about me."

"He's dreading the moment," Ivan agreed, looking at his work and not my eyes.

I hummed. "I knew it."

"Dmitri doesn't want to give you away to the rest of the world either," Ivan revealed.

"Oh?" My brow inched up. "I would have thought he'd want to strut me through the faire naked and brag that my ass was his."

Ivan chuckled and shook his head. "The moment he

does, half of the wolves in the forest will start sniffing around for you."

I tensed. "You don't think people will try to kidnap me, do you?" I asked. They had apparently tried to steal Gregor from his pack more than once, though I was still unclear as to whether that was Sascha's pack or the one he'd been part of previously.

"Don't you worry about that," Ivan said. "Sascha will make good and certain everyone knows they're taking their lives in their hands by so much as looking at you wrong."

Which was the advantage of fostering a deep emotional connection as well as mere ownership where Sascha was concerned.

"So you think he will let me go to the faire?" I asked again.

Ivan moved back to clean his razor and apply soap to my legs. I brushed a hand across my damp chest. Actually, that did feel much better. "You'll have to come with us to the faire," Ivan said consideringly. "As dangerous as it will be for you there, it would be more dangerous to leave you here unprotected. We might be isolated, but after our antics in Novoberg, I'm sure rumors about you have spread all through the forest."

I tilted my head to the side, considering that, as I watched Ivan shave my legs. I supposed it would be perilous for me to stay in the house by myself. Even if it would have been highly entertaining to snoop through every room on my own, which I still hadn't had an opportunity to do. I wanted to go to the faire more than anything, though. I'd only ever been to the tiny faires outside of Novoberg. The one in Berlova would be much bigger. My companions had discussed it so much in the past week that I was as eager to go as I was to experience new and erotic ways of having sex.

I let my thoughts drift to the upcoming faire and how much of a danger it might be, but I also imagined all of the wonders I might see there. I hadn't been outside of Novoberg in my life—which was normal for young noblemen from the cities—and from what my companions had told me about the treats and treasures to be found at larger faires, I was in for the day of my life, no matter the risk. I'd always known the world was bigger than what was contained within Novoberg's walls, but getting to experience that for myself was invigorating.

"Right. That's that," Ivan said as he shaved away the last of the stubble on my legs. The entire process had taken far less time than the first time. Ivan smacked the side of my leg with a companionable smile. "Why don't you go soak in the pool to wash off any remaining soap."

My heart leapt at that idea, and I stood as Ivan did. The warm pool was one of my favorite things about Sascha's house. Whatever minerals were contained in the water, it was downright luxurious to soak in. It had proven to be exactly the antidote my body needed for frequent sexual use, and I credited it, along with Gregor's medicines, as the reason I felt as hale and hearty as I had before anyone had thrust their cock up my ass. I gathered my folded clothes, not bothering to put them on again, but planning to take them outside with me.

"Oh, why don't you take a platter of snacks out to the others who are working," Ivan said as an afterthought.

I veered off of my path toward the door so that I could take the large, wooden plate of biscuits, dried fruit and tarts Ivan had prepared earlier in my arms. As I carried it and my clothes outside, I stole one of the jam tarts and ate it with relish as I walked.

It was a lovely day. Spring was in the air, and even though it had rained the day before, the skies were clear now, and the breeze was balmy. Sven was hard at work erecting netting of some sort over a long row of freshly-sprouted plants he'd just put in the ground a few days before. As he'd explained, even though the weather was still tricky, the hot springs under the house meant he could plant early crops now, as long as they were covered, instead of waiting until after the last frost. I took the plate of snacks to him, offering him his pick, before carrying my clothes the rest of the way to the still-covered pool. It remained covered when not in use, Sascha had explained, so that forest animals didn't fall in and drown, spoiling the water.

Once my clothes were set aside, I continued on to Gregor's workshop with the tray.

"So they've got you walking around naked after all, eh?" Gregor laughed as I presented the tray to him.

I grinned along with him. "I didn't see any point in

dressing for the sole purpose of delivering snacks just to undress again once I take a dip in the pool."

"Clever and practical," Gregor said, selecting a few biscuits, then nodding to me in thanks.

I lost my grin as I approached Dmitri's workshop. It was in an even worse condition after his last few days of successful hunting. The smell coming from it made me blanch. I was grateful that Dmitri wasn't inside, but rather was in the smokehouse, checking on the meat he was preparing.

"Ivan sent snacks," I called to him, my voice hoarse with nausea.

Dmitri turned from the strips of fresh meat he was hanging in the house. At the sight of me, nude and freshly shaven, he broke into a toothy grin. "Yes, he did."

I was only just able to control my visceral reaction to him as he stepped out of the smokehouse to study me the way Gregor had studied the plate of snacks. Dmitri even licked his lips and handled his crotch. In the end, he popped a dried apricot into his mouth instead of striking the tray of treats out of my hand and bending me over, like I half expected him to.

"You're lucky I've so much work to do this afternoon, pup," he growled, stepping closer to me. "The way you look right now, all I want to do is tie those delicate wrists of yours together and string you up in my smokehouse so I can fuck your sweet ass into oblivion."

I gulped, answering his ravenous look with one that said I probably would have enjoyed it. Dark side indeed.

Something inside of me must have been broken to enjoy the pain Dmitri inflicted along with the pleasure he gave.

"Run along, little pup," he growled, gripping my arm and turning me aside, then smacking my ass hard. "Before I choose your meat over this." He gestured into the smokehouse with his thumb.

I took his advice and scurried on toward Sascha's workshop. My ass still smarted with the memory of the way he'd pushed me to my limits the day before, all while forcing me to watch the way he'd fucked me in the mirror. If "forced" is a word that could be used for something I got off on watching.

"Peter, what in God's name are you doing?" Sascha snapped as soon as I appeared in the doorway of his workshop with the platter.

My thoughts were far away, so the vehemence of his question startled me. "Bringing you a snack?" I asked, pausing in the doorway. Sascha's workshop was littered with woodchips, some of which were sharp, so I was hesitant to enter in bare feet.

Sascha frowned, lips pursed, and got up from the lathe, where he was turning a bowl. Several bowls in various states of completion were stacked around the shop, and the scent of stain and raw wood filled the air. Sascha's frown remained in place as he crunched his way across the woodchips to meet me at the door.

"I told you that I don't want you doing any manual labor," he said, snatching the platter out of my hands.

I backpedaled into the grass as he advanced on me,

gaping. "Carrying a tray of snacks out to my pack members is hardly manual labor," I argued.

"It is to me," Sascha said with a scowl.

Perhaps it was the sense of belonging that I was finally starting to have within the pack, or perhaps it was something as silly as standing in front of Sascha naked, my skin still tingling from being shaved, but I was in no mood to play the fainting violet. "I'm hardly likely to strain a muscle or injure myself my carrying a tray," I snapped.

"It's work," Sascha snapped right back. "And more importantly, it's work I don't want you to do."

"What harm can there be in me simply lending a hand when a hand is needed?" I asked, raising my voice in a way I hadn't done since arriving at the house.

"Your hands are needed for other things," Sascha argued.

"Oh, yes." I threw up the hands in question in a frustrated gesture. "The only thing you want my hands to do is stroke cocks all day."

"That's not what I meant at all." Sascha's scowl was as frustrated as I felt.

"Really?" I took a half step closer to him. Even though he was so much taller than me, I didn't feel at all intimidated. "Because that's not the way I see things."

"And just how do you see things?" he asked with more than a hint of sass.

Well, he'd asked. "The way I see it," I spat, "you just want to see me as weak and dependent. You want to believe that I'm so soft in the head that I'll be happy to act as nothing more than a receptacle for pricks. You don't want to see me as an actual person, you just want a living doll to fuck. Because dolls can't think for themselves. They can't challenge your authority or question your decisions."

Sascha's eyes flared wide in shock and offense. I could see at once that I'd inadvertently hit a nerve I hadn't known was there. "How dare you speak to me like that?" he hissed.

"How dare you rob me of my personhood?" I snapped right back.

Another wave of shock and hurt flickered through Sascha's eyes. "Are you trying to tell me that you don't like it when I touch you, when I fuck you? Because if you are, you're lying."

"I'm not saying any such thing," I said, holding fast to my pride. "I enjoy being with you. I like everything about it, and I'm not too proud to admit as much. But that doesn't make me less of a man, and it isn't an excuse for you to treat me like a helpless child." I paused, noting the way Sascha was breathing heavily with anger. I wasn't quite done, though. "Frankly, your obsession with me as a child is disturbing, considering how much *you* enjoy fucking *me*."

It felt good to finally assert myself, though it ran counter to my original strategy of playing meek and relying on Sascha's protection for survival. I supposed I wasn't as biddable or capable of tolerating being belittled as I'd assumed. And as uncomfortable as it made me, the fight had me questioning whether what I felt for him was deep or merely shallow infatuation.

Sascha gaped at me. I could see the emotion in his eyes, but he took his time forming that emotion into words. I wasn't in the mood to wait around to see what he would come up with to insult me with his overprotectiveness either. I had held his gaze for long enough, so I turned and marched away from him.

Only then did I notice Dmitri leaning against the wall of his workshop, watching the scene with a smirk. Gregor had stuck his head out of his shop to see what was going on as well, and Sven had glanced up from his garden plot. Their witness of the scene only made me walk with my head held higher—in spite of being stark naked and pale in the early spring light. I didn't acknowledge any of them as I strode over to the pool, where I'd left my clothes, and grabbed hold of the cover to wrench it open.

The cover was heavier than I'd anticipated, and my show of strength didn't extend to grace as I muscled it to the side. It felt good to strain, though, and it was satisfying to remove the cover all on my own. I stepped angrily into the pool, splashing as I went, and sat sullenly in one of the embedded seats, my back to Sascha and everyone else, crossing my arms.

After a few minutes, I uncrossed my arms and let out a breath, realizing I probably looked like a pouting child.

The exhaustion I felt after arguing with Sascha was every bit as heavy as post-orgasm exhaustion, but not as sweet. I sank up to my chin in the pool, closing my eyes and leaning my head against the lip. As good as it felt to finally stand up for myself and call Sascha out for his ridiculous behavior, I had to admit that I hated fighting with him. He deserved it, but I felt hollow in the aftermath all the same.

Perhaps it wasn't surprising that nobody disturbed me in the pool for a good long while. I floated where I was, eyes closed, listening to the sounds of the forest, which were becoming familiar to me. A breeze rustled the treetops above me. Songbirds called out to each other as they flitted from tree to tree. Squirrels chirped to one another. Something rustled in the grass at the edge of the tree line. It was all peaceful and soothing, and before long, my body relaxed and my temper calmed. This wasn't the life I'd been raised for, but it was the one I was stuck with, and it wasn't as bad as it could have been. I could work with it.

I heard footsteps approaching the pool through the grass well before whoever it was reached me. I figured it was either Sascha come to address the fight or Dmitri coming to gloat over it, and probably fuck me. I wasn't sure which I was less in the mood for.

"You could have told me that you didn't like being coddled," Sascha's voice said high above me.

I opened my eyes and squinted up at him. With the afternoon sunlight behind him, he looked like some sort of angel. The anger was gone from his expression, but not the frustration.

"No, I couldn't have," I said frankly. "You wouldn't have listened."

I waited for him to argue, forming my rebuttal. Instead of taking me up on it, Sascha let out a sigh and bent to remove his shoes. I pushed away from the pool wall, floating to the center, but staying in the water up to my neck. As I expected, Sasha undressed. I enjoyed the sight openly. If he was going to ogle me like I was a piece of meat, then I would do the same to him. He glanced to me out of the corner of his eye and smirked at the way I studied him. Finally, he finished removing his clothes and stepped into the pool.

"I'm only trying to act in your best interest," Sascha said once we were on the same level. And it was the same level. He sank into the water up to his chin, which eliminated any height difference between us. I rather liked it.

"How is rendering me useless in my best interest?" I asked, trying to remain calm instead of turning spiteful.

Sascha looked surprised. "You're not useless. You're exceptionally valuable."

I let out an impatient breath. "My ass is exceptionally valuable, you mean. And my cock."

"That's not what I mean at all." He looked even more surprised by my statement. "Peter, you are so much more than a bedmate."

I narrowed my eyes at him. "Do you actually believe that or are you simply avoiding the truth?"

"You are *not* just an object," he insisted in a louder voice. "Not to me," he added in a softer tone.

"Then let me fend for myself now and then," I demanded. My heart wanted to soften to him, but my pride was still wounded. "I won't chop wood or hoe garden beds or do anything that might cause me to pull a muscle, but I can carry a platter, I can clear a supper table. I can even run a dust-cloth over the furniture, because God knows the house could use a tidying."

Sascha flinched back, his eyes widening. "I had no idea you thought our home was such a stye."

"Don't be dramatic," I said.

"Take your own advice," he shot back at me.

"I'm not being—"

"I thought I was honoring you," he interrupted me, his face flushing from more than the heat of the water. "I thought that by seeing to your every need, showing you that you would not be treated like a slave, that I was showing you how precious you are to us, to me." He didn't look at all happy to reveal something so vulnerable.

I gaped at him. "Do you actually think that forbidding me to do anything but service the lot of you sexually would be seen as a compliment?"

"Yes," he barked, laughing humorlessly. "Your life should be all pleasure and no pain."

"There are different kinds of pain, Sascha," I told him. "And different sorts of pleasure. There's the pain of boredom, the pain of humiliation, and there's the pleasure of pride in a job well done, in accomplishment."

He let out a breath, his shoulders sagging. "I didn't see it that way," he admitted, looking a bit relieved. He glanced out at the forest for a moment before turning back to me. "My whole life has been one of work and hardship. I've been laboring since before my memories start. All I ever wanted in life was to rest and enjoy the finer things of life. I just wanted the relief, just for once, of not having to constantly fend for myself."

"You've always wanted someone to take care of you," I said in a low enough voice so that anyone who might be tempted to strain their ears to listen in wouldn't be able to hear.

Sascha's answering look of vulnerability was followed by an uncomfortable frown. Clearly, he didn't like opening himself up that way. But I was infinitely grateful that he had.

I floated closer to him, wrapping my legs around his waist and draping my arms over his shoulders, but I didn't smile. "I understand that you were trying to express affection," I said in a soft voice, meeting and holding his gaze. "I appreciate that more than you could possibly know. But your methods of taking care of me are not what I need. In fact, they chafe horribly."

"Then what can I do to show you that I care for you?" he asked, his voice low and deep as well. His hands rested on my sides, stirring need within me. "What can I do to show you that you are valued, as a pup and as a man? To...to make up for all the hardship that comes with a position like yours?"

I felt like he'd handed me something golden—a greater understanding of his soul and his motivations. Sascha cared for me, just as I'd suspected from the start. The others had said he had a sentimental streak, and I could see it was a mile wide. Whether I was actually who he wanted as a more intimate form of lover or if he was simply imposing those things on me to fulfill a fantasy, he wanted to be in love with me. I found it achingly endearing, but the temptation to give in to his fantasy and play along weren't as strong as they had been after the first few days.

"Let me be me," I told him. "Let me be useful in ways that satisfy *me*, not just you, or anyone else. Let me have some sort of employment and a greater measure of self-respect."

He let out a heavy breath, resting his forehead against mind and closing his eyes. "All right," he said.

My mouth twitched into a grin. I'd won that victory far more easily than I'd expected. Who was the leader of the pack now?

"And I wouldn't say no if you wanted to fuck me right now," I added in a mischievous whisper.

Sascha opened his eyes and grinned at me, the look full of heat and need. "I know just the thing," he said, floating back to the edge of the pool, as though he would get out.

"We could do it right here, in the pool," I said coyly.

Sascha's mouth twitched to one side. "Not with what I have in mind," he said, stepping out and helping me out behind him. "Besides, I don't think we want an audience."

He was right. Sven was nearby and clearly interested in what we were talking about. Dmitri had stepped out of his smokehouse and watched us with a frown. We took a moment to dry off using towels from the chest beside the pool before gathering up our clothes. Sascha grasped my hand and led me around Sven's garden beds and into the house.

"Did you bring the tray back?" Ivan asked as we entered, then let out a quick, "Oh," and returned to his food preparations with a smile and a chuckle.

I didn't feel half as submissive as I could have as Sascha drew me down the long hall and into his bedroom. The power of winning our spat continued to surge toward me. We hadn't bothered to actually dress again after drying off at the pool, and as soon as Sascha tossed his wadded clothes on the chair near his fireplace, he pulled my load from my arms and tossed that aside too before advancing on me.

I laughed deep in my throat as he backed me toward the bed with a ravenous grin.

"This is more like it," he said, reaching for me.

I slipped out of his grip as I lost my balance and sat heavily on the side of the bed, but there was nothing wrong with the level that put me at relative to him. "Most certainly," I said on a sigh, sliding my hands over his hips to his ass.

Rather than going straight for his cock, I let my hands

rove freely over his warm, still slightly damp skin. We'd fucked more times than I could count in the near fortnight since I'd come to be with the pack, but I'd never really given myself free reign to explore his body with touch until then. He was all muscle and sinew covered by soft skin and manly hair that had my breath hitching in my lungs as I threaded my fingers through what grew on his chest. He had all the power of a man who regularly chopped down trees combined with the grace of an artist. I might have been his fantasy, but he was certainly mine.

"I like it when you touch me like that," he growled, stroking a hand through my hair in turn. "Like you want me."

"I do want you," I said, glancing up at him. I didn't bother to change the lust I felt into a look of innocence. "I've always wanted you."

"I can see that," he chuckled, glancing momentarily to my cock, which stood up for him.

I drew my hands down his sides to his abdomen with a wicked look. My mouth was already watering to taste him, and I could tell from the heat rippling off of him and the excitement in his eyes that he wanted me to devour him. I teased my hands over his hips and thighs, taking my sweet time on my way to what we both wanted. He let out an impatient breath and shifted his legs farther apart for better balance, nudging my knees apart as he did. That gave me more room to tease my way between his legs, testing the weight of his balls and stroking my fingers across his taint toward his hole.

He sucked in a surprise breath when I added enough pressure to my explorations to push a finger into him. "Do you have ambitions of flipping things between us?" he asked, his voice gruff with lust.

"Perhaps," I said coyly. I closed my free hand over his thick cock and stroked it lazily. "Would you like that? Would you like me to fuck you?"

I felt a tremor go through him that left me panting with excitement and my cock beading with pre-cum. The idea had never occurred to me. I was happy in the role that I'd been given. But now that it was a possibility, I found myself wanting to at least experiment with being the aggressor. Judging by the difficulty Sascha was having in catching his breath, the possibility titillated him too.

"Not today," he answered at last, voice shaky. "I have something else in mind."

"Do you?" I asked, arching one eyebrow before leaning close enough to close my mouth over the flared and sensitive tip of his cock.

He growled and gripped both hands in my hair, as if he needed to hold on in order to maintain his balance. I loved the feeling that I could undo him that way and continued to lick and caress his head with my lips. I kept my hands firmly in place where they were, playing with his head only and waiting to swallow him until I knew he was desperate for it. He breathed heavily, vocalizing his pleasure with deep sounds as I licked pre-cum from his slit and added pressure by sucking.

"I can't decide if you're an angel or a devil," he

groaned, jerking just enough to sink deeper into my mouth as he did.

I pulled back long enough to ask, "Which do you want me to be?" in a sensual voice.

Another shudder passed through him. "Both," he said.

In a flash, he took charge, pushing me to my back, then climbing on top of me, like a wildcat who had caught his prey. His mouth slanted over mine, and he kissed me hard enough to evoke a passionate sigh from me. His hands roamed my sides, drawing one leg so high over his side that I was almost bent double. With his other hand, he reached between us to stroke my cock.

It was my turn to let out a cry of pleasure so carnal I almost embarrassed myself.

"This is why you're so good to fuck," he rumbled between kisses that spun my head and left me panting for more. "You make me feel like you'll die if you don't have me balls deep inside you."

"I think I might," I gasped, digging my fingertips into the broad muscles of his back. I was already dangerously close to coming and working with everything I had to keep myself in that heady, heightened pleasure for as long as possible.

"I want to see your face when you feel me come inside of you," he hummed, moving away from my mouth to nuzzle and bite my neck. The way he sucked hard for a moment thrilled me. He was deliberately marking me with passion. It felt so good I could hardly hold on and undulated against him, hungry for release.

He moved away long enough to snatch at the jar of ointment on the table beside his bed—a clear sign he couldn't hold out much longer either. I'd learned his rhythms well in the last ten days as well as his moods. I could see in his face that he was going to be aggressive and make me feel so, so good. I wriggled impatiently as he slicked his cock, then took two fingers of the ointment to slide across my hole.

I sighed loudly as he tested me, spreading my legs wide and penetrating me with his fingers. I'd stretched and limbered up considerably in the time that I'd been with the pack, so he didn't have to work hard before I was more than ready for him. But instead of flipping me to my stomach and pounding into me, like I expected, he tugged me to the edge of the bed instead.

"You're my angel," he growled, drawing my legs up and out to the sides, almost to the point where my heels could have rested on his shoulders. "But I'm going to make you scream like the devil."

I started to smile when he lifted my hips enough to push his cock into me. It was a whole new sensation, being taken while facing up and able to look into his eyes as he fucked me. It was worlds away from how I'd been able to meet Dmitri's eyes in the mirror when he used me. Sascha groaned and sighed as he worked deeper and deeper into me, all while watching my reaction. It was fiery and intimate, and easily the best experience I'd had so far.

It got even better when he adjusted himself to bring his chest as close to mine while still thrusting. It felt so good to be filled and stretched and to be able to see how much he enjoyed it at the same time. I spiraled quickly toward orgasm, everything within me building up to the moment I knew was coming. Best of all, I was able to thread my fingers through Sascha's thick hair and look deep into his eyes, letting him see everything I was feeling as he fucked me.

"God, Peter, you're everything," he panted, clearly close to the edge himself. "I want to give you everything. I want to fill you and love you."

"Yes," I mewled, face contorting as I passed the point of no return. "Yes, yes. Oh."

I shot over the edge, coming on both of our bellies as his thrusts grew more frantic. Everything within me was suddenly wildly over sensitive, but the discomfort was worth it when Sascha let out a roar, erupting inside of me. The way his face took on a glow of ecstasy and pinched as he cried out was the most amazing thing I'd ever seen. All I ever wanted to do for the rest of my life was have sex with him that way, while we could watch each other and feel the full impact of what each of us was experiencing.

It felt too soon when he pulled out, but the way he rolled with me onto the bed, his body encompassing mine as we lay spent together was enough to make up for it.

"You know it's never been like this for me with anyone before," he panted, drawing me against him.

Part of me was tempted to make a sly comment about how little experience I had to compare my experience with, but instead, I embraced him, closed my eyes, and whispered, "I know."

At the same time, I was left wondering if sex could feel that good or better with men other than Sascha. I did care for him, and he satisfied me in ways I didn't know I needed to be satisfied, but he couldn't quench my curiosity all on his own. I just knew there was more out there in the world to experience. I didn't know how I would be able to experience it, but as I drifted into a well-deserved nap, I refused to worry about it. Things would sort themselves out in good time.

12

The day I had been waiting for almost from the moment I'd found myself with Sascha's pack came just a few days later: Faire Day.

"I still don't like it," Sascha said as I walked into the main room for the fourth time.

I glanced down at the clothes I wore as Sascha frowned at them and let out an annoyed sigh. "This is the most unobtrusive outfit I own," I argued, my patience at an end. I felt as though I'd pored through every piece of clothing I owned to pick out something suitable for a faire that also met with Sascha's approval. What I had come up with on my fourth try was a simple pair of dark green trousers, a plain, white shirt, a deep purple vest embroidered with lilies, a dark green jacket, and a lavender scarf tied around my neck.

"It's the scarf," Dmitri said, coming to stand near

Sascha and surveying me with the same critical eye. "It screams 'pup'."

I clenched my jaw. "The marks littering my neck scream 'pup' even louder."

I glanced between the two men. In the last few days, since Sascha had left his particularly large, bright mark, it was as if the two of them had been in competition to see who could lay the most visible claim on me. Sascha's marks had been left with passionate sighs, his heart laid bare as our bodies joined eagerly. Dmitri's had been inflicted as he'd held me down, arms and legs contorted at uncomfortable angles, fucking me until I'd begged him for mercy that he knew I didn't want him to show me. The rest of the world wouldn't have seen any difference in those marks. All they would see was a pup who was thoroughly enjoyed by his masters.

Sascha sent a scathing look to Dmitri that Dmitri either didn't catch or didn't care about.

"He has a point," Ivan said as he and Sven prepared to take the last basket of baked goods he would sell out to the wagon. "He's going to be obvious enough with his face alone. Showing off to the faire that he's a good little pup is only going to draw interested wolves like flies to honey."

I shuddered. The last thing I wanted was to be noticed for the wrong reasons. I didn't want to be noticed at all. I wanted to do the noticing.

"I know just the thing," Gregor said, a look of inspiration in his eyes.

He headed back to his bedroom as the others finished carrying goods for sale and the tents we would sleep in overnight out to the wagon. Sascha let me carry out a very small crate of Gregor's medicine bottles and my change of clothes for the morrow, but that was it. He'd been somewhat repentant after our argument, but I could see he still wanted to treat me like something that needed wrapping in as much straw and cotton-wool as Gregor's bottles.

"Here we go," Gregor said, coming out of the house with what looked like an old, grey cloak over one arm. "It'll be too big, of course, but it'll do the trick."

He shook out the cloak and threw it over my shoulders. Sascha finished the job, tugging it into place, then lifting the hood over my head. The cloak was heavy and itchy. It fell almost all the way to the ground on me. I felt as though my head might drown in the hood.

"That's perfect," Sascha said, stepping back.

"I can hardly see a thing," I groused, attempting to adjust the hood so that I could.

"Which means no one can see you." Sascha grabbed the front of the hood and covered my face with a wry grin.

I pushed the hood back again, sending him a half sullen, half teasing look. "The whole point of me going with you is so that I can see everything there is to see at the faire," I said.

"No, the whole point in you going with us is that we

can't leave you here on your own for two days," Sascha said with overexaggerated patience.

I huffed at him, which only made him laugh. It was actually quite a pleasant exchange. Banter was a sign of friendship, which was quickly developing between us right along with lust. Sascha drew me over to the wagon, then lifted me, his hands around my waist, into the tall bed.

"Now, Peter," he said, purposely addressing me like a child as he pushed my knees apart and yanked me forward until our groins ground together. He *would* be devilish enough to tempt me right before we departed for the faire. "I want you to be on your best behavior today," he said in an almost sing-song voice. "You've never been to a faire this large before, and while I know there will be a lot there for you to see and to tempt you, I want you to stay by my side at all times. No running off, and no touching merchandise unless I intend to buy it."

"God, you're insufferable when you're giving orders," I grumbled, eyeing him heatedly.

He pulled my hips even tighter against his and undulated in a way that nearly had me crying out with an impassioned and undignified sound as my cock strained against my trousers. "Don't speak to strangers," he went on, mischief shining in his eyes. "Don't even look at anyone who watches you with any interest at all. Be meek, but make sure everyone knows you're taken, and that your protectors will kill anyone who so much as winks at you."

I could tell he was serious about that last bit, but the indignity of being lectured to was too much. "Perhaps you should tie me to your belt with leading strings if you think the danger is so acute," I snapped.

"Perhaps I will," Sascha growled. He leaned in and stole a quick kiss, then patted my head and said, "And if you're very good, I'll buy you a sweetie at the end of the faire for you to suck on as we make our way home."

"I'll give you something to suck on all right," I growled, meeting his eyes with defiant fire.

"And I *will*," he replied in a whisper against my ear. "I'll suck you off so hard in the tent tonight that you'll swear I'd swallowed your soul along with all the cum you can give me."

That comment nearly had me spewing that cum into my trousers then and there. Which was, of course, the cruelest part of Sascha's teasing. He let go of me and shoved me deeper into the back of the wagon, leaving me hard and unsatisfied. Those feelings were even more uncomfortable as Dmitri snapped the leads over the backs of the two horses that had been hitched to the wagon to start us on our entirely-too-bumpy journey to the faire.

"It should be my turn for a go at you today," Dmitri complained sullenly as I scrambled through the packed and moving wagon bed to stand behind the seat. "Sascha needs to learn to share his toys."

"Sascha's not the one who throws me out of his room the second he's done with me," I reminded

Dmitri, wincing as my erection rubbed against my trousers.

Dmitri chuckled. "I just want to fuck you. I don't want to kiss and cuddle and pretend everything is all happily ever after with you."

"Then we're in agreement," I said in a low, shrewd voice. "All I want is for you to fuck me and make me come. I don't even want to be your friend."

Dmitri laughed aloud, earning a sudden, sharp look from Sascha as he rode one of the other horses several yards to the side of the wagon. "Does Sascha know you're such a cold-hearted, sick fucker?"

"Of course not," I said, glancing around the back of the wagon for a comfortable place to sit for the journey.

Dmitri shook his head and glanced over his shoulder at me before focusing on guiding the horses through the forest. "He's going to be so disappointed someday, when he finds out."

Those words sent a chill through me as I settled in for the ride. They were a threat and a promise. I'd deliberately kept everything I did with Dmitri a secret from Sascha. I wasn't certain how I felt about it myself. If sex with Sascha was heaven, then what I did with Dmitri was...well, not hell, that was certain, but it fed a different sort of need.

Dmitri was a hard taskmaster. He deliberately sought out to inflict pain along with pleasure. The mechanics weren't that different, but he knew how to clamp my balls too tight, fuck my ass without enough lubrication to ease things, and fist my cock for minutes after I'd already come, making me cry with pain because it was too sensitive. He could tie me up until I felt utterly helpless as he fucked my mouth until I choked, or clamped his hand over my mouth and nose so that I couldn't breathe as he fucked me until I almost passed out. All the while, he made me watch the cruel things he did to me in the mirror. Not once did I disappoint him by failing to get and stay rock hard, and often I came more than once... except for the times he refused to let me come at all.

All those things filled me with strange, new forms of guilt that I hadn't known existed, but also relief. It seemed utterly wrong for me to enjoy being mistreated by Dmitri like that. But it also satisfied something deep and dark within me, something that believed every horrible thing my father and brothers had ever said about how disgusting and broken I was. Letting Dmitri abuse me felt like a consummation of those horrible things, like I owned them, fulfilled them, instead of being put down or belittled by them. And on top of that, Dmitri certainly didn't view me as a child when he dominated me.

"What's wrong, pup?" Gregor asked as he rode up to the side of the wagon on the other horse. "You look as though you've swallowed a burr."

"Oh. Nothing," I lied, putting on my best innocent look. "I was just worrying about whether I'll see anyone I know at the faire."

"Doubtful," Gregor said with a wink. "Berlova is far away from Novoberg."

"You're probably right." I smiled and pretended to be reassured. In fact, Berlova was just short of a day's ride from Novoberg, which was hardly any distance at all, considering the vastness of the frontier.

As soon as Gregor rode on, I fell back into contemplation about my embattled feelings. If Sascha had tried to do the things to me that Dmitri did, it would be horrible and wounding—not just on a physical level. From Sascha, those same actions would be destructive. Likewise, if Dmitri ever tried to kiss and caress and snuggle with me, whispering endearments in the middle of the night, I would have found it repulsive. Each man fulfilled a very specific need in my life, but I knew I wouldn't be able to maintain the balance for long.

More than that, being forced to share me had caused things between Sascha and Dmitri to deteriorate further. The two barely spoke to each other anymore. They only glared. I wished Dmitri would go off and be a lone wolf or form his own pack. And yet, I knew I would miss the sweet torture he provided me with once he was gone. But if that's what I had to give up to feel safe—not to mention for Sascha to find a truer sort of happiness—I would be willing to part with it in a heartbeat.

I thought about the thorny matter for as long as I could before it threatened to overwhelm me. The day was meant to be fun and festive, not agonizing, so I forced myself to think of other things on the long journey. And it was long. We set out shortly after sunrise, but the sun was well on its way to its zenith by the time we began to encounter other wagons hauling their wares toward the faire. It had dipped well toward the horizon by the time the trees thinned a bit as we neared the city of Berlova, and a great mass of tents and wagons came into view in a ring around the city walls.

"The faire," I gasped, scrambling to stand and pushing back the hood I'd let fall over my face while contemplating dark things.

"Careful there, Peter," Sascha warned me. He'd been riding closer to the side of the wagon since we'd come across the first of the other wagons on the road. "You're being watched."

Alarmed, I glanced around. Ivan and Sven had started out the journey walking behind our large wagon, but as soon as we'd come across a slightly smaller wagon driven by a trio of women, they'd hopped on to ride with them. There were at least a dozen wagons in line with us now—most of them driven by men, but a few by women—stretching ahead and behind us. All it took was one sweep of my head to see that Sascha was right. I'd been noticed.

Several men amongst our companions on the road sat straighter in their saddles or twisted and craned their necks to get a better look at me as I revealed my face. It came as a shock to realize none of my pack members had been exaggerating when they'd said I was a rare find and that others would show an interest in me. You would have thought I was made of diamonds the way the other men gaped and stared. It was enough for me to quickly replace my hood so that I was mostly hidden.

"I told you," Sascha said with a smirk. "But don't worry. Like I said, stay close to me and trust me, and let everyone see that you are mine, and no one will bother you."

All I could do, under the circumstances, was trust Sascha. Dmitri drove the wagon to a long stretch of empty booths that were filling up fast as more people joined the faire, laying out various wares on tables in the booths. There didn't seem to be any rhyme or reason to who claimed which booth or what goods were sold next to each other, which wasn't the way things were done at faires outside of Novoberg. Sascha set up his furniture, bowls, plates, and cups next to a man selling what looked like whips made of leather. Dmitri took the booth across the central aisle with his smoked meats, furs, and treated hides. Ivan and Sven laid out Ivan's baked goods beside that, and Gregor took the booth beside Sascha for his medicines. He also set up a slate detailing medical services he provided and the prices he charged. I helped him arrange the bottles of his herbs and tinctures, and a line had formed in front of his booth before I was even close to finishing.

"That's enough help for now," Sascha told me in a warning voice well before I was finished lining up bottles in rows.

I was tempted to be frustrated with him, until I noticed that not all of the men lining up in front of

Gregor's booth looked ill. Worse still, as soon as I moved over to stand beside Sascha, a few of those men came to stand at his booth, scrutinizing me as though I were for sale instead of Sascha's wooden wares.

As it turned out, I wasn't exactly mistaken.

"How much do you want for him?" a man who was too gnarled for his relatively young appearance asked. He licked his lips and grabbed his crotch as he studied me.

I shifted hard toward Sascha, disturbed enough to want to grab his arm. I tugged on the hood of my cloak, trying to hide my face. It was some sort of ironic punishment that, now that I wanted to hide from the scrutinizing gazes around me, the softness of my hair meant it kept sliding back, revealing my face. At least I'd won the battle to wear a scarf around my marked neck. I suddenly worried that my mouth looked as sensual as it had the last time I'd checked my appearance in a mirror.

"He's not for sale," Sascha barked, loud enough for the small crowd that was beginning to form around his booth to hear.

"How much for an hour with him?" another man in the crowd—young, but missing an eye—asked, baring his rotting teeth at me.

"He's not for rent either," Sascha snapped.

Several of the gathering men let out sounds of disappointment and moved on. A few lingered, but when Sascha removed his traveling cloak to reveal a long knife in his belt, and when Sven moved away from Ivan's booth to stand at the end of Sascha's with a spiked cudgel and a nasty look, those men moved away too.

"I stand corrected," I breathed, sounding as weak and effeminate as I had that first night with the pack.

"I knew you would," Sascha said with a sympathetic smile. That smile was not only reassuring, it was leveling. Sascha wasn't speaking down to me, he was treating me as his equal. That, more than anything, convinced me to obey all of the things he'd said earlier to the letter.

It was a good thing, too. That first crowd of men cleared out in a hurry, but within fifteen minutes, another, larger group had formed.

"I'll give you a thousand marks for him," a middle-aged man who was dressed far more richly than most of the other faire-goers offered. Unlike the other wolves crowding the booth, he had a look of surprising intelligence about him. He watched me with calculation that sent a shiver through me—a shiver that wasn't fear. I was intrigued. The man couldn't be a wolf. He had to be from one of the cities, but I couldn't tell which one from his accent. It had me wondering whether there were actually city-dwellers who kept pups as well as wolves.

"He's not for sale," Sascha told the man with the same ferocity he'd displayed for the rougher men.

The refined man looked offended. "Do you know who I am?" he asked.

"Yes," Sascha snapped. "You're not his pack leader."

Surprisingly, the wealthy man looked momentarily thwarted. At least, until he went on with, "I'll give you a thousand marks to let me have him for the night. My caravan is right over there." He pointed off to the left-hand side of Berlova's main gate. "I'll even let you watch so you can see no harm comes to him."

My brow shot up and my cock twitched at the idea of the wealthy man having me while Sascha watched. Apparently, my darker side extended beyond just having Dmitri brutalize me.

The wealthy man caught my heated look before I could school it to neutrality, and he grinned knowingly at me. I forced myself to smile up at Sascha, indicating where my loyalties resided, but my heart pounded against my ribs all the same.

"He's not for sale, and he's not for rent," Sascha growled, taking the knife out of his belt.

"My apologies," the wealthy man said, holding up his hands, then backing away. "I did not mean to offend you."

He turned to walk off. I risked a last peek at him only to accidentally meet his eyes for a sizzling moment. He broke into another grin, and I was left with the curious feeling that it wasn't the last I would see of the man. The whole idea of pups being kidnapped rushed back to my mind, except instead of finding the notion terrifying, I considered that there could be some scenarios in which being kidnapped wasn't the worst thing that could have happened to me.

That second group disbursed as well. As they did, I noticed Dmitri watching the exchange with narrowed eyes. Clearly, he didn't approve, but a chill raced down my spine as I wondered what it was Dmitri didn't approve of. A thousand marks was a staggering amount of money. I remembered Gregor say that money was one reason Dmitri hadn't set out on his own yet—although I questioned that, based on how swiftly he was selling out of the wares he'd brought to the faire—a thousand marks would have been more than enough for him to live in luxury somewhere.

"How much do you want for that uncommonly sweet pup's ass?" yet another man asked, this time in an almost jubilant voice, as he approached from the line of wagons behind the booths.

Sascha turned, thunder in his expression and started to shout, "He's not for—" His growl stopped dead, and his expression broke into a wide smile.

I knew why in an instant. Two men approached us from the wagons, and one of them was the spitting image of Dmitri. So much so that I stood there gaping at him. Mikal was a perfect copy of his brother, but with one exception. Where Dmitri had a definite air of menace to him, Mikal radiated happiness and good will.

"Sascha. Long time no see, my friend." Mikal stepped forward, and he and Sascha embraced like brothers.

"It's good to see you, Mikal," Sascha said. "You too, Jakob."

He embraced the second man. Jakob was younger than I expected him to be, though still several years older than me. He had wild, curly, brown hair and mismatched eyes. One was blue and the other was green. As soon as Sascha let go of him, he shifted to stand with his arm around Mikal. "I'd heard you found a pup wandering in the forest, but I had no idea anything like this was even possible."

He glanced to me, and immediately I wanted to hide in my cloak. Even though I knew the story and knew Sascha trusted Jakob. Jakob had the air of a good man, but the way he raked me with a frankly appreciative glance—as if I were a trinket for sale and not a man—made me squirm and chafe against the submissive role that had been assigned to me.

"I didn't find him, Dmitri did," Sascha confessed, as though that were an important bit of information.

"I should say hello to my brother," Mikal said in a serious voice, moving away from Jakob and stepping around Sascha's table.

I twisted to find Dmitri staring at Jakob with a look of pure hate. He could pretend to be terrifying all he wanted while fucking me, but the look he gave Jakob was genuine spite. Ironically, it made me wonder if Dmitri liked me more than he let on. All the same, I swallowed hard and inched even closer to Sascha.

"So this is the remarkable pup I've heard so much about," Jakob said, looking me over again while keeping an eye on Mikal and Dmitri.

Sascha turned to study the way Mikal and Dmitri embraced stiffly and fell into conversation before facing Jakob again. He slipped an arm around my shoulders and drew me close. "This is Peter," he said, sending me an affectionate smile.

It was all calculated, I could tell—the possessive touching, the emotion in his smile. He was telling Jakob I was his, but also that I was cared for. For once, I genuinely didn't know how to react. I erred on the side of caution and kept quiet, clinging to Sascha.

Sascha glanced back to Jakob with a frown. "But how did you hear about him? We've barely left the house for the past fortnight."

Jakob chuckled and shook his head. "You made quite a scene in Novoberg when you terrified Duke Royale to retrieve your pup's things. There were more than a few wolves in the crowd that day, listening to your speech and secretly cheering you on."

So wolves walked free in the cities by day after all. I'd been increasingly convinced they must since coming to live in the forest as one of them.

"Everyone from Tesladom to Good Port is talking about the blue-blooded lord who is now pup to a pack of common forest-dwellers," Jakob went on. "You'll have your hands full keeping the gawkers away from him." He stared at me again, as if he, too, couldn't quite believe a nobleman had fallen so low.

"Yes, I'm already fighting them off," Sascha snarled. He turned to a man who had approached his booth, his eyes on me, and barked, "He's not for sale nor for rent."

The man snapped his mouth closed and scurried away.

Jakob seemed to find the whole thing funny. "I hope you know how lucky you are to have landed in the pack of a man as moral and fair as Sascha here," he told me. "Half the pack leaders I know would have you rented out by the hour for all three days of the faire, and they'd go home ten times wealthier for it."

I swallowed, sick at the prospect, tilted my chin up, and answered with a fiery look, "I know how lucky I am."

Jakob's brow went up. "Beautiful, soft-spoken, and feisty as fuck."

"You don't know the half of it," Sascha said with a proud smile for me. He turned back to Jakob. "But I'll slice your balls right off, just as surely as the next man, if you so much as make him uncomfortable."

Jakob laughed and thumped Sascha's shoulders. "You always were a sentimental bastard." He leaned suddenly close to me and whispered in my ear, "Have a care for this one. He needs more minding than he knows."

He straightened and winked at me. I grinned in spite of myself. I liked Jakob. What was more, I trusted him. And I was not swift to trust, not after the life I'd lived.

"Excuse me. I was told you had a prime pup for sale, and I'd hoped—"

"He's not for sale," Sascha and Jakob barked at the man simultaneously.

"Nor for rent," Sascha added.

The man nearly shit himself as he backpedaled and hurried away.

Sascha and Jakob shared a laugh.

"Do you need help manning your booth?" Jakob asked.

Sascha relaxed further, resting a hand on my shoulder. "To be honest, yes, I do," he said. "I've several things I need to purchase before the day is through, and I told Peter here I'd show him what a real faire is all about."

Jakob blinked at me with a look of disbelief. "Don't tell me you've never been to a faire before."

"Not a large one. Novoberg only holds small ones," I answered honestly. "Even then, my father never let me do more than ride through in the family carriage. I was never allowed to mingle with the people or examine the goods."

Jakob tilted his head to the side consideringly. "That doesn't surprise me." His smile returned. "Take your pup and show him around. Show him off, even. I'm sure every wolf prowling this place will be green with envy at the sight of him."

"That's what I'm afraid of," Sascha said with a wary look.

He gave Jakob a few instructions about the prices of his wares. I immediately had the impression that Jakob had played salesman for Sascha in the past. It had me wondering what particular skills Jakob and Mikal had brought to the pack and what the pack had been missing since they were banished. There certainly didn't seem to be any hard feelings between Sascha and Jakob over the whole thing, which reminded me of something I'd heard either Gregor, Ivan, or Sven say about inviting them back.

I wouldn't have minded at all. I wouldn't have if either Jakob or Mikal wanted to fuck me either, but I certainly wasn't going to tell Sascha that. But like Ivan and Sven, Mikal and Jakob seemed very taken with each other.

"Is this faire just for forest-dwellers who live in the area and Berlovians?" I asked Sascha in a hushed voice, not wanting to be overheard, as we walked away from his booth and started to wander the ring of booths around the city wall. I stayed glued to his side, going so far as to grasp his belt with one hand. It made me feel like the worst sort of pet, but it also made me feel protected from the leers and stares that surrounded me. Particularly since I gave up trying to keep my hood over my head and walked with my face in full view.

"Not at all," Sascha laughed. "If you look around, half or more of the attendees and vendors at the faire are city-dwellers from neighboring cities. As long as they're within a day's ride, anyone is welcome to come to a faire. Faires make up a far larger percentage of the frontier's economy than you've probably been told in the cities."

I nodded, believing his answer. The list of things I hadn't learned in my education in the Novoberg palace school could fill a library. I looked around, my curiosity bubbling. The booths we walked through sold everything from food to weaponry, fine silks to bags of grain. In fact, I saw so many foodstuffs for sale that I started to wonder how much of their food supply the cities imported from forest-dwellers. I hadn't seen any farmland at all in the forest, but the forest was extensive—far more extensive than the fields that were enclosed within Novoberg's walls. I suddenly felt stupid for believing that those few fields were enough to feed the population of the cities.

The more we wandered, the more I drooled over bolts of silk and rolls of linen and muslin. Sascha caught me lusting after them and actually bought a few.

"You'll want to make new clothes, I assume," he teased me as he paid for the luxuries.

"I should make a few things for you and the others too," I said, considering some of the plainer fabrics.

Sascha nodded. "Yes, you should. It will save us the trouble of buying ready-made. Which ones do you want for us?"

I pointed to a bolt of rich blue broadcloth, two bolts of muslin in white and cream for shirts, and three other bolts in colors that might actually brighten the pack's dull wardrobes and give us all something more interesting to look at. Sascha laughed the whole time—particularly when I took on a bossy, no-nonsense tone with the vendor, who was trying to bilk Sascha—but indulged me, going so far as to let me purchase an entire case of embroidery thread and enough needles to keep me busy sewing for the rest of the year. He paid for the purchases from a fat sack of coins I hadn't realized he had concealed in his jacket, then sent the booth's runner back to our booths with the purchases. I noticed that booth runners were busy all through the faire and saw more than a few receive fat coins as tips. It must have been a profitable job during the run of the faire.

There was far more to see at the faire than just that. Sascha purchased some honey-drenched pastries for us—he'd long since discovered my love of honey—that we ate while watching a troupe of contortionists. The sweets were delicious, and once mine was gone, I continued to lick and suck honey off my fingers. Until Sascha stopped me abruptly and forced me to hide my still-sticky hands under my cloak. Fully three men nearby were rubbing themselves as they watched me, and one appeared to reach climax before Sascha put a stop to the show.

"I should have charged him for that," Sascha growled as he led me to a small well near to the city gate and sheltered me from view while I washed my hands.

The faire held other wonders besides just food and entertainment. I nearly came undone at the sight of a pen filled with fluffy, blue-eyed puppies near the castle gate.

"Can I get one, Sascha?" I asked. "Please, please?"

Sascha laughed at me. "You realize those are wolf pups, don't you, Peter?"

I snapped my mouth shut, jerking away from the puppies. "But they're adorable."

"They don't stay that way," he said, sending me a particularly sentimental, longing look.

"I may not be an adorable pup for the rest of my life, but I'll always be devilishly charming," I told him, chin tilted up with mock arrogance.

Sascha laughed louder, pulling me closer and walking on with his arm tight around me.

That was a wiser move than I thought at first. We

drew an astounding amount of attention as we walked through the faire. I became aware of at least a dozen men who were following us, gaping at me, though they tried not to draw our notice as they did. Not all of them had the same sort of lustful glance that the ones who had offered to buy or rent me had. Some just seemed astounded. There was even a woman among them who bore a distinct resemblance to an old maid my father had once thrown out of the palace for a reason I had never discovered. In fact, as we continued on our rounds, I was certain it was her.

"I think some of these people know me," I whispered to Sascha as we approached a stretch of booths that held common household wares.

"They probably do," Sascha said, glancing over his shoulder with a scowl and tightening his arm around my shoulder. "Or, at least, they might know *of* you, if what Jakob says about the rumors of our scene at your father's palace are true. You're a celebrity."

"I'm not sure I like that," I grumbled.

"I don't like it either," Sascha confessed.

He purchased a few more things for the house, sending runners back to our booths once they were paid for—everything from axe heads to chicken feed to a broom. Faires happened every few weeks in the warmer months, so it was like a trip to market where Sascha needed to pick up the things we needed to get by until the next one.

As we reached the far side of the city wall, I spotted

the wealthy man who had offered to purchase me overseeing a collection of booths selling the same sorts of common items that half the other booths sold, only more of them. A shiver of attraction zipped through me. I counted fully a dozen other men who were clearly under his command. He glanced enviously at me, rubbing his mouth, then turned a resentful look on Sascha.

"Who is he?" I whispered. "He asked if you knew who he was when you turned down his offer for me."

Sascha huffed. "His name is Magnus, and he's the leader of a pack of fifty men, or so rumor would have it."

"Fifty?" My eyes practically bulged out of my head.

"I told you some of the packs were like villages," Sascha said. "His is one of the larger, and more prosperous, ones."

"Fifty men," I said in a faint voice. "And I thought five was a challenge."

Sascha laughed, but with less humor than before. "If I had to guess, I would say that any pup under Magnus's authority would be saved for Magnus himself and for those who earn his favor."

"I'm not sure if that would be better or worse," I said, eyes round.

I was about to speculate more when a sharp, anxious call of, "Peter! Peter Royale!" came from a booth we had just passed.

I jumped at the sound of my name, immediately on the alert. As it turned out, I had good reason to be alarmed. I whipped around to see who had called out to me, but what I saw instead was a large cage—like the kind I'd once seen at a traveling zoo that had brought exotic animals to Novoberg—filled with naked men. And not in a nice way. They were filthy and most of them were emaciated, and their hands were bound with shackles.

A barker of some sort stood to one side, calling out to everyone passing. "Slaves here! Finest slaves from all corners of the frontier lands. Strong backs! Fine bums! We've even got a few choice pups just waiting for a pack to give them a home. Come and see! Come and see!"

I reeled away from the cage. Sascha caught me and held me steady, wrapping both arms around me as if to show the barker and everyone else who might be curious nearby that I was most definitely taken and protected.

But what shocked me nearly to the point of losing control of my bowels were two of the young men near the front of the cage. I knew them.

"Peter! Peter Royale!" Lord Oscar Beiste called out to me, a wild and frantic look in his eyes. His younger brother, Lord Neil stood next to him, shaking and weeping and trying in vain to cover his genitals with his hands. "Peter!" Oscar cried out again. "You have to tell these people who we are. You have to get us out of here."

13

The sight of Oscar and Neil was so unnerving that I shrank back into Sascha's arms as if I were the one trapped in the cage with flocks of men hovering near, eyeing me like pastries they wanted to take a bite of. It was just short of three weeks since Oscar had tormented me along with my brothers at Father's formal supper and Neil had shrunk away from me, the two of us unable to help each other. How they had managed to end up captured and naked in a cage at a faire in Berlova in that time was an utter mystery. Then again, they might have been wondering how I could end up with a broad man over six feet tall, his arms wrapped possessively around me, as if it were a mystery as well.

"Shut up, you!" The barker shouted at Oscar. "No one wants to hear your whining."

"Do you know him?" Sascha asked. His breath on my

ear was a comfort, and the solidity of his form caging me calmed me down.

I nodded sharply. "The one who called out to me is Lord Oscar Beiste. The shivering one beside him is his brother, Lord Neil."

"They're noblemen?" a man standing nearby who had overheard my comment said, his eyes going wide.

"That's what I said, isn't it?" the barker snapped.

Claims of nobility must have been commonly made by men like the barker as they tried to unload their wares. I had the feeling those claims weren't usually true.

"Peter, you have to save us," Oscar demanded, trying to look dignified as he stood straighter, his too-thin body on full display.

Out of the corner of my eye, I noticed Sascha scowl. "He's a bit full of himself, isn't he."

I drew in a deep breath, weighing the consequences of what I was about to do. I told myself that Oscar deserved it, that he was a colossal prick, and that he'd had something like this coming for years. I wasn't as certain that Neil deserved his fate, though. Before speaking, I considered my words, then sighed. I was an angel and a devil, after all. I had my good side, and I had my dark side.

"Lord Oscar used to torment me along with my brothers," I said, turning toward Sascha and meeting his eyes with a look meant to communicate what I wanted to happen.

"Understood," Sascha said. He glanced around, as if looking for someone in particular.

I rested a hand on his arm as he went to raise it. "Lord Neil is all right, though," I added. "He's a bit of a coward, but he never raised a hand against me. In fact, I wouldn't be surprised if he was more like me than I've given him credit for in the past."

I realized the truth of my words as I spoke them. I didn't know for certain—I couldn't know, as it was something one didn't speak of—but it occurred to me that Neil could have shied away from me at supper because he was afraid of being found out as the same kind of man I was.

Sascha nodded, then went back to searching the crowd. He caught the attention of the wealthy pack leader who had tried to purchase me earlier and waved to him.

Perhaps predictably, Magnus dropped what he was doing and hurried through the crowd, shoving people out of his way, to reach us.

"Have you changed your mind?" he asked breathlessly as he met us near the slave cages.

"Not on your life," Sascha said. "But my pup has just informed me he knows two of the men in the cages."

Magnus frowned. "Don't waste my time." He started to turn away, but Sascha grabbed him by the arm and turned him back to the cage.

"That one who is glowering, near the front, and the one beside him, the one who is crying and trying to shield himself, are noblemen," Sascha said.

Magnus scoffed. "A likely story used to sell rotten goods."

He tried to turn away again, but this time, I stopped him with, "I swear it on my life. They are Lord Oscar and Lord Neil Beiste of Novoberg. I've known them my entire life."

Whether it was the shock of me, a pup, speaking, my high-pitched, delicate voice, the borderline flirtatious look I fixed him with, or whether Magnus knew I was the son of Duke Royale, like everyone else seemed to know, and believed me, he turned back and gave Oscar and Neil another look. I wanted to explain more, to attempt to determine both Oscar and Neil's fates, but I sensed it would be bad for me to speak. Instead, I glanced up to Sascha.

Sascha seemed to understand. "The glowering one is a right ass, according to my pup," he told Magnus. "He made my pup's life miserable for years because of who he is, how he is."

"I see." The corner of Magnus's lip twitched malevolently.

"The weeping one is nicer and might be our sort. My pup isn't certain, but he thinks that might be the case. If true, I think the poor young lad could do with some protecting." Sascha nodded to Neil in the cage. "Clean him up, make him feel at home, and there's no telling what sort of a prize you'd have on your hands. I shouldn't be the only one with a blue-blooded pup."

"An interesting tip." Magnus stroked his chin, considering Neil. "I might have to owe you for this one, Sascha Kerensky. I'll let you know in the future." He looked at me as well and nodded in gratitude.

Magnus nodded to Sascha as well, then walked on toward the barker. Sascha drew me on, out of the way, but we stayed close enough to watch as money exchanged hands and two of the barker's men opened the cage to extract Oscar and Neil. It was a gruesome scene to witness, as several of the other slaves attempted to escape while the cage door was open. They were pushed and beaten back mercilessly. Blood was spilled as noses were cracked, and the wailing of the men who failed to escape after the cage door was shut again chilled me to the bones.

"Peter! You've saved us, Peter," Oscar called to me. "You've—"

Oscar's hopes were dashed and he was silenced as Magnus slapped him across the face. "You belong to me now, boy," Magnus said. He gestured to some of his men, who ran forward. "Take this one to work in the fields," he said. "I don't care what else you do with him." The men growled and licked their lips. "Take this one to my caravan tent," he instructed another man, pushing Neil toward him. "Give him a bath and as much food as he requires. Cut his hair while you're at it. It's too long for my tastes. Find a nice robe for him, and prepare some tea for when I return to my tent at the end of the day."

A strange feeling twisted through my gut, especially when Neil glanced at me, question and terror in his eyes.

I nodded to him, standing as straight as I dared with so many people looking on. I held his eyes for as long as I could, attempting to communicate that whatever happened to him next was my doing, for good or for ill. Although, honestly, how the rest of his life turned out was entirely up to him.

"I think it's time we return to our booths," Sascha said judiciously, sliding an arm around my shoulders and heading back the way we'd come.

By the time we reached our booths, my nerves had steadied a bit, but I still felt as though something momentous had happened.

"So the faire wasn't to your liking after all?" Jakob asked, relinquishing his spot behind the booth to Sascha. A good portion of Sascha's wares had been sold while we were gone—enough to make me wonder if there would be anything left to sell on the morrow.

I still didn't feel like speaking to anyone who wasn't a pack member, even though I liked Jakob, so I glanced up at Sascha.

"He liked the faire, all right," Sascha answered, sending a look to Ivan and Sven, who were watching from across the aisle. "He ran into a few friends."

"Friends?" Dmitri snorted, evidently paying attention to us as well. The only one who wasn't paying attention was Gregor, but that was likely because he was treating a man for what looked like gout behind his booth while others lined up for his services as well. Mikal was nowhere to be seen.

"A pair of young lordlings of Peter's acquaintance," Sascha answered. "In the possession of one of the slave masters."

Jakob let out a long, low whistle. "That must have been a shock indeed." He glanced sympathetically at me.

"They weren't friends," I said, barely audible. Or, at least, Oscar wasn't. I still felt a guilty sort of wistfulness about Neil. I trusted my hard expression to convey the rest of my feelings.

Jakob looked both surprised and impressed. "And what, pray tell, was the fate of these two not-friends?" He glanced to Sascha.

"They are now the property of Magnus Gravlock," Sascha replied with a self-satisfied grin. "One as laborer, one as pup."

Jakob glanced back to me, "Remind me not to cross you, Sascha's pup. Ever." There was more seriousness in his voice than his teasing grin conveyed.

"Where is Mikal?" Sascha asked after quickly selling a set of bowls to a woman who appeared to be a city-dweller.

"He went off to purchase a few things we need," Jakob answered as he went to stand by Gregor's booth, selling a few bottles of herbs while Gregor tended the sick. "I only hope we have enough to cover all necessities." He sent Sascha a particular look.

Sascha let out a weary sigh and glanced across to Dmitri. Dmitri was busy haggling over the price of one of his larger, finer pelts. "Let me know what you need and I'll slip it to you when he's not looking."

Jakob huffed a laugh. "You'll have to make sure Mikal doesn't see either. He's fired up about the two of us fending for ourselves now."

That made Sascha scowl. "And are you fending for yourselves?"

Jakob suddenly looked exhausted. "It was a hard winter. We're lucky we finished constructing the hut before the first snowfall, and we were fortunate to manage a few weeks' labor for a brewer in Berlova." He nodded at the city wall. "But there were a few unpleasantly lean weeks before more work was to be had tilling fields."

"I'm sorry," Sascha grumbled, pausing to sell a large wooden serving platter. "I should have seen to it that you had more when I...." His shoulders sagged as he let his words drop.

I moved closer to him, resting a hand on the small of his back. I made it look like a meaningless gesture, careful to keep my expression vacant and sweet for those looking on or passing by, but I could tell by the way Sascha's back muscles flinched and the way he stood straighter that he'd taken the gesture as the comfort it was meant to be. By the look of things, Jakob also recognized what he was seeing. His exhausted expression turned to a sly grin.

"You're welcome to join us for tonight's feast," Sascha went on, perking up a bit. "And to pitch your tents near ours. For obvious reasons, I plan to keep close to the wagons and to avoid the revels. I know you and Mikal don't go in for that sort of thing these days either."

Jakob laughed. "Our days of hard reveling are long behind us, but we wouldn't say no to a little light celebration." I had the feeling he was including Sascha in his statement as well as himself and Mikal.

A surge of buyers ended the conversation. I was pleased to see that Gregor's medicines and concoctions were in as much demand as he'd hinted they were back when I first started helping him make labels. I'd thought the prices he was charging were exorbitant, but his bottles flew out of his booth with lightning speed. As the faire day seemed to be winding to a close, every single mixture and tincture Gregor had brought with him had sold out, and it was only the first day of the faire. Even the more dangerous concoctions that Jakob had handed off in deals designed to make it look like neither party was actually talking to the other were gone. I could only imagine the money Gregor had made in one day.

"That will be the end of that," Gregor said, receiving payment from his last patient of the day. I'd heard him make arrangements to meet with others the next day by appointment. He would travel to them instead of having patients line up for him. "Well," he went on, parceling some of his money into a pouch around his waist. "I'm off to the revels."

I opened my mouth to ask Sascha what the revels were, but before I could manage the question, a pair of men swooped in and claimed Gregor's booth. They unloaded crates and barrels of jars and bottles of all sizes. What surprised me was that they didn't even have to put up a shingle or post prices before the booth was swarmed with men waving money at them.

"Grab a few before they're all sold out," Sascha told Jakob, handing over his entire purse of coins.

Jakob rushed to do as Sascha had instructed, managing to purchase an entire, small crate of jars from one of the men before it could be unloaded onto the table.

"What in heaven's name is that about?" I whispered, edging closer to Sascha.

Sascha glanced from Jakob to the now swamped booth to me and started to laugh. Not only that, his face colored bashfully in a way that had my blood racing. "They sell ointment," Sascha said in a low, sheepish voice. "You know," he added significantly.

I blinked, then caught his meaning. Then I burst into a loud laugh that drew more attention than I needed. So much so that I covered my head completely with my hood—which was also convenient as I continued to laugh uproariously. The men beside us sold lubrication. I hadn't stopped to question where the jars both Sascha and Dmitri kept on their bedside tables came from, but now I knew. No wonder they were in such high demand.

Perhaps it was the stress of the day or the wonder of the faire, but I remained in a giddy mood even after Sascha, Dmitri, and Ivan packed up their remaining goods and returned everything to the wagon. By then, all of the booths were closing up for the day and the activity of the faire moved to an outer circle, around where the wagons were parked and young people were paid to care for the forest-dwellers' animals. I noticed that very few young *men* were tending the animals. It was mostly young women my age and girls. That could only be out of a fear that the young men might never make it back inside the city walls. The atmosphere around the wagons was cheerful and light as fires were lit and food was cooked and served.

Jakob and Mikal joined our pack for the supper Ivan prepared over the open fire Dmitri and Mikal had made near where our tents were set up. I was happy to have them there and eager to learn more about them, not to mention to glean whether there was any chance of them rejoining the pack.

"What are your plans for after the faire?" Sascha asked Mikal, drawing me to sit on the ground between his legs as he sat on a short stump behind me. I knew better than to argue against being caged between his thighs as the meal got started, or to complain when he served my food. If I'd been unnerved by the number of men inquiring after me during the daylight, the number who seemed to lurk interestedly around our camp was terrifying.

Mikal and Jakob exchanged a look, then Mikal shrugged. "To continue on with life," he said. "To find enough food to eat and to keep a roof over our heads." He glanced covertly to Dmitri.

Dmitri was pretending not to listen to his brother, or any of the conversation, as he rushed through his supper. The only indication I had that he was listening at all was the short scowl he sent Mikal.

"I rather like the life of leisure," Jakob said, smiling at Mikal as though he'd hung the stars. He rubbed Mikal's shoulder. The two men were clearly deeply in love.

I finished the skewer of roasted meat and vegetables I was eating as if that were the most interesting thing in the world, but in reality, I watched every nuance of what was going on around me. Dmitri obviously cared for his brother, or at least felt possessive of him, and being separated from Mikal made him bitter. The fleeting thought that he took out that bitterness on me when he dragged me into his bedroom crossed my mind. Mikal cared for his brother as well, if the sad looks he sent Dmitri were any indication. But it was a hopeless, frustrated sort of sadness, like Mikal had given up any chance of a true reconciliation. Dmitri and Jakob clearly hated each other. It didn't take a shrewd observer to see that.

The one person whose reaction to the dynamic I couldn't see at all was Sascha's. Not while sitting between his legs, my back to him. I tried to gauge his reaction by the tension in his thighs and torso, but Sascha had been tense all day. Tense and protective of me.

The other clear emotional thread I was able to pick up from the stilted supper—in which my pack shared news and gossip from the last year and asked about men they all knew but I didn't—was that Mikal and Jakob wanted to come home. And everyone but Dmitri wanted them home as well. As the meal wound down, I found myself contemplating ways that it might be possible to accomplish that goal and make everyone happy.

"Well, that's enough for me," Dmitri said, tossing his empty skewer into a basket Ivan had laid out near the fire. He stood and stretched with a keen grin. "I'm off to join the revels."

"Hold up for a minute or two and I'll join you," Gregor said, hurrying to finish his food.

Dmitri laughed dismissively as he crossed to the small crate of ointment Sascha had purchased earlier and helped himself to a jar. "I'm not waiting for you, old man. You'll scare all the best ones away."

My brow shot up, but Gregor laughed at the jab. Dmitri headed off on his own as Gregor tossed his skewer in the basket and stood. "I'm sure there will be plenty left," he said with a bright look in his eyes.

"Er, Sascha, I'm assuming you're not going to participate this year?" Ivan asked, peeking at Sascha and me with an impish grin.

"Not on your life," Sascha laughed, resting a hand on my shoulder.

"Then you wouldn't mind cleaning up here, would you?" Ivan's mouth twitched mischievously. "We sort of, er, made arrangements with a fresh young thing that stopped by to buy some tarts while you and Peter were exploring the faire." He exchanged a wink with Sven.

"By all means," Sascha laughed.

Mikal and Jakob exchanged a look as well and stood. "I think we'll see what's out there for the having too, if it's all the same," Jakob said.

I watched them finish up their meals, toss their skewers into the basket, gather a few personal belongings and jars from the crate, then wander off with high spirits and spring in their steps, feeling oddly aroused by the whole thing.

Once we were alone, I turned to Sascha and said, "It's an orgy, isn't it. They're all rushing off to be part of an orgy."

Sascha laughed, the same arousal in his eyes. "It's a bit more than that." He stood, nudging me to get up and help him sort out our camp.

"A whole series of orgies?" I suggested.

Sascha grinned, looking positively coy as he gathered up remnants of uneaten food and the basket of skewers. "Wolves live in small packs, for the most part, or on their own," he explained with a shrug. "Faires are the perfect opportunity to get together to let off a bit of steam and to soothe the ache of loneliness."

My mood was still slightly giddy from earlier, and I snorted with laughter at the idea. I set to work helping Sascha tidy the camp—although he put his foot down and forbid me from helping him set up the tent we would sleep in, right up against the shelter of the wagon. That meant there was nothing for me to do but sit back on the stump Sascha had used as a chair during supper and observe the strange new world of wolves around me.

I could see at least a dozen camps from where I sat. The sky was darkening quickly, which made everyone's campfire stand out in the night. They also illuminated the activity around the wagons. Somewhere in the distance, a band of musicians had started playing. The laughter of men rang out from the area of the music and other camps as well. It was a cheery and uplifting scene, unlike anything I'd ever found myself in before. Parties and revels at the palace had always been formal, stilted affairs, where everyone was there to be seen instead of to enjoy themselves.

And the wolves of the forest were most certainly there to enjoy themselves.

A sound caught my attention that wasn't singing or laughing or music. I turned my head to seek it out and flinched, heat rushing to my face, when I spotted two men leaning up against the side of a wagon only a few dozen yards from me. The larger of the two was thoroughly engaged in fucking the man in front of him while they both stood. Both made sounds of pleasure that matched anything I'd ever heard. I couldn't bring myself to look away until their movements turned fast, then subsided altogether as one, then the other man cried out. They sagged against the side of the wagon for a moment, then peeled away from each other. After that, they shook hands, shared a laugh and a pat on each other's backs as they pulled up their trousers, then each walked on in different directions as though all they'd done was say hello.

The larger of the two men passed by our camp and did a double-take when he spotted me staring at him.

"Is he good for a go?" he asked Sascha in a disbelieving voice. "I'll be ready again in twenty minutes or so."

"No," Sascha growled at the man. "And if you want your cock to remain attached to your body, you'll walk away and not look back." He pulled the knife out of his belt and showed it to the man. And a few others who were inching neared.

The large man held up his hands and walked on, as if he didn't particularly care. I would have bet he'd find another willing partner in a matter of minutes. Twenty minutes, to be exact. The other men who had seemed interested in me rushed on to greener pastures as well.

Once the whole episode was over, I turned toward Sascha and asked, "Did I just see what I think I just—"

My mouth stayed open as I gaped past Sascha to see a naked man on all fours a few campsites down. He groaned as he sucked off a man on his knees in front of him while a third man fucked him from behind. All three were thoroughly and vocally enjoying themselves.

Sascha twisted, unconcerned, to see what I was gaping at. When he spotted them, he laughed. "Keep watching," he said with a wry grin as he moved to pound the last tent stake into the ground. "You're likely to get quite an education if you do."

"Are they just going to—" I stopped once more, my eyes going wide as a fourth man walked unapologetically up to the man who was being sucked off, grabbed him around the waist, bent him forward, and unceremoniously thrust into him. I wasn't sure if the men even knew each other, but the man who was now being fucked went right along with it, submitting and clearly enjoying himself. They were close enough that I had a full view when come spurted out of his cock.

"Revels," Sascha said, humor thick in his voice.

"I'll say," I answered him with wide eyes.

In fact, the more I looked around, the more there was to see. Supper was definitely over throughout the campsite, and more men than not were stripping naked to enjoy each other. In every manner I could have imagined. In pairs and in groups that were ever changing. There didn't seem to be any rules about what was going on, only pleasure. At least everyone seemed to be enjoying themselves. I even spotted a young man who had to be a pup being handed around to several men in succession. Thankfully, the pup seemed more than happy to be the object of everyone's attention. Though when a short line of aroused men handling themselves lined up to fuck him in succession as he bent forward over a laughing man on his hands and knees, I had to look away.

"It is consensual, isn't it?" I asked Sascha with a wince. "For everyone, I mean."

Sascha's amused expression turned circumspect. "I wish I could tell you it always was," he said, finishing with the tent and coming over to offer a hand to help me to stand. "I'm sure there's a fair amount of rape going on as well. Though if it makes you feel better, the punishments that will be handed out in the morning will be severe."

"What do you mean?" I asked, standing and inching closer to him—particularly since I'd once again garnered interest.

"Don't even think of it," Sascha growled at the men who tried to approach us. "He's mine, and I'm not sharing." That chased the men away enough for Sascha to say, "The penalty for any man proven to have raped someone is removal of a testicle. And not with a blade either. The removal is accomplished by smashing between two stones."

I flinched hard and leaned into him.

"Let's just say that it's rare for a man to commit the crime twice," Sascha said with a smirk.

"Is that why men are backing away from us without putting up a fight?" I asked, feeling relieved.

"That's exactly why they're backing away," Sascha said. He moved toward the tent's flap, tugging me with him. "And now I suggest we retire for the evening so that we don't tempt anyone to risk punishment. You're worth losing a ball for."

"That sounds like a very good idea," I said hoarsely, in spite of the odd compliment.

Before we made it to the tent flap, though, I flinched in surprise to find two of the men at the camp no more than a few yards from ours had joined the revels themselves, but in a way I hadn't even thought of before. One of them lay on his back with his hands behind his head, his face transported with pleasure. His partner straddled his hips and was thoroughly enjoying fucking himself on his partner's cock. My brow flew up so fast and hard I thought my eyebrows might come right off.

Sascha saw my reaction and laughed as he pushed me ahead of him into the tent. "I have no objections whatsoever if you want to fuck that way," he said, his voice low and hungry.

"What, here?" I gaped incredulously at him as I ducked into the darkness of the tent. "Tonight? With an entire field of men all around us?"

Sascha shrugged and dropped to his knees, reaching for the bedroll he must have put in the tent when I was watching the activity around us. "It isn't as though anyone will notice one more couple fucking each other senseless."

I continued to stare at him as though he'd taken leave of his senses. "I absolutely will not engage in any such activity in what amounts, for the most part, public." I unhooked the clasp of my cloak, relieved to finally be able to take it off. I was boiling hot for several reasons.

Sascha spread out the bedroll, then scooted toward me, starting in on the buttons of my jacket. "And what if I demanded it?" he asked, his voice vibrating through me. I couldn't help but be aroused, In spite of what I perceived of the danger of that state.

"You wouldn't," I challenged him, one eyebrow raised. Even though there was barely any light in the tent.

Only that which was reflected from the campfires around us.

"You don't know that," he went on, peeling my jacket off and moving on to my waistcoat and shirt.

I slapped his hands to stop him from doing more than tugging the hem of my shirt out of my trousers. "Stop. I'm not undressing all the way in a camp full of aroused men looking for fuck partners for the night. Or the next half hour."

Sascha chuckled, removing his own clothes instead. "I had no idea you were such a prude, Peter."

"I'm not," I snapped back. "But I have my limits."

"And I love testing those limits." Sascha discarded his shirt, then pulled me into his bare chest for a kiss. I didn't dare tell him that he couldn't hold a candle to Dmitri when it came to testing my limits.

His kiss was intoxicating, but I fought to keep my senses about me. "We can't go fucking where anyone passing will hear me," I said, hoping he knew how conspicuous I was in the throes of passion.

"You'll just have to be quiet," Sascha murmured, continuing his glorious assault on my mouth.

"I don't want to," I managed between kisses.

His hand reached into my trousers, stroking my hard cock and caressing my balls. I let out a moan. "Liar," he whispered against my ear, then nibbled on my earlobe.

His hand continued to pleasure me as he moved on to my neck. Somehow, he managed to untie the scarf I wore and drop it to the side so he could add another mark to the constellation already there. I braced my hands against his chest, intending to push away, but the way he fondled me shattered any resistance. It didn't help a damn thing that, all around the tent, the sounds of groans, cries of pleasure, and fucking were growing louder.

"You need to stop unless you want me to come right now," I gasped all of a sudden as the tell-tale signs of orgasm started to creep up on me.

Sascha immediately pulled his hand away, leaving me aching and disappointed. "We wouldn't want that," he said. I could just make out the teasing glint in his eyes. "I said I'd suck you off tonight, and that's exactly what I intend to do." He reached for my trousers, unfastening them all the way and tugging them down my thighs so that my straining, leaking cock jumped free. "You can keep your shirt on, if you'd like," he added with a wink.

"Bastard," I muttered, trying not to grin, as I fell back on the bedroll and removed my shoes so that I could yank my trousers off. Sascha finished undressing as I did, grinning like a fiend the whole time. There was just enough light for me to see his thick cock spring straight up as he shucked his breeches. "I'm beginning to think there's something wrong with you, you're so randy all the time. Perhaps you should see Gregor for some sort of treatment."

"I don't need treatment," Sascha said, helping me pull my shirt off over my head, then shoving me playfully to my back. "I just need you. As often as possible."

He covered my body with his, slanting his mouth

hungrily over mine. Our tongues twined as we teased each other's mouths. In spite of my protests, I was as hungry for Sascha as ever, digging my fingertips into the muscles of his back and wrapping my legs around his hips. He had me breathless and swimming in arousal in no time. The chorus of sex outside the tent only heightened my feelings.

"Every man at this faire wants you," Sascha growled, kissing his way down my neck and chest to tease one of my nipples with his tongue. "But I'm the man who gets to have you." He pushed my leg off of his thigh, prompting me to spread my legs wide. "Because you're mine, only mine, forever mine."

It was the wrong time to point out the semantics of the fact that I was technically Dmitri's too. But Dmitri wasn't there. He was probably off fucking as many men as he could before passing out, whereas Sascha was there with me—body and soul—kissing his way across my smooth belly.

In spite of swearing to myself that I would swallow my tongue and not make a sound, I cried out with undiluted passion as Sascha took my cock in his mouth and swallowed it deep in one movement. I tilted my head back, fisting my hands in his hair, as he pulled up slowly and kissed and suckled my head. He was so wildly good at what he was doing that I undulated in time to his swallowing, crying out in a high voice with abandon. The noise I made was probably drawing a crowd of men who were getting themselves off on the sound of me alone, but instead of embarrassing me, I found that image incredibly erotic.

I knew I wouldn't last long, but I was surprised by the force with which I came, deep in Sascha's mouth. He groaned as though I were the one getting him off and continued to move on me and swallow until my body lost all strength. He finally let me go with a wet pop and slithered his way up my body to rut against my hip, rubbing against my sensitive cock and balls.

"You are remarkable, Peter," he panted, reaching for one of my hands and drawing it between us so I could help finish him off. His mouth crashed over mine as he stifled a groan, but he was panting too hard to kiss for long. "You undo me. I'm desperate for you all the time. Your body is sinful, and your mouth is sharp as a whipcrack."

His words went straight to my soul, filling me as surely as his cum would have if he'd been penetrating me. Which I'm certain he would have done if he wasn't already so close to coming that there wasn't time to seek out any ointment.

"Oh," he groaned, moving faster. I closed my hand more fully around him so that he had something more to thrust into. "Oh, Peter. I love you. I—oh!" He came with a hard jerk, spilling warmth across my hand and belly. That combined with his confession of love would have made me come a second time, if I'd been able to.

"I love you too," I panted. And in that moment, I

meant it. Whether I would still feel that transported with sentiment in the morning remained to be seen.

"I love you," Sascha repeated drowsily, his body losing all tension as he sagged over me. I liked his weight and would have wrapped my arms and legs around him to hold him there longer, but he rolled to the side and used the last of his strength to tuck us together inside the bedroll.

I closed my eyes and smiled as I settled against him, our bodies tangled together. Outside, the sounds of men moaning and rutting continued, but it might as well have been crickets on a summer night for all I cared.

14

The camp I awoke to just after dawn the next morning was very different from the one I'd fallen asleep to. It was nearly silent, for one. If, by silence, you included the sounds of songbirds, a dog or two barking in the distance, a few, muffled shuffles and the clank of pots, and indistinct snoring from far and wide. I was instantly alert as soon as I woke all the same. I didn't feel I could afford to let my guard down by languishing in Sascha's embrace, like I did when we were home. Particularly since Sascha already lay alert and tense in the bedroll with me.

"I was about to wake you," he said, sitting and pulling me with him, then kissing me. "It's safer if you're up, washed, dressed, and cloaked before too many other people are up."

"Agreed," I said, though I was in no hurry to move away from his naked form. We'd only been together for three weeks, but it felt like a lifetime. And it felt like hardly enough time at all. I couldn't get enough of the sight of his bare torso in the scant light that made it through the tent's canvas, or his half-erect prick resting against his leg. But it would have been madness to indulge in any of it.

All the same, I remembered the words we'd spoken to each other the night before. I checked my feelings, disappointed to find that I wasn't nearly as certain of my love in the morning light as I had been with my cock down his throat. I leaned into him, kissing him soundly all the same. Just because I didn't feel it like a raging fire in the middle of a practical and potentially dangerous situation didn't mean the same tender love wasn't inside of me. I wanted to be in love with Sascha, I just didn't know if I could afford to be.

He smiled and closed his arms tenderly around me when I tried to move away, drawing our kiss out for a few more, heady seconds. It was clear to me his affections hadn't diminished at all. If fantasy affections even could diminish. When he finally let me go and I pivoted away to search through the satchel of clean clothes we'd bought, he smacked my ass with a smile.

"Make sure you don't look too appealing today," he teased me. "You're like honey to these flies, and I don't want anyone else touching my honey."

I gave him exactly the sort of sultry, bashful, submissive look I knew he wanted before reaching for the satchel.

The others weren't exactly up when we exited the tent, but they were strewn and draped around the camp. I nearly missed a step and did a double-take to find Gregor asleep over a log, naked from the waist down, his ass red and crusted with the remnants of his revelry.

"That's not a sight that inspires one to have an appetite for breakfast," I commented to Sascha in a wry voice.

He laughed, threw an arm around me to draw me against him, and kissed my head.

The others weren't in any more decent of a state. Ivan was already up and grinding coffee beans next to a fire where he'd set a pot to boil, but Sven lay asleep on the grass beside the fire, completely naked. His flaccid prick was red from overuse. Mikal and Jakob were at least under a blanket on the other side of the campfire, but a third man that I didn't recognize was asleep between them.

"Don't they have any sense of decorum or modesty?" I muttered, sneering probably more than I should as I kept hard on Sascha's heels as he crossed to Ivan at the fire.

"Lighten up," he told me with a teasing grin. "It's not often that we wolves get a chance to really let loose."

"The least everyone could do is let loose in the privacy of their own tent and not lie around with everything hanging out first thing in the morning," I insisted. Sascha laughed and shook his head as he checked what Ivan was doing. "You would never be so gauche."

Ivan laughed out loud at my statement. "I wouldn't be so sure of that. You should have seen him at the Seymchan faire last July."

"Ivan," Sascha warned him.

Ivan cleared his throat and focused on dumping the ground coffee beans into the boiling pot.

"No, I want to hear this." I grinned from ear to ear, glancing to Sascha with a gloating, imperious look.

"No, you don't," Sascha mumbled, sulking away from the fire and drawing me with him.

I glanced over my shoulder to Ivan with a look that dared him to spill the story.

Ivan threw caution to the wind and said, "This one had far too much of some very strong mead. He stripped naked, propped himself against a stack of barrels, and called out to every passing buck to come ride him. Legend has it, he set a record for number of times he came up someone's ass in one night. Eight, I believe it was?"

I snorted so hard I started coughing and had to cover my mouth. "Sascha, you depraved whore," I ribbed him.

Sascha was as bright red as the logs on the fire. "It wasn't eight. And I honestly don't remember the whole thing. Much," he added in a mumble. He looked beautifully embarrassed as he sat on his stump from the night before and drew me down to sit on his lap.

I would have been appalled at the indignity of sitting on him that way, but I was too busy laughing to care. "I should have known you are the sort to fuck as many men as possible in one night."

"I'm not," he told me with a flat look. "That mead was stronger than I'd anticipated."

"Doesn't alcohol loosen inhibitions?" I asked, still teasing. "Doesn't it remove the impediments that would prevent us from doing something we know to be wrong, but that we want to do?"

"Shut up, pup," he scolded me.

I let him get away with the slight. I was too giddy, knowing that Sascha was just as human as the rest of us, to care. Perhaps he wouldn't take it so badly if I wanted to experiment and experience other men after all.

The others awoke gradually. Gregor cussed with embarrassment at the shape he was in and staggered off to stick his head—and probably his ass—in a barrel of wash-water several camps down. Mikal and Jakob awoke and said goodbye to their friend for the night—who was astonishingly young, or at least looked it.

"You shared someone's pup last night?" Sascha asked the two of them—asked them the question on the tip of my tongue—as they cleaned up, dressed, and joined us by the fire.

"We're very generous with each other," Jakob said.

Sascha shook his head. "You'd better have a care for your balls."

"Don't worry," Mikal said. "We paid a good price for the pleasure."

I arched one eyebrow, especially when Sascha sent

Jakob a stern look. I had the feeling Sascha was actually the one who had paid for it. I wanted to ask if the young man had been a willing part of the transaction, but it seemed like an unforgivably rude question. And considering that the youth had stayed the night with them and taken his time gathering his things to go, I figured it was all good—and profitable—fun for him.

Sven eventually woke up and cleaned up as well, but it wasn't until all of us were seated around the fire, enjoying a rough breakfast, that Dmitri returned. He had two friends with him—one balding and missing an eye, but still young and muscular, and another with sharp bone structure and hair so blond it was nearly white. All three looked as though they were still slightly intoxicated.

"There he is, lads," Dmitri said, nodding to me. "That's the gem of a pup I told you about."

The way the other two looked at me killed any feeling of warmth or mirth I had. I huddled closer to Sascha.

Sascha, in turn, circled his arms around me in a show of possession. "Gunter, Axel," he nodded to Dmitri's two friends.

I wanted to ask if he knew the men, but not only was that obvious, I suddenly had no desire whatsoever to open my mouth.

"I thought you were lying," the bald one, Gunter, laughed, leering at me. "I mean, I always assumed your cozy little pack would find a pup eventually, but you're right. That one's a wonder."

I didn't like the way he talked about our pack. It sounded as though he was laughing at us for being cozy.

"The things I could do with him," the blond one, Axel, growled. His voice was much rougher than I'd assumed it would be by the chiseled, god-like look of him —as though his throat had sustained an injury.

"He's not for sale, nor for rent," Sascha said in a forceful voice, looking at Dmitri rather than the two other men.

I swallowed hard. Never in a million years would I have thought Dmitri could so much as entertain the idea of selling me. I still wasn't sure that was what he was thinking as he shrugged and moved closer to the fire.

"Thanks for the night of fun and debauchery, lads," he told his friends. "We'll catch up again soon."

He was dismissing his friends, but they were slow to leave. The two of them continued to stare at me, and Gunter leaned over to whisper in Axel's ear. Axel's face split in a toothy grin, and he whispered something back.

Something about the exchange left me shaking. Sascha obviously felt it. "Move along," he told the men, a threatening look in his eyes.

"Sorry, we were just resting a spell and talking about how to spend our money this afternoon," Gunter said in a somewhat mocking tone.

"You can do that elsewhere," Sascha told them.

The two sent him scathing looks, then walked on. When Sascha turned his furious frown on Dmitri, Dmitri just sighed.

"You've no reason to be so rude to my friends," he said.

"I'm not sure you need friends like that, brother," Mikal told him. Every one of our pack had grown grave, censuring Dmitri with their looks, but Mikal's was the scowl that seemed to have an effect on Dmitri.

"I'm sorry if you don't approve," he said, spitting his words slightly. "Next time, I'll have anyone I choose to spend a night reveling with run by you first."

"You would do well to do that," Mikal said in a serious voice.

Dmitri let out a bitter laugh and shook his head. He turned to me and asked, "What did you think of my friends, pup?"

I swallowed hard and answered in a high voice, "I don't think I care for them."

"But why not?" Dmitri asked, pretending to be baffled. "You have so many of the same tastes."

It took everything I had not to tremble harder. I could see as clear as day which particular tastes Dmitri had in mind. But if Sascha felt my fear even a little, he would start to ask questions. Questions I wasn't ready to answer. All I knew was that if I never saw Gunter and Axel again, it would be a blessing.

The rest of breakfast passed less eventfully. We cleaned up our camp, prepared to depart later that afternoon—Sascha apparently never wanted to stay for the third and final day of any faire, saying he was usually sold out of his wares and had purchased everything he needed by then, and that the last day was little more than fucking—and returned to our booths with the remainder of our wares. I could see at once that he was right about everything selling out. By noon, Ivan's baked goods were all sold, Gregor's medicines had sold out the day before, and there was barely enough between Dmitri's and Sascha's things to fill a single booth.

"What do we do for the rest of the day once everything is sold?" I asked Sascha. We were the only two left at the booths. Gregor was off treating patients privately, and the others were off enjoying what there was to see, do, and eat.

Sascha finished selling the second to last of Dmitri's pelts, then opened his mouth to answer, but was cut off by an odd procession traveling down the center of the aisle between the booths.

"Justice!" a man on a horse called out in a loud voice. "Come and see justice served. Justice!"

Behind him was an ox-drawn cart carrying three naked men. They were tied up and weeping profusely, but they didn't seem to be slaves. All three were large and muscular with the rough look of the forest about them. Each of them had one testicle painted red.

"Come and see justice served!" the man leading the procession called out. "Justice!"

A long line of men—and a few women—followed the cart, throwing refuse and shouting insults at the men in the cart.

I shrunk back against Sascha's side as they passed.

After what Sascha had told me last night, I didn't need to ask what crime the men in the cart were guilty of or what justice was about to be meted out. My own balls ached at the mere thought of what was about to happen to the three men to the point where I was tempted to shield them in sympathy.

Sascha reached for me and pulled me against his chest—probably as a show to everyone passing that I belonged to him. "Punishments have no teeth if they aren't carried out now and then," he said. "There are always a few men who leave a faire with one smashed ball, because there is always someone stupid enough to think they can take what doesn't belong to them."

He said the last bit loud enough for anyone passing to hear. A few did hear and steered clear of the booth, eyeing both of us askance. I had the feeling Sascha wouldn't be getting as many offers for me on that second day, and that I wouldn't be bothered by as many lascivious looks.

"If you were any more obvious about that pup of yours, I'd think your head was going soft."

The deep-voiced call came from a small group that was part of the procession following the rapists—a group of women. I blinked and leaned into Sascha a little more as the curious group broke from the procession and made their way over to us. The woman who had spoken was as tall and broad as Sascha—almost enough to be mistaken for a man—and was dressed in breeches. She was followed by a trio of women who stayed close to her sides, as though she were their leader. One was also dressed in breeches and had short hair, one was dressed as a woman but looked like she could wrestle any of the wolves she came across to the ground, and one was no older than I was and astoundingly beautiful, with long, blonde hair and downcast eyes. She carried a toddler on her hip.

"Katrina," Sascha greeted her with a smile. He stepped forward, offering his hand. The two shook like men. "I would have introduced you to Peter yesterday, if your gang hadn't been so busy catching up on gossip with Ivan and Sven."

I realized immediately who the woman and her friends were, and my curiosity perked. "You're our closest neighbors," I said, gazing up at Katrina in awe.

"So Sascha here has mentioned us?" Katrina asked, amused.

"In passing," I said, putting on my best manners. I offered my hand the way Sascha had, figuring I had nothing at all to be afraid of where the women were concerned. If what Sascha had told me was accurate, they weren't the least bit interested in men. "How do you do? Peter Royale," I introduced myself.

Katrina looked as though I'd presented her with a gem-encrusted crown. Her wide face split into a broad grin, and she glanced from me to Sascha and back again. "Well I'll be," she said, then shook my hand. It was like having my hand enclosed by a giant. "He really is something special."

"Peter hasn't learned the etiquette of the forest yet," Sascha said with amused apology.

"The forest doesn't know etiquette, full stop," I snapped in reply, eyeing Sascha impishly.

Katrina laughed so hard I thought it might start an earthquake. "It all makes sense now," she laughed. "Everything Ivan and Sven said. You didn't catch the pup, the pup caught you."

Sascha glanced around as if hoping no one had heard Katrina. With a voice like hers, it was next to impossible not to hear her. Fortunately, if anyone did hear, they ignored the comment. Everyone was too interested in following the justice procession, which passed by completely in no time. Katrina and the others didn't chase after them, though.

"This is Lena," Katrina introduced the tough woman who was dressed as a woman to me. She put an arm around her shoulder and yanked her in before smacking a kiss on her lips. Lena winked up at her in reply. "And this is Ox, short for Oksana."

"Don't call me that," the woman in breeches said, rolling her eyes.

"I'll call you what I want," Katrina barked back at her, but with good humor. "And this—" she drew the beautiful, young woman with a child out to the front, "—is a new member of our family, Annika."

"How do you do?" I asked Annika with a friendly smile.

I was surprised when the poor woman gasped and

pulled away, hiding against Katrina's side. The gesture was not unlike the way I'd fallen into the habit of clinging to Sascha when something unnerved me. That realization served both to make me feel embarrassed for my own actions—where was my spine, after all—and certain that Annika had been abused in some way.

"We rescued her from a cruel husband just a month ago," Katrina said, confirming my suspicions. "Her father married her off far too young. I know her sister. Beka came to me before the last snowfall and asked me to take her away. That bastard of a husband actually shit himself when we kicked in his door and scooped the poor thing up."

"She's far better off with us," Ox said with a proud grin. "And I, for one, enjoyed meting out the punishment of the forest." She cracked her knuckles for good measure.

"Speaking of the justice of the forest, we need to catch up so we can see the show." Katrina gestured with her thumb over her shoulder to the receding procession. "Are you coming?"

"No." Sascha sent me a sideways look and rested a hand on my shoulder, as if I were the reason we wouldn't be attending such a brutal spectacle. I wasn't sure if I wanted to see three men have one of their balls each smashed to a pulp. It would be a sick thrill, especially given the reason for the punishment, but I was certain I'd have nightmares about it for weeks after.

"Suit yourself," Katrina said, moving away. "Now

that the last frost has passed, we should get together for a feast one of these days."

"You know you're welcome whenever you'd like," Sascha called after her, waving. "Besides, I think Sven will need help with the planting in a week or so anyhow."

"Just send someone over to fetch us and we'll be there," she said.

I waved to the group as they walked on, feeling a strange sense of satisfaction. "How long of a walk is it from our house to theirs?" I asked. I had been too busy contemplating dark thoughts when we'd set out for the faire the day before to pay much attention.

"An hour or so," Sascha said, moving back to the edge of the booth as another customer stepped forward with an interested look in his eyes. "We visit frequently when the weather is nice."

It felt good to know that, like the existence I now lived with Sascha's pack wasn't as isolated as my first few weeks there had led me to believe. Once again, I had the feeling that there was an entire society in the forest that had gone completely unnoticed—or at least un-commented upon—by city-dwellers. The suggestion of punishing Annika's husband by "forest law" only deepened my conviction that, with a little imagination, everyone living in the forest could come together to form one community, if they ever needed to.

Half an hour later, the last of Sascha's platters sold. We have officially sold out of everything we'd brought with us to the faire.

"What do we do now?" I asked as Sascha tucked the last of our money into the coin purse inside his jacket.

Sascha shrugged. "We enjoy what's left of the faire. Although the good merchandise will have sold yesterday. Really, all that'll be left at this point is entertainment. Do you want to walk around?" he asked with a hopeful look.

I nodded, adjusting my cloak and stepping around the booth with him.

Unlike the day before, when so many men exhibited interest in me that I had to stick close to Sascha's side, I was able to walk beside him now, as an equal. Whether word had gotten around that I wasn't for sale or the men who would have been interested in purchasing me had sated themselves the night before, I was left alone. That left me far freer to look around at my surroundings and to marvel at the people milling outside of Berlova's wall.

It truly did appear to me as though forest- and city-dwellers mingled freely at faires. Which begged the question of why my father had never allowed me or my siblings to walk freely through the small faires outside of Novoberg. Then again, as I began to notice soldiers patrolling here and there, I wondered if Father simply didn't trust his military to keep the peace the way Berlova's was. Or perhaps there just wasn't anything interesting at a Novoberg faire worthy of my interest.

After some time of wandering, Sascha reached out and took my hand. I was so occupied watching everything around me that I hadn't noticed the two of us veering closer to each other. The moment he threaded his fingers through mine, I grinned, my face heating. Sascha flushed as well, though neither of us said anything. I remembered the words we'd spoken the night before, let them swirl around my heart. There couldn't be any harm in letting myself pretend to be in love. Life was harsh enough without little joys like holding hands with a man who I shared a desperate passion with.

That point was proven a few minutes later when a blood-curdling cry rent the air several dozen yards ahead of us. The crowd that had gathered around the front gate of Berlova burst into a brutal cry, throwing fists and hats in the air.

I swallowed hard, stopping my steps. "Someone just received their punishment," I said in a small, thin voice, my balls squeezing in sympathy.

"Let's just walk in the other direction," Sascha said with a wince.

We turned and headed back, but there was no escaping the second howling cry.

"You don't care for violence, do you?" I asked Sascha as we walked on.

"No," he admitted. He turned to me, huffing a laugh. "It probably surprises you that a man who abhors violence is the leader of a pack."

I tilted my head to the side and made a considering face. "There are other ways to lead besides violence. A wise leader knows how to guide without fear and how to impose discipline without punishing." As had been drilled into me through the many years of my education. I was supposed to have been a Justice, which meant I was raised to be a leader.

Images of being with Dmitri also came to mind. One might argue that he employed violence against me on a regular basis. Then again, he was careful never to leave a mark—aside from one made with his mouth. If I were ever to walk out of his bedroom with bruises, cuts, or scratches, Sascha would have his hide. Perhaps it was the lack of any physical mark of the pain I enjoyed with Dmitri that made it so cathartic for me.

"You get this odd look sometimes, you know," Sascha said, narrowing his eyes as he studied me. "I wish you'd tell me what you're thinking when you look like that."

I glanced up to him with a firm look. "No, you don't," I said quietly.

A third cry of pain and terror rent the air. This time, when the crowd shouted in response, there was a note of shock and disgust in their jeer. I glanced over my shoulder with a frown, wondering what could have gone wrong to cause such a sound. I even spotted one man lurch away from the back of the crowd to vomit into the grass.

"I don't even want to know," Sascha said in a vaguely sick voice, picking up his pace.

Neither did I, come to think of it. Whether it was the shift in atmosphere from the punishments or my own, troubled thoughts, I was ready to leave the faire and go home. I walked on with Sascha, hoping the others would return to the booths soon so that we could gather our things and leave.

My newfound urgency was arrested, though, when Sascha and I stumbled across Magnus and Neil walking in the other direction. My eyes went wide at the sight of Neil. He had changed profoundly in just one day. Instead of being naked, dirty, and shivering, he was dressed well—if a bit childishly in a flouncy style boys in short pants usually wore—and he'd had a haircut. He had a slightly glassy look in his eyes, as if everything were so overwhelming that he didn't know what to think. As soon as he saw me, his gaze snapped into focus.

"Sascha." Magnus nodded to us as he and Neil passed.

"Magnus." Sascha nodded back.

That would have been it, but Neil called out, "Wait!"

All four of us froze. Magnus frowned at Neil. "Pups do not give orders," he said, as though instructing a naughty child. "They do not speak unless spoken to."

Neil's mouth fell open and his jaw worked for a moment, but no further words came out. He glanced to me with a desperate look, though.

I tilted my head up to look at Sascha as though asking permission to speak. Of course, I had no need to ask, but I always had been a stickler for protocol. Sascha's mouth twitched with amusement for a moment before he schooled his expression to seriousness and nodded.

I glanced to Neil. "Are you well, Neil?" I asked as though we were meeting in the grand hall of the palace during a formal ball. "Are you satisfied with your new position?"

For a moment, Neil gaped at me. Then his expression ran through about twelve different emotions, from disbelief to guilt. He glanced to Magnus.

"Perhaps we could give the pups a moment to speak to each other in private," Sascha said.

"If you think that wise," Magnus said, stroking his chin as though he considered the idea quaint.

"I trust my pup with my life," Sascha said gravely.

Magnus sighed. "Very well."

He winked at Neil, then he and Sascha stepped aside. They didn't go far enough to give us any real privacy, but if Neil and I spoke quietly, we wouldn't be overheard.

"Truly," I said, swaying slightly closer to Neil and keeping my voice down. "Are you well?"

"I...I don't even know how to answer that," Neil said, letting out a breath. He was clearly dazed and perhaps suffering lingering effects of the tea I was certain he'd been given last night. "Do you know what he did to me last night?" he asked in a tight whisper.

"Yes," I answered frankly. "Did you enjoy it?"

Neil gaped at me in outrage. That outrage evaporated into guilt, then the slightest of smiles. It was all the answer I needed.

"Enjoy it," I rephrased my question as a statement. "I know you're inclined to." In fact, I knew no such thing. But if I could plant the suggestion that there was nothing wrong with being fucked by another man—or several—and if Neil accepted that and believed me, his life would be much easier. "You're in the safest possible position you could be in as a pup to a wealthy pack leader," I told him frankly. "Magnus is smart and powerful. I don't know him, but even I can see that. Do as he says, and he'll protect you. It's a far better life than either of us could have hoped for in the palace."

"Is it?" Neil suddenly looked bereft. "I wasn't certain I'd be able to walk today," he whispered, his face going red. "And my jaw hurts."

I knew what he was telling me and grinned. "Give it a few weeks and your ass won't be so tight. That's when it gets really good. And as for the other, breathe through your nose and keep your tongue as relaxed as possible. You can take it deeper if you make small swallowing movements. And believe me, there's nothing better than watching the way you hold them in the palm of your hand when they're coming down your throat."

Neil gaped at me, but I could see a spark of arousal in his eyes. He nodded very slightly/ My guess about him might just have been right after all. I wanted to clap a hand on his shoulder in reassurance, but I had a feeling it would have been a violation for me to touch him.

"There's nothing wrong with it," I whispered. "You're not doing anything wrong by enjoying it. In fact, the more you enjoy it and let him know you're enjoying it, the kinder he'll treat you." I paused before adding, "I did you a tremendous favor yesterday, Neil Beiste. I might just have saved your life."

Neil shut his mouth and nodded tightly, the guilt in his expression mingling with resignation.

"Remember that," I added in a harder voice. "Remember that I saved your life and that you owe me."

He met my eyes with a startled look, but said, "I will remember."

"I think this conversation has gone on long enough," Magnus said, stepping forward to fetch Neil. "Come along, pup. We've an invitation to join Dushka Nobrovnik for lunch."

Sascha returned to my side. We watched the two of them walking away before heading back to our booths. I noticed both Neil and Magnus giving me one final look before Magnus leaned toward Neil, as if asking him something. Neil responded enthusiastically, but I was too far away to make out their conversation.

"What was that all about?" Sascha asked, taking my hand again. There was a touch of uneasiness in his look. "You look as though you've won a particularly large prize at a hand of cards."

I shrugged. "Neil just needed someone to give him permission to enjoy being fucked by a man." It was true enough. I didn't need to add that Neil now had a lifelong debt to me. One I might be able to call in someday.

By the time we reached our camp, Ivan and Sven were there, seeing that everything we'd purchased during the faire was loaded up and secure in the back of the wagon. Before too long, Mikal and Jakob joined us for a final, comfortable conversation. Although they spent most of the time describing everything they'd done with the pup they'd rented for the night in intimate detail. They were funny about it, but the story had me curious and hard the more they described. It didn't help that I sat on Sascha's lap in the back of the wagon as they told their tales, with his cock pressed hard against my ass.

"If there weren't so many people around, I'd take those trousers of yours down and have you ride me right here, sitting like this in the wagon," he growled against my ear.

"Then you'd have to endure a hungry audience," I snapped back, breathless and bothered, "because I'd make so much noise as I came that I'd draw men from miles around."

Sascha laughed, resting his head against my shoulder. "You always have a smart reply for everything I say to you."

"It's more fun that way," I whispered, grinding my ass against his erection.

"Where are Gregor and Dmitri?" Sascha gasped, sitting straight. "I want to get this imp home as quickly as possible."

"And we all know why," Ivan laughed.

Gregor came striding up through the camps a few minutes later, his medical sack slung over one shoulder. "Sorry, sorry," he said. "I've been busy. The first faire after the winter is always filled with people in need of my services."

"Did you see everyone you need to?" Sascha asked.

"No," Gregor said with a disappointed sigh. "I could easily stay here for two more days and still not get through everyone in need of my help."

"If you want to stay, we'll take you home when you're done," Mikal offered. "That is, if Sascha doesn't mind visitors in a few days."

I could feel the tension in Sascha's body lighten. "I wouldn't mind at all," he said with a smile.

"It's settled, then," Jakob said. "We'll bring him home in a few days."

I was thrilled at the prospect of getting to know Mikal and Jakob better—perhaps much better—and in the privacy of our own home. Arrangements were made, then the two men walked off with Gregor. The rest of us returned to preparing the wagon and hitching the horses.

Half an hour later, Dmitri showed up with a satisfied look on his face. "Well?" he asked as though we were the ones holding him up. "What are we waiting for?" He hopped up into the wagon's driver's seat and took up the leads. "Did you have a good faire, pup?" he asked me, snapping the leads and starting the wagon forward.

"I did," I answered, struggling to maintain my balance, then sitting.

Sascha and Sven rode our two extra horses on either side of the wagon, and Ivan settled into the wagon bed with me, immediately curling up as though he would sleep most of the way home.

"I'm glad," Dmitri told me. "I'm glad you had a chance to meet so many new people. I'm sure it widened your horizons fantastically."

"It did," I said. I had the feeling he had more in mind than just the wonders and oddities of the booths and entertainers.

"This faire has given me quite a few ideas," he went on, lowering his voice. "Ideas I'm sure you'll be interested in." He sent a sultry look over his shoulder. "But we'll talk about it once we're home."

I met his sly look with one that said I wasn't intimidated, then found a seat in the wagon bed for the journey. No doubt Dmitri had discovered some new way to cause me agony and ecstasy. God help me, but I was looking forward to the novelty of whatever it was.

15

I'll admit, I expected worse than what I got from Dmitri just after midday two days later.

"Deeper, pup, deeper," he demanded, thrusting hard into my mouth as he pulled my hair with one hand and pinned my hands above my head on the wall behind the head of his bed with the other. He had them smashed so hard against the wall that I would have to come up with an excuse for the bruises to satisfy Sascha later. "Take it all," he growled, finally managing to push so hard I gagged—something that was becoming harder for him to achieve as I mastered the art of focus.

I will admit that the knot tricks he'd learned were diabolical. He had me seated at the head of his bed, pillows propped behind the small of my back, legs spread wide. He'd purchased some rough twine at the faire and had learned to fasten it into a curious sling around my genitals. The harder I became, the tighter and more restrictive the twine, until every movement had me crying out in pain and pleasure. His little trick had the added bonus of a large, rough, monkey's paw knot that ground deeper and deeper into my asshole, opening me without the addition of any of the ointment Sascha had purchased at the faire.

The whole thing was raw and glorious, and I fulfilled everything Dmitri wanted from me by weeping, choking, and coming hard shortly before he did.

"Is that the best you could do?" I panted after he released my hands and collapsed onto his back across the foot of his bed.

Dmitri lifted his head and stared incredulously at me. "You were sobbing and sweating from pain and begging me for mercy."

I let my arms drop to my side, wincing at how sore my muscles were from being wrenched at odd angles. "What I may do or say in the moment is not an indication of how I feel overall," I said in a soft voice, chin tilted up smugly.

Dmitri laughed, letting one arm fall over his forehead. "You're a liar."

"Am I?" I hadn't quite caught my breath, but I did my best to be imperious.

"Believe in your own superiority all you want, pup," he said, eyes closed. "I terrify you. And you get off on that terror."

"I do not," I said in a low, quiet voice. I was lying, and Dmitri knew it too.

He turned his head toward me, a slow, toothy grin

spreading across his handsome face. "That cum splattered across your belly says otherwise."

I touched a hand to the spots he nodded toward, then shifted so that I could untie the knots he'd made. Every part of me was still raw and sensitive, and the rough, wiry ends of the twine felt like being raked with needles as I plucked at it.

"Have any of them ever just asked you outright to leave," I said, venom in my voice and eyes narrowed at him.

Dmitri's eyes widened, then his face grew as hard and cold as stone. "They wouldn't dare," he growled. "You wouldn't either," he added with a nod.

"Wouldn't I?" I asked in clipped tones.

Dmitri laughed breathlessly. "You need me, pup," he said in a deadly serious voice.

"I beg to differ," I said, gasping in the middle of my rebuttal as I worked the main knot at the base of my sore cock loose.

"You think you don't need me?" Dmitri said with a challenging sneer. "You think you would do just fine without me to release the pressure that builds up in you like a geyser about to erupt?"

I stopped picking at the twine—stopped panting and held my breath too—and stared incredulously at him.

"Oh yes, I see it." Dmitri rolled to his side, then pushed himself into a wolf-like crouch. "The others don't. Certainly not Sascha. But I see it in you, as plain as day. The fury. The hate. The need to lash out."

He grabbed me by the arm, muscling me until I was on my back as he straddled me. He grabbed the ends of the twine that I'd managed to loosen and pulled hard. The money's paw knot ground into my throbbing ass. I let out a pained yelp as fire erupted through my ass and balls.

"Sascha thinks you're so sweet and pure and innocent, but I know otherwise," he growled, bringing his face to within inches of mine. "You don't have the temperament to be a pup. You're too filled with anger and bitterness."

I didn't argue with him. I couldn't.

"You know full well you're a slave here, and it burns you up inside." He fisted the twine harder and harder, until the knot pressing against my asshole felt like it would tear right through me. "You're trapped in the role of a pet, and you despise it. Just like you despised your family before coming here. You've been boiling with rage for years, and I've finally given you a way to feel it down to the marrow of your bones."

He clamped a hand around my cock—which was still tender from coming—and jerked, rubbing the tip with his palm, until I cried out. The sensory overload was so acute that I wanted to peel out of my skin, but the emotion storming within me felt so good.

"You need me so that you can hate me," Dmitri growled against my ear, still torturing my cock. "So that you can gnash your teeth and rage against me for tormenting you. Because if you didn't have me to hate, you'd be forced to hate Sascha. And that would kill you." He whispered the last bit in a surprisingly empathetic voice.

"Stop, please, stop," I begged him, reeling from the most painful thing he'd done to me yet—told me the truth. Tears streamed out of the corners of my eyes.

Dmitri let go of me at once, backing away and standing as I lay, devastated, on the bed, weeping real tears for a change. It was so horrible that I covered my face with my hands, shaken at how deeply his words wounded me. Because he was right. I was a prisoner, and the only way I could justify loving my jailor was if I had someone else to resent.

"It's your own damn fault for falling in love with him," Dmitri grumbled, untying the rest of his rope trick from my groin with a surprising amount of care.

"I'm not in love with him," I insisted, sobbing.

He fixed me with a flat, disbelieving look. "We're damn fools for letting anyone have our hearts."

I knew he was talking about Mikal, but I was too blinded with my own pain to find a way to console his. And part of me thought he deserved it. He deserved to feel as broken and miserable as I did.

I grunted as he took the twine away fully, then twisted to my side. The paradoxical pleasure that always came after pain was released hit me. Relief and release were powerful emotions, and for a moment, I could only lie there, tucked into a ball, and sigh with it.

Dmitri gave me just enough time before saying, "Get

up and go away. I'm sick of looking at you, and I need to go hunting anyhow."

I sucked in a breath and dragged myself first to a sitting position, then, when I'd gathered more strength, to stand. My clothes lay strewn over the chair in the corner, and once I'd retrieved them, I shuffled to the door, thinking about nothing but a nice, long soak in the pool.

"Peter," Dmitri stopped me before I reached the door. I glanced to him, surprised he'd used my name. Our eyes met, and I was arrested by something vulnerable I saw there. "We understand each other," he said in a hoarse voice.

So much seemed to coalesce into that moment, so many different kinds of need. I nodded. "We do," I replied, then turned away and left the room.

Our lives had returned to their normal routine. Ivan was busy cleaning up after lunch in the kitchen and acknowledged me with only an understanding nod as I walked gingerly through the main room, naked. I'd left my clothes in Sascha's room to change back into later. Sven barely acknowledged me at all as he worked laying seeds in one of the freshly-turned garden beds. The sound of Sascha sawing trees somewhere on the other side of the house was a godsend. That meant he wouldn't see me grimace and wince as I pulled the lid off the pool, set it aside, and sank into the water. I let out a groan of relief as the warm, bubbling water caressed my aching joints and muscles. I wondered if pups entered the later stages of their lives with bad joints and hunched backs from all the ways they were folded and twisted and used in their youth.

I'd finally relaxed fully, letting the water do its work, and my thoughts had drifted to Neil and how he might be faring in his new life when the sound of loud, happy voices drifted around the corner of the house.

"We're home!" I heard Jakob shout.

His greeting was welcomed by Sascha's indistinct cry of welcome. I smiled at the notion that we might just have a jolly few days, depending on how long Mikal and Jakob stayed and how Dmitri faced his own pain, and sank deeper into the pool, eyes closed. All I wanted to do for the moment was listen to people who were happier than me.

"And you should have seen the amount of pus that spewed out of that boil the moment I lanced it," Gregor's voice sounded distinctly as the group marched around the edge of the house. "You would have thought he was storing a waterskin under his armpit."

The others laughed. I made a face, but kept my eyes closed.

"At least you were there to end the poor man's pain," Sascha said. They were all definitely coming toward the pool.

"Yes, and you should have seen the size of the purse Duke Ferdlova gave him," Jakob said, accompanied by the sound of someone, presumably Gregor, being slapped on the back.

My eyes popped wide, and I twisted to watch them

approach, wincing as my body twinged with the last remnants of the afternoon's pain. "Duke Ferdlova?" I asked, astounded.

"Peter!" Jakob greeted me loudly, his arms stretched wide. "Good to see you again. And by the look of things, we'll get to see all of you this time."

If it weren't for my earlier activities, I might have been more amenable to his joke. As it was, I could only manage to smile politely and float into the center of the pool, sinking back to my neck, so I could face them. All three of the new arrivals, and Sascha too, immediately began removing their shoes and clothing.

Jakob flinched halfway through removing a shoe as he studied me. "What's wrong, pup? You don't look as wide-eyed and bushy-tailed as you did at the faire."

"Don't," Gregor warned him in a suddenly hushed voice.

"Sorry, have I said something wrong?" Jakob asked.

"He was with Dmitri earlier," Sascha said, barely above a murmur, his face an expressionless mask. He hurried to throw off his clothes and wade into the pool with me, closing his arms around me and drifting to the far side to sit with me cradled against him.

"What did my brother do to you?" Mikal asked, looking murderous.

"Peter doesn't like us to ask," Gregor explained.

"It's nothing," I recited by rote. "He didn't hurt me, I was perfectly willing, there's nothing to talk about and nothing to be concerned with." I held up my arms, in spite of Sascha holding me, as if to ward off any further questions.

Sascha grabbed my right hand and brought it closer to his face to study the fresh bruise flowering there. "You said you would tell me if he hurt you, Peter," he murmured in a deadly voice.

"I dropped the pool lid on my hand when I was uncovering it earlier," I lied, sounding peevish at being asked as I did.

"On the *back* of your hand?" Sascha didn't believe me for a moment.

I met his eyes with a look that dared him to call me out, trying with everything I had not to tremble in rage. Particularly since I didn't know who that rage was directed at.

He stared right back at me, unbending. "This isn't good," he said so that none of the others could hear.

"As if any of it could possibly be good," I whispered back with venom.

I'd gone too far. I could see it in his eyes and feel it in his body right away. My barb was too pointed, and likely poisoned by Dmitri's painful words. Sascha glanced away, wounded and guilty. I hated the way his shame seemed to press down on him. We both knew who was responsible for my position and for Dmitri to begin with. But I was determined to salvage the situation and to direct my hate where it was supposed to go. I shoved it and Dmitri out of my mind and let out a sigh, resting my head against Sascha's shoulder and curling into him like a child. Sascha's arms tightened around me, and he rested his cheek against the top of my head.

"Well, that's my brother for you," Mikal said, stepping into the pool. "He isn't even here and he's managed to kill everyone's joy in an instant."

"Where is the bastard anyhow?" Jakob asked as he and Gregor stepped into the pool as well.

"He's gone hunting," I answered, nuzzling against Sascha's neck, not even bothering to ogle Mikal's and Jakob's nakedness. As conflicted and uncertain as I was about Sascha, it felt good to rest in the arms of someone who truly loved me.

"Sounds like there'll be a feast when he gets back," Jakob said with a sigh, sinking into the pool up to his neck. "Oh, this feels nice. I miss the pool."

"It certainly is wonderful to come home to after a long journey." Gregor groaned as he settled into one of the seats along the wall.

"So what other medical wonders did you encounter at the end of the faire?" Sascha asked. It was a clear order to return the conversation to lighter, pleasanter topics.

"Oh! I delivered a baby," Gregor announced. "Only the third time I've ever done that."

Even I lifted my head from Sascha's shoulder, excited to hear about that.

Whether it was for me alone or whether everyone needed an afternoon recounting miraculous, funny, or cheerful stories, the pack was full of chatter for the next several hours. As warm water and camaraderie soothed my earlier, emotional aches, I let go of the lingering resentment I had for Sascha and let myself enjoy the way he stroked my arms and sides under the water. His touch was meant to comfort more than arouse, which meant the world to me. Perhaps I'd been a fool to let Dmitri's words pierce me so deep. I could care about Sascha, whether he was my captor or not, if I tried hard enough.

"I take it you wouldn't mind if we stayed in our old room? Jakob asked a while later, as we all stepped out of the pool.

"Is it still intact?" Mikal asked. "Or has my bastard of a brother turned it into a storage room for his hunting trophies.

"If he's a bastard, wouldn't that make you one too, since you're twins?" I asked, glad that my spirits had been lifted by the friendship that clearly bound the men together, whether they were all part of the same pack or not.

Mikal laughed and began to say, "I suppose it would," but his cheer tapered off as he glanced at my body.

Jakob looked with interest too, but it was obvious as soon as the light of day hit my pale skin that they weren't studying me with lust or appreciation. The twine Dmitri had used on me earlier had left criss-crossing red marks all around my hips and groin. Anyone with a hint of imagination could have interpreted what those marks meant.

I pretended nothing was wrong and walked to the chest to fetch myself a towel. There was a certain amount of power in being the only one who knew the full story and pretending that that story didn't exist. The red welts that the others stared at felt like a badge of honor to me. They meant I had endured something that none of the men around me had. And frankly, the more I thought about it, the more I wondered if they *could* endure it. They might have had muscle, but I was stronger than they were.

"Is your old room the one that looks out on the gardens?" I asked with deliberate casualness, daring them to comment. I dried myself off, then wrapped the towel around my waist to hide what they were all squirming about. "The one next to my and Sascha's room?" I deliberately claimed the room as mine. I'd claim the whole house and the entire forest as mine and dare them to take it away from me.

"Yes, that's it," Jakob said slowly, blinking rapidly. He seemed to be the first one to catch on to my stalwart display of nerve. He straightened slightly, facing me like a man, like an equal. It was instantly arousing, and if my body hadn't already been exhausted, I was certain everyone looking on would have been able to see my curiosity about Jakob plainly.

"I was in there just the other day, looking for extra crates to carry the wares we took to the faire," I answered, starting toward the house. "The bed has been stripped, and if you ever had curtains, they've been used for something else, but the furniture is all still there."

"That's a relief, at least," Jakob said. I had the feeling he was trying to sound as normal as possible.

"I, for one, am eager to unpack my things and take a short nap before supper," Mikal said, recovering next.

"Supper which I should help Ivan and Sven prepare and serve," Gregor added. "Just as soon as I put the last of my things away and prepare my instruments for a deep cleaning."

I walked ahead of them into the house, knowing Sascha would follow me to ask questions—or rather, to demand answers—without having to turn around. Sure enough, I heard his footsteps right behind mine as I crossed through the main room and started toward our bedroom.

As soon as we were alone in the bedroom, Sascha grabbed a corner of the towel around my waist and yanked it off. "Sit," he said, tossing the towel aside and pointing to the bed.

There didn't seem to be any point in resisting his order. I walked to the bed and sat. I even opened my legs for him to get a good look at the marks, since I knew that was what he wanted to see.

Sascha came forward and knelt in front of me, glowering as he traced a few of the brighter lines with his fingertips. I flinched at his touch, both because it stung and because the tenderness he used felt good. Which was an accurate description of the muddle I found myself in where Sascha was concerned.

"What caused these marks?" he asked, stone in his voice.

I kept silent, debating what to tell him and how. I was far from ready to confess the darker side of my desires to the person who saw nothing in me but light.

My silence must have been too much for him. Sascha glanced up, meeting my eyes with a combination of anger and worry. "I have told you over and over to tell me if he hurts you," he said, his voice shaking. He spread his hands possessively over my thighs. "You've been lying to me when you say he hasn't."

"Not everyone sees pain and pleasure the same way that you do, Sascha," I said. I hesitated for a moment before attempting a strategy of interaction I hadn't dared to try yet. I stroked the side of his face the way he liked to pet and coddle me, running my hands through his hair. "It's best not to ask questions about things you won't understand," I said, talking down to him for once.

I couldn't tell if my strategy worked or if it was a disaster. Sascha's expression pinched with hurt. "I understand what love is supposed to be," he insisted, "and this is not it."

"I don't love Dmitri," I said, almost dismissively. "I love you."

It was a cheap trick, one I felt guilty about instantly. I had no right to manipulate Sascha with sweetness I wasn't sure I was even capable of feeling. But I'd started down the path and needed to finish the journey. I cupped my hands around his face and leaned in to kiss him.

Our kiss extended for a few, lovely seconds before Sascha broke away, rocking back and meeting my eyes. The worry was still there in him, as was the vulnerability, and along with that, I could see he didn't know what to do.

I counted that as a blessing. It meant I could dictate the terms between us.

"I told you it was nothing to worry about and I stand by that," I said. "What Dmitri and I do together has no bearing whatsoever in how you and I are together. Put it out of your mind entirely. Forget it exists at all. I do as soon as I step out of that room, and I wish you would do the same."

Sascha's eyes narrowed slightly, and he held perfectly still. For a moment, I wasn't sure how he would react. The air between us crackled with tension. I could see a thousand thoughts forming and dissipating in Sascha as he tried to make sense of everything. I'd made up my mind that I would have to take charge of the situation further and order him to go about his business as usual when he let out a breath and lowered his head.

"No one prepared me for this," he said, shaking his head. He drew in another breath, then squeezed my thighs before standing. "No one prepared me for it at all."

I figured there was an equal chance he was talking about either love or jealousy. Probably both. I didn't need to know all of the answers right then and there, though. Sascha stepped away, which meant I could rise and retrieve my clothes to dress again. It felt as good to feel the slip of fine linen and cotton over my tired body as it had to sink into the pool.

"How long are you going to allow Mikal and Jakob to stay?" I asked, watching out of the corner of my eye as Sascha dressed as well.

"As long as they want to," Sascha answered. His tone wasn't quite back to normal, but I could tell he was battling with himself to be as circumspect about the whole thing as possible.

"Why not just ask them to return to the pack, then?" I asked the question I really wanted an answer to.

Sascha finished pulling his shirt on over his head, then turned to me. "I've been asking myself that for almost a year now," he admitted in a tired voice as he did up his buttons.

"And what is the answer?" I sat on the bed to put on the slippers I wore around the house when I knew I wouldn't have to go outside.

Sascha didn't answer at first. He frowned at himself as he pulled on his breeches and tucked his shirt into the waist. I had the feeling the debate within him was as old as the conflict he'd been charged with resolving the year before.

"Maybe there's still a way to sort the entire mess out without damaging anyone's feelings," he said at last in a grumble.

"I think the time may be long past for that," I said, rising once I was finished dressing. Dmitri was long past the point of being able to forgive and forget. I figured Sascha knew that, so I said nothing.

"I wish it weren't," Sascha sighed, slipping into a waistcoat I'd embroidered for him the week before.

Once he'd buttoned it, before we left the room, Sascha crossed to fold me into his arms. I hadn't thought I was in the mood to be coddled, but it felt remarkably good to crush against him, his arms tight around me. I closed my eyes and rested my face against his shoulder, breathing in the scent of his skin with a satisfied sound. It was so easy to pretend I was just a boy in love with his protector, one who didn't have another care in the world and who was as light and innocent as Sascha thought I was. I'd missed out on the simple comfort of an embrace for my entire life—enough to make me wonder who I would have turned out to be if I'd had that kind of affection from boyhood. I might have been the man Sascha thought I was.

"We should go join—"

"Wait." I cut Sascha off, pressing into him and tightening my embrace. "Just a few more seconds. This feels good."

Sascha let out a laughing breath and continued to hold me, resting his cheek against the top of my head. "You do beat all, Peter. One minute you're a warrior, the next you're a lover."

"And who knows who I'll be after that?" I teased him.

Sascha laughed. The clouds that had been hanging over me all afternoon seemed to part. He leaned back, stroking the side of my face before bending down to kiss me with fire. "I'm sure you'll be anything you want to be, my honey sweetness," he said, then kissed me again.

I reveled in the kiss, but my heart was anything but sweet. Whether he knew it or not, what he said was a lie. I couldn't be anything I wanted. As his pup, I could only be what he told me to be.

16

The next few days were every bit as jovial and peaceful as I could have hoped for. Mikal and Jakob were good company. They were useful around the house—particularly when it came to helping Sven with the spring planting—and they fell back into what I assumed had been their old routines within the pack almost at once. It was glaringly obvious that they belonged right where they were. We all knew it. Everyone except Dmitri, that was.

Dmitri made himself scarce for most of the daytimes the first few days, saying he was hunting. He only came back for supper, but when he did, he joined in the conversations as though nothing were out of the ordinary. For Dmitri, at least. By the fourth day, though, he seemed more inclined to stick around the house.

"A man can only hunt for so long before he has to rest," he said, fixing me with a wolfish look as he did.

It was mid-morning on an overcast day. Ivan, Sven, and Gregor had gone to Katrina's house for the day to help plant their garden patch and because one of Katrina's women needed Gregor's medical advice. Sascha was hard at work carving a table that had been commissioned at the faire. Mikal and Jakob were engaged in some sort of leathercraft, constructing satchels or something, which I assumed was their special talent. I was hard at work cutting out patterns for new trousers for Sven and Gregor at the dining table. I knew by the look Dmitri gave me that I would be twisted into some new and devilish position later that afternoon as he fucked me raw.

"I should really be seeing to things in the smokehouse," he went on as though nothing were unusual, "instead of idling away with you lot." He grinned at Mikal.

It was a relief to see that he and Mikal were getting along. The two had gone off for a long walk the night before, and I trusted they'd worked out at least some of their differences. The entire mood of the house was lighter somehow. Or, it was until Sascha caught the look Dmitri had sent me.

"Perhaps you should tend to your work instead of unnerving Peter as he does his," Sascha said.

I blinked at the harshness of the comment, and at the way it was so unexpected. I sent Sascha a surprised look, then glanced to Dmitri. Dmitri wore a look as though he knew all of my secrets—which, as related to the pack, he did—and was about to divulge them. I hadn't been unnerved until that moment.

I glanced back to Sascha and said, "I'm fine. He doesn't bother me."

Sascha got up from his chair near the fire, brushing off one of his carving tools, and carrying it toward the kitchen sink, as though he needed to clean it. On the way, he swayed close, arching over me as I bent across the table, marking fabric.

"You need to stop lying to me, Peter," he murmured in my ear with a combination of frustration and seduction. "He does bother you. Too much."

I let out a breath and straightened, standing right up against him, careful to make certain his back was to the others and his massive body shielded me from their prying eyes. I cupped the sides of his face and stared hard into his eyes. "You *have* to learn to trust me," I said in a low voice.

Sascha's expression darkened. "I'm trying," he ground out, "but—" His whole body went rigid for a few seconds until he let out a defeated breath. He rested his hands on my hips and did the only thing I figured he could have done to soothe himself and prove that he was still in control, he slanted his mouth over mind and kissed me searingly.

I returned his kiss eagerly. I liked it when he was aggressive. I liked it when he was tender as well. I liked it pretty much any way Sascha wanted to give it to me. But as he peeled away and continued on to the kitchen to clean off his carver, I bristled with impatience with him. If he was so aggravated by Dmitri's interest in me, why didn't he put his foot down as leader and do something about it?

I turned back to my work, catching the looks of the others before bending over the table again. Mikal and Jakob clearly didn't know what to make of the ever-shifting dynamics between me and Sascha and Dmitri. They seemed to be communicating silently with each other, which I found endearing.

Dmitri's grin had only grown more voracious through my entire exchange with Sascha, though. "I like the look of you bent over the table like that, pup," he called out to me. "It gives me ideas."

"I'm certain it does," I said with pretend nonchalance, wondering if a table would feature in our fucking later.

"Your ass looks delectable lifted up like that," he went on.

Sascha dropped something in the kitchen.

I straightened slightly and glared at Dmitri, ordering him to stop his games at once before a fight broke out.

Dmitri arched an eyebrow at me, as though challenging me to step up and control the situation. "It's been a few days," he went on in an incendiary tone. "I bet you're disappointed that that sweet ass of yours isn't sore and tender anymore. I could fix that, you know."

I narrowed my eyes at Dmitri, shaking my head slightly to tell him to shut up.

"That's enough out of you," Sascha said, his voice tight, as he walked back to his chair. He didn't take the matter further, though. His control was only surface deep.

"So Mikal and I were wondering how you would feel about the two of us extending our stay a while," Jakob started in the sort of tone men used when they wanted to steer the conversation away from something controversial. Though to me it felt more like jumping out of the frying pan and into the fire of controversy. Jakob turned to me. "Peter, what do you have to say about that?"

"It's not my decision, is it?" I said, reaching for the scissors to cut out the patterns I'd traced. "Sascha is the leader. He doesn't trust me to carry my own supper plate to the sink, let alone to make a decision like that."

I'd let my temper get the better of me, and Sascha felt the sting. He sent me a look of indignation, but said nothing. Which only seemed to prove my point. I'd stepped out of line, and he did nothing. My estimation of him sank, paradoxical as it was. I wanted my freedom, but I also valued a strong leader.

"A few weeks might be a nice amount of time to visit with old friends," Mikal said, glancing between the two of us. "I'm sure we can find plenty of ways to contribute to the group while we're here."

"Yes," Dmitri said with a smirk. "Contribute right up our pup's ass, I'm sure." He stood, moving slowly across the room toward me. "How long has it been since you've been fucked by more than just one of us at a time?" he asked me. "I bet you've been fantasizing about the way we all had you that first night ever since then." He came to stand on the other side of the table from me. His trousers were tented, but I knew him well enough to know that was from the power play he was attempting more than from the memory of that night.

The trouble was, he wasn't wrong. Guilty though it made me feel, there was a certain, erotic appeal to being used by multiple men simultaneously. All the hands, all the mouths, the feeling of being the center of sensual adoration. It was just another part of the darkness within me that Sascha refused to see.

"That whole incident was a mistake on our part," Sascha said, confirming my sullen thoughts. He was perched on the edge of his chair, as though he would leap up and wrestle Dmitri away from me at a moment's notice. "Peter doesn't care for that sort of activity."

Dmitri snorted, glancing over his shoulder at Sascha. "Is that what you think? You think this little pup is as sentimental and soft as you are? That he doesn't like it rough?"

"Don't," I growled at Dmitri, hoping my voice was too low for Sascha to hear. "He can't know."

I intended my words to mean that Sascha wouldn't identify with that sort of need because he didn't feel it himself. Dmitri, of course, took my words differently.

"You can't keep your secret forever," he whispered, leaning across the table to me. "One of these days, I'm going to make you scream so loudly when you come that Sascha will hear it. And won't he be green with envy."

"Enough of this." Sascha stood, marching across the room. The way his eyes were fixed on Dmitri, I was certain they were about to come to blows. "Stay away from Peter."

Dmitri surprised me by backing away. "Oh, yes," he said. "Because we wouldn't want our sweet, innocent pup to hear anything untoward."

"Dmitri, I'm warning you," Sascha growled.

Dmitri had the gall to turn away from Sascha as though he were a bothersome gnat and not the leader. "You and I need to talk," he told me. "The time has come. I have a proposition for you that you're going to want to hear."

I frowned in confusion, no idea what he could be thinking of. But before I could say anything, Sascha clamped a hand around Dmitri's arm and pulled him away from the table.

"I think you need to go for a walk," Sascha growled. "Leave Peter alone."

Dmitri glanced between me and Sascha, his mouth pinched into a smirk. "Yes, I think I do need to go for a walk." He looked at me with a particularly calculating look. "And when I get back, you and I will—"

"You'll do nothing," Sascha said. "I'm ending this... this whatever it is that you're doing to torment Peter right here."

"Sascha," I turned to him with a warning look.

"Please do not interfere with something you don't understand."

The offense and hurt was back in Sascha's eyes in a moment. "How can you tell me not to interfere? What could there possibly be between the two of you that I wouldn't understand?"

They were deceptively simple questions. But because of the clear and sharp jealousy in Sascha's eyes they were a flashpoint moment. I wasn't going to let the secrets or the bitterness go on for another second. I stood straight, tossing the scissors on the table.

"You," I said to Dmitri, "need to go on your walk. And you and I," I faced Sascha, "need to have a conversation."

Dmitri stepped away, holding his hands up as though he'd been put in his place. "Yes, pup," he said in a mocking voice. "Whatever you say, pup." He walked across the room, grabbing his coat from its peg by the door and leaving the house.

I glanced past Mikal and Jakob, highly aware that they were listening. I didn't want to have what was bound to be an unpleasant conversation with Sascha in front of them, so I stepped around the table, heading for the short hall.

"Come with me," I ordered Sascha.

He followed me, radiating frustration and desperation as we headed out to the backyard.

As soon as we were alone in the dreary afternoon,

under a canopy of clouds and trees, I whipped to face him.

"If you are so terribly jealous of Dmitri, why don't you send him away, like you should have last year?" I snapped.

Sascha clearly wasn't ready for any of what I had to say. He reeled back, his mouth dropping open in shock.

"I'm not jealous," he said, unable to meet my eyes.

"Sascha, if you were any greener, you'd blend into the forest," I said.

"It's not jealousy, it's anger." He managed to look squarely at me. He was angry. That much was true. "Dmitri hurts you, Peter. I've let him get away with it for too long because you've sworn to me that he *isn't* hurting you. But I know he is. I've seen the marks. I've let it slide for too long."

"Yes, Dmitri hurts me," I shouted, at the end of my patience. "He hurts me because I want him to, because I get off on it when he does."

Shock splashed across Sascha's face, quickly followed by denial. "No, I don't believe that. You're too young and too innocent."

"Is that what you believe?" I said, nearly laughing, I was so incredulous. "You believe that I'm just a sweet, soft-headed pup who wants nothing more than to be fawned over and pet?"

"You are the last person I would call soft-headed." Sascha frowned, pacing slightly as emotion got the better of him. "You're the most hard-headed man I've ever known."

"And why do you think that is?" I asked, standing my ground and crossing my arms.

"Because you're stubborn," he flung at me, more restless with every passing second. "And arrogant. You think you're better than the rest of us."

I laughed out loud at that one. "And so you counteract that by treating me like some fragile doll without a thought in his head, who only wants to be fondled and fucked?"

"When have I ever treated you like that?" Sascha shouted.

"Every damn day," I shouted right back. "You won't let me serve my own food. You won't let me engage in any labor that might give me callouses. You won't let me stay alone in the house."

"I care for you," he countered. "I love you. I don't want any harm to come to you."

"Yes, heaven forbid anything should break your favorite toy," I snapped.

"You are not a toy." He towered over me, passion of every sort in his eyes.

I refused to back down or be intimidated. "I was broken before you found me, Sascha," I said, trying to be dispassionate as I told him what he didn't want to hear. "Dmitri saw that in me. He understands it."

"Are you saying that Dmitri understands you better than I do?" Sascha's voice was low and hurt.

"Yes, I'm saying that." He didn't want to hear it, but I had to get it out. "He understands that pain isn't always a bad thing, that hurt is cathartic. He is an expert at inflicting that pain in a way that helps me to see myself and transcend it."

"What does he do to you?" Sascha inched closer. "Tell me how he hurts you."

"No. It's personal," I said in an iron voice. I could see he wanted to know so that he could attempt to give me everything I needed himself, but that would never work. Sascha didn't have enough hate in him to be effective.

"Why are you shutting me out when all I want to do is be close to you?" he growled, more frustrated than before.

"You are close to me, Sascha," I insisted. "But you cannot give me everything I need."

"I should," he spat. "I should be everything to you."

I knew he meant it from his own perspective, but my emotions were too raw to let the opportunity pass. "Oh, you are everything to me, Sascha. You're my lover and you're my captor. You're my friend and you're my owner. I live at your whim and I love at your command."

"How can you say that?" His voice was raw and wounded.

"Because it's true," I laughed, throwing my arms wide. "I'm your pup. You're the leader of the pack. Though your leadership skills are sorely lacking."

A whole new level of offense washed over him. "What is that supposed to mean?"

I wasn't ready to answer him yet. Once I said what I had to say on that score, I'd have a far bigger mess to clean up than the one brought on by my revelations about Dmitri. Instead, I took a step toward him.

"Do you know what my life was like before I came here?" I asked.

"Yes," he said. "You were bullied and tortured by your brothers. You grew up in a family that didn't love you, that was revolted by you. You weren't touched or shown any affection at all. That's all I want to do for you, Peter. I want to make up for all that."

I ignored him, shaking my head. "I was raised in a palace. I was given the finest education possible. I was supposed to be a Justice, a leader, someone in the center of governance. I had knowledge at my fingertips and a palace filled with servants to answer to me at all hours of the day." I hadn't appreciated how precious my freedom had been until finding myself worse than a servant myself. "Do you know what my life would have been like if I hadn't been found by Dmitri and made into your pup?"

"You would have lived a sad, loveless life," Sascha said, though his certainty was waning. "You would have been tucked away in that cold, heartless palace, forgotten and reviled."

I shook my head. "I would have been made a Justice in my father's court. I would have had the power to determine men's lives. My studies were directed toward the law, toward leadership and organization. I knew about geological formations that first day when you asked me how I knew about potential sinkholes under the house because I had studied the natural resources of the entire frontier, how to mine them, and what their uses and value are. My curiosity about the ways of the forest is because I have had the ins and outs of the law as it pertains to the entire kingdom, Old Realm and frontier, drilled into me so that I might be the executor of that law someday. I would have been respected and important, whether I was liked or not."

Sascha stared at me. If he weren't so angry, I was certain he would have been impressed.

"But what is my life now? I'm a fuck toy for two men who cannot stand each other and who use me against each other," I went on.

"You're so much more to me than that," Sascha insisted. "Dmitri is the one who sees you as an object he can use."

"Yes," I said. "I'm an object he can use to take out the fury and the aggression that you left him with when you sent his brother, his only family, the man he nearly gave his life for, away." I hadn't realized how true that was until I hurled the words at Sascha. "And he's the object I use to bring the pain and the darkness inside of me out into the open so I can face it and conquer it."

Dmitri had been right all along about me needing him, but I hadn't realized how desperately he needed me. He needed me to punish to stop him from wanting to punish his brother. We were more deeply entwined than I'd thought. I wasn't comfortable with the idea at all.

"So this is my fault?" Sascha's voice was hoarse. "I'm to blame for whatever Dmitri inflicts on you?"

"He inflicts nothing," I said. "I invite it. I'm not as innocent as you think. Dmitri sees that in me and feeds it."

"But it's my fault because I'm such a piss-poor leader," Sascha said, face pinching with resentment.

"Not everyone is born to lead," I said, trying to rein in my raw frustration over everything I'd been made to endure without comment for the past several weeks. "I don't know how you became leader of a pack, but it wasn't because of your ability to make hard decisions."

"I was made leader of this pack by agreement of the rest of the pack," he insisted, gesturing toward the house. "It was a near unanimous decision."

So many things suddenly made sense to me. "Let me guess. The other choice for leader was Dmitri."

"No one else wanted him." The way Sascha answered was as much a confirmation of my suspicion as anything.

"So they chose you," I said, sweeping him from head to toe with a gesture. "They chose a kind, sentimental man who would never cross them, who would allow them to get away with whatever rule-bending they wanted, and who wouldn't mete out any sort of brutal, forest punishment if there was trouble."

Sascha's mouth hung open for a moment, as if he

were only just realizing it as well. "They have faith in me. They trust me. You don't." The last was fired at me as though it would wound me.

In fact, it did hurt my heart, but only because it proved just how in over his head Sascha was. "You would have done well, if you didn't have Dmitri to challenge you," I said. "But when the moment came when you should have been strong and banished him, you couldn't do it. Because you need everyone to like you, Sascha. You care more about being loved than you do about being respected."

"They're the same thing," he argued, starting to grow restless and pace again.

"They're not," I told him. "If there's one thing that I learned growing up as my father's son, watching him rule Novoberg, it's that love and respect are most certainly not the same thing."

"I made the best decision at the time," Sascha said.

"By banishing Jakob and then letting Mikal go with him instead of telling Dmitri to put up or shut up? Instead of sending him off on his own to start a new pack or be a lone wolf himself? Didn't you tell me that the leader in the pack you used to be with sent contentious men off to start their own packs instead of keeping them around? Did you learn nothing from him?"

"Mikal might have gone with him," Sascha shouted, stopping in front of me again. "And if he went, Jakob would have gone too."

"But Mikal wouldn't have gone, because he loves

Jakob, and Dmitri hates him," I argued. I blinked, then asked, "Did you ever consult with him, ask what he wanted? Or did you let your heart guide your decision?"

Sascha winced. "Jakob and Mikal deserved to be together without Dmitri's interference."

"Away from their home and pack?" I asked. "Pitted against the entire forest on their own? I will admit, I don't know them well, but they seem far more suited for this domestic sort of life we've all made for ourselves here. Dmitri is the one who could handle a rougher sort of life. Even Gregor, Ivan, and Sven know that."

"You've spoken to them about the whole thing?" Sascha seemed alarmed.

"They told me about it right at the beginning," I said. "I see the truth of it all now. You've made the wrong decisions, Sascha. You acted from your heart, not your head."

"That isn't true." He leaned closer to me. "If I acted solely from my heart, I would forbid Dmitri from ever touching you again. But I let him have you. As much as it tears me to shreds inside, I let him have you, because the law of packs says that he has a right to you." I could tell from the vivid emotion in his shaking voice that he believed what he was saying, even though it wounded him.

I shook my head. He still didn't see. "Because I'm nothing but a pup." I shrugged. "The property of the pack, free to be shared with anyone who wants me."

"You're not a pup to me, Peter." He surged into me,

clasping the sides of my face. "You're everything I've ever wanted. You're perfection."

"I'm not," I said, my voice cracking as my own emotion got the better of me. "I'm an angry, bitter, petty, broken man who has had everything taken from him. Don't let my appearance fool you. I'm a man who loves the idea of being used because it absolves me of responsibility for my darkness. Who likes to be hurt so that he has a reason to revel in that darkness. I'm a man who felt a rush of lust when Dmitri mentioned being used by multiple men at once, because the idea of being stretched thin feeds a sick need in me." I let out a breath. "But yes, I'm also the man who feels alive and loved in your arms, who could want nothing more than to spend the rest of my life lost in you. If I could only do it as your equal and not your slave. I'm not one thing."

Sascha dropped my face and took a step back. "You don't love me at all, then," he hissed. "If you did, you wouldn't hurt me like this."

"If you don't start seeing me as I am and accept me as myself, you're only going to hurt yourself," I threw back at him. "Over and over. Because you can't face hard truths. And any man who cannot face hard truths shouldn't be a leader."

"Is that what you think of me?" he asked, face twisting with bitterness.

"Part of what I think of you, yes," I said, knowing the damage was done. I might have just ruined the best thing that had ever happened to me. But to be honest, if that was the best thing, life had a lot of explaining to do. I deserved better.

"I'm sorry to be such a disappointment to you," he said, backing away. "I'm sorry that loving you with my whole heart isn't good enough for you."

"If I believed you loved me, the true me, with all my faults and flaws, and not some idealized image of me you've created in your mind, then nothing could stop me from giving you everything I have and more," I said.

His expression pinched, and for a moment I thought he would continue the argument. Instead, he blew out a breath, all energy leaving him. He turned and strode back toward the house, raising a hand to his face.

"Sascha." I followed after him, worried that I'd gone too far. But at the same time, a new sort of relief filled me. I'd finally said everything I needed to say. I'd liberated myself as much as I could.

Sascha tore across the main room grabbing his coat from its peg by the door and throwing it over his shoulders before charging out the front door.

"Is everything all right?" Jakob asked. He and Mikal stood slowly, glancing between me and the door Sascha had left through.

"No," I said honestly. "I told Sascha some things he wasn't ready to hear."

"Let me guess," Jakob said. "He needed to hear them."

"Badly," I said. I wished it hadn't had to be that way. A huge part of me wanted Sascha to rush back into the house and take me in his arms to kiss me and make it all better. "You'd better go after him," I said in an exhausted voice. "He's not in a good state of mind to be alone."

Jakob stood a bit straighter, studying me with a shrewd look. Sascha might have been blind to what made a good leader, but Jakob knew one when he saw one. He nodded and started for the door.

Mikal marched after him. "We'll talk to him," he said.

"You might want to talk about more than a few things," I told the two of them as they left. "I told him he made a terrible decision in banishing the two of you last year. I think I might have made him see just how bad that decision was."

Jakob and Mikal seemed to catch their breaths. They looked at each other as though a confrontation they'd been expecting for a while had come. Then they nodded to me and marched out of the house.

I felt an odd sense of depression, but also relief, once they were gone. I felt powerful on top of that. The one thing I didn't feel like was a pup. I was a man, and a strong one at that. And for the first time since being cast out of the city and finding myself in the forest, I was alone.

17

I returned to work at the table, picking up the scissors and continuing to cut out pieces of the trousers I intended to sew. The silence that filled the house was unusual, but also peaceful. I went so far as to open a few windows—even though it was just a bit too cold still to keep them open long—so that I could hear birdsong and the early spring breeze in the treetops. The rich, moist scents of Sven's newly-planted garden beds wafted in along with the cool air. Before long, I found myself humming some of my favorite old folk tunes that I'd learned in music lessons at the palace.

I felt full of myself in the best possible way. I felt like a man. I'd asserted myself, spoken my truth, and stood up for what I believed in. Anything was possible. Sascha would recover from the emotional wounds I'd inflicted the same way I recovered from the strains and bruises of the way Dmitri liked to fuck me. Like I'd recovered from the initial soreness of those first few days. It was all a matter of getting used to things. Once Sascha got used to me as I was and the truths he needed to learn about himself, we would be able to speak to each other as man to man. We would be able to reach a deeper understanding with each other as well. Perhaps then we could even fall in love for real.

That prospect left me with a smile on my face as I finished cutting out the first patterns and laid out another length of fabric on the table to trace pieces for more trousers.

I was startled when Dmitri returned from wherever he'd gone skulking off to earlier.

"Are you here alone?" he asked, stepping into the house but keeping the door open behind him.

I should have recognized something suspicious about his manner, but self-satisfaction had me blind. "Ivan and the others aren't back from Katrina's yet," I said, glancing to Dmitri, but focusing on my work. "And I upset Sascha, so he ran off to lick his wounds for a while. I sent Mikal and Jakob after them. Who knows how long it will take him to—"

I stopped, instantly on edge when Dmitri stepped to the side and gestured to someone through the doorway.

Those someones turned out to be his friends, Gunter and Axel, from the faire. They stepped into the house, managing to look even more imposing indoors than they had outside. Both looked weathered. Gunter's eyepatch was frayed around the edges, and his other eye narrowed at the sight of me as he broke into a toothy grin.

Axel licked his lips, hunger in his eyes as he said in his damaged voice, "He looks even better than I remember him."

I gripped the scissors tightly, pulse racing. "You shouldn't have guests when Sascha isn't here," I told Dmitri.

"Gunter and Axel are friends, aren't they?" Dmitri started across the room to me, gesturing for Gunter and Axel to stay where they were.

"We hope to become very good friends indeed," Gunter growled, grabbing his crotch.

I stepped away from the table, scissors still in hand, edging my way to the short hall and thinking of nothing but escape. Dmitri sped up, shifting into my path to keep me from getting away.

"I've got a plan, Peter," he said, gripping my upper arms, prying the scissors out of my hand, and staring pointedly into my eyes. Something deeper than lust flashed there. "It's a plan you're going to like."

"I don't think I will," I said in a weak voice, glancing past him to Gunter and Axel.

The two strangers stood with their heads together, muttering to each other as they studied me. I had the horrible feeling that they were discussing how to divide me up and eat me alive.

"You want out of here as badly as I do," Dmitri whispered quickly. He tossed the scissors to the table and grabbed the side of my face, forcing me to look at him. "Neither of us wants to live at Sascha's will anymore."

"I wouldn't say that," I said in a hushed voice.

"I've been working on getting out of here for a year," he went on. "I've got contacts in the forest, people who will supply me if I go lone for a while. I've got men who will join me to form a new pack."

"Gunter and Axel?" I asked, my voice shaking.

Dmitri scoffed. "No, not them. They're as stupid as dirt, for one. They have no redeeming skills either."

"Then why are you friends with them? Why are they here?" My voice began to shake. I fought not to tremble all over.

"They're part of a wealthy pack," Dmitri whispered. "We got to talking at the faire. They fancy you. A lot. Enough to meet the price I asked."

My eyes went wide, and I could feel the color drain from my face. "I'm not going with them," I said, terrified.

"It's just for an hour or so," Dmitri insisted. "They're offering a fortune for you. More than enough for us to get away from here and start out on our own."

"I don't want to go anywhere with you." I tried to pull away from him, but he held me.

"Fine, you don't have to come with me," he said. "But before you say no entirely, hear me out. We could make a fortune, you and I. We could live like kings."

"By selling me to men like them?" I nodded toward Gunter and Axel.

Dmitri looked confused by my reticence. "But you like it," he whispered. "You gag for it."

"Not like that. Not with them." My voice grew smaller and higher. It was almost as though I could feel myself shrinking as Dmitri's intent became clearer.

"What's wrong with you, Peter?" Dmitri shook me hard. "You never balk when you come with me, and believe me, I'm ten times more creative than either of those two."

"I won't do it," I said, trying to get away from him in earnest. "I don't want them touching me. I don't want them anywhere near me."

"What's taking so long?" Axel growled. "My balls are about ready to fall off."

"Yeah," Gunter added. "You said your pup was insatiable, that he'd be offering that sweet ass of his to us on a silver platter."

"No," I told Dmitri, shaking. "I won't do it. Let me go. Let me out of here."

Dmitri held fast as I yanked and tugged to get away from him. Panic raged through me now. My hands and feet were beginning to go numb.

"This isn't like you at all," Dmitri said, disappointed. "One hour. That's all. They've been without since the faire, and probably for a long time before that. They'll be over and done before the hour is through, mark my words."

"This isn't what we were promised, Dmitri," Gunter boomed, shifting restlessly.

"Come on." Dmitri shifted around me, clamping a hand over my wrist and dragging me across the room.

The closer we got to Gunter and Axel, the more I struggled against him. "No, I don't want to, I won't," I said, increasingly desperate.

"Ooh," Axel said, as though Dmitri were bringing him a treat. "I like it when they fight. It makes it so much more fun to force them into submission."

"This one will be especially sweet when he's submitting," Gunter said, grabbing my face with one, large hand when Dmitri dragged me close enough.

As soon as he touched me, the panic flared so strong that the edges of my vision blurred. "No. I don't want you. Don't touch me."

"Yes, he'll be fun to play with," Gunter said, lust in his one eye.

"You can't make me do this," I gasped, thrashing and trying to strike anyone who came near me.

"I swear, he isn't usually like this," Dmitri apologized. He glared at me, as if the fault in the situation were mine. "Get his clothes off and I'm sure he'll calm down."

"Not too much, I hope," Axel laughed, yanking my shirt out of my trousers.

"Stop." I burst into tears. "I won't let you do this. Don't touch me. Stop!"

They ignored me, pulling at the buttons of my waistcoat and trousers in spite of my efforts to fight them off.

When my struggles annoyed them too much, Axel grabbed my arms and pulled them back behind me so that I couldn't move. I kicked instead, trying with everything I had to fend them off. All my kicking did, though, was lift my feet off the ground. As soon as they were out from under me, Axel hoisted me up enough so that Gunter could rip my trousers off my legs, exposing me from the waist down.

Gunter sucked in a breath. "Look at that cock."

"Impressive for a pup, eh?" Dmitri said, as casual as you please. "Just wait until it's hard and dripping for you."

Gunter looked at him for a moment as though he didn't quite believe it, then moved in to wrap a hand around my prick and stroke it.

"No, stop," I cried, panting in terror.

Traitor that it was, my cock responded to being handled, even if I found the man handling it to be horrific and repulsive. I didn't give quite the response I usually did, which was a small victory.

"We'll soon get that sword pointed in the right direction," Axel laughed. "Where can we have him?" he asked Dmitri.

"In one of the back bedrooms," Dmitri said, pointing to the long hall.

Axel hoisted me against him and turned to drag me down the hall.

"No!" I shouted, using every bit of strength I had to

fight back. "I don't want to. I won't let you. Get off of me. Sascha!" The last cry was proof of how desperate and afraid I was. Sascha was off in the forest, furious at me for hurting him. I'd left myself vulnerable, and he wouldn't be rushing to my rescue.

The only hope I had was to fight as I'd never fought before. I kicked, I flailed, and I growled. I'd have enough experience being manhandled by my brothers that I knew where to aim my blows, but Gunter and Axel were so much bigger than my brothers. They were miles bigger than me.

"This goes beyond feisty," Gunter growled, somehow tearing the rest of my clothes off in spite of the effort I made to impede their progress in dragging me back to the bedrooms.

"Stop struggling, pup," Axel growled, trying to grab my arms and hold them behind me as I lashed out. "Stop it."

He slapped me hard across the face. That stunned me for a moment, but as soon as I felt myself being pulled toward the hall again, I redoubled my efforts to get away.

"No! Dmitri, do something! Stop them," I shouted in a last-ditch appeal for help.

"Stop fighting them, Peter. It'll be over with soon enough," Dmitri shouted back. "This is absurd," he added.

"He'd better be worth what we're paying for him," Gunter growled.

"Oh, he will be, he will," Dmitri insisted.

"Let go of me." Struggling was all I had, and I'd be damned if I would give up and let myself be raped by a pair of brutes who turned my stomach.

"I've got an idea," Dmitri said, breaking away from Gunter and Axel and heading to Gregor's apothecary counter. "We gave him something on that first night that made him amenable to whatever we wanted."

"No," I shouted, more alarmed than ever. I remembered full well what that tea had done to me. It had made it impossible for me to move. I hadn't wanted to that night, but in the situation I found myself in now, the idea of being rendered immobile chilled me to the bone. "I won't drink the tea."

"This is it," Dmitri said, plucking a bottle from one of Gregor's high shelves and bringing it back over to where I continued to struggle. "It's just the tincture and not the tea, but it's the same concoction."

"I won't take it," I raged. "I won't do any of this. Let me go."

"His struggling is making me hot," Gunter growled, unbuckling the belt holding his loose trousers up. "I'm going to enjoy every second of this."

"With a body like that, I don't know how we wouldn't enjoy ourselves," Axel laughed. He managed to run his hands over my naked torso while also stopping me from breaking away from him.

"Hold him still so I can give him this," Dmitri said.

"I won't take it, I won't swallow it," I insisted. I glanced desperately toward the door, praying that Sascha and the others would return and put a stop to things.

"You'll swallow everything you're given to swallow, pup," Axel growled against my ear. "And when we've recovered, you'll swallow it all again."

"I won't," I insisted as Dmitri uncorked the bottle and tried to get closer to me. "Let me go."

"You're embarrassing me, Peter," Dmitri sniffed, looking irritated. "Open up. This will make it all feel good."

"No." I kept my teeth clenched.

I'd never particularly liked Dmitri, but I'd thought we had enough of an understanding to respect each other. As Axel wrestled my arms behind my back and trapped my legs between his to keep me from kicking, I hated Dmitri with a fire I hadn't known was possible. The more annoyed he looked, the fiercer my hatred for him grew.

I thrashed my head to keep him from getting near me with the bottle, but Gunter stepped in from the side and clamped a hand around my jaw. "The best ones always put up the biggest fight," he said and licked his lips. "That just makes it sweeter to master them."

I put up a struggle for as long as I could, writhing and squirming in a vain attempt to break free. I refused to open my mouth, and in the end, Gunter had to pinch my nose hard—hard enough to make it bleed—until I was forced to open my mouth to gasp for breath. As soon as I did, Dmitri thrust the neck of the medicine bottle in my mouth and poured. Gunter shoved my head back so the majority of the bottle's contents spilled into my mouth, then held my mouth closed until I was forced to swallow.

I knew something was wrong in an instant. The tea they'd given me on that first night tasted of mint with a bit of honey. The tincture Dmitri poured down my throat tasted strongly of bitter herbs and earth. I'd reacted quickly to the tea, and it was a vain hope to think I could hold out against the effects of the tincture.

"That should do it," Dmitri said, staring distastefully at the bottle, then scowling at me. "It takes a few minutes to work. Let me fetch some ointment for you."

"No." I resumed my struggles, but the fear of what would happen once the tincture took effect made my fear of rape even stronger, which made me clumsier. "Let me go."

"Might as well," Axel said as he dragged me down the hall, following Dmitri. "I like it better when it's smooth anyhow."

"Then you'll really love this pup," Dmitri said, as though describing the prize traits of a horse he was selling at a faire. "They just shaved him again yesterday."

"I can see that," Gunter said, handling his cock as he followed Axel dragging me down the hall.

"You can have him in there." Dmitri pointed down the hall to one of the empty bedrooms.

By the time Axel dragged me into the room, the tincture was working.

"No, stop," I wept, talking to my body more than Axel and Gunter as they closed in on me. My limbs felt heavier and heavier with each passing second. My body started to relax against my wishes. My balls grew heavier and felt fuller, and as Axel threw me down on my back on the bed, then nudged my legs apart and closed a fist around my cock, I went hard fast.

There was more to it than just that, though. The feeling that something was horribly wrong continued to sink down on me. I tried to move, but it was like swimming through mud. Everything seemed far away, but sharp and acute at the same time. I was beyond terrified, shaking in fear, but my body wanted to be touched and used and made to come so desperately I thought I might lose my mind if I didn't come.

"That's what I was promised," Axel growled. He yanked me to the edge of the bed, shoved my knees apart, then knelt so that he could slide my prick into his mouth.

I let out a protest, but it didn't form into words. Physically, it felt pleasurable. Emotionally, I was in agony. I willed my body to move, screamed at myself to fight back, but not only could I barely move, within a minute I came in Axel's mouth.

"God, that's sweet," he growled, rocking back and wiping his mouth with the back of his hand.

"And look, he's already filling again," Gunter laughed.

"It's the concoction," Dmitri said, walking into the room and handing a jar of ointment to Axel. "He was good for about four or five goes the first time he had it. You should get a full hour out of him and more now." He slapped Axel on the back, then headed for the door. "Enjoy. I'll keep a look-out for the others and warn you if they come home."

I opened my mouth to scream every foul name I knew at Dmitri, but all that came out was a feeble groan.

"Looks like he's already begging for more," Gunter said, rubbing his hands together. "I should have asked for a bit of that magic sauce myself. I already feel like I could blow." He gestured to Axel. "Hold him up so he can suck my cock."

In my mind, I screamed and cried and ordered, begged, and pleaded with them to stop. I kicked and bit and scratched until they backed away. In reality, I was as limp as a rag doll as Axel pulled me to a sitting position, then tipped me forward. Gunter grabbed my head and brought it to the level where he wanted it, then pried open my mouth and thrust his prick inside.

"Ah, yes," he growled, moving slowly at first. "That's what I wanted."

My senses were both heightened and immobilized by the drug. Gunter's cock seemed unbelievably large in my mouth as he thrust harder and deeper. It was more than just horror of the moment. My mind played tricks on me. He seemed to grow fatter and fatter until it wasn't just my mouth he was fucking, but my entire head. I was losing my mind.

"Oh, he's too much." Gunter pulled out of my mouth with a strangled sigh. "I want to come in his ass."

"I don't care where I come as long as I do," Axel laughed. "Sit on the bed."

Axel wrenched me to stand, though how I managed to stay on my feet as Gunter sat behind me was a miracle. My head flopped down—even as I screamed at myself to move or fight back—but as my gaze dropped to the floor, I shouted in earnest. Somehow, the entire floor was covered in spiders. At first, there were hundreds of small ones, scurrying this way and that, running over my bare feet and Axel's. Then they grew larger—to the size of peas—then the size of coins—then the side of my fists. I screamed at them, but they just kept getting bigger, and there wasn't a damn thing I could do about it.

"Ease him back."

I felt hands around my waist, and a moment later, Gunter's cock pressed against my asshole. I snapped my head up—or so it felt, the gesture, in reality, was little more than a loll—as I was breeched. I let out a long, low cry of protest.

"He wants it, all right," Axel laughed.

Gunter clamped one arm around my waist and used the other to brace against the bed as he jerked his hips into me. "Oh, that's good," he groaned. "That's so good."

"He's ready to burst," Axel panted. He wrapped a hand around my cock—which was somehow slick—and fisted me. "Look at him."

I came a second time, but something was still horribly, horribly wrong. Cum seemed to gush out of me like a fountain, in greater and greater amounts. The pleasure I felt was like a nightmare, and the gushing just kept going and going. I felt as though my insides were spewing out through my prick, and there was nothing I could do to stop it.

"Bend him this way," I heard Axel say somewhere above me. The world tipped precariously. I wasn't sure if anything was coming out of me after all or if it was my mind unraveling. "Yes, like that."

Axel grunted, and his cock filled my mouth. Only it didn't feel like a cock, it felt as though someone were shoving flaming logs deeper and deeper into my throat. My whole body was being split in two, from the front and the back, as the two men used me. I could feel them invading me deeper and deeper, their cocks thickening and extending as they burned away my insides, reaching for each other. I knew that the moment their tips met and fused in my gut, I would never be free. I'd disappear inside of them, disintegrating into nothing.

Vaguely, what felt like a thousand miles away, I heard Gunter cry out and felt something warm spread through me. Axel's thrusts were frantic, and he, too, made a noise as warmth hit the back of my throat. I tried to fight it, tried not to swallow. If I did, I knew the poison would spread all the way through me and I would die. The room around me wasn't just spinning, it was warping, folding in on itself, and turning colors. Terrifying shrieks sounded in my ears, like giant night birds flying through the forest, intent on finding me and pecking my eyes out.

"Is he supposed to do that?" I heard someone ask high, high above me, like I was at the bottom of a well.

"Not on your life," came the answer. "Dmitri!"

I felt myself jerk and fall. My body hit the hard floor. Spiders still skittered every which way. I tried to strike out at them, but couldn't move. I feared opening my mouth lest they crawl inside of me, but I couldn't stop myself from screaming over and over, louder and louder. It occurred to me that the sound of night birds was actually me screaming, but I couldn't grab hold of the idea or the sound.

"What did you do?" someone asked.

"What's going on here?" another voice shouted. In the very corners of my mind, the last part of me with even a tenuous hold on reality, I thought it might be Sascha. There was no way to tell for certain, though. Someone had opened up floodgates, and the sound of water rushing furiously filled the room, drowning out everything else.

There was movement everywhere, more noise than I could grasp hold of. One moment I thought that someone else hit the floor with me. The next I was certain I was being lifted up. Hands tried to close around me, and I screamed and flailed for all I was worth again. I hit against something, no idea what it was. The more I moved, the more I felt as though my insides were leaking through my skin, like my entire body was turning inside out. The night birds were furious in my ears.

And then all of the movement, all of the sound clamped around me, throbbing into silence. I went rigid, jerking and trembling. That tiny, back corner of my mind that though it'd heard Sascha's voice observed dispassionately that I must have been having a seizure. That part of me was curious for a few seconds before snapping into blackness.

18

"...Meant to be diluted, you fucking bastard! That's why it's made into a tea!"

"I didn't know. How was I supposed to know that?"

"I've never heard of anyone ingesting that much straight."

"Will he die?"

"I don't know. I just don't know."

"You made the bloody stuff. You should know its side-effects as well as its uses."

"I've never known anyone stupid enough to drink it undiluted."

"I want you out of here. I want you gone, now."

"Sascha, he's starting to seize again."

"Hold him down. Turn him so he doesn't bite his tongue this time."

. . .

"...penalty for rape is. I have half a mind to execute it myself."

"It wasn't rape, I swear."

"We paid for him fair and square."

"...signs of a struggle all over the house."

"You'd better run."

"You need to run too. I'll kill you myself."

"No one deserves what you did to this boy."

"He was in on it, I swear."

"Dmitri, you need to go. Even I think you need to go. And never look back."

"...doesn't come out of it soon, I don't know what I'll do."

"Can you give him more water? Flush him out?"

"It's in his blood now, not his...."

"Sorry. I'm so sorry, Peter. I never should have left that day. I should have stayed with you, forced myself to be the man you needed me to be. I should have been here to protect you. I'll never forgive myself for...."

Every part of my body ached. My head felt thick, my limbs disjoined, my joints as if they'd all been pulled apart and forced back together again at the wrong angles. My insides were even worse. My stomach felt like

I'd swallowed embers and my gut as if I'd shit them out in a steady stream of fire. I could feel myself trembling, but every other sensation struck me as wrong, bad.

As soon as I realized large, strong arms were wrapped around me, I broke out into screaming at the top of my lungs and flailed, punched, and kicked, desperate to get away.

"He's awake again," someone said in a grave, exhausted voice.

"Hold him down so we can get some water into him." That voice was Gregor's. "Someone fetch Sascha."

I screamed and battled against the arms holding me. They were going to hurt me. It had to be Gunter or Axel. I could already feel the way they would fuck me, going deep until it hurt. When something slid into my mouth, I screamed even louder, sputtering and thrashing.

"No! No, I don't want to. Stop! I won't. Let me go," I screamed, my voice already hoarse.

"Peter? Peter!" Sascha's voice was far away at first, then right near me.

Whoever held me still let go. I tried to push off of whatever I was lying on, struggling to get away, but another set of arms clamped around me, holding me hard. I thought it might be Sascha, but I was still desperate to get away. I thought the sob I heard might have been Sascha too, but I was too busy screaming myself hoarse and battling for my life to do anything about it.

"Can you give him that tea that made him sleep?" Sascha asked, his voice strange and tight.

"I can't keep giving it to him forever," Gregor answered.

"I can't stand seeing him like this. You said it could be weeks before the drug worked its way out of his system."

"And I can't keep sedating him for weeks. He's going to have to come around and deal with the hallucinations soon."

"Not today," Sascha said. "Not today."

I fought and cried, then gagged and sputtered as whatever it was slid into my mouth again. Then I drifted off, falling back into the blackness.

I don't know how much time had passed the next time I came to. It was dark and quiet. I could hear the sounds of night insects outside an open window. A horrible stench filled the air, like piss and shit. I was too warm, and after a few minutes of listening to myself breathe, I realized that was because I was wrapped tightly in blankets. My entire body was just as sore as the last time I'd almost come around, but my head didn't feel quite as thick.

I moved slightly, half to see if I even could move. It was difficult, but the more I tried, the more I realized that was because I was swaddled tightly in the blankets, as if I were an infant. Bits and hints of the last few times I'd drifted close to consciousness hit me. I'd lashed out, which explained why I was restricted. At least I wasn't being held down by a man's arms. That was the only, tiny bright spot in a never-ending sea of darkness.

I realized I was on my side and tried to roll to my back. The motion made me realize just how badly my body ached. I drew in a deep, steadying breath, realizing my throat was sore. That was probably from all the screaming I'd done.

I sucked in a breath. I'd made the connection between my throat being sore and screaming. That had to mean my mind was coming back from wherever it had gone due to the tincture Dmitri had forced me to drink. Unfortunately, realizing that brought everything back with it—Dmitri's betrayal, the rape, my argument with Sascha, the spiders.

I'd been a complete and utter fool. I'd trusted the wrong people, and that included myself. I'd lashed out at Sascha and chased away my greatest protector. I'd deliberately wounded the man who loved me. And my punishment had been severe.

Tears streamed out of my eyes as I wriggled in an attempt to free my arms. Then again, what was the point in breaking free? I was as safe as I was going to be, and at least where I was, I couldn't hurt myself or someone else. My crying grew worse when I realized the horrible stench was coming from me. I'd messed myself while passed out, and there wasn't a damn thing I could do about it.

"Peter? Are you awake?"

I gasped sharply and flinched away from the voice that sounded from the chair next to me.

A heartbeat later, I realized it was Gregor and let out a breath. "I am." My voice came out as a croak.

Gregor slipped off his chair and knelt beside me. I was wrapped up on the sofa in the main room. It was night. Everything was dark, but for one lantern on the table.

"I'm not going to touch you," Gregor said in a soothing voice. "Not until you tell me it's all right. You've been in and out for a week. It took us four days to figure out that if someone is touching you when you wake up, it causes you to have a fit."

"Is that why I'm swaddled?" I asked groggily.

"You've lashed out at anyone who comes near you," Gregor said. "I can't say I blame you. Mikal told me how they found you."

I blinked at him in the dim light. "How did they find me?" I asked, barely above a whisper.

Gregor swallowed. "On the floor. Bleeding. Those men had—" He shook his head, squeezing his eyes as if he were about to cry. "Mikal said you were screaming your head off, and then you fell into a seizure. It was the tincture Dmitri gave you. It's meant to be diluted into a tea, no more than twenty drops at a time. You must have had three dozen doses all at once."

"I told him I didn't want it," I managed to croak. "I told them to leave me alone, that I wouldn't do it. I fought so hard, but they held me still and Dmitri forced me to drink it."

"That's what we figured," Gregor sighed. "In spite of what Dmitri tried to say."

My eyes went wide. "Is Dmitri here?"

"God, no," Gregor said. "Sascha banished him days ago. It's a miracle he didn't kill him, or the other two. You'll never have to see Dmitri again."

I nodded, gladder than I could express. Then I burst into a fresh round of tears. "They hurt me," I said. It was all I could say, but it was enough.

"Poor boy," Gregor sighed. He hesitated, and for a moment the only sound in the room was my pathetic keening. "I can give you something to make you sleep, if you'd like."

The ghost of a conversation I might have heard when I was near consciousness before drifted back to me, and I shook my head. "You said it's been a week since…it happened?"

Gregor nodded. "Seven days tomorrow. We managed to get you to drink water and broth."

"Is that why I'm festering in my own shit?" I asked, screwing up my nose.

"It's hard to take someone to the washroom when they strike out at anyone who touches them, and when they continue to have seizures every few hours."

I nodded slowly. "Can you help me there now? Or… or help me out to the pool? I just want to be clean." I wasn't sure I would ever feel clean again.

Gregor looked doubtful. "You're still having seizures, and since you have a fit every time someone touches you, the pool isn't a good idea." He stood, studying me as though he wasn't sure how to go about helping me now.

I thought I understood his concern. "I'm feeling lucid now. I think I'll be aware that it's you touching me and not...them."

Thankfully, I didn't need to explain further. Gregor untucked the ends of the blanket that constricted me gingerly all the same. The smell was terrible, but it felt so good to have fresh air hit my skin as I was unwrapped that I started to sob again.

"Are you certain you're all right?" Gregor asked, helping me to a sitting position, then to stand.

"No," I sniffled, allowing myself to feel as pathetic and morose as I wanted. "I'm not sure I'll ever be all right again."

"I know," Gregor said in a sad voice.

I tried to take a few steps toward the hall on my own, but I was as weak as a newborn. Even with Gregor supporting me, I had to go painfully slowly. My muscles ached, but they weren't the only thing about me that throbbed. With bitter irony, I was highly aware of my balls and cock. I knew it was one of the effects of the tincture, but the desperate need to come was maddening.

"What time is it?" I asked in a whisper to distract myself, loath to wake anyone else as Gregor helped me shuffle to the nearest washroom.

"Well past midnight," Gregor answered. "Long before dawn."

I'd picked the perfect time to come out of my stupor. Everyone else was asleep, so I could clean myself up undisturbed. I wasn't comfortable with complete silence, though.

"Did Sascha tell you we argued right before it happened?" I asked in a hollow voice.

Gregor let out a heavy breath. "He did. He feels terrible, Peter. I've never seen him like he's been for the past week."

"It was my own blindness to Dmitri's plan," I said, every part of me aching as we finally reached the washroom. "And my own pride that made me argue with Sascha."

I leaned against the sink, attempting to turn on the spigot, surprised that I couldn't manage it. Gregor turned it on without me needing to ask.

"Sascha said you had some good points," Gregor said.

I also didn't need to tell him I was too weak to wet a rag and run it over my stinking body. He reached for the rag and did the honors for me, being gentle but thorough, as I leaned against the sink. It took all of my strength just to stay upright. I was mortified that, in spite of everything I quickly went hard.

"I was too harsh," I whispered, unable to speak any louder, desperate to distract myself from my prick. "He didn't deserve to be the target of my frustration like that. Not when I know he loves me."

"And you love him too," Gregor said.

It took everything I had not to cry out in remembered fear and pain as he wiped the wet rag over my backside. I could feel ghost hands grabbing at me, and I swore the sink in front of me started to fill with spiders. They had to be hallucinations, but that didn't make them seem any less real.

"I love him," I repeated Gregor's words, though they rang hollow in my ears. "Inasmuch as I am capable of loving anyone."

"Of course you're capable," Gregor said, using almost comical care to wash my genitals. "Everyone is capable of love."

I shook my head. "Not me. Not before, and not now."

"Don't say that," Gregor said. "What happened to you was abominable, but it doesn't mean you aren't capable of loving anyone now."

"Gregor, I'm sorry, but I can't—" I panted, close to losing my mind as he washed my balls. "I'm going to—"

"It's the tincture," Gregor said gravely. "Not you. It doesn't mean anything. You're likely to feel the effects for a while still. If it helps, I could—"

I nodded quickly, bracing myself against the sink. It only took a few gentle strokes before I came. The release of tension was such a relief that I groaned and burst into fresh tears.

"That's a good lad," Gregor cooed, rinsing his hands, then finishing up washing me. "All better now."

I smiled weakly. Gregor was nearly twice my age, but

it felt as though I were an old man being tended to by a green youth. I'd seen more pain in my twenty years than he'd probably known in his lifetime. And I was tired. Beyond just the physical. I felt as though I wanted to put down the burden of my life and sink into a rest I would never wake up from.

"You're looking better."

I snapped my head up at the sound of Sascha's voice. He stood in the washroom doorway, watching me with pained, uncertain eyes.

"If this is better, I shudder to think what I looked like before," I croaked.

Sascha let out a breath and surged toward me, but before he could reach me, Gregor stood and blocked him.

"Don't," Gregor said. "You remember what happened the last few times you tried to touch him."

"I have to hold him," Sascha pleaded with Gregor. "This is all my fault. I can't stand you forcing us apart like this."

"I'm doing it for both of your own good," Gregor said, glancing warily between us. "Peter's mind is still in a fragile state, and every time he has a fit, you react badly," he told Sascha.

"This is intolerable," Sascha said. I could hear the stress in his voice.

In fact, I wanted him to hold me. I wanted to curl up in Sascha's arms and forget the entire thing had happened. I wanted him to make me feel safe and loved. But I had a horrible feeling the memory of what had happened wasn't finished torturing me. I had a horrible feeling I couldn't pretend to be in love anymore.

"I...I think I need someone to carry me back to bed," I admitted sheepishly, glancing to Sascha.

Sascha flinched toward me, but looked to Gregor, as though he were the gatekeeper.

"If Peter says it's all right...." He shrugged, then stepped out of the way.

Sascha moved forward, lifting me into his arms quickly and cradling me like a baby. The touch of his skin against mine sent waves of confused feelings through me. It felt so, so good to be close to him again, but at the same time, I felt trapped, threatened. I didn't know whether I wanted to disappear into him or thrash until I was free, so I tensed harder and harder. That only brought me close to the edge of the sensation that I was going to drown.

"I'll get rid of the soiled blankets and find more to wrap him in," Gregor said, hurrying out of the room ahead of us.

"I thought Peter could go back to sleeping in my bed," Sascha said, sounding vulnerable.

"Not a good idea yet," I said, forcing myself to breathe as steadily as possible. I was starting to shake harder and harder as Sascha carried me into the main room. I forced myself to think and to speak honestly. "It's too much. All of it. I don't know if it's the drugs. Gregor says they're still in me."

"And they could be for a while longer," Gregor said

as he hurried to gather up the blankets and take them to the back hall.

"It feels like...." I couldn't think of how to finish the sentence. My breathing came harder and harder, and the edges of my vision blurred. "My mind isn't working. I want.... It's all mixed up. What happened. Now. I want to feel...but it's all mixed up together."

"I've got you," Sascha murmured, as tense as I felt. "Nothing is ever going to harm you again. I won't let it."

I knew he was only trying to show how much he cared for me, but the tighter he held me, the more panic overwhelmed me.

"They held me tightly," I said, unable to form the thought of what I wanted to tell him fully. "I couldn't get away. This is...I can't...there are spiders everywhere, Sascha. Let go before I—"

It was too late. I started to convulse in his arms.

"Peter?" Sascha's voice sounded as though it came from the end of a tunnel.

"Put him down," Gregor's voice answered. "Stress is what's causing him to have these fits. If you put him down, it might pass quicker."

I wasn't sure how quickly it passed. When I drifted up from the morass I'd sunk into, I was dripping with sweat and panting. It was still dark. I sat on the sofa, wrapped in a blanket. Sascha sat to one side of me and Gregor to the other. I groaned as I let out a breath and flopped my head against the back of the sofa.

"Has anyone done any research at all on the properties of that tincture and the long-term effects of overdose?" I panted, closing my eyes.

"I'll prepare my paper to send to the Royal Institute of Medicine right away," Gregor answered.

I somehow managed to laugh weakly.

"You have to do something," Sascha said. "Peter is suffering. There has to be a medicine you can give him, something that will make him well again. We can't go on like this."

I agreed with Sascha, but didn't feel particularly hopeful about a miracle cure.

"Time," Gregor said with a shrug. "All we can do is give it time and see what happens. These are uncharted waters we're swimming in."

"But they can't be," Sascha argued. "I want to...I need to be able...This is all my fault."

Sascha leapt off the sofa, holding a fist to his mouth as he strode toward the back hall and out into the night.

I closed my eyes and let out an exhausted breath. "You'd think that he was the one who was drugged and raped," I said, but without much emotion.

"He was," Gregor said, a note of surprise in his voice. I peeked at him. "He loves you, so whatever pain you feel, he feels too."

He was right. I nodded. "Oh, I feel his pain. Believe me, I do."

"I believe you," Gregor said.

It was probably easier for him to believe my pain, considering the tears that squeezed out of my eyes as I closed them again and rolled to my side so that I could sleep.

The sun was up the next time I awoke. I was immediately aware of activity in the room. My first instinct was to flinch and gasp and try to get away, but sense reached me quickly, and I stopped myself from screaming in the nick of time. I forced myself to breathe, rolling to my back and blinking up at the ceiling. A few more breaths and a quick assessment of the state of my body, and I realized I hadn't shit or pissed myself when I was out. I considered it a small but vital victory.

"You're awake," Jakob said from somewhere nearby.

I twisted, glad that the blankets weren't wrapped so tightly around me this time, and managed to muscle myself to a sitting position. That was another mighty victory.

"Am I?" I asked, blinking around at the room.

It seemed different, in spite of everything being exactly as it was before. Ivan was working in the kitchen, which smelled wonderful—like baking bread and chicken roasting with herbs. Gregor was busy at his apothecary counter, grinding something in a pestle and making notes. Jakob was seated in the chair beside the sofa—the same chair Gregor had been in the night before—sewing something leather. He smiled as I turned my bleary eyes to him.

"Would you rather be awake or asleep?" Jakob asked. His expression communicated sympathy and sadness, but also respect.

"Awake," I said, catching my breath. I winced and strained as I found a comfortable way to sit. What surprised me was that I actually found one. As soon as my body settled into it, I was reasonably comfortable. Except for a renewed heaviness in my balls and throbbing in my prick that said the tincture was still raging in my body.

"Do you need anything?" Jakob asked, leaning forward in his chair as if he would get up. "Water? Coffee? Something to eat?"

I nodded. "Water."

"And give him one of the buns I made," Ivan called from the kitchen. "Gregor says he needs to start eating again or he'll waste away to nothing."

I lifted the blanket to look down at my frame as Jakob went to fetch water and a bun. I had lost weight. I could see my ribs. Skinny wasn't attractive on me.

Jakob brought me a glass of water and a bun, then sat to the side, at the ready as I ate and drank painfully slowly. It felt good to eat, and I was surprised by how hungry I was, but I knew enough to eat only tiny bits at a time.

"So," I said at length as awkwardness pressed down on me. "Lovely weather we're having."

Jakob laughed and moved back into his chair. "Well, at least your humor has returned," he said. "I'm sure the rest of you will be back in no time to join it."

"I wish I were as certain," I said in a hard whisper.

Jakob shrugged. "You'll heal from this. You're

stronger than you look."

"And you know this how?" I asked, then took a slightly larger bite of the bun.

Jakob narrowed his eyes and studied me. "From what everyone has said. From what I've observed myself."

"I'm glad someone has faith in me," I said before taking a drink.

"We all have immense faith in you, Peter," Jakob said with a serious look. "More than you know."

I looked at him, trying to figure out what he could possibly mean by a comment like that. Faith was not something I expected anyone to have in me, particularly not my pack and its tangential members. Lust, yes. Affection, certainly. But the way that Jakob looked at me hinted at an entirely different emotion.

"Did something happen when I was…ill?" I asked, pushing myself to sit up straighter.

Jakob was an intelligent man. I wondered what his life had been like before he had been thrown into the forest and become a wolf. He leaned forward, resting his elbows on his knees. "You are what happened, Peter. You walked in here and changed everyone's lives."

"By giving them all someone to fawn over and fuck," I said, almost as an afterthought, as I finished my bun. I wasn't happy that the morose frustration I'd felt before… what happened happened would return so soon.

Jakob laughed and shook his head. "Is it because your family were such pricks?" he asked. His mention of the word "prick" did nothing to help distract me from the embarrassing and uncomfortable state of mine. "Is it because they spent your whole life looking down on you and kicking you around? Are you just used to doing the same to yourself?"

"I'm terribly sorry, I don't know what you're talking about," I said with perfect manners.

"You're a gem, Peter," Jakob said with a wry smile.

"So I'm constantly being told, and so my ass periodically reminds me when it's uncomfortable to sit down," I replied, finishing my water and setting the cup aside.

Jakob gawked at me. "You really don't know what you've come to mean to this pack, do you?"

We were going to keep going around in circles if I didn't put an end to things. "They care for me. I also caused a conflict that—if it's true that Dmitri is gone—split them down the middle. Sascha fancies himself in love with me, but he's only in love with a fantasy."

Jakob studied me with a silent frown for so long that I wanted to squirm. "You don't know what life is like in the forest," he said at last, leaning back. "How long have you been here now?"

"To be perfectly honest, I'm not certain," I admitted. Weeks. Perhaps as long as two months. My entire lifetime? It was beginning to feel that way.

"Sascha's house is not the norm," Jakob went on. "This place is a paradise, compared to what most of us live through."

I felt bad for him, even though something seemed off about his assessment of forest life. That man, Magnus, hadn't looked as though he were living through hardships. "Is that why you and Mikal are so keen to move back?" I asked, pushing my doubts aside.

"Yes," Jakob answered with an honest shrug. "You missed that while you were ill, by the way. Mikal and I are formally members of the pack again."

I was relieved, though I couldn't explain why. I tilted my head to the side, enjoying the feeling of nourishment spreading through me after eating the bun. "Is there a formal ceremony one undergoes to be made a member of the pack?"

"Not per se," Jakob said, "but the unanimous agreement of the pack is required."

His words weren't intended to sting, but they did. "Unanimous agreement of all of the members of the pack except the pup," I said, hugging myself under the blanket and indulging in self-pity.

Jakob could see right through me. "Peter Royale," he said in a mockingly formal voice. "Do you vote in favor of Jakob Brewer and Mikal Glinkov officially rejoining Sascha Kerensky's pack?"

My mouth twitched into a wry grin before I could stop it. "Yes, I do," I said.

"There." Jakob spread his hands in a gesture of acceptance. "It's settled."

"I'm glad my opinion matters," I sighed, settling back into the sofa. Relaxing only made me realize I needed to use the washroom, though.

"Your opinion does matter, Peter," Jakob said.

"Because you matter. You matter to all of us."

I was touched, but at the same time, I didn't feel comfortable with any sort of tender emotion yet. I was still raw with pain, and any new layer of emotion would be too much. To avoid it, I concentrated on gathering my strength and shifting in preparation to stand.

"Do you need help?" Jakob asked, sliding forward on his chair.

"I need to use the washroom," I said. I glanced askance at him. "Did Gregor tell you I can't abide being touched after...."

"He did." Jakob nodded. "But if you need a hand standing, just let me know."

I nodded, grateful that he didn't simply invade my space and hoist me to my feet. I managed to struggle to a standing position, then shuffle through the main room with Jakob hovering nearby, ready to catch me if I fell.

"It's ridiculous, really," I sniffed, angry at the whole thing. "My whole life, hardly anyone ever touched me. I come here, and that's all anyone wanted to do. And I adored it." My voice took on a maudlin tone. "I loved being touched more than anything else. The more hands the better." I let those painful words die and shook my head. "And now, it brings back horrific memories. I can't stand it."

"You will again," Jakob promised. "Give it time. No wound that deep heals in a day."

I was concentrating too hard on walking to reply with more than a nod. I considered it a victory when I made it to the washroom on my own power. Jakob hesitated, as though he wasn't sure whether he should enter the room with me or not.

"Would it be too much to ask for a few moments of privacy?" I asked in a wispy voice, turning like I would shut the door behind me.

Jakob took a step back. "Call out if you need help."

"I will."

I shut the door. If it had had a lock, I would have locked it. Instead, I dropped the blanket around my shoulders and moved toward the commode. A moment later, I sighed in consternation. Thanks to the blasted tincture, I was too hard to pee. At least there was an easy solution to that problem. I leaned against the wall, closed a hand around my cock, and stroked myself off.

The whole thing felt bizarre, and it had a paradoxical effect on me. I was in no mood to pleasure myself. I resented the concoction that had me aching with need. Sex was the absolute farthest thing from my mind. But it did feel good in a purely physical way, and I was in complete control. I was hardly a threat to myself. In fact, my mind wandered back to lonely nights in the palace as a youth, shortly after discovering what I could do to myself. Back then, the object of fantasy for my self-abuse had been various of my father's guards or courtiers. I always had liked the tough, muscular ones. And now I had a whole stable of them all to myself—six, now that Dmitri was gone, but Jakob and Mikal had joined our ranks. Fifteen-year-old Peter would have frigged himself raw on a daily basis if he'd known he would have so many fabulous specimens of masculinity at his disposal in the future.

My orgasm wasn't spectacular, but it still felt good. There was a shred of desire left in me after all. Maybe Jakob was right and I would heal from my inner wounds to the point where I wanted Sascha again. And who knew? Maybe someday I would be back to wanting to pleasure all of my packmates at once. Maybe.

I rested against the wall, catching my breath, until I was flaccid enough to pee. That added even more relief to my frustrated body. I would have liked a full bath, but I settled for washing my hands and face before wrapping the blanket around my shoulders again and opening the door.

Sascha was waiting on the other side, leaning against the wall, his arms crossed, when I shuffled into the hall. He wore a troubled scowl that dropped into an anxious look as I stepped out. "Peter." My name on his lips said everything from wondering if I was all right to begging forgiveness.

Whether it was the relief of bringing myself off or the simple fact that I felt stronger, I was genuinely happy to see him. "Sascha," I spoke his name in return.

Sascha jerked toward me, then stopped himself. He grimaced in frustration, balling his hands into fists. "Can I please, please embrace you?" he asked, rippling with tension. "You have to know that I'm not a threat to you, that I would never force you to—"

"All right. Let's try it," I cut him off. If I had my way, neither Sascha nor anyone else would so much as whisper about what had happened to me ever again.

I inched closer to him. Sascha took a huge step forward, closing his arms around me. I could practically feel him vibrating with need as he pulled me against his broad chest. It wasn't sexual need, just a profound need to have me accept him. Panic seeped in around the edges of my consciousness all the same. I wondered if it was strictly the damage done by the rape or if the drugs still in my system were making something I had once adored so painful. Having the blanket wrapped around me as a buffer helped dull the sensations, though—physical and mental.

"This feels nice," I said in a small voice as Sascha cradled me against him.

He let out a wry laugh. "One of these days, you're going to have to stop lying to me," he said.

Ironically, that made me smile. I rested my head against his shoulder, fighting through the discomfort. "How about I say that I really want this to feel nice, so I'm going to pretend it does until the darkness bleeds out of me."

Sascha dipped down to kiss the top of my head. "I'll accept that." He held me there for a few more seconds before loosening his grip. "It's a lovely day. Will you come sit outside with me? You could use some sun." He paused. "And I need to talk to you." He glanced down slightly with his last words.

I could tell Sascha was in a delicate place, that our relationship was in a delicate place. Whatever fears and misery I still felt didn't matter as much as making sure he had the opportunity to let his own darkness bleed out by saying what he needed to say.

"You're going to have to carry me out, though," I said, letting every drop of exhaustion show in my voice.

He looked warily at me. "You're sure that's all right? It won't cause you to seize again?"

I managed a weak shrug. "Honestly, I don't know. But if I spend the rest of my life shying away from things because they might hurt, I won't be living at all."

Sascha smiled, though there was a great deal of sadness in his eyes as he did. "This is exactly what I need to talk to you about," he said.

That piqued my interest, but I didn't get an answer to what he meant straight away. He scooped me carefully in his arms and carried me through the house and out to the backyard. Jakob had gone back to sewing whatever purse or satchel he'd been making in the main room, and Ivan was still cooking lunch or supper—I wasn't actually certain what time it was. They both watched us for a moment before returning to their tasks.

"Spring always surprises me," I said as Sascha brought me out into the sunlight and sat with me against a large tree in the side yard, farthest away from any of Sven's garden beds or the workshops, where we wouldn't be disturbed. "I always think winter and the snows are going to last forever, and then one day, it's warm, the grass is green again, and the sun is shining."

"I want to tell you something," Sascha said with sudden intensity, ignoring the light mood I was trying to create.

We sat shoulder to shoulder. That small touch didn't seem to bother me. I turned my head to look at him questioningly.

"I want to tell you that you're an arrogant, cold-hearted prick," he told me.

My eyes snapped wide with indignation. "I beg your pardon," I said.

"You are a complete jackass," Sascha went on. "You're overly proud, and you refuse to let anyone past that prickly armor you wear. And you're a reprehensible liar."

"Tell me what you truly think?" I snapped. Something warm and wonderful began to spread inside of me.

"And you use sarcasm to push people away when you come close to being vulnerable," Sascha continued, shifting to face me more fully. "And I love you." He rested a hand on the side of my face. It felt like stings and fire, but I didn't want him to move it. "I love you in spite of all that. I love you *for* it," he came close to laughing. Aggravation pinched his face hard on the heels of that aborted laughter. "And if you ever accuse me of not truly loving you, of being in love with a fantasy version of you, again, I'll smack you so hard it will make whatever Dmitri used to do with you look like child's play."

It was my turn to make a sound that was almost laughter. Not because I thought anything Sascha had said was funny, but because nothing that anyone in the entire world could have done to soothe or coddle or appease me could have come close to feeling as good as Sascha's pissy little declaration. I couldn't tell him I loved him in return, but I liked him, and I felt as though there was peace between us again. "I think it would be a good idea if you were to kiss me right now," I whispered, feeling a surge of passion, like new shoots reaching up through charred earth, trying to reach the sun.

Sascha shook his head and pulled away, sitting so that he partially faced me again. "Not until we talk about all the things we need to talk about first."

I drew in a breath, forcing myself to admit that I was relieved he'd stopped touching me. "Fair enough."

I waited. Sascha took his time to gather his thoughts.

"You cannot possibly imagine what it was like for me to burst into that room," he said, his voice haunted and shaking, unable to meet my eyes. "To find you naked and bruised, thrashing on the floor, screaming as those two devils—" He clenched his jaw hard and blinked off to the side, face going red. He had to take a steadying breath before he could face me. "I nearly beat the blond one to a pulp. That face of his will never be pretty again." He paused. "I would have killed them both, and Dmitri too, if Jakob hadn't wrestled me away and pinned me to the floor while Mikal dealt with Dmitri."

"It was my fault for putting myself in that situation in

the first place," I said, hoarse with shared grief. I reached out and rested a hand on his knee. I might have had qualms about being touched, but apparently me touching someone else didn't bother me at all.

Sascha snapped his eyes to mine, incredulous. "You were in no way responsible for what happened to you. Dmitri was. Did you know he'd had the whole thing planned since the faire?"

I swallowed, then nodded slowly. "I suspected, based on things he said to me, but I didn't know. It all seems so obvious now—the way those two looked at me at the faire, how cagey Dmitri was once we returned."

"He did it for the money." Sascha paused, studying me. "He said you were in on it with him, that you were planning to leave with him."

"I wasn't," I insisted. "He assumed I would go with him, but he never told me his plan, never asked if I wanted to leave. I didn't," I rushed to add. "I don't."

Sascha rested his hand over mine on his knee. His hands were so much larger than mine that for a moment, sharp prickles broke out not only on my hand, but traveling up my arm. "I know." Sascha smiled weakly. "You might shout at me, you might say cruel things to me, you might call me a terrible leader and a fool of a man, but I know you would never leave me. At least, not like that."

I wasn't as sure as I could have been.

"I shouldn't have said those things," I sighed, squeezing my eyes shut for a moment. "If those had ended up being the last things I ever said to you, I don't think I could have lived with myself." I smirked, showing him that I was aware of the paradox in my words.

Sascha laughed softly. He raised my hand to his lips and kissed my knuckles, my palm. It was strangely erotic, and it didn't send me into a seizure, which was progress. It did, however, start the cycle of overexaggerated need that had my cock filling. But I couldn't decide if I minded. More than anything, I wanted to enjoy fucking again.

"I am a terrible leader," Sascha admitted as though it took a great deal of strength for him to admit it. I opened my mouth to contradict him, but he raised a hand to stop me. "No, I am. I have been from the start. If I was a good leader, this wouldn't have happened to you."

"Sascha, you can't—"

"If I was a good leader, Dmitri would have been gone a year ago," he spoke over my protest. "If I was a good leader, you wouldn't have been treated like a slave just because Dmitri found you wandering in the forest. You didn't come here willingly. You weren't even cast out, the way the rest of us were. You were the victim of a prank. You have been the victim of my mismanagement. And because of me, you were the victim of a—"

"I am not a victim," I said, meaning it as I'd meant nothing so much in my life. "I refuse to be a victim. Of any of it."

"Which is why I love you so much." Sascha leaned toward me, cupping my face in both of his hands. "You have the face of an angel—"

"And the body of a devil?" I suggested, one eyebrow raised.

"Yes," he said, his mouth quirking into a wicked grin. "But what I was going to say is that you have the soul of a lion. You, Peter Royale, are a better man than I will ever be."

"I'm not," I insisted. "I'm arrogant and cold and spiteful, remember?"

"I never said you were spiteful." Sascha lowered his voice to a warm purr and stared at my lips. I thought I might get that kiss after all.

Strangely enough, I wanted it. Not because every fear and anxiety had left my body or because the drugs suddenly vanished from my blood, but because the joy I knew I would feel with a man I'd found peace with wrapped around me was stronger than the fear and the pain. I was willing to risk a seizure for it.

But once again, when I tried to lean into him, he warded me off, saying, "Not yet."

I let out a heavy breath. "For someone who has been tearing himself into pieces with the need to hold me, it astounds me that you can resist when I'm throwing myself at you."

"I'm resisting because I've had a lot of time to think and come back to my senses, now that I'm certain you will make a full recovery. Gregor didn't know if you would survive the overdose," he added in a grave voice. "For the first few days, he kept preparing me for the worst. But you managed to pull through."

"I'm too stubborn to die," I said.

Sascha grinned. "I know." He let go of my face and took my hands, threading my fingers through his. "This is all right, isn't it?" he asked with a quick frown. "I'm not pushing you too much, am I?"

"I'm pushing myself," I said as honestly as I could. "Yes, it's uncomfortable in some ways, but I believe that's the drug speaking. It's not what I truly want." For good measure, I added, "I want to feel lust again. I want to feel alive."

He let out a breath and nodded. I had the feeling he'd been holding that breath for a week, possibly longer. A moment later, he sucked it in again, then paused before saying, "I made a deal with myself when we weren't sure if you would live or die. I made a promise to you."

"Was it a good one?"

He ignored my attempt at humor. "I made a promise that if you lived, I would abolish your status as pup."

I flinched. "I didn't even know that was possible."

"Oh, it's very possible," he said. "It's always possible to free a slave."

A surge of excitement raced through me. "Is that a law of the forest?"

"I'm not sure if there are any actual laws of the forest," Sascha admitted with a wince.

I considered it, then said, "There has to be, though. Otherwise, who was it that authorized those three men to be punished at the faire? Who set that law in stone so that people would follow it without question in the first place?"

Sascha's brow inched up, and his eyes took on a distant look. "I've never thought of it that way. I always assumed every pack was governed by its own laws."

"But who suggested those laws to begin with?" I asked. "Clearly, there is some sort of understanding that extends across all packs, through the entire forest. Even if each pack has its own variation of the laws—like every city does—it's obvious there are certain laws that everyone recognizes and abides by. Who administers those laws and carries out punishment when they are broken? It has to be more than a few scattered wolves or packs. Is there more out there in the forest than people, even wolves, know about?"

"I don't know." Sascha shrugged. His face pinched. "This is why I'm a terrible leader. This is why I need to correct the mistakes I made. And the first correction I need to do is to elevate you to full member of the pack."

My mouth dropped open, but a moment later, I snapped it shut. "Does Jakob know about this?"

Sascha blinked. For a moment, I thought he looked jealous. "No. What does Jakob have to do with anything?"

"Earlier, he told me the pack had officially voted to welcome them back as members," I explained. "I joked that I hadn't had a vote, knowing full well pups don't get a vote. He formally asked for my vote."

"Did you vote in favor?" Sascha asked.

"Of course." I shrugged with every bit of imperiousness I had learned during my life at the palace. "I like Jakob and Mikal." I paused. "I think they are valuable men to have around."

Sascha answered my sentimental statement with a teasing grin. "Very judicious of you, Peter."

"What? What did I say?" I loved the fact that we were bantering. Especially since the subject of our banter wasn't anything having to do with what had happened or how wounded it had left both of us. It made my cock as hard as stone, though.

Sascha's sly, sideways look didn't help my arousal at all. "You want them," he said. "Or, at least, you're curious about what it would be like to fuck with them."

"I do not," I lied, feeling my face go bright pink. "I've thought nothing of the sort." Realistically, I simply wasn't ready for anything even remotely close to that. But at some point in the future, the idea intrigued me.

"The thing about you and lying," Sascha said, a familiar, exciting heat filling his eyes, "is that even though you do it all the time, you're actually terrible at it."

"I am not," I laughed. "I'm an excellent liar."

"You turn bright red, Peter," Sascha informed me. "And you can't look me in the eyes."

"Well, you can't look me in the eyes when you feel guilty," I fired back. "Even though you have nothing to feel guilty about."

"I have everything to feel guilty about," Sascha

sighed. Thankfully, the fire in his eyes only lessened, it didn't disappear entirely. "So very many things."

"Then we're even," I said, moving my hand so that it covered his. I slid his hand farther up my thigh toward my erection. "You feel guilty, I feel broken. You think you're a terrible leader, I think I'm a horrible person. You're hurt, and I've been violated. We're both guilty of a dozen, unforgivable wrongs."

"That just makes us equals," Sascha said, catching on to where I was going.

"If you're abolishing my status as pup, we are," I agreed.

"Peter Royale," he said, shifting to his knees and moving toward me, "as leader of this pack, I hereby officially dissolve your status as pup."

"Thank you, I accept," I said, suddenly breathless. I wriggled away from the tree so that I could fall to my back in the soft, spring grass. Sascha crawled forward until his knees were planted between my parted legs and his hands rested on either side of my shoulders, but without touching me. I could feel the heat rippling off him all the same.

A war raged within me. I wanted him so desperately that I could taste it, but a knot of fear pulsed in my belly. It felt as though the fear were foreign, as if someone had cut me open, thrust it inside of me, and sewn me shut, trapping it there, but I could still feel it.

"Are you all right?" Sascha asked, staring down at me

with great care. "I want you so badly I can hardly breathe, but I don't want to rush things."

I drew in a long, calming breath. "I can't control the fear," I admitted. "I don't want to feel it, but I do."

"You're afraid of me," Sascha said, grief darkening the desire radiating from him.

"No, I am not afraid of you," I insisted, gripping his shirt and feeling the warmth of his sides through it. "I could never be afraid of you. But I have fear inside of me now, whether I like it or not."

"What do we do about it?" There was a hint of teasing in Sascha's voice, but I knew his question was serious.

I considered for a moment. "Lower yourself onto me slowly," I said. "Gently. Until you're resting your weight on me."

"Won't I crush you?" he asked, doing as I'd asked.

"No. I like the feeling of your weight on me," I answered.

He followed my order until our bodies were flush against each other, but before he could press down on me fully, he laughed. "For God's sake, Peter. Have you been this hard the whole time?"

I broke into a guilty laugh. My hard cock was pressed between our bellies. "It's not my fault. It's that tincture. You know what it's intended to do."

"True." He tilted his head to the side for a moment as he rested fully atop me. "It makes sense that you're still feeling those effects along with everything else. And that would also explain why you kept shooting off, even though you were terrified and fighting us, for those first few days."

"Was I?" Humiliation raced through me. "That's horrifically embarrassing."

"Trust me. No one had a spare second to think less of you for it."

"I do trust you," I said in a suddenly serious tone. "I trust you with my life, Sascha."

I glanced up into his eyes, willing him to see just how deep my trust was. I couldn't love him, but I could trust him. He had to know that. The alien fear fought to get the best of me even as Sascha gazed lovingly down at me, but I refused to let it win. I refused to let the reverberations of what had happened to me stop me from feeling the passion that I had for the man in my arms. I refused to let it take away the part of me that enjoyed sex, even the part that entertained the notion of having it with men other than Sascha.

"You look very much like you want to be kissed, Peter Royale," Sascha said in a sultry voice.

"That's only the half of it," I murmured, wriggling under him to cause friction against my cock. "You see, I find that I now have this bothersome affliction that causes me to feel a desperate need to come. It's nearly constant. I have a suspicion I'll need someone to bring me relief on a regular basis until the drugs I ingested fully leave my body. Even then, this particular affliction might not ever leave me."

Sascha chuckled. The vibrations of his body against mine sent pleasure rocketing through me that managed to outweigh the prickles of fear clawing at me. "The mad part is, I don't think you're lying now, or exaggerating."

"I'm not," I said with wry seriousness. "Gregor hinted this could be a problem for me for a while."

Sascha hummed mischievously, tugging at the blanket wrapped around me and pulling it aside so that our skin touched. "Whatever am I going to do, as leader of the pack, to alleviate this problem?"

Panic surged dangerously in me, but I fought it off, tooth and nail. I focused on Sascha's eyes, on the slip of his hand between us. "I haven't the faintest idea," I answered breathlessly.

Sascha slanted his mouth over mine, kissing me long and lingeringly. At the same time, he lifted his hips enough to brush my cock. But instead of fisting me and finishing things, like I thought he might, he fumbled quickly with the fastening of his breeches, then pushed them down to his thighs.

I sucked in a breath, willing myself not to fly over the edge into full panic as he flexed his hips against mine, rubbing his prick against me. It felt wonderful and horrifying at the same time. I forced myself with every ounce of effort I had to concentrate only on the pleasure and to ignore the trembling that started deep within me. Sascha was being as careful as he could, I knew. He groaned with arousal and kissed me repeatedly, grinding his cock slowly against mine. I had to hold out and give him what he needed, in spite of the terror lodged inside of me. He needed this more than I did, but I needed it too.

He reached between us again, closing his hand around both of our cocks and fisting us slowly. If we'd had ointment, he could have gone fast, driving us both wild with pleasure. I was already close to coming, thanks to the drugs, so it didn't take much for me to erupt across his hand and my belly with a rending cry. Sascha sighed with pleasure and spread my cum across his prick, pumping himself faster, until his seed spread across me in a warm spurt.

The release felt good. The sense of communion with Sascha felt better. Being strong enough to tuck myself against his side when he collapsed to the grass next to me felt best of all.

"I thought I was going to lose you for a second there," he panted, turning his head to study me with worried eyes.

"You almost did," I admitted. "It took everything I had not to seize up."

Sascha nodded, squeezing his eyes shut for a moment and swallowing. "But you didn't," he said, letting out a breath and breaking into a smile. "You stayed with me."

I closed my eyes and smiled, stretching an arm and a leg over him and covering us with my blanket. It was a good moment, and I needed good moments, because whether Sascha liked it or not, everything had changed. I was free now, and free birds tended to fly.

19

"We have things to discuss," Sascha announced the next evening, as the seven of us sat around the table, finishing an exquisite supper.

It was the first time I'd joined the rest of the pack at the table for supper, and Ivan had outdone himself in my honor. Not that my appetite had returned to the point where I could gorge myself. After a week of not eating solid foods, I had to go slowly. My recovery was far from complete, but I'd felt well enough since spending the afternoon napping in the sun-dappled grass with Sascha the afternoon before—then returning to sleep in his bed that night—to attempt something that resembled my usual routine again. I'd washed and dressed in my regular clothes that morning. I've even appealed to Ivan to cut my hair—which had grown ridiculously long since I'd come to the forest. I'd gritted my teeth to keep from trembling with panic the whole time Ivan's hands were near me, but we'd made it through, and I felt like myself again.

Ivan and Sven were still busy clearing the table. The others settled into their seats as though they were royal advisors attending one of my father's meetings.

"I'm sure you all know the decisions we now face," Sascha went on. "This pack has undergone a major trial—not just in the last couple of weeks, but in the last year. We cannot continue to pretend nothing has happened or that mistakes weren't made." He glanced to Mikal and Jakob, who joined hands on the table between them and exchanged a meaningful look.

"But first," Sascha continued with a smile for me, "and perhaps most importantly, as you all know," he glanced back to the others, "I dissolved Peter's status as pup yesterday. So today, I ask for your vote. As leader of this pack, I hereby ask for an official vote on whether Peter Royale should be admitted as a full-fledged pack member, entitling him to equal rights and an equal say within the pack. All in favor?"

"Aye," all five of the others called out in unison, Ivan and Sven from the kitchen.

"There you go." Sascha grinned, then winked at me. "Congratulations, Peter. You're a full member of this pack."

I beamed from ear to ear, warm from the tips of my ears to my toes. "Thank you so much for your kind consideration."

"You deserve it, Peter." Gregor nodded across the

table to me.

"You've been a member of this pack and more than just a pup, almost from the start," Sven said, taking the seat at the table next to me.

"Hear, hear," Ivan agreed, sitting beside him. "Although I'd be lying if I didn't say you were an excellent pup." He winked.

"I can drink to that," Gregor laughed, raising his cup.

"And just because he's a full member of the pack now doesn't mean he isn't free to enjoy himself with the rest of us to his heart's content," Sven added.

I couldn't help but laugh at that, even though it would be a long time before I wanted anyone but Sascha touching me, and even Sascha's touch wasn't always welcome. The afternoon before and the night and morning we'd just spent together—while pleasurable in their own way as Sascha had helped me relieve the pressure of the drug's lingering effects—had pushed my ability to control my panic to the limit. I'd fallen into a seizure both the night before and in the morning when the stress of pleasure overlaid with panic became too much for me. I could only hope and pray that I'd find myself in a state where I wanted to indulge in other men someday—not because I didn't trust or respect Sascha, but because willingness to play would mean I'd conquered the forces that sought to conquer me.

"Now that that's settled," Sascha went on, a twinkle in his eyes, "It's time to move on to other business."

"Oh?" I asked. "And what business is that?"

"Leadership business," Sascha told me, still looking as though he were up to no good. He cleared his throat. "I hereby renounce my authority as leader of this pack."

I was stunned. "Sascha, you can't do that. You formed this pack."

The others looked as though they knew something I didn't know.

"I formed it," Sascha said, "and I have the right to step down as leader."

I eyed him suspiciously. "Is that codified in any lawbook regarding the ways of the forest or are you just making it up?" I already knew the answer to my question.

"There is no codified lawbook of the forest," Jakob said, also looking as though he were a part of whatever was going on. "But wouldn't it be a grand thing if someone wrote one?"

"Someone with experience in the law," Gregor added. "Who grew up with the expectation of administrating the law, and who is, therefore, educated in the law like no one else I know of in the forest."

"That would be something indeed," Mikal agreed, lifting his glass to me before taking a drink.

"I would gladly undertake a study of the law of the forest and attempt to codify it into some sort of set of standards that all packs could follow," I said. In fact, the prospect thrilled me. What a fascinating study it would be to speak with heads of packs throughout the forest to learn how they managed their men. And with the women of the forest too, like Katrina, to see if there were any similarities. And if all forest-dwellers could unite under one set of laws, there was no telling what sort of power we might have. Our civilization might even come to match that of the city-dwellers.

"Good," Sascha said. "I'm glad you feel that way. And that being the case, I nominate Peter to replace me as leader of this pack. All in favor?"

"Aye," all six of my packmates, including Sascha, said enthusiastically, without hesitation or debate, before I could stop them.

My jaw dropped. I could see at a glance they'd all contemplated and perhaps even discussed this wild turn of events amongst themselves. I was flattered, but I was also incredulous.

"Are you all out of your minds?" I asked, glancing at each of them. "I've barely lived in the forest for more than two months. I'm still suffering the consequences of being drugged and of a brutal attack. And yes, I can assure you, even though I have tried to hide it, I am still *suffering* those consequences. I don't know all the ways of the forest. I hardly know anything about the forest at all. I cannot possibly be your leader."

"To be honest," Gregor said with a sheepish grin, "now that Dmitri is gone, we don't actually need that much leading."

"It's true," Sven agreed. "We each already know our jobs and responsibilities within the pack, and we carry them out without prompting."

"Then why have a leader at all?" I asked, glancing

around the table, but settling on Sascha, who had taken his seat. "Why not just operate the pack as though it is a collective?"

"Because we need someone to sit in authority when hard decisions need to be made," Sascha admitted. "We need someone who can look at things dispassionately and put aside their own interests to decide what is best for all, no matter how difficult that might be." His shoulders dropped almost imperceptibly, as though he knew he was not that man.

What remained to be seen was whether I was. "I might be educated and I might have been through more than most people endure in a lifetime—" especially now, I thought to myself, though I didn't want to say it aloud, "—but that doesn't necessarily translate to me being able to make difficult and complicated decisions."

"Doesn't it?" Sascha asked. The look he sent me was a clear challenge. "Let's put it to the test, then."

"And how do you propose to do that?" I asked.

Sascha studied me intensely for a moment. It was as though everyone else at the table faded into the distance. "We need to decide what to do about Dmitri," he said quietly.

I swallowed, the fear and trembling starting deep in my center. Now was not the time for me to give in to the panic or risk falling into another seizure. "I thought you banished Dmitri," I said in a hoarse voice. "I assumed he's run off into the forest to make a new life for himself."

"He has," Mikal answered, pulling my attention away

from Sascha. "But he's not gone entirely. He's taken over the hut Jakob and I built last summer."

"We found him there after the others voted to readmit us to the pack, when we went to gather our things," Jakob said.

Mikal hesitated before adding, "The other two are there with him."

My body began to shake visibly. I could have sworn I saw tiny spiders crawling out of the cracks in the floorboards and flooding in from the walls. "So, we know where he is," I said. My voice felt as though it were coming from another room.

"We do." Sascha rested a hand over mine.

At first, I flinched, gasping as panic closed in on me. I couldn't let it win, though. The men around the table with me wanted me to lead them. I couldn't do that and give in to hallucinations and seizures every time my stress levels rose. So I fought back the only way I knew might work. I flipped my hand on top of Sascha's so that I was the one holding onto him and not the other way around.

I sucked in a breath, closed my eyes for a moment, and tried to clear the emotion from my mind. "If we approach them directly, it's three against six," I thought aloud. "But Dmitri is an expert hunter, and the other two are strong. Mikal is Dmitri's brother, and even though I trust your loyalty, it could be a disadvantage. And I'm sorry, but the rest of you may be strong and brave, but you're not fighters, nor are you hunters. You're a cook, a gardener, a doctor, and a woodworker. Numbers give us no advantage."

"Then what should we do?" Sascha asked. I could tell by his tone that the question was a prompt to encourage me to think harder, to solve the riddle in a way he never could.

"Criminals return to the scene of the crime, if they feel they can get away with it a second time," I said, racking my brain for examples of crimes my father had been faced with in Novoberg. "Or else, if they are not punished, criminals grow cocky and boast of their misdeeds. Either way, they grow careless and expose themselves to capture, even if it takes time to do so."

"So are you saying we should pretend nothing happened and wait for them to it again?" Jakob frowned at the idea.

"No." I turned to him. "At least, I seriously doubt any of the three of them would be stupid enough to come back here."

"If they're smart, they won't stay in the hut for long," Mikal said. "They'll gather their resources and get as far away from here as possible."

"But there's only so far they can go," I went on. Ideas began to rush in on me. Ideas that had a direct connection to everything that had excited me so much just minutes before. "Eventually, they'll return to a faire," I said. "And the law of the faire is very clear when it comes to the punishment for rape," I added in a croak.

"But only for rapes that occur at the faire, during revels," Gregor said, shifting uncertainly in his chair.

I hesitated, gathering my thoughts for a moment, then asked, "What if the law of the faire extended for all time? What if whatever governing body that metes out punishments during a faire existed between faires as well? What if there were a way for members of any pack—or lone wolves, or even the women of the forest—to bring cases against those who have wronged them to a central judicial body?"

"Do you mean forming a court system for the forest?" Jakob asked in disbelief.

"A court system would be easier to form than a centralized government," I argued. "As long as the leaders of the packs agreed to abide by whatever decision the courts made."

"I could see men like Magnus and some of the others agreeing to a set of laws," Sascha said, energy and excitement rippling off of him. "As long as they believed something was in it for them."

"Where does Magnus live?" I asked, deeply curious all of a sudden. Wherever Magnus lived is where Neil lived now. I still felt responsible for Neil's fate, be it good or bad. "How does a pack of fifty men conceal itself in the forest?"

My packmates shrugged.

"I've always been told that the larger packs live farther to the south," Gregor said. "The farther south you go, the farther away from the cities you get. And those bigger packs want as little to do with the cities, outside of faires, as possible."

"You two have wandered." I turned to Mikal and Jakob. "Have you come across any of the larger packs in the south?"

Mikal and Jakob exchanged a look. "To tell you the truth," Jakob said, "even though we wandered, we didn't go far from here. Just in case."

"But I've heard those rumors about larger packs in the south too," Mikal said. "I've even heard rumors that there's another river, even bigger than the River Kostya, in the south."

I snorted with laughter. "That's impossible," I said. "I was educated at a palace school—one of the finest schools in the frontier. The Kostya is the only major river west of the mountains. I've seen dozens of maps that prove it."

The others didn't dispute my claim. Rumors or not, everyone knew there was only one river in the frontier, just like they knew there was only one safe path through the mountains to reach the Old Realm, where the king lived.

"Either way," Sascha went on, "if there were some sort of a court system that spread throughout the forest, one that encompassed those larger packs rumored to be in the south and the smaller ones, like us, I think everyone would be interested in it."

"Those large pack leaders could send representatives

to sit on the court," I offered. "Or they could sit on it themselves if and when a case was brought forward."

"How would you organize something like that, though?" Mikal asked, leaning against the side of his chair and rubbing his chin thoughtfully.

It was not a rhetorical question. He was literally asking me.

"I would start by convening a meeting of the leaders of the most significant packs during a large faire," I said. "I would present an idea that was already clearly worked out and offer up examples of how it might benefit everyone in the forest."

"Like the example of two rapists and an accomplice roaming the forest freely, threatening any unprotected pup, or even pack members they thought they could prey on," Ivan said with a sympathetic look for me.

"Yes." I let out a nervous breath, clasping my hands on the table in front of me to keep them from shaking. "I would be willing to use my story as an example. And by sharing it with the leaders of other major packs, if they are sympathetic, it would mean Dmitri and the other two wouldn't be able to show their faces at a faire again—or anywhere with significant numbers of pack members abiding by the law code—without risk of being captured and brought to justice."

"You might be able to accomplish more by not capturing Dmitri and the others immediately than you would by hunting them down tomorrow and making them pay," Jakob said, eyes narrowed in thought.

"They would serve a better use as examples instead of martyrs," I whispered, uneasy with how calculated my suggestion felt. "Because there will always be those who see them as heroes for what they did and who would try to emulate them."

"Just as there are always those who end up having a ball smashed at every faire because they think the law doesn't apply to them or that they won't be caught," Gregor said.

"The next major faire is in a fortnight, outside of Mayskova" Jakob said. "That might be too far away, though."

"It is," Sascha agreed with a nod. "The next faire that is close enough for us to travel to is the one at Neander, in seven weeks."

"We must go to that one, then," I said.

"We could use the faire at Neander to get the word out to all of the pack leaders about this plan. The biggest faire of the summer is in three months, outside of Hedeon. We could ask to convene a council then to discuss the matter."

"Three months would be more than enough time to travel the forest, interviewing pack leaders about their rules and laws, and to put together a single law code for leaders to vote on," I said.

"And you would be willing to take on the project?" Sascha asked.

My heart raced, and I couldn't help but smile. "Three years ago, as an academic exercise, my tutor charged me with inventing a law code for an imagined nation," I said. "It was the most fun I've ever had learning. I never dreamed I'd have a chance to write a real law code that actual people might follow."

"Then you see?" Sascha said. "This is why we were so quick to vote for you as our leader."

"Hear, hear," Sven said.

The others joined them, all raising their glasses.

"To our leader, Peter," Jakob boomed.

"Wait, wait." I held up my hands before they could start knocking glasses and throwing back their toasts and, knowing them, breaking off to enjoy some revels of their own for the night. "If I'm busy interviewing forest leaders and writing a law code, how will I have time to lead you all?"

"Like we said," Gregor shrugged, "we don't need that much leading."

"Personally," Sascha said with a lively grin, "I'd follow you wherever you go and give you whatever assistance you need."

"We don't need him making platters and carving chairs," Sven said with a snort. "Gregor's medicines alone earn enough money to pay for our lavish lifestyle anyhow."

The others agreed, laughing, and completed their toast. They leaned out of their seats to clink glasses, then drank deeply.

All except Sascha. Sascha continued to smile at me

with pride, lust, and longing in his eyes. "See what becomes of you shouting at me and serving up some hard truths about my horrible leadership skills? It gets me to thinking. And when I actually take time to think, I come up with reasonable solutions to problems."

"If you're willing to go along with this," I told him with a hesitant sigh, "then so am I."

"Good." He nodded. "Now drink up. Let's see if a bit of alcohol makes your affliction better or worse."

It was the stupidest experimental suggestion I'd ever heard. Alcohol never made any medical problem better. But that didn't stop me from sipping away at half a glass of the mead Ivan kept pouring for the others. And even though just a few sips were enough to leave me feeling fuzzy and daring, I didn't push things too far.

Neither did Sascha. I watched him pretend to drink more than he actually did as the meeting turned into a ribald conversation, that turned into storytelling and singing, and the singing led to all of us getting up from the table and disappearing by couples into our bedrooms. Sascha was sober but relaxed as we stood. He took my hand with a grin and a wink and led me toward our bedroom with a look so mischievous it was almost sheepish.

"You truly are a wonder, Peter," he said as soon as we were alone in our room with the door shut. "And if you'll let me, if you're feeling up for it, I want to fuck you into oblivion tonight."

I laughed in spite of myself, ignoring the twist of worry that prickled through me. "How could I say no to that?" I asked in a soft, coy voice.

"You could, you know," Sascha said, reaching for the buttons of my waistcoat and undoing them almost lazily. "You could tell me to back off and never touch you again, now that you're the leader of the pack."

My smile turned into a wry grin as I tugged his shirt out of his trousers. "Now why would I want to do something that silly?" I glanced up to him, feeling as though my insides were on fire, but in a good way. The fear was there—I feared it would always be there now—but I could turn it into something exciting.

Sascha finished with the buttons of my waistcoat and pushed it off my shoulders, but instead of going right for my shirt, he paused. "You could always have said no, you know. To me, at least."

"Even though I was your pup and you were so desperate to fuck me that I could smell it on you?" I asked, one eyebrow raised.

"Even so," Sascha said, seriousness and affection in his eyes. "I never would have forced you. If you hadn't wanted me, I wouldn't have touched you."

I wasn't entirely certain I believed him. I hadn't exactly been given a choice that first night. Luckily for him, though, I'd been a willing participant in everything he'd wanted to do to me. I didn't see that changing anytime soon.

"Kiss me," I said, sliding my hands over the flesh of his sides as I pushed his shirt aside. "Kiss me and make me forget everything else."

"Yes, my leader," he replied, half teasing, half deeply earnest.

He moved into me, closing his arms around me and bending to slant his mouth over mine. He tasted of mead as he parted my lips and invaded me with his tongue. That kind of invasion was exactly what I wanted, but it still sent prickles of approaching panic skittering through me. I pushed them aside, tried to ignore them, and dug my fingertips into Sascha's back as if I could cling to him and ward them off. I concentrated on how good it felt to mold against him, how much I liked his kisses, the way his lips pressed to my jaw and neck before he returned to trust his tongue against mine once more. I focused on my cock as it hardened, making my trousers tight, and the way Sascha pulled my shirt up and fumbled with my trousers' fastenings so he could slide his hand down to caress me.

I groaned into his mouth as his fingertips reached my balls and dug deeper, teasing and tempting, but I also started to shake.

"Too much?" Sascha panted against my mouth. His hand went still, but he still cradled me.

"I don't want it to be," I said breathlessly.

"But it is," Sascha finished my thought.

I glanced up at him, keeping my mouth tightly shut

rather than admitting what neither of us wanted to hear. It didn't help matters that the phantom spiders that always seemed to precede a genuine fit started peeking up through the floorboards and the joints of the wall.

"We'll slow down," Sascha said, withdrawing his hand from me and lifting my shirt off over my head instead. "There's no need to rush."

"No need except the fact that I want to fuck so badly I think I might lose my mind," I said, undoing the fastenings of his breeches once my shirt was cast aside.

He arched one eyebrow at me as he removed his shirt. "It sounds to me like you're going to lose your mind one way or another."

I huffed a humorless laugh, then stepped out of the soft slippers I wore around the house. "It almost sounds desirable to ask you to fuck me so hard I have a seizure."

Sascha shared my gallows humor and laughed. He stepped out of his breeches, revealing his magnificent body to me fully. The sight of him still made my breath short and my prick hard. I could have looked at him all day—his broad chest, his trim waist, his powerful muscles, and his long, thick cock, which immediately stood stiff and tall for me. In my current condition, after a week of barely eating, my body was pathetic in comparison to his. But he still swept me with a ravenous look as I tugged off my trousers, tossed them aside, and backed toward the bed.

"One might argue that you've already made tremendous progress recovering from—" He didn't finish the sentence. Instead, he pulled back the bedcovers, lifted me against him, then rolled into bed with me, pinning me on my back under him. "It's a miracle you aren't having a fit with me all over you like this."

I didn't want to tell him how close I was to breaking down. Not when he seemed so pleased with himself and with me. And side by side with the encroaching panic was my favorite kind of pleasure. I was aroused, and I was minutes away from being fucked. It was a bitter shame that any sort of fear gnawed at me, especially since it felt imposed on me from an outside source.

"I need you to touch me," I whispered, brushing my hands up Sascha's sides and digging my fingertips into the muscles of his back. "I need you to help me fight off the lingering effects of the drugs by making me feel good, making me feel loved."

"You are loved," Sascha said, doing exactly what I asked and brushing his hand up and down my side while balancing himself on his other arm. "You are good too. So, so good." He whispered against my lips, kissing me softly when he was done.

I wriggled under him, grinding my erection against his. His praise felt as good as his body, which sent me into a paradoxical fit of giggles—which was just one more, mad emotion on top of everything else I felt.

"What?" Sascha asked, laughing himself as he muscled himself above me. He continued exploring my body with his hand, stroking my chest, rubbing my nipples, and dragging his fingertips across my belly. It felt good enough to battle against the spiders of fear circling in on me. "Why are you laughing at me?"

"I'm laughing at myself," I admitted. "Because every time you coo and compliment me, I feel like a puppy at your feet, hungry for praise."

Sascha's smile grew. "It turns you on when I tell you you're a good boy?"

"Yes," I laughed, face heating ridiculously. I was so embarrassed by my quirks that I couldn't look him in the eye.

"Well then," Sascha growled, closing a hand lightly around my cock and stroking. "You're such a good boy, Peter. You're such a sweet, sweet lad. You're so lovely."

I sighed with pleasure, and then, with very little warning, I came in a warm gush against his hand.

Sascha laughed. "You weren't joking." He grinned devilishly at me and spread my cum across my belly.

"Don't congratulate yourself too much yet. That was the after-effect of the drugs," I panted. "But don't worry, I'll be hard again in no time."

"I wouldn't have it any other way," he hummed, sliding against me and kissing me passionately.

It was absolute heaven, even if it was tainted. The way Sascha overwhelmed me and claimed me made up for the way I'd been overwhelmed against my will. The way he slipped his hand under me, caressing my ass, and lifting my leg over his hip canceled out the hands that had grabbed and forced me. Everything within me wanted to give myself to him in every way, even though those things had been taken from me.

"I want you inside of me," I whispered between kisses, tilting my head back as he nipped and licked my neck.

He paused, holding himself above me and looking down at me. "Are you certain?" he asked. "That's a big step after—"

I nodded jerkily, panic welling inside of me as I did. I didn't know how I would react to being fucked, if the darkness in my mind would take over, in spite of me not wanting it to. All I knew was that if I wanted to reclaim every part of myself, I needed to charge fiercely into the heart of the things that terrified me.

"I trust you," I told him, meeting and holding his eyes. "No matter what happens, even if I'm overcome with darkness or if I have a fit, I want to try. I have to. If I don't, I'll be at their mercy forever. And I refuse to be defeated."

"I love you so much, Peter," Sascha murmured, grinding against me and kissing me with enough emotion to ignite the room.

"I love you too," I told him, meaning it for the moment.

He devoured my mouth, almost to the point where I wondered if he'd forgotten my request. He moved against me in a way that had both of us gasping for breath and sweating in no time. That was beautiful in itself, but I wanted so much more from him.

At last, he peeled off of me long enough to reach for the jar of ointment on the side table. I forced myself to breathe steadily battling bad memories, including the echo of my own screams for mercy, as he scooped a large amount and spread it across my asshole, between my open legs, I shimmied to adjust some pillows, glad for the distraction, then watched him transported by the erotic sight, as he slicked his cock.

He was glorious. Just the sight of his hand working the length of his thick cock had pre-cum beading on my prick. It made no sense. He was so much bigger than me, so much stronger. He could have crushed me or snapped my neck or hurt me in a hundred different ways. I remembered how huge his prick had felt the first time he fucked me, stretching and filling me until I thought I couldn't take anymore. I wanted to feel all of those things again, and I wanted it to be pure. But in the meantime, I would take what I could get until I won my personal battles.

"Tell me to stop at any time," Sascha said, bending over me. He balanced with one hand and teased my hole with his other, testing and stretching me to make sure I was ready. "If it's too much, don't be a hero, don't lie to me, just tell me."

"And if it's so good that I have a fit while you're inside me, just hold me until it passes," I replied, pretending to joke with him. In fact, I was dead serious.

Sascha sent me a playful, heated look, then held himself as he moved into me. He didn't hesitate or make apologies, he simply pushed past the slight resistance my body put up, penetrating and filling me. I gasped and let out a muddled cry, praying he would think it was pure pleasure and not panic trying to burst through my seams. I would not give in to panic, even though the way he invaded me felt like a loss of control. It was world different from what had happened to me, though. Sascha and I were face to face. I could look into his eyes, see the love and the concern there as he rocked gently in and out of me.

"That feels amazing," I panted, willing myself to believe it.

He leaned into me, parting my legs farther and drawing my knees up to my sides as he moved faster, gazed into my eyes more intimately. "You are amazing, Peter," he said in a passion-hazy voice. "You're so brave. I'm so proud of you."

The sound that I made was supposed to be a laugh—he'd caught on quickly to my love of being praised—but it came out more like a ridiculously sultry cry of need.

"That's it," he whispered, finding just the right angle to thrust that gave both of us the most pleasure while allowing our bodies to be as close as possible. "Make those sounds. Let it all escape, even if you scream. In fact, I'd consider it a compliment if you screamed my name."

I did manage a laugh then, but it turned into a definite moan of pleasure as he picked up his pace even more, fucking me in earnest. In spite of the black edges around the corners of my vision and the second-hand terror leftover from the drugs, it felt so good that I thought I might explode. I wasn't the only one making sounds of pleasure, and every noise that ripped from Sascha as he enjoyed me to the fullest sent me closer and closer to the edge.

"Peter," he called my name in a strained voice. "Oh God, Peter."

He shifted one hand to hold my cock, stroking fast as he thrust desperately. I could tell when he was about to come and reached for it myself. When he gasped in glorious completion, spilling warmth inside of me, I let myself go, coming hard in his hand. It was as close to perfect synchronicity as it was possible to get, and it was almost enough to stop the seizure that roared through me. Almost.

Whatever happened to me, it was short. I lost track of the next few seconds as my eyes rolled back and my body convulsed, but when it passed and I relaxed as the edges of my mind settled into place again, I was resting relatively comfortably, all things considered, Sascha curled around me. I sucked in a deep breath, then let it out in a sigh.

"Thank God." Sascha let out a breath as well a moment later. "I thought I'd lost you."

"How long?" I panted, wriggling so that my back and ass were firmly spooned against him. I felt safe that way, sheltered.

"No more than ten seconds," he said, stroking my side and cradling me as though I'd been gone for days again.

I smiled, grabbing his hand and bringing it to my lips to kiss it. "Worth it," I said.

"You might think so," he growled, holding me close, "but let's work toward no seizures at all in the future, thank you very much."

I opened my eyes fully, twisting to look at him. "You said thank you." I grinned at him. "You're learning manners after all."

He smacked the edge of my ass, but not hard. "You're impossible," he sighed, resting his head against the pillow beside me.

"And you like me that way," I sighed happily, sagging against him.

"I do," he admitted. "And I always will."

I laughed hazily, closing my eyes and reveling in the feel of his arms around me. We'd come so far in such a short amount of time. I knew in my heart I had been waiting for someone like Sascha, waiting for the life I was about to have in the forest, for ages. The tasks we had ahead of us were monumental. Dmitri would be found, and so would the other two. Justice would be served, and with any luck, a whole new era would dawn for the forest-dwellers. I had so much healing to do, but I knew that, in time, I would heal fully.

I HOPE YOU HAVE ENJOYED *PETER AND THE WOLVES*! This is a story that I wrote for myself as entertainment and as self-care during the pandemic. And then I fell head over heels in love with Peter (and a couple of other characters who become a MUCH bigger deal in the rest of the books) It was never intended for others to read... until I gave it to a few friends and they said, "Oh my gosh, Merry, you HAVE to publish this!" So if you didn't enjoy it, blame them! And if you did enjoy it, which I sincerely hope you did, please, please stay with me and Peter on this journey and continue along with us to the next incarnation of Peter's journey, *Peter and the River*...

THERE IS A WHOLE WORLD OUT THERE IN THE FOREST that Peter is only just beginning to become aware of, and he wants to be a part of it. But he also knows he'll never be able to reach his full potential—as a man, a leader, and a lover—if he stays with Sascha. Of course, finding just the right man to attach himself to opens a whole can of worms that Peter isn't quite ready for. It also brings him back to someone from his past who he could have loved, if only it hadn't been forbidden. Will that love blossom now? How about falling head over heels in love with two men? Find out all about this and more—and by more, I mean an entire civilization hidden in the forest and the potential collapse of the kingdom—in *Peter and the River*! Keep reading for a preview of things to come for Peter... namely, Neil and Magnus. ;)

PETER AND THE WOLVES

From Peter and the River....

Our discussion—I refused to call it an argument—was halted by the sound of my name.

"Peter Royale."

I started, looking away from Ox and past the bored wolf manning the boot booth to see a familiar face striding toward me from a caravan parked behind the entire row of booths. I blinked, hardly believing my eyes.

"Neil?"

Neil Beiste had changed immensely in the months since I'd seen him at Berlova. He'd put on enough weight to be back to the size and strength he'd been when I'd known him in Novoberg. Beyond that, his skin was clear and flushed pink in the summer sun, his hair was neatly brushed, and he was dressed in fine, albeit juvenile, clothes. He looked happy.

"I was hoping I'd see you again," he said, eagerness in his eyes. "I've looked for you at ever faire since Berlova, and here you are."

"Here I am," I repeated.

"I have been dying to thank you," he said, his voice full of emotion. So much emotion that he blinked away tears. "Thank you so much for changing my life."

Relief washed through me. Neil was happy. My

gambit of having Magnus Gravlock purchase him had been a good one. "You're welcome," I said.

"Neil, what have I told you about speaking before being spoken to?" an authoritative voice sounded from behind Neil.

Neil flinched, but not in a way that indicated he was afraid, and stepped aside. As soon as he did, Magnus Gravlock himself walked up to the booth across from me. He broke into a sly, admiring smile as soon as he saw who Neil had been conversing with.

"Well, well," he said, raking me with a look from head to toe. "If it isn't Sascha's pup."

I felt more than saw Sascha step up behind me. Before Sascha could speak, I said, "Actually, I'm no one's pup anymore. I was emancipated and am now my own man." I would never get tired of saying that, and I probably sounded like an arrogant prick every time I did.

Magnus's brow shot up, and he glanced behind me to Sascha questioningly.

"It's true," Sascha said, clamping a possessive hand on my shoulder all the same. "Peter is the leader of our pack now."

Magnus laughed aloud at that. "Don't go telling the other packs you're ruled by a pup. You'll be a laughing stock."

My smug look evaporated in an instant. "I was born and raised to be a ruler," I informed Magnus with an imperious air.

Again, Magnus's brow went up, this time with a

distinct glint of calculation in his eyes. "You certainly have the attitude mastered."

I could tell he was impressed. "Ask Neil," I said, unable to resist the chance to be arrogant to a man that radiated the same sort of arrogance. "He will tell you that I have been educated with the intent that I become a Justice in my father's courts."

Magnus glanced to Neil.

"He was," Neil confirmed. "We were students together."

Magnus turned back to me. "Justice Peter," he said.

"In fact," I went on, even though he hadn't asked me to elaborate, "I am in attendance at this faire because I have taken it upon myself to do a thorough study of the laws and rules that each of the packs, particularly the larger ones, use to govern themselves. It is my hope that a single, central law code can be devised that all forest-dwellers could live by."

I had Magnus's full attention. I could tell by the interest that flared in his eyes. It was more than just interest in fucking me, although I could see that as plain as day too. He crossed his arms and rubbed his chin with one hand. "You think wolves are willing to abide by any sort of central code?"

"From what I have discovered so far, most packs employ similar laws to begin with," I said. He didn't need to know that I had talked to a total of four small packs so far, two of them being my own and Katrina's band of woman. "Of those codes, most of them bear strong resemblance to the laws of the cities anyhow. It would be a small step to codify forest law and bring some sort of unity to wolves from Tesladom to Good Port."

"And why would anyone want to do that?" Magnus asked, cagey as hell. He shrugged and picked at the cuff of one of the boots on the table in front of him, but I could tell he was interested in my answer. There was too much shrewdness in his eyes and in the way he studied me for him to simply be humoring me. And why would he humor a former pup anyhow?

"In case the situation in the forest changes and wolves find themselves in need of allies," I said carefully. I didn't want to divulge too much, particularly since I felt I didn't have enough information to truly know anything. All I had were hunches and ambitions. But the banter felt good somehow.

"Hmm." Magnus nodded, then rearranged some of his boots. "Who have you spoken to about your theories so far?"

"We've only just arrived at the faire," I said, stretching the truth a bit. "I've been making a list of pack leaders that it would be in my best interest to speak to." I paused, wondering if Magnus was an ally or a foe. "Who would you speak to first if you were undertaking this endeavor?"

"Me?" He looked surprised, but I suspected it was his way of pretending he wasn't that interested when, in fact, he absolutely was. He blew out a breath and shrugged. "Boris Gresky is here. You would definitely want to speak to him. And you must speak to Dushka Nobrovnik at some point."

"That's what I think too," Jakob added. I hadn't seen either Jakob or Mikal approach our conversation, but they were both there now. In fact, Jakob, Mikal, and Sascha stood protectively around me, staring daggers at Magnus.

"Let me know if you need an introduction to either men," Magnus went on casually. "Boris and I go way back. Ludvig and I are on friendly terms too. You should speak to him."

"You knew his brother," Sascha said, sounding as if the thought had just come to him.

"I did," Magnus asked, his gaze suddenly downcast. I caught my breath at the sorrow that filled his expression. It was only there for a moment, though. He quickly pushed it aside, drawing in a deep breath. "You look as though you're in the market for a pair of boots, Peter Royale," he said. "Choose any pair here, they're yours."

It was my turn for my brow to shoot up in surprise. "Truly?" I asked, unable to hide how genuinely pleased I was with the offer. "They're all so lovely. I've seen boots from the king's city that aren't this fine."

"Take whichever pair you'd like," Magnus said again. "It would be the least I could do to thank you for prompting me to purchase the finest pup I've ever known in my life." He smiled at Neil—though with a possessive sort of fondness rather than the affection Sascha always showed to me—and clapped a hand on Neil's shoulder.

For his part, Neil blushed and lowered his head,

looking every bit as pleased as a puppy who had had his ears scratched by his master.

I sent Sascha a teasing smile over my shoulder. He was in no mood for jokes and silliness, but he softened his scowl and smiled at me all the same.

I turned back to the booth, poring through the selection of boots in earnest. I liked just about every pair, so I made my selection based on which ones fit me the best. That involved having a seat on a stool right behind the booth and trying on several pairs. The entire process reminded me of how much I enjoyed shopping. I hadn't had so much fun since coming into the forest, even though Sascha, Jakob, Mikal, and Ox all hovered nearby, looking like they would murder anyone who touched me.

When I finally selected a pair, Magnus himself wrapped them in a muslin bag for me.

"I used to be a cobbler," he said, handing me the bag. "I know the proper care and maintenance of fine boots. I've included polish and a cleaning cloth in there for you." He winked suggestively, and our hands brushed as the bag was exchanged. "You should put these on as soon as you can."

A surprise jolt of lust shot through me. Magnus was nearly old enough to be my father—which wasn't saying much, since I had only just turned twenty-one and father had been married to mother when he was nineteen—but he was fit and handsome in spite of his age. His dark hair was greying a bit at the temples, and he had fine lines around his eyes, but he had a certain shrewdness and maturity about him that I found irresistible. He radiated confidence and power. And judging by the way Neil smiled and fawned over him, he must have been proficient in bed. It was far too soon to tell, since I hadn't even spoken to the other pack leaders yet, but my pulse raced with the idea that Magnus might be exactly who I was looking for.

IF YOU'RE READY TO READ MORE, PICK UP PETER AND the River today!

IF YOU ENJOYED THIS BOOK AND WOULD LIKE TO HEAR more from me—not only about M/M Romance, but about Historical Romance as well—please sign up for my newsletter! When you sign up, you'll get a free, full-length novella, *A Passionate Deception*. Victorian identity theft has never been so exciting in this story of hope, tricks, and starting over. Part of my West Meets East series, *A Passionate Deception* can be read as a stand-alone. Pick up your free copy today by signing up to receive my newsletter (which I only send out when I have a new release)!

SIGN UP HERE: HTTP://EEPURL.COM/CBAVMH

. . .

Are you on social media? I am! Come and join the fun on Facebook: http://www.facebook.com/merryfarmerreaders

I'm also a huge fan of Instagram and post lots of original content there: https://www.instagram.com/merryfarmer/

ABOUT THE AUTHOR

I hope you have enjoyed *Peter and the Wolves*. If you'd like to be the first to learn about when new books in the series come out and more, please sign up for my newsletter here: http://eepurl.com/cbaVMH And remember, Read it, Review it, Share it! For a complete list of works by Merry Farmer with links, please visit http://wp.me/P5ttjb-14F.

Merry Farmer is an award-winning novelist who lives in suburban Philadelphia with her cats, Justine and Peter. She has been writing since she was ten years old and realized one day that she didn't have to wait for the teacher to assign a creative writing project to write something. It was the best day of her life. She then went on to earn not one but two degrees in History so that she would always have something to write about. Her books have reached the Top 100 at Amazon, iBooks, and Barnes & Noble, and have been named finalists in the prestigious RONE and Rom Com Reader's Crown awards.

ACKNOWLEDGMENTS

I owe a huge debt of gratitude to my awesome beta-readers, Laura Stapleton, Scarlett Scott, Erin Dameron-Hill, MeShe Bryant, and Jackie North, for their suggestions and advice. And double thanks to Jackie North, for helping me figure out how to write a blurb in a genre I don't usually publish in, and to Cindy Jackson for being an awesome assistant!

Click here for a complete list of other works by Merry Farmer.

Printed in Great Britain
by Amazon